# STRIKE DOG

# STRIKE DOG

## JOSEPH HEYWOOD

THE LYONS PRESS

GUILFORD, CONNECTICUT

AN IMPRINT OF THE GLOBE PEQUOT PRESS

Copyright © 2007 by Joseph Heywood

First Lyons Press paperback edition, 2009

The Lyons Press is an imprint of The Globe Pequot Press.

Text designed by Georgiana Goodwin

ISBN 978-1-59921-364-4

The Library of Congress has previously cataloged an earlier hardcover edition as follows:

Heywood, Joseph.
    Strike dog : a woods cop mystery / Joseph Heywood.
    p. cm.
    ISBN-13: 978-1-59921-160-2
    1. Service, Grady (Fictitious character)—Fiction. 2. Game wardens—Fiction. 3. Upper Peninsula
(Mich.)—Fiction. 4. Serial murderers—Fiction. 5. Psychological fiction. I. Title.
    PS3558.E92S77 2007
    813'.54—dc22

                                                                              2007033864

Printed in the United States of America

10 9 8 7 6 5 4 3 2 1

To Shanny, who can spell but can't read,
and seems to prefer it that way.

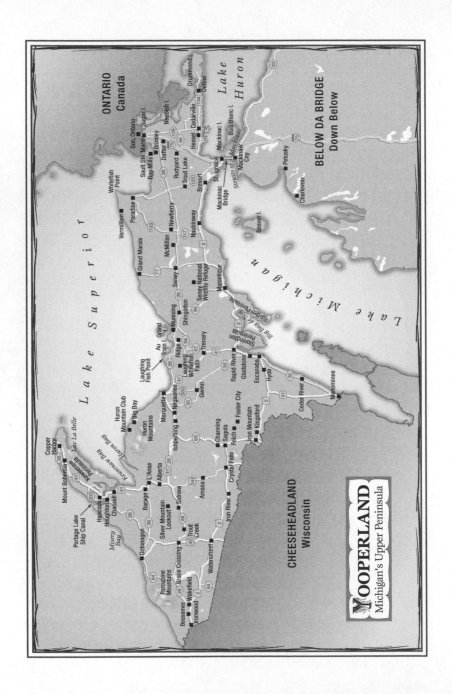

# STRIKE DOG

# PART I
## MADSTONES AND DEVIL'S SMILES

*Commune periculum concordiam discors parit.*

Common danger brings forth discordant harmony.

# MARQUETTE, MICHIGAN
## APRIL 28, 2004

Grady Service stared down at the large white metal drawers, his mind cluttered by unconnected thoughts, mostly fragments: spring, the season of change, breakup and runoff, a time of sloppy excess; his old man, whom he'd never gotten along with; more than two erratic decades as a conservation officer, mostly alone; the divorce from his late first wife; and finding Nantz, and learning he was a father—all of this rolling around in his aching head as he stared at the drawers. He felt blood rushing to his head, then racing away, his insides in chaos, at the edge of an abyss—one he knew he could not back away from.

"Grady," Captain Ware Grant said from beside him. "You don't have to do this." The captain grasped his detective's arm.

Service pushed the hand away. "Open them," he ordered the hospital orderly.

"Which one first?"

The captain pointed.

It seemed like the man took forever to pull out the drawer and unzip the black plastic bag. There was a bright yellow biohazard label on it. *The plastic didn't look strong enough to contain a human being,* he thought, his mind grasping for details to cling to, something to process that would make sense. Anything but this.

He stared down, saw Maridly Nantz's face, unmarked, like she was asleep. "The other one," Service whispered, his legs reducing to gelatin.

It was the same in the second drawer, Walter asleep, his son, his only son, the only one he was ever likely to have, his dead son, at eighteen.

"No," Grady Service said. It was not a word born of thought, but a defensive thing, a verbal arm instinctively raised to ward off an assailant.

Captain Grant stood nearby, saying nothing. The orderly left them alone in the small, chilled room.

"But she was a pilot," Service said after a long time.

"Accidents happen, Grady."

"Not to her, not to Maridly Nantz. Safety was in her blood."

The captain kept quiet.

A sign in the room said NO SMOKING. Grady Service lit a cigarette and inhaled deeply.

He smoked the cigarette down to embers, GI'd the butt, and put it in his pocket. He stood between the drawers, with one hand on the love of his life and the other hand on his son, both killed in an accident on the way back from Houghton.

Grady Service wanted reasons, tears, anything to take the ice out of his blood, but nothing came. Inside all he could feel was a cold rage, at chance, at God, at anything, everything. He had spent his life around death in all forms, but this was different.

Eventually he felt the captain move his hands away from the bodies and he watched as his superior zipped the bags and slid the drawers into the wall. The drawers squeaked, needed oil. Nantz would hate a noisy drawer, would take it as a personal affront. Walter would not pay attention. Nothing bothered the boy.

In the corridor outside the orderly stepped in front of Service. "You can't smoke in there, dude."

The blow sent the man backward, sliding down the waxed floor like a human stone in a curling match.

The captain ignored the man with the bleeding face, took a tight hold on Service's arm, and kept him walking away from the morgue, up the stairs, toward the light.

||||||||||||||||||||||||||||||||||||||||||||||||||||||||||||||||||||||||||||||||||||||||||||||||||||||||||||||||||||||||||||||||||

2

## SCHWEITZER CREEK, MICHIGAN
### APRIL 28, 2004

M-35 was curvy where it crossed Schweitzer Creek about four miles south of Palmer, but the hardtop was dry, the shoulder wide, and the county road commission had brushhogged it, providing plenty of room for a sliding vehicle. Grady Service stomped up and down the road, studying the marks left by Nantz's pickup truck, trying desperately to make sense of them.

"She was a pilot," he said, as if this alone explained why Maridly Nantz could not be dead.

Captain Grant said, "Even the best pilots have accidents."

"Not this pilot—not her," Service growled. "Look, she skidded to the right here," he said, walking along the rubber marks, "fought out of it, and rolled the other way. Not that tough to get out of. We all do it in the snow every winter, and in summer on washboard roads that will rip the steering wheel out of your hands. She's done it a million times. We all have." It had been a dry day in early May. There was no excuse.

"Sometimes there's no explanation," the captain said. "It just happens."

"Not to Nantz, not to Walter. Where's her truck?"

"U.P. Autobody and Collision in Negaunee Township," the captain said.

"They should have left it here so I could see."

"You're not a trained accident investigator."

"Bullshit," Service said. "They took it away before I could look it over."

"They took it away because it's standard procedure. The removal had nothing to do with you."

"I want to see it."

"The Troops are looking at it."

"I want to *see* it," Service demanded.

Marquette deputy sheriff "Weasel" Linsenman drove up, parked, got out of his cruiser, and approached sheepishly, his head bowed. "I just heard, man. Jesus, Grady. I'm so sorry."

Linsenman started to step closer, but stopped.

"U.P. Autobody," Service said.

"You want me to show you where it is?" the deputy asked.

Service and Linsenman had been friends for a long time, and had shared some tense professional moments together, but both men tended to lead solitary lives, Service with his girlfriend and son, and the deputy with his dogs. They were friends who barely knew each other, yet willingly covered each other's backs.

"I'm so sorry, Grady."

Service looked up and seemed only then to recognize his friend. "She was a pilot."

Linsenman glanced at the captain, who shook his head almost imperceptibly, a signal for the deputy to keep silent.

U.P. Autobody & Collision was in Negaunee Township, not far from the state police post. There were two main buildings, basic pole barns, painted taupe, a metal fence around the property, and rows of wrecked vehicles strewn around. Service looked at the buildings and said "Taupe," to the captain, who raised an eyebrow. Service had never heard the word *taupe* until Nantz taught him. He was the old dog, nearly twenty years older than she, yet it seemed he learned more from her than the other way around.

They went inside a door marked OFFICE and asked about Nantz's truck. A woman at reception sent them to the back building, where they found a large man with a potbelly and muttonchops that hung down the side of his face like feathers.

Neither the captain nor Service was in uniform. "Hey," the man said. "Sorry, but youse can't just waltz in here."

Service grabbed the man by the throat, backed him over to a metal wall, and slammed him against it. The metal reverberated like a reluctant steel drum. "Red Ford, just came in," Service said.

The man shook his shoulders, took a step away, and pointed. "The state's not done with it yet," he stammered.

Service walked over to the wreck, which was in the back of the shop, partially covered with a black plastic tarp. The roof was flat, but had been cut open with the Jaws of Life. Both sides of the truck were caved in, the grill shattered. Two deflated air bags lay on the floor near the wreck. Powder residue from the bags spackled the floor and hood of the truck like gray pollen.

"When will the accident investigation team be back?" the captain asked.

"AIT's business, their time," the man said.

Service turned toward the man, felt fire rippling along his spine.

"His girlfriend and son were in it," the captain said.

The man's demeanor immediately changed. "I'm sorry. They said they'd be back tonight; they got called out to another accident all the way down by Traunik."

Service stared at the man. "Who're you?"

"Ptacek."

"You the honcho?"

The man shook his head. "I just drive the wrecker."

"You tow it in?"

The man nodded.

"How long you done this for a living?"

"Seventeen, eighteen years."

"You see anything that catches your attention?"

The man held up his hands. "I just haul them."

"You've got eyes and a brain," Service said.

"Nobody wants to hear what the wrecker driver has to say."

"I want to hear."

"The AIT will kick my ass."

"The Troops want to get to the truth," the captain said, intervening. "Anything that helps will be welcomed."

"I heard them talk when they come in. They think it's a rollover, pure and simple."

"You have a different view?" the captain asked.

"Over twenty years you see a heckuva lot of wrecks. You didn't look, you'd be bored outta your bloody mind, eh?"

Service lurched, his face flushing, "You think wrecks are for your *entertainment?*"

The man quickly raised his arms. "No. I'm just saying, when you see so many, you get to looking at them pretty closely."

"Have you seen something to suggest it's not a simple rollover?" the captain asked.

The man shook his head. "I could lose my job. The boss has contracts with the state in four counties."

The captain was adept at interviewing reluctant witnesses. "You won't lose your job for telling the truth. We're conservation officers . . . cops."

"Youse're game wardens, no fake?"

"The Troops will draw their own conclusions," Captain Grant said.

The man looked conflicted, crossed his arms, and approached the wreckage. "Maybe it *was* just an accident," he began.

"But?" Grady Service interjected gruffly.

"I don't have 'er all worked out in my head yet," the man said, "but as I looked it over, it seemed to me that something else might have happened."

"Work it out now," Service said.

"Here," the man said, leaning over the rear of the truck. "There's paint here, just a few flecks."

Service and the captain flanked the man, leaned over, looked down. "Green paint," Service said.

"Or blue," the man countered. "Can't tell for sure unless you actually lift a sample and analyze it."

"That paint wasn't there before," Service said.

"She might have backed into something over in Houghton," the captain offered.

"This didn't come from backing into something," the wrecker driver said. "I'd say it came from her being hit."

"Rammed?" the captain asked.

"Not rammed . . . not exactly. The bumper don't show it; in fact, nothing shows it, but look at the left rear taillight."

"Gone," Service said.

The man nodded. "Left one's gone, right one isn't. And where's the foreign paint?"

"Near the left rear light," Service said. Nantz took good care of her vehicles, would not abide even marginal damage. If she'd dinged her truck, she would have gotten it fixed immediately. It was a matter of pride for her, almost a fetish. The plane she owned, her vehicles, her house, everything had to be in working order and cosmetically shipshape. *Why had she cut him slack?* he wondered. He'd never worked that out: Her the neat freak, him the slob. It made no sense.

The man suddenly seemed to withdraw from his observations. "All these years I seen me a heap of wrecks, and after a while you get to recognize some things. I'm not saying this is how it went down, but it's possible."

"Say what it is you have to say," Grady Service said.

"Ask me, it looks like somebody put a PIT against this truck." PIT was short for precision immobilization technique, a maneuver used by police officers to spin a vehicle and end the chase.

"The state police agree?" the captain asked.

"I didn't say nothing about it to them. I didn't really see it until I got back here and started looking."

"But they'll see it," the captain said.

"Maybe, maybe not. Most cops have to PIT somebody, they're so jacked up over what they done and the fact they survived it, they don't really look at the damage. You know, if you get through it, who cares about dings in your patrol car? And why look for PIT damage on a civilian truck off the cement by its lonesome?"

"PIT," Service said.

Ptacek said, "Not just a PIT, but a PIT by a smaller vehicle against a bigger one, say a big pickup like this Ford, and probably the PIT driver in the smaller car wasn't so good at the maneuver. When you get a mismatch in vehicle size, the smaller one ain't gonna drive away without damage."

Service said, "Walk me through it."

"Walk *us* through it," the captain said, correcting his detective.

The man grabbed some bricks, set them on the shop floor, and reconstructed the accident as he thought it could have happened. When he was done, he stood up and fumbled with a pack of cigarettes. "Okay if I smoke?"

The captain nodded. "You work here."

Grady Service looked at Nantz's Ford, the dark flecks, the missing taillight, and closed his eyes, trying to match what the man had just shown him with the bricks with what he had seen out on the highway. He worked his way through the events several times and felt a wave of dizziness begin to envelop him.

"Not an accident, Cap'n." Service put his hand on the back of Nantz's truck to hold himself up. "Not an accident," he repeated.

Without remembering why or how, Grady Service had his .38 snub out of the holster in the back of his belt and was staring at it in his hand.

"Detective!" the captain said in his sharpest command voice. He looked at the wrecker driver and waved for him to get out.

The man backpedaled out the door.

"Grady, give me your piece."

"Murder, Captain. Not an accident. They were murdered."

"The gun, Grady. *Now.*"

Service pondered the captain's request and finally held out the small pistol, grip toward the captain.

"I got more guns, Captain."

"Grady."

"Captain, I am going to hunt down the cocksucker who did this and I am going to blow his fucking brains out."

The captain grabbed Service's arm, but the bigger man swept him away and barged outside.

Ware Grant found him sitting in his Tahoe and got in beside him.

"You're off duty until further notice, Detective."

"I'll find who did this—one way or another," Grady Service said, grinding his teeth. His mind was in overdrive. If Nantz had been deliberately forced off the road, there could be only two reasons, and one of them—the most likely in his mind—was revenge *against him.*

"I'll talk to the Troops. Let the process work, Grady."

Service's face twisted in a rictus of pain and anger. "Yeah, do that—but I promise you this: Whoever did this is never going to make it to trial. This is personal."

Only then did tears come, and he wasn't sure if they flowed from grief or the need for vengeance.

On his way home he called Nantz's cell phone and landline providers to request the bills from her phones. Maybe there was something there. Anything.

"I'm sorry, sir, are you related to the lady?" the cell phone company woman asked.

"I live with her."

"I'm sorry, sir, but the phone is not in your name."

"I'm with the DNR," he said, his temper spiking.

"I'm sorry, sir, but you'll need to get a warrant from the regular police."

*Regular* police! He broke off the call and pounded the steering wheel with his fists. He inhaled to settle himself, and considered calling the captain to see what he could do, but decided against it. Why the fuck didn't you marry her? he asked himself.

He then called the Marquette County Sheriff's Department and learned that Linsenman was off duty and called him at home.

"It's Grady."

"How're you doing?"

"I need a favor."

There was a pause on the other end of the line. "Like what?"

"I need to get Nantz's current phone records, but the company won't give them to me because we weren't married, the house phone is in her name, and I'm not *regular* police. Can you get them for me?"

"No problem," Linsenman said. "What do you want?"

"Home phone and her personal cell phone." He gave his friend the numbers.

"I can do this by fax. What's the rationale for the affidavit?"

"Needed for an ongoing investigation."

"The accident investigation is still open?"

"Just do it, okay?"

"Okay, drop them at your house or your office?"

"Slippery Creek."

"Your house is in Gladstone."

"I'm relocating."

"Huh," the deputy said. "I'll drop them out at the camp. Anything else?"

"I appreciate this," Grady Service said.

# 3

## GLADSTONE, MICHIGAN
### APRIL 28, 2004

It was dark and Korea-born Candace McCants was inside Nantz's house on the Bluff overlooking Gladstone, rubbing the ears of Newf, Service's 154-pound Canary Island mastiff, a breed the Spaniards called *Presa Canario*. The dog had been given to him by his former girlfriend, veterinarian Kira Lehto. Before Newf, he had been deathly afraid of all dogs, any size, breed, or shape, but over time he and Newf had bonded in ways he never would have predicted.

McCants was a damn good CO, and a close friend. She got up, came over to Service, and put her arms around him. He was more than a foot taller. No words passed between them.

He pushed her away. He went up to the bedroom and came back minutes later with a bulging canvas hockey bag he often used as a suitcase.

"Grady?"

He turned and faced her. "Either help or get the fuck out of my way," he said.

McCants didn't move. "You intimidate a lot of people, Grady, but I'm not one of them. What the hell do you think you're doing?"

"Going back."

"Going back to what?"

"Who I was before—"

"—Nantz civilized you."

"Yeah, that worked out," he said bitterly.

"Put down the freaking bag."

He stared at her.

She took a deep breath. "You're not thinking. You're doing—hell, I don't know what's going through that twisted mind of yours, but you're not thinking. The Grady Service I respect thinks before he acts. He thinks about everyone and then he does the right thing."

"I *am* doing the right thing," he countered.

"Packing your stuff and running away?"

"Not running away," he said. "I'm going to get it back."

"*It?*"

"*It*," he repeated.

"And who's keeping *it* from you?"

"Me," he said. "But not anymore."

"What about the funeral? Have you made arrangements?"

"No funeral," he said. "No memorial, no words at the grave, no nothing."

"You haven't answered the question."

"Cremation," he said.

"Is that what she wanted, or what you decided?"

"What Nantz wanted," he said. "Walter was too young to have an opinion."

"Cremation and no memorial, no effort to come to grips with this, let us all grieve?"

He looked at her and showed a half-grin. "Oh, I am most definitely going to come to grips with it."

"I?" McCants said. "You. What about the rest of us—all their friends, all of us who cared about Nantz and Walter?"

"You mourn your way and I'll mourn mine."

"I thought you were growing up," she snapped.

"I am," he shot back.

"You are not making any sense, Service."

He saw that McCants was on the verge of an emotional outburst and put his hands on her shoulders. "It wasn't an accident, Candi. Somebody ran them off the road and killed them."

The younger officer's jaw hung open and she blinked.

"We all got a voice message from Chief O'Driscoll this morning. He said it was an accident."

Service said, "It wasn't."

McCants began to chew her bottom lip. "The whole world thinks it's an accident, but the great Grady Service knows better."

He tapped his stomach. "Gut first, then evidence. When your gut twists into a braid, you can't ignore it. I won't," he added with a glare. "Call the captain, ask him."

McCants went to her truck, got her cell phone, and punched in the number as Service looked on.

"Captain, McCants here. I'm with Grady and he says it wasn't an accident. What's going on?"

Service watched as she nodded, her face impassive. She then flipped the phone shut. "He says you've been relieved of duty for now and that you are being irrational."

He studied her eyes. "He said more, didn't he?"

"Yeah. He said you may be right, but that the Troops have to make that determination."

He quickly talked her through what he knew, and when he had finished, she said, "Okay, you want to move back to your camp, you've got it. But if the investigation comes back as an accident, all this bullshit is done and you will sit down and do the things you are supposed to do in a way that will honor your woman and your son. Am I clear?"

"You always are," he said, heading back to the house for another load.

They carried loads to his truck in silence until the bed of his personal pickup was nearly full. "What is this going to prove?" she finally asked.

"Somebody killed them," he said.

"Maybe," she corrected him.

"Maybe," he echoed. "But if it was homicide, I plan to be in shape to do something about it, and I can't do that here."

"You mean living in luxury," she said, filling in the blank.

"Right. I got soft here—I lost my edge—and if somebody killed them, I'm sure it was to get at me."

"Why do things always have to be about *you?*"

"They don't, but when they are and I don't focus, I'm asking for it."

"Your logic scares me," she said.

"It's not logic," he said. "It's all gut."

"So it's back to sleeping on footlockers in an unfinished camp in the woods."

"It's finished," he said in his own defense.

"Jesus, you big dumb bastard, it has four walls and some doors stacked around a toilet and a shower in the corner. It's not much more than a wall tent made of plywood and half-logs."

"It works for me," he said.

She followed him into the garage, where he began moving his free weights out to the truck, and she began to help.

"Maridly would want you to slow down and think," she said again, trying to reason with him.

"What Mar would want is for me to find out who did this to her and Walter and to settle it."

"Who hates you so much they'd kill your girlfriend and son? Allerdyce?"

Limpy Allerdyce was one of the state's most notorious poachers, and Service had once put him in jail for seven years for attempted murder. Allerdyce was the leader of a tribe of lawbreakers, mostly his relations, who lived like animals in the far southwestern reaches of Marquette County.

The clan killed bears and sold the galls and footpads to Korean brokers in Los Angeles for shipment to Korea and Taiwan. They killed dozens of deer each year, took thousands of fish, and got substantial money for their take from buyers in Chicago and Detroit. Despite a probable huge income, the tribe lived like savages. Since his release from Southern Michigan Prison in Jackson, Limpy had pretty much followed the law, and even claimed to have been a snitch for Service's father, who had been a CO of the old school. Since getting out of prison, Limpy had begun feeding information to Service. Allerdyce was a lot of things, most of them too vile to contemplate, but this wasn't his style. Limpy did things Yooper-style, head-on and toe to toe, and whatever the challenge, he fought his own battles.

"Not Limpy," he said. "But whoever it is, they knew that Nantz and Walter were my vulnerabilities. Now they'll come after me."

"Maybe they know they can't get you and they're settling for Nantz and Walter," McCants offered.

"They'll come," he said. "They'll come."

"Tree called," she said. "He's on his way north."

Luticious Treebone and Service had finished college the same year, Service graduating from Northern Michigan University, where he had been only a fair student and a competent hockey player. Treebone had played football and baseball at Wayne State and graduated cum laude. They both had been on the verge of being drafted when they volunteered for the marines, met at Parris Island, and served together in the same unit in Vietnam. They had been through hell and rarely spoke of the war since. When they got out of the marines, they both joined the Michigan State Police, went through the academy in East Lansing with honors. When the opportunity came to transfer to Department of Natural Resources (DNR) law enforcement, both had made the move, but within a year, Treebone left the DNR for the Detroit Metropolitan Police, where he was now a much-decorated lieutenant in charge of vice. They had remained close friends since boot; each thought of the other as his brother.

Service grinned. "Good. Tree knows how payback works."

"Listen to yourself! Payback? What kind of shit is that? You're a cop."

"Somebody does your partner, you go after *them*."

Later, while McCant's was outside with the dog, he went through last month's house telephone bills to see if there had been any unusual activity, but he saw nothing out of the ordinary. He also checked Nantz's personal cell phone bills. Apparently she called Walter's cell phone almost every day, which surprised him. He talked to his son perhaps once a week. There was also a number he didn't recognize that came up repeatedly, and out of desperation he dialed it.

"Hello?" a familiar voice answered. His son's girlfriend? Why the hell was Nantz calling her?

"Karylanne? I saw your number on Nantz's cell phone record and just thought I'd see who it was," he explained clumsily.

"It's me," she sighed. "Ah, when's the funeral?" she asked with a weak voice.

"I don't know yet," he said. Not her goddamn business. "Nantz called you often," he said.

"We were friends," the girl said.

When the hell did they become friends? Jesus Christ, was he blind to everything?

"OK, thanks," he said, and abruptly hung up.

He threw the records back in a drawer in Nantz's desk with disgust. What else could he check? He couldn't think of anything and felt even worse. You're supposed to be a detective, asshole, but you couldn't find a turd in a toilet. When the fuck would Linsenman bring the current records? He thought about going through Nantz's checkbook, but he wasn't sure where it was.

When McCants came back he was sitting alone in the kitchen looking out at the gray water of Little Bay de Noc, and trying to force his brain to give him something to work with, a place to start. Anything.

# 4

## SLIPPERY CREEK, MICHIGAN

## MAY 1, 2004

Luticious Treebone and Service sat on the porch of the cabin. "The whole woods cop clan is going to close ranks around you," Tree told him.

Service took him through the facts as he knew them, and Treebone listened without interrupting until his friend had finished.

"I've seen your gut in action," Tree said. "What do you need from me?"

"Just keep people off my tail while I get myself ready."

"Kalina will be up tomorrow," Treebone said. Tree had brought his duffel and a sleeping bag, declaring he'd be staying for two weeks, like it or not. He was under Kalina's orders, and no one defied his wife.

Kalina Treebone had been named for the great Detroit Tiger Al Kaline, but where Kaline had been humble throughout his Hall of Fame career, she was outspoken, resolute in her beliefs, and intimidating to her husband and most of his friends.

Three days had passed since Service had seen the wreck. The captain drove out from Marquette and said that the state felt 70 percent certain it had been an accident, but they were not going to declare it so until they had ruled out other possibilities. Service was not happy with the news, but it didn't change his mind about what he had to do, which was to get himself into top shape by living a spartan existence, with as few distractions as possible.

Each morning and afternoon he lifted weights. In between he ran six miles down Slippery Creek and into the Mosquito Wilderness Area, which he considered to be one of the state's natural jewels. Before Nantz, the Mosquito had been his one true love, and he had guarded it with the tenacity of his father before him. An unexpected promotion to detective in the

Wildlife Resources Protection unit removed him from the Mosquito, and it had become Candi's. So far she had been as fierce in protecting it as he had been.

Two hours after the captain left, Kalina Treebone arrived toting an enormous cooler filled with food and sent Tree to her van for two more coolers.

"You two aren't going to be eating cold beans from a can if I can help it."

Tree and Service hoisted the coolers into the cabin. Kalina confronted Service, one hand on her hip and the other waving like a flick-knife. "You've always been a selfish, self-absorbed man," she said. "Just like my Tree. Why any woman would want either of you is beyond me. What you need to be doing is getting your woman and your son properly buried and prayed over. Until then there ain't nothing else matters."

"They're dead," he said coldly, "and nothing can change that. What I have to do is deal with the things I can deal with. The state has ordered autopsies and I can't do a damn thing until they release them, so if you don't mind, put your finger back in its holster and let me get on with what I've got to do." He was sick of being hugged, advised, and lectured about what he ought to be doing, and he was fed up with hangdog faces and pathetic sighs. He didn't need sympathy; he needed space. Why couldn't they understand that? Couldn't they see or sense that whatever this was—and he wasn't in any position yet to describe it—it was just starting, not ending.

He knew she didn't buy it, but Kalina was like her husband, the sort who would do what a friend needed, even when they didn't agree.

Kalina manned the phone, which kept ringing with sympathy calls. Ever since he'd arrived, the cabin had been overflowing with a stream of friends, bearing food and cringing sympathy, most of them at a loss for exactly what to say. His friends and fellow woods cops came one after the other. Gus Turnage, CO from Houghton County, and a fly-fishing friend, arrived just after Treebone. Gus hugged him but had little to say. He had lost his own wife many years back, raised three sons on his own. He had never remarried.

Their friend Yalmer "Shark" Wetelainen and his wife, Limey Pyykkonen, came in the next morning, followed by Simon del Olmo, the Cuba-born army vet, and his girlfriend and conservation officer, Elza "Sheena" Grinda. Lars and Joan Hjalmquist came over from Ironwood; Wink Rector, the resident FBI agent for the U.P., drove down from Marquette; and DaWayne Kota, the tribal game warden from Bay Mills, also showed up. Last to arrive were the giant CO Bryan Jefferies from Luce County, and Gutpile Moody, and his young girlfriend, Kate, also an officer and close friend of Nantz's. Moody and Nordquist lived together in nearby Schoolcraft County.

Vince Vilardo and Rose came up from Escanaba. Vince was the retired medical examiner for Delta County, and a longtime friend.

Linsenman showed up with an envelope and handed it to him, and Service took it to the side and opened it and scanned May's phone records. They looked like last month's, mostly calls to him, Walter, and Karylanne. She had called Walter the day before the accident, but not Karylanne. Nothing there. Shit! He stuffed the records back in the envelope and threw it in a cardboard box in a corner.

Lieutenant Lisette McKower and her husband drove in from Newberry. McKower was five-five, 120, with short brown hair, a long neck, and the tiny hands of a doll. Service met her for the first time when she had been sent to him as a rookie to train. He thought they had sent him a cheerleader, but she had been twenty-four, had three summers under her belt as a smokejumper out of Montana, and turned out to be as tough as moosehide. She'd risen through the ranks and Service was proud of her, though he'd never have admitted it.

"I'm sorry for our loss, Grady. Hear that? Ours, not just yours."

Nantz was to have entered the DNR academy this fall.

"I talked to the captain," McKower said. "He told me what you found at the auto-body shop."

Service nodded.

"The evidence doesn't prove anything," she said. "Are you prepared to deal with it if it's ruled an accident?"

"It wasn't an accident," he said.

She sighed. "You always see the world in black and white, Grady. Remember, the Chinese say black has five colors and the Ojibwa have fourteen words for snow, including several colors other than white."

He didn't respond. She was one of those people who was pathologically rational, a woman who overrode intuition with pure intellectual power and had risen because of it. But she had also been a smokejumper and had considerable fire inside. Even if she wouldn't admit it, she understood the call to vengeance.

"I know you, Grady; you only *think* you know me," she said. "You classify me according to what's convenient for you. If this is not an accident, that does not mean it is automatically a homicide. There are shades, Grady, and there is a system and a process, and we are sworn to uphold both. We both know that the system and the process are no more than social algorithms, not final arbiters of right and wrong; they are only methods we use to determine guilty or not guilty, which has nothing to do with morality. Vengeance is not part of the system or the process," she concluded, looking directly into his eyes. "I know you will do the right thing," she said. "The captain says we are to assume this is an accident until the Troops issue a formal report to the contrary."

"Nice speech. It won't be me talking about it," he said.

"Not you talking, period," she said.

"Never been much good at it," he said.

"Nantz made you better," McKower said. "We don't want any backsliding."

"Is that the departmental 'we'?"

"That's the personal we, you big hardhead—me, and all your friends."

It seemed like half of Michigan Tech's hockey team trooped in the second morning, led by Walter's girlfriend, Karylanne Pengelly. Her eyes and nose were red and swollen, but she walked with her head up in a gesture of pride and resolve that caught Service's attention and choked him up for a moment.

His son had been in his first year at Michigan Tech and was working out and practicing with the team. Next year he would have been on scholarship. Not now. The Tech players mumbled as they shook his hand, and he understood. Elite young hockey players were like all young jocks. They hated dealing with injuries and death. Athletics was about feeling invincible, and when one of their own went down, it caused most of them to pull away so that they didn't have to face the reality or their own potential vulnerability. He couldn't blame them. He had been there once, had been a player who could have signed a pro contract if he'd wanted, but he had chosen the marines and gone to Vietnam instead of the NHL. It was a decision he'd never regretted, though it had been a hard, often nasty road from then to now.

He held Karylanne and felt her sob, but he had no words to soothe himself, much less her. All he could do was prepare to act. Why couldn't they all understand this?

That morning he had gotten a visit from the past.

The silver-haired man who walked into his cabin was tall and straight-backed with a weather-beaten face, accompanied by a small, gray-haired woman who was stunningly beautiful. "Grady, Bowie Rhodes," the man said.

Service said, "We're all getting gray."

Rhodes smiled. Service had met him when Rhodes was a UPI reporter in Vietnam. He and Tree had watched him trying to fish in a rice paddy that was actually a minefield, and they had helped get him safely out. They had known each other for decades, though they seldom got to see each other. Rhodes had a job that was the envy of fishermen: He wrote a column for an outdoor magazine and traveled around the country doing nothing but fishing.

Tree came over and embraced Rhodes. "What it is, bro." They dapped in the elaborate Vietnam style and laughed, like the kids they had once been.

Service went outside with Rhodes. "I'm not much for giving advice," the old reporter said, "but I've been through this one."

"Ingrid," Service said. Ingrid Cashdollar had been Bowie's first wife. She had been a deputy in Luce County and Service had known her. She had been beautiful, funny, and an effective cop, and when she died it had affected a whole county, not just her husband. Since then Bowie had remarried and seemed happy with Janey.

"What you have to do is keep your mouth shut and let people do and say whatever they need to get out their feelings. The funny thing is that when a wife dies, everyone is concerned about everything except the husband."

"We weren't married."

Rhodes smiled. "Yeah, like paper matters." He fished in his pocket and held out a key. "When all the company clears away, you need to go off somewhere and be totally alone for a while. That key opens the door to a camp I have in west Chippewa County. You have to come in through Fiborn and drive ten miles up a two-track. There's a coded lock on the gate. What was your last day in Vietnam?"

"December 19," Service said. "1969."

"Okay, the lock will be coded 1219, and you have the key to the camp. There's no well or running water, and no electricity. There's heat from propane and kerosene lamps—very old-style, unheated outhouse included. The camp sits at the end of a finger in a huge swamp. Go when you want, stay as long as you need, and take in your own water. You remember Ironhead Beaudoin?"

Beaudoin had been a contemporary of his father's, also a conservation officer. "Out of Trout Lake, right?"

Rhodes nodded. "He was a pistol. He tracked a poacher named Carvolino for years. The camp is built where the old poacher's stand sat. Carvolino used Indian pulpies to haul in timber and built a cabin on state land in the swamp. Beaudoin didn't find it until after Carvolino died, and when it got logged and came up for sale, he bought it. After Ironhead passed, I bought it from his daughter."

The name Carvolino seemed familiar. "He the one—"

Rhodes interrupted him by nodding, opening his mouth and pointing a finger inside. "Carvolino used to sell buck racks to downstate sports in bars in Moran and Brevort and Trout Lake and Ozark and St. Ignace. He was a major lush, but he knew his way in the woods. Ran traplines. Come deer season he'd park his car somewhere for two weeks, walk into his hunting ground in a roundabout way, and stay until the season was over. He'd ship out the meat and racks using a sidecar that the Indians used to go back and forth to town. Beaudoin never could catch him. Just after deer season, Beaudoin's last before he retired, Carvolino and his wife had separated and he was drinking like a fish. He called her at the phone company in Iggy one morning and begged her to come back and give him another chance, but she was fed up and refused, and he said, 'Okay, then listen to this.' He put the shotgun in his mouth and squeezed it off. I think it broke Beaudoin's heart that he never pinched the guy."

Rhodes told a good yarn, and had a conservation officer's appreciation for stories.

"I'm serious, Grady—use the camp. And trust me: Over time, the pain will be replaced by scar tissue, which will thicken. It will never completely cover the wound, but it will make life tolerable."

That night there were twenty or thirty officers and friends in the cabin, but Grady Service was alone in the dark, several hundred yards away on a ridge, and when he began firing his pistol at a paper target he had tacked to a tree, several woods cops appeared, their 40-caliber SIG Sauers in hand, ready to rock and roll.

Treebone was winded from the run through the woods to the site of the gunfire. "What the hell are you *doing,* man?"

"Getting ready," Grady Service said.

"There it is," Treebone said quietly.

Service was certain that all of them understood exactly what he meant.

# 5

## SLIPPERY CREEK, MICHIGAN
### MAY 3, 2004

Grady Service and Tree sat on the porch of his cabin. Newf and Cat stayed close. The sky was the color of sun-baked slate. He had found the cat years ago in a cloth bag with seven kittens someone had dumped in the creek. Why the one had survived was beyond him, but she had lived and turned into a feline misanthrope that he never got around to naming. Newf's color was brindle, an unappealing mix of brown, gray, and ocher, all slopped together like cheap cake mix in a bowl. She had intelligent brown eyes and a wide black snout.

The crowds of well-wishers had dwindled. There were just the two of them, alone finally.

His watch said 2:40 p.m., but time had lost all meaning. The only numbers registering now: Five reduced to three, death in a flash, sudden, unexpected, too familiar, too permanent, the way he knew it best, had experienced it too many times before.

Intellectually he understood they were dead, but he was still trying to process the reality. Somebody had tried to drown Cat and she had survived. Nantz and Walter wanted only to live, but had died. It made no sense. Was God a jokester, or just an asshole?

Sadness had changed to anger. What the hell had Nantz been doing on M-35 south of Palmer, and why the hell was Walter with her when he was supposed to be at school? Something inside him kept telling him that if she had not gone down that road they would still be alive, but he knew the truth. Death came in its own time and in its own way. Nantz had wanted to be a conservation officer and had already adopted a game warden's habits. Like him, she never came home the same way. His fault! She had tried to copy a lot of his behaviors. Jesus.

For three years he had lived with Maridly Nantz as friends, lovers; they were a couple. In three years with Nantz he had almost become civilized—and even soft—but he had also been deeply and undeniably in love. Now she was gone and not coming back, and he had returned to sleeping on a thin mattress on military footlockers set end to end.

The autopsy results were still pending, and there had been no funeral service and no memorial. He refused to hear of it. When it was time, he would have them both cremated.

"You remember Erbelli?" Tree asked, and answered his own question. "One day in country, base camp, sniper round to the head. Wouldn't know him if he walked up on the porch right now. How many we lose from the company?"

"Fourteen dead."

"There it is," Treebone said. "We are born to die."

"God's will, that junk?" Service asked, feeling uncomfortable. Of all his friends, Tree was closest. They had been through the most together, including Vietnam, and Tree would be the one to try to reach out to him, toss him a net if he thought he needed it.

"A while back Kalina tries to get me down to the AMC, the Reverend Thelonious Jones, proprietor—Thelonious Jones of Howard, Harvard, and Jackson. He did fifteen for a plethora of transgressions, now reformed, his life an open book, all sins pronounced and denounced, can I hear an amen, *brother?*"

"You went to church?" This was a revelation. Neither he nor Tree put much stock in organized religion, but Kalina was undisputed queen of Treebone's kingdom.

"Ain't no quit in the sister. The reverend and me circled and sniffed each other and we both saw the truth of the other: two pit bulls with a philosophical fence between us, him wanting to redeem lost souls in order to redeem his own, and me wanting to go up the side of bad-ass motherfucking heads—his included."

"This story have a point?"

"Are who we are, is what it is," Tree said.

"Meaning?"

"We choose to walk through the Valley of Death, Grady. We don't have to like it, but we got to keep on keepin' on."

"Trucking until we retire."

"After all the shit we've been through, a retirement ain't something to throw away, man."

"You telling me to rein it in?"

"No, man. There's got to be payback. All I'm sayin' is that payback can be in degrees—hear what I'm sayin'?"

"I hear." Grady Service had enough years of service, between the marines, state police, and DNR law enforcement to pack it in now, but he had begun to conceive of retirement in the context of Nantz and his son—not alone. Now they were gone.

"I never married her," Service said, his voice cracking.

## 6

## SLIPPERY CREEK, MICHIGAN
### MAY 4, 2004

Service came back from a run and found Tree tying flies on the porch of the cabin. He was sitting next to a small man with a ruddy complexion and white hair in a buzz cut, smoking a cigar and rubbing Newf's ears.

"This is Father O'Brien," Tree announced.

"I'm not a mackerel snapper," Service greeted the man caustically.

"Call me OB," the man said. "Technically we don't have the Friday fish rule anymore, and in any event, I'm not here as a Catholic. I'm here as an informal grief counselor. Your captain suggested we talk."

Newf came over to Service and poked at his hand with her drooly snout. "So talk."

"As you reenter the melee, you're apt to carry a bit of anger, and maybe your judgment will be frayed. It helps to talk things through with somebody neutral, bounce feelings off."

Service started to object, but he held back, understood O'Brien's presence was the captain's way of gauging and monitoring his readiness. He had no choice but to go along with it. He could hear Nantz whispering, "Back off, you lummox."

"Whatever floats your boat, OB," Service said, going into the cabin. *If everyone would just leave him alone he would be fine*, he thought. Like Tree had said, no choice but to keep on keepin' on.

"Okay then," the priest said, following him. "I guess that's a good introduction. I'll leave my card with you. Feel free to call me every couple of days."

"One time better than another for you?"

"It's your choice. I'm mostly retired and my time is open."

Service turned around to face the man. "What sort of work did you do?"

"I taught psychology at Marquette University for thirty years. Also I was in the Marine Reserve as a chaplain, and served in the first Gulf War."

"Retirement a tough adjustment?"

"*All* of life's adjustments are difficult, son. Semper Fi."

"You're not gonna call him," Tree said after the man was gone.

"Back off," Grady Service said. "I don't need help."

"You mean you don't *want* help, man. We all *need* it."

"I called the funeral home today. I have to stop and sign papers tomorrow. They'll be cremated tomorrow or the next day."

"And the memorial?"

"Not yet."

"What does that mean?"

"It means not yet."


Two days later the two of them drove to the funeral home in Gladstone and picked up the ashes. They were in sturdy cardboard containers made to look like marble. They brought the ashes back to Slippery Creek and Service set them on the counter in his kitchen and broke open a bottle of Jack Daniel's. Tree would be heading back to Detroit in the morning.

Treebone held out his glass and touched Service's. "She was a fine woman, your Nantz, and Walter was a fine kid. It don't mean nothing."

This was what they had said in Vietnam every time something bad or inexplicable occurred. A drunk marine second lieutenant named Ploegstra once explained, "Think of a huge honker of a log floating down the Colorado River, and on that log there's billions of pissants and each one of the little assholes thinks he's steering. It don't mean nothing."

But it did, Grady Service knew. It meant he was alone and would never again feel the soft touch of Maridly Nantz or smell her hair after she got out of the tub. And he would never again hear his son shout in triumph as he hooked a big brook trout with a fly. What it meant was that he had lost not just a lot, but everything, and that meant something. It meant that he would not rest until he figured out what the hell had happened and settled accounts. He looked over at his friend and Tree nodded. He understood.

# MARQUETTE, MICHIGAN
## MAY 19, 2004

Service sat in his captain's office.

"But she was a pilot," Grady Service insisted. "Don't you *people* get it?"

Captain Ware Grant looked across the table at him. "You *people?* Grady, pilots are not invincible," his captain said gently. "Have you got something to say to me?"

"I've been on the shelf three weeks," Service said.

"Take as long as you need," the captain said. "There's no hurry to come back."

"If I don't get back to the field, I'll go out of my mind," Service said. "You have to let me come back to work."

"You don't seem ready."

"I can't sit around. I need focus. I need my boots in the dirt, dealing with what I know best."

"We can't afford to have a loose cannon out there," his supervising officer said.

"You know me. You know that's not what I am."

"Sudden loss can induce a form of PTSD," the captain said. "Mourning can bring a severe form of the disorder."

"I lost my father suddenly. I've lost men in combat suddenly. I've lost friends suddenly—this is not something new. And, dammit, it wasn't me in the accident!" It was difficult to keep his voice at a reasonable level.

The captain studied him.

"We each mourn in our own way and in our own time. The aftermath of some situations is nearly as traumatic as the situation itself."

"Please, Cap'n." This was as close to pleading as Grady Service could bring himself.

The Upper Peninsula's DNR law boss took a long time to reply. "Okay, you can come back, but if you need downtime, take it. Just let me know. I won't ask questions."

"You won't be sorry," Service said.

"The night this happened, you said, 'But she's a pilot.' And you said it again today."

"She wasn't *just* a pilot, Cap'n. She was a damn good pilot, experienced. She was born to vehicles, didn't panic, kept emotional control when all hell was breaking loose. How does somebody like that lose control of a truck and hit a tree on a dry road? I haven't seen the report."

Grant reached into a neat pile of folders, extracted a stapled document, and slid it across the table. "Straight off the road, down the embankment and into the tree. The cab roof absorbed the main impact, buckled flat. The case is closed—official ruling is that it was an accident."

Grady Service had expected as much. He took the folder out to his Tahoe and drove from the pagoda-like Marquette Regional DNR building called "The Roof," over to an abandoned gravel pit on the Carp River behind Marquette Mountain. He parked in the shade and spent an hour smoking and reading and thinking, and when he was done, he decided he needed to see photographs—but not now. He didn't want to wallow in their deaths. He wanted to move on and find out *why* they were dead, and he knew that if he went back to the captain, Grant would be suspicious of his focus. Right now he was glad to have the green light to work.

One thing was for sure: He was no longer a family man. Now he had only the clan of conservation officers in gray shirts and green pants, a gigantic dog, and a bad-tempered cat. He had been left with less previously. He would make do with what remained.

|||||||||||||||||||||||||||||||||||||||||||||||||||||||||||||||||||||||||||||||||||||||||||||||||||||||||||||||||||||||||||||

8

## SLIPPERY CREEK, MICHIGAN

### MAY 20, 2004

Today he was finally going back to work. Grady Service woke up thinking not about Maridly and Walter, but about this past Easter night when he had gotten disoriented in the dark and rain as he pursued three people illegally spearing pike at the bottom of the Stonington Peninusula. It had been raining hard, dark, air at thirty-seven degrees, and for reasons he had still not figured out, he had fallen into Wilsey Bay Creek, which was swollen with winter runoff; he had fought, but the current had swept him through a culvert. He had managed to struggle out of the water seventy-five yards downstream, his teeth broken, his pride and body bruised.

Ten days later he was sitting in an ergonomic tilt-a-chair in an oral surgeon's office in Green Bay trying to focus on a pair of blue jays feeding on a platform feeder a few feet away. There had been multiple injections of anesthetic into his gums and the roof of his mouth; his tongue felt like a burrito on steroids.

"We'll give it a few minutes," the surgeon said. Service had met him two days before, to "create an extraction plan." The male blue jay pushed the female aside and pecked her on the head.

The surgeon and his assistant returned. A tray was rotated under his chin. The doctor poked a metal instrument in his mouth: Service felt nothing. The doctor slid a mask over his nose, jacked open his jaws with clamps, and hung hissing tubes in his mouth.

"Feel anything?" the doctor asked.

His mind sorted possible answers: angst, shame over a stupid accident, the curse of poor dental genetics, gravity? What he said was, "Uh-uh."

"The gas will take you to the edge of consciousness," the oral surgeon said. "You'll be here, but not here."

Did that mean the doctor and his assistant were likewise here, but not here? Long ago he and Tree had been on a mission in Laos, watching hundreds of North Vietnamese black ants moving war materiel south along the Ho Chi Minh Trail. Publicly both countries were saying they had no troops in Laos, and Tree had whispered, "They here, but not here." That night they had sprung a brief but deadly ambush, leaving enemy bodies there that weren't there, and bugging out for their extraction point ten clicks west.

His mind would not settle into that zone where his thoughts would turn off. His girlfriend, Maridly Nantz, was a lot younger and had all her teeth. How would she handle a toothless boyfriend? If he was here but not here, did that mean that the teeth being pulled were not really being pulled?

"Okay," the surgeon said enthusiastically, "here we go."

*We:* Did the man have a mouse in his pocket?

Thirty minutes later his cheeks were distorted with cotton wads and he was biting down on sterile gauze pads as the assistant led him from the surgeon's office through the waiting room of the prosthodontist, blood on his chin, pink drool cascading. He saw Nantz watching him wide-eyed.

After another forty minutes he walked out to the truck with Nantz trying to steady him by holding his arm. He kept pulling away. The surgeon had extracted twenty-two teeth, upstairs and downstairs, and the prosthodontist had installed new false teeth, insisting as he gagged almost continuously that he would "over time" adjust to them.

"Don't smoke, and use your pain meds liberally," the prosthodontist concluded.

"You're handling this pretty well, hon," Nantz said as they got into the truck.

"Smoke," he said, staring out at the late April rain, the word feeling like a foreign object in a mouth full of foreign objects. He could not feel his tongue, lips, cheeks, jaw, most of his lower face.

"You won't be able to hold a cigarette," Nantz said. "You'll drop it and burn yourself."

"Smoke," he repeated, adding, "*Goddammit.*"

She handed him a pack, which he looked at. It was too hard, something not right.

"Candy smokes," she said. "They'll take care of your oral fixation and they can't burn you. The upside is that you don't have any teeth for the sugar to rot."

He flung the candy into the back. "Could use sympathy," he said, the multisyllabic word causing him to drool.

"That's what pain pills are for," she said.

"No pills!" he said. "*Embrace* pain."

"You *would* say that," she said, starting the engine.

*Embrace pain.* That was the thought in his mind as he climbed into his truck and started the engine, feeling here but not here. This is all you have, he told himself. Get your boots in the dirt, get it done.

|||||||||||||||||||||||||||||||||||||||||||||||||||||||||||||||||||||||||||||||||||||||||||||||||||||||||||||||||||||||||||||||||||||||||||||||||||||||||||||||||

9

## MORMON CREEK, MICHIGAN
### MAY 20, 2004

Nantz's last words just about every morning had been to ask if he had his teeth in. The things still felt like alien invaders in his mouth and already had drastically altered what and how he ate.

This morning he had gotten to the truck and realized the teeth were back in the cabin. He went back, fetched them, and drove off into the unknown, back at work after more than three weeks.

Grady Service parked his truck in a gap in a grove of aspens, grabbed his ruck, silently closed the doors, locked them, and started hiking west. He considered leaving the false teeth in the truck, but on the long shot that he might encounter someone, he left the diabolical pieces of shit in. The public might be unhinged by the visage of a toothless game warden. The sky was gray and threatening, the air heavy. As he crossed through a cedar swamp, he detected movement. It was a deer, a ribby buck, one-inch nubbins of antlers in coppery green velvet, its hide still winter-gray when it ought to be reddening for summer.

A two-year-old, he guessed, standing beside a puddle of black swamp water, its legs splayed apart, ears droopy, muzzle in the water. Service passed within ten feet of the animal, which ignored him and continued to drink. Come spring and early summer, deer were often bold, their interest in food after a tough winter overriding any inborn fear of humans.

There had been neither an unusually deep snowpack over winter, nor abundant spring rain, and what snowpack they did have had melted off slowly, leaving no floods. Even with a workable water level in Mormon Creek, a lot of the local trout-takers and most old-timers wouldn't venture out to dunk red worms and crawlers until after Independence Day. Rivers were usually fishable before the Memorial Day weekend, but locals waited to fish until blackflies were on the wane. Never mind that trout fishing with flies was far better in May and June when Hendricksons, brown drakes, and giant Hexagenia were hatching. There were few Yooper fly fishers and even fewer catch-and-release types. Up here it was catch-and-release into grease, and once a tradition took hold, it was difficult to change the mind-set, especially for natives who believed all fish and game that inhabited the peninsula were their personal birthright. At best, Service knew, he might encounter some hardy down- or out-stater after brookies. Most dedicated fly fishers in the U.P. were elderly males, twenty to thirty years his senior. For some reason flies had not caught on with his generation, and he had never understood why.

It still amazed him the lengths to which some brook trout chasers would go in search of a species of fish where eighteen inches was a lifetime trophy in Michigan. It amazed him, but it didn't surprise him, because serious brook trout fishers knew that the further you hiked off the grid, the better the fishing was likely to be. Chasing trout, he had decided a long time ago, was a lot like being a game warden. If you kept too close to the easy marks, you missed the good cases, and the bigger fish. The worst poachers, like the best trout, had to be hunted in their natural habitat, which was neither easy to get to nor particularly hospitable after you reached it. Good game wardens and successful trouters learned how to ignore pain and discomfort to do the job, no matter what.

Because of the state's law enforcement manpower shortage, he had, since the first of the year, continued to double as a detective for Wildlife Resources Protection, the Department of Natural Resource's statewide investigatory unit, as well as handling slices of Marquette, Delta, Schoolcraft, and Alger counties in a more-traditional game warden role. It felt good to be back doing what he knew best, but all winter his gut had churned with foreboding, a feeling that something terrible was looming. Even in the wake of the deaths of Maridly and Walter, the feeling persisted. What could be worse than losing the two people who mattered most to you? *Don't think about it,* he told himself. *Keep your mind in the game.*

It had been several years since he had been into the Mormon Creek meadows area where an old Civilian Conservation Corps camp had once stood. As he passed it he thought about the Creekateers, a jug band made up of CCC men back in the late thirties. Why had he thought of this? He had never actually seen or even heard the band, only of them—and only from his father and his hard-drinking cronies. It struck him as odd to think of something his father liked. For the most part he rarely thought about his old man, had no reason to. *Don't let your mind wander, asshole,* he lectured himself again.

The old camp was only a few miles north of Nahma Junction and US 2. Mormon Creek originated in a swampy marsh south of Lost Lake and flowed south for a mile or so before sharply turning east to dump into the Sturgeon River. All that remained of the camp was a crumbling stone foundation, spackled by patches of scratchy gray-green lichen. There were no vehicles parked along the way, and this allowed him to concentrate less on violators and more on fishing possibilities.

He liked what he saw, and cut southwest on foot down to the creek and made his way across squishy, bouncy, sphagnum moss meadows toward the headwaters, more interested in what bugs might be hatching than in any major expectation of encountering fishermen. He used a small digital thermometer to check the water temperature: fifty-seven degrees, just about perfect for brook trout. And it was unseasonably clear if you ignored the tannin that stained the water the color of liquid rust year-round.

Most trees had some new leaves, but serious foliage was still to come. The sticky May air was in the low seventies, and the humidity brought forth blackflies that landed on his hands and neck looking for places to nail him. Unless the area got significant rain soon, the fire danger was going to soar, and with the state's severely pinched budget, there were fewer fire officers to manage the blazes. Service wondered if this summer would be spent more on fire lines than regular law enforcement duties. Nantz had been a fire officer when he met her. "Stop it!" he said out loud.

When it began to drizzle he hoped it would continue, and when he heard thunder rattling to the west he smiled and returned his attention to the water. This time of year fish were starved from the long winter, and thunderstorms seemed to turn them on—until the storm got overhead. If the wind stayed down after the storm passed, the fish would start eating again. He took comfort in knowing the cycles and moods of fish and other creatures. Knowing such things helped him to find violators and poachers, who often also knew the same things.

He stopped below a riffle in the narrow, meandering creek, hunkered down, lit a cigarette, and watched and listened to the softly chuckling water. The rain was light, the thunder distant, and he guessed the cell would pass north of him, which would be good for fishing. Caddis flies began to emerge and frantically pop through the surface film. A few flies were soon followed by a steady flow of bugs, and as some of the insects got trapped in the surface film, trout began to rise and slurp cripples for quick meals. Because caddis tended to emerge from the nymphal stage to dun, and hatch more energetically than mayflies, trout tended to go after them aggressively. It was like mealtime in a boardinghouse: Grab fast or go hungry. More than once he had seen trout come entirely out of the water, taking such bugs in splashy somersaults.

Squatting beside Mormon Creek watching trout feeding on small black caddis, he reminded himself he could be content doing this for the rest of his life. He loved being a conservation officer, and after his unexpected and unwanted promotion to detective, he felt he was adjusting to the new job and learning to enjoy it, but he didn't need work to define himself. He knew that if the job ended tomorrow he'd be content wandering the Upper Peninsula's hundreds of miles of beaver ponds, pothole lakes, streams, and rivers, searching for brook trout. Being alone in the middle of nowhere was one of the greatest gifts of both his vocation and avocation, and he appreciated the solace and the silence. He could heal out here.

Tree had once told him he'd been born two hundred years late. They had been on a fifteen-day recon in the tri-border area at the time, a place cluttered with triple canopy jungle, plastic-wrap humidity, swarms of carnivorous insects, bad water, poisonous snakes, smells only maggots could embrace, and trigger-happy Pathet Lao and North Vietnamese Army regulars.

"You get off on this shit," Tree had said. "And that ain't normal."

It was not so much that he got off on it as he knew what his job was, and had the freedom to do it. Service smiled at the memory. Tree had grown up in the city, but he was a natural outdoors, and if not for keeping peace on the home front, he'd still be humping the woods as a CO and complaining about how much he hated it. The two of them shared a passion for fly fishing and brook trout.

When the caddis hatch began to wane, Service continued downstream, careful to watch where he put his feet lest he drop into a sinkhole or through one of the quivering, porous humps of muskeg tussocks that covered the meadows and lined the banks. The footing only looked solid, a potentially lethal illusion; it was strictly veneer over bottomless, frigid black loon shit.

A half-hour after the caddis petered out, a few dark Hendrickson mayflies began to rise and the fish, which took a while to catch on to what was happening, eventually noticed and began to rise steadily along the length of a long, curving dark slick with dense logjams and thick tag alder cover on both sides. Because of the state's budget crisis, all conservation offices were working eighty hours every two-week pay period, but being paid only for seventy-six. And, like every state employee, every so often they were taking unpaid furlough days off, accumulating 104 unpaid hours over the year, which could be taken as vacation, or banked for retirement when it would then be reimbursed. *If* the state could afford to pay then, a big *if* in the minds of many state employees, who dutifully took orders from elected politicians, but rarely trusted them.

Like Social Security, the state's future fiscal health was anything but secure. The budget crisis had been brought on by recently departed governor Samuel Adams Bozian, who had decimated the state, hit term limits, and moved on to greener, higher-paying private-sector pastures. Few people other than hard-core Republicans regretted Bozian's departure, and although Democrat Lorelei Timms had been easily elected over a Bozian protégé, she remained unproven and was starting deep in a hole, with a helluva steep hill facing her.

Service's next furlough period would be on the weekend, and with two regular pass days tacked on, he would have four days to spend with Nantz and not think about anything except fishing and each other. He corrected himself. He would be *alone* for the furlough. He could no longer allow himself to think in terms of *they*. Life was reduced to him and the job. Still, this was a very sweet-looking spot, and probably tomorrow night there would be a spinner fall at dusk—if the wind didn't come up or the temperature drop precipitously. Most mayflies lived only forty-eight to seventy-two hours, and if they didn't mate and the females deposit their eggs, the whole purpose of their short lives was wasted. He could understand their desire to get on with their biological imperative. He sometimes thought his own drive to defend natural resources was biologically driven. Certainly he was no less zealous than his old man, who had been a CO before him. The difference was that the old man was rarely sober, and it had cost him his life. *Jesus!* Nantz and Walter. Why? Goddammit, why had she gone to Houghton and come back through Palmer? And why the hell had Walter been with her?

He was tempted to contemplate life from the perspective of an insect, but decided against it. Life was life: You got what you were born into. If there was a God, did he choose which spirits would be bugs or humans? The Indians believed that all things, animate and inanimate, had spirits, which he thought probably meant souls. Certainly, all living things were part of the cycle of life and death—but rocks? This was the problem with codified religions. When you began to try to dissect them in detail, they didn't quite work, and invariably that's when the most fervent types went to their fallback: You just have to believe—to take things on faith. He wasn't one to blindly accept anything on hope alone. He conceded that he could be deceiving himself, but he had also concluded over more than fifty years of life that a man made his own opportunities and luck, and if not, it helped to think so. Was this faith or hubris? He didn't know. Had Nantz made her own bad luck? He could not, would not believe this. No way. She was the *best*.

Why was he thinking about such things? After his divorce from his first wife, Bathsheba, he had gone through a series of girlfriends and had never felt a particular urge to remarry, much less to father children—until Maridly Nantz. She had been scheduled to enter the DNR academy in October with the goal of becoming a conservation officer. Last year's session had been canceled because of the state budget crisis, and Nantz had gone through the roof. Her raw emotional outbursts made him wonder how she—*they*—would handle it if the academy got canceled again. Worrying about others was not the sort of thing he had given much thought to in the past. Now it didn't matter.

The mercurial Nantz's interests and aspirations had become as compelling as his own. She was the major change and force in his life, even more than finding out he had a son. For the first time in his life he learned what it meant to put someone else's needs before his own. He didn't think much about love or what it meant: It just felt right, and this had sufficed. Love persisted; objects of that love did not.

He checked his watch. Time to move down the creek, cross out to the road, and get back to his truck. There was almost continuous thunder to the north, and he could see shafts of sunlight piercing the dark clouds, what his old man had called "devil's smiles." The rain was beginning to pick up, which suggested the storm cell was closing.

After fifty yards of stumbling, he decided he'd followed the meandering stream long enough. He looked for the nearest high ground and started directly for it. As he got close to the cedars he thought he saw a flash of light to his left and above. He flinched, thought his heart skipped a beat, nearly threw himself on his face, waiting for the inevitable thunder, but heard only the steady patter of soft rain and saw no more light. What the hell had it been? He sniffed the air. No ozone, which meant the strike, if there had been one, had not been that close. Still, the light had the suddenness and intensity of a close strike, and he was virtually exposed in the open, a perfect target. There was no point bending over to lower his profile. He did not move for nearly a minute, then eased up his binoculars and scanned the tree line for nearly five more minutes. Maybe there had been a light flash, maybe not. It could have been a play of light from the instable sky, or an animal's movement. Why had he overreacted? Weird. Whatever had been there was gone, and he had a long walk back to the truck. A black bear possibly, more likely a deer. Young bears were out scavenging and does were throwing fawns, the whitetails not that long out of their winter yards and still dispersing, some of them en route to their summer ranges up to fifty miles away. Come fall they would reverse course and seek denser winter thermal cover and the sparse food of cedar and spruce swamps.

He smiled as he moved. The backcountry: There was always something new to be experienced, and often it was inexplicable. The forest was an unnerving venue for people with fecund imaginations. The rain was softer now, something between a drizzle and mist. The main cell, he saw, was moving north of him. *Good fishing,* he told himself.

All officers were taught and encouraged to hide their trucks a good distance from where they intended to go, but Service tended to dump his vehicle further away than most, believing that the further away you were, the less chance you had of being detected by shitballs. Some violators used scouts to patrol roads and search for game wardens' vehicles, and with the advent of CBs, cell phones, and other radio systems, instantaneous communications was becoming the rule rather than the exception for habitual violators. A good game warden had to be willing to walk, and put his boots in dirt, mud, ice, and snow, and Service took pride in being a damn good game warden. *Maybe too much pride,* he chastised himself.

He diverted toward the area where he thought he had seen the light and began playing with the ear mike, which was irritating his ear. He was still skeptical about the devices Michigan conservation officers had recently been ordered to use, and more than anything he was constantly picking at his ear, trying to make the damn thing comfortable. Between false teeth and the ear mike, he felt anything but comfortable. He was becoming a damned android, more technology than human. He had heard that some downstate districts had told their officers to forget the new devices, but he wasn't ready to give up on it quite yet. Naturally, younger officers—Generation X or Y or whatever the hell they were being called now, those from the Nintendo generation—embraced any and all new technology, but Service thought it made game wardens look like they were playing at being Secret Service agents or James Bond wannabes. He had the microphone rigged under his shirt, and in order to transmit, he had only to press his hand to his heart. It seemed silly, but he knew there would be times when having silent radio contact and two free hands would be a good thing—*if* he could make it less annoying, Or he could stuff it in his ruck. But he had kept his teeth in and they were uncomfortable. Better to gut it out, try to adjust.

"Twenty Five Fourteen, do you have TX?" a voice asked over the 800-megahertz radio. He had it turned down and didn't catch the caller's code. He glanced at the digital display on top of the 800 stuck in its belt holster and saw he was on the district's channel.

"Twenty Five Fourteen is out of vehicle, TX in fifteen minutes," he said, touching his chest, adding, "Twenty Five Fourteen clear." He had left his cell phone in the truck. Even there he'd be lucky to get a signal. There were vast reaches of the U.P. where cell phones refused to operate with any regularity, and other places where they would not work at all.

He heard the cell phone buzzing as he unlocked the Tahoe, unclipped the tiny phone from the sun visor, and flipped it open to activate it.

"Grady? Lorne O'Driscoll."

"Chief." O'Driscoll led the Law Enforcement Division for the Michigan Department of Natural Resources Law Enforcement Division in Lansing. Why the hell was the chief calling *him*? He had already called several times to express condolences and check on him. Enough was enough.

"Where are you?" O'Driscoll asked.

Service toyed with a smart-ass answer and rejected it; the chief was a good man, but a stickler for professional communications etiquette. "Uh, eastern Delta County—more or less." Hell, if the chief had the Automatic Vehicle Locator up on his computer screen, he could damn well see where he was—to within 25 meters of accuracy.

"We need for you to get over to Florence, Wisconsin. Check in with Special Agent T. R. Monica at the Florence Natural Resources and Wild Rivers Interpretation Center. It's a half-mile west of town at the intersection of US 2 and Highways 70/101; got it?"

The term *special agent* usually added up to one thing. "Feebs, sir?"

"That's affirmative. You'll be there in a consulting role. The order comes directly from the governor's office. Your mission is to remain with them until they kick you loose."

*Just great,* Service thought. "When?" he asked. A consultant to the FBI? *It sounded like a goat rodeo in the making,* he told himself. It figured that the governor was interfering in his life, but he kept this to himself. Governor Timms had been a good friend of Nantz's. He'd already received the expected condolence call from her. He had been through Florence before and knew where the center was. CO Simon del Olmo in Crystal Falls often worked closely with a Wisconsin warden from Florence County. Service had met the man several times, once at the center, where he maintained a satellite office. Florence was about ten miles due south of Crystal Falls. He had a Wisconsin map book somewhere in his truck, and he eyeballed the backseat, but couldn't see it.

"Get there ASAP. I assume you're rolling," the chief said. "Check in as you can. Any questions?"

"Nine thousand one hundred and twenty-two," Service quipped, aiming his vehicle south toward US 2.

"Join the club," the chief said.

"Sir, I've got two furlough days this weekend."

"Negative. You're working and the feds are paying for your time."

The state budget was in bad shape. If there was a chance to pick up reimbursement from the feds, O'Driscoll would jump on it. The order to join the FBI was mostly about money, he concluded.

He was about to pull away when he thought about the deer he had seen earlier. Something had registered vaguely as not being right with the animal, but he had been anxious to get to the creek and had shrugged it off. He got out of the truck and went back to where he had seen the deer and found it in the same place, still drinking—and urinating at the same time.

"Oh boy," he said out loud. The department and the state's 800,000 licensed hunters were worried about Chronic Wasting Disease moving into the state from Wisconsin and devastating Michigan's herd. So far CWD had not been detected here, but all officers had been briefed on symptoms, and this animal was showing some of the classics: spread legs, droopy ears, no fear, constant thirst, and urination. He trotted back to the truck and got on the cell phone.

It was answered after two rings. "Wildlife, Beal."

Buster Beal was a biologist in the Escanaba office, a man who loved white-tailed deer, took care of the herd as a sacred responsibility, and killed them with equal fervor during rifle and archery seasons. Beal was well over six foot, burly and hairy and known throughout the DNR as Chewy, after the hirsute *Star Wars* character.

"Chewy, it's Grady."

"You find me a big boy?" Beal expected calls from COs who saw large bucks and most of them complied. "I'm up near Mormon Creek. I've got a buck here, spread legs, droopy ears, doesn't seem the least bit bothered by me, and he's drinking and pissing at the same time."

"Oh, man," Buster Beal keened. "Shit, fuck, shit."

"Hey, I'm not giving it a label; I'm just reporting what I see. How do you want me to play it?"

"Wait for me," Beal said. "I'll be in my truck in thirty seconds, there in thirty minutes."

Service explained his current location. "I'll move my truck, meet you where Mormon is cut by the forest service road, but you've got to step on it, Chewy. I just had a call from my command and I have to get somewhere posthaste."

"Sit tight," the biologist said. "Neither of us wants the first case of you-know-what in the state to be on our watch." Last year Michigan had sold 800,000 hunting licenses, and this money, and that spent by hunters, remained a major plus in the state's crippled economy. Even so, there were fewer hunters every year. Not long ago the state was selling more than 1.5 million licenses every year.

The biologist was there in less than thirty minutes, his face red with excitement and nerves. Service led him back to where he had parked earlier and walked him to the deer, which had not moved. They stood six feet away and Beal observed for a couple of minutes until he shook his head and said, "Still in its winter coat."

"What do you want to do?" Service asked.

"Well, if it's you-know-what, the animal hasn't started to waste. He's thin, but coming out of winter, that's not abnormal. But we need to play this safe. You want to put it down?"

Service took out his 40-caliber SIG Sauer and walked over to the deer. Beal told him to wait, ran back to his truck, and returned quickly with a blue plastic tarp and a box of disposable latex gloves.

"Not the brain," Beal said. "Pop the heart. I want the brain and spinal column tissue in good shape. And don't put him down in the water. Let's limit blood loss just to be safe."

Beal waded into the water beside the deer and poked it with a stick, but the animal refused to move. Finally he had to put both hands on its back haunches and shove. Only then did it reluctantly stumble up to higher ground, its ears finally perking up, its movement still clumsy and uncoordinated.

Service took aim and fired. The animal collapsed, kicked once, lay still.

The biologist handed him latex gloves, and the two of them pulled the animal onto the tarp and dragged it back to the biologist's truck, where they loaded it in the bed.

"You gonna send it to a lab?" Service asked. The state wildlife laboratory was in Rose Lake, just north of Lansing.

"After I take a good look for myself. Let's don't get too many bowels in an uproar over this," the biologist said. "There are several diseases that present similar symptoms, and coming out of winter yards, most deer are not at their best."

Service knew the biologist was trying to think positively.

"Well, if it turns out to be bad news, we've at least got a governor who won't sit on her ass," the biologist added. "Lori's got the best interests of sportsmen and resources at the center of things."

Service shared the biologist's opinion. Despite Republicans calling her Limousine Lori, the governor was a lifelong hunter and sportswoman. Shortly after taking office, Governor Timms had transferred responsibility for the inspection of commercial put-and-take game farms with captive elk, deer, and more exotic animal populations from the department of agriculture to the DNR. It previously had been the DNR's responsibility until Governor Sam Bozian suddenly reassigned part of it to Ag, a move which had upset sportsmen and conservationists alike. Now it fell to conservation officers to inspect the state's nearly eight hundred game farms and operations, and being so short of people, this was pulling officers away from other law enforcement duties. Time management issues aside, the governor's decision had been the right one, and he was hearing from other officers that at least half of the game operations were out of compliance with the most essential regulations.

Service knew a necropsy had to be done—and fast. The outbreak in Wisconsin was thought by some to have originated with animals, probably elk on a cheesehead commercial game farm—animals allegedly imported from Colorado, which reportedly had been infected by Canadian imports. The whole thing with fenced-in hunt clubs and game farms bugged Service. They were playgrounds for the lazy and well heeled—a quick way to bag a trophy if you had the cash, but no time for a real hunt outside the enclosures.

The two men discarded their rubber gloves in a white plastic pail in the rear of the biologist's truck and headed their separate ways. Service had a hard time shaking the image of the strange-acting deer. He did not enjoy putting any animal down, but this was necessary. The first one he'd had to dispatch had been during his first year near Newberry. An elderly man had called during the summer to report that a deer had been hit by a car. Service's sergeant suggested the man shoot the animal to put it out of its misery, but the man wasn't a hunter, didn't own a gun, and said he couldn't kill anything. Service was sent to handle it.

The old man came out of the house to greet him and led him to the big doe, which had two broken forelegs and was entangled in an old wire fence. Service told the man he didn't have to watch, but the man insisted on staying. Service took aim with his .44 and tried to neatly clip the animal's spinal column just behind the head. Result: It began to thrash.

The old man, who was wearing white slacks and a long-tailed white shirt said, "Oh my."

Service took aim a second time, and fired into the deer's skull. Suddenly the air was awash with fine pink mist and the old man was gasping and saying, "Oh dear God . . . oh God!"

Both of them were covered with blood. Apparently the first shot had caused extensive bleeding into the ears of the animal, which had filled like cups. When Service fired the second round, the animal's head had snapped sideways, showering both of them. Since then he had learned to be more efficient, and over the years he had killed so many animals with potential and actual problems that he normally didn't even think about them afterwards. It still irked him, however, when someone brought up the story of his "red rain-deer." COs were fond of repeating stories about other COs' screwups.

## 10

## FLORENCE COUNTY, WISCONSIN

### MAY 20, 2004

Grady Service kept most of his equipment in his unmarked Tahoe, including a couple of changes of work clothes. As a detective he operated mostly in the western half, but sometimes across the entire Upper Peninsula, which was the size of Vermont and New Hampshire combined, and larger than Delaware. Despite making it home most nights, there had been times when he had to sleep in his vehicle somewhere in the woods.

The chief had made it clear that he was to get over to Wisconsin PDQ, but no way was he going until he stopped at home in Gladstone to see Nantz. He punched in the speed dial on the cell phone, caught the mistake, and flipped the phone closed. He deleted the speed-dial numbers for Maridly and Walter and lectured himself to stay focused. *Stop feeling so damn sorry for yourself,* he thought as he drove out to US 41 and headed south toward Escanaba.

A gray-black Humvee coated with red-gray dust was parked in the lot behind the interpretive center, which was jointly run by the U.S. Forest Service, the Wisconsin DNR, and Florence County, a three-way marriage that sounded to him like a bureaucratic management stretch. There were two men in the vehicle. Service eased alongside the Humvee, got out, stretched, and showed his credentials to one of them. "Special Agent Monica?"

The man studied the credentials and pointed. "Go seven miles west on Wisconsin Seventy, turn south across the ditch at Lilah Oliver Grade Road. There's a gate there. Check in with the agents. I'll let them know you're rolling."

Service thanked the man, pulled onto highway W-70, and headed west, passing a billboard, black type on a white background: IF YOU'RE AGAINST

LOGGING, TRY WIPING WITH PLASTIC. There was a yellow steel tube gate across the road and behind it, a dusty gray Crown Victoria with two men in it. They let him pull up to the gate, got out, looked at his credentials, and manually swung open the yellow gate. "Command Post's a couple miles in," one of the men said. "They're expecting you."

The road was deeply rutted, the area recently logged, with twenty-foot-high stacks of maple and assorted hardwoods piled neatly along the two-track, bark chips scattered all over the road like confetti. Discarded beer and pop cans twinkled with reflected light on the edges of the road. The forest in the area was thick. Along the way he saw two red logging rigs nosed into the tree lines.

There could be only one reason the FBI would be set up so far out in the boonies: They had a crime on their hands, and no doubt a crime scene nearby as well. An unmarked navy blue panel truck was snugged close to a copse of birch trees where a camouflaged plastic tarp had been strung to create shade. Service parked and walked toward a group of people under the tarp. A crude, hand-painted slab of quarter-inch plywood nailed to a nearby tree read BEER, WEED, GAS, OR ASS—NO ONE RIDES FREE. *Life at its most basic,* he thought. The sign wasn't new, and suggested that the logging company's gate was ineffectual in deterring visitors, especially kids who obviously used the area as a party spot. As any soldier, border guard, and game warden knew, outdoor security was impossible unless you had the rare perfect terrain and a lot of bodies in the security detail.

A dark-haired woman with a prominent nose got up. She had short black hair and dense black hair on her arms. She wore khaki pants and sleeveless black body armor over an open-collar, short-sleeved polo shirt. A badge dangled from a navy blue cord around her neck. "Detective Service?" she asked.

"Special Agent T. R. Monica?"

"Tatie," she said, adding, "Follow me." She led him to the panel truck, slid open the massive door, and nodded for him to step inside. He could hear a generator humming softly. The cramped interior was filled with banks of communications equipment; the air was cool. "Take a seat," the agent said, nudging a wheeled stool over to him with her boot.

She opened a blue-and-white cooler and took out two bottles of beer. "It's sticky out there," she said, pushing a longneck Pabst Blue Ribbon at him.

"No thanks. I'm working," he said. "Tatie?"

She smiled. "When I was a kid, all I wanted to eat were potatoes: fried, boiled, baked, you name it—like that Bubba dude and his shrimp in *Forrest Gump?* You don't drink when you work, or is it my brand?"

He shook his head and wondered what this was about. She had a soft air to her, but a commanding, slightly imposing voice. She was also slender and obviously long shed of her childhood starch fixation.

"At ease," the agent said, opening her beer and taking a long pull.

Service ignored his beer.

"Is it because of your father?" she asked.

"Is *what* because of my father?"

"Your not drinking on duty."

"It's because that's the rule." What the hell did she know about his father, and why? He felt his blood pressure rise, took a deep breath, and tried to adjust his breathing.

"It's my understanding that you're sort of a cookbook Catholic when it comes to rules," she said.

"Whatever," he said, not wanting a confrontation, but if she kept this up she might get one. This gig was starting off oddly and he sensed it was not going to improve.

Special Agent Monica leaned back. "I heard you can be pretty tight-lipped," she said. "This isn't a deposition. We're on the same team."

"I don't know what *this* is. My chief told me to report and here I am," he said.

She tilted her head, sizing him up. "I take it you've had some less-than-satisfactory experiences with the Bureau?"

"Mixed," he answered, adding, "at best."

She smiled. "I'd hate to depose you," she said.

"So don't," he said. "What's this about?"

"I say again, we—you and I, all the people here—are on the same team, Detective. You are a federal deputy, correct?"

She was well briefed. "All of our officers who work state or international border counties are deputized," he said. This had taken place just more than a year ago. Anyone committing a game violation in one state and crossing the border of another state in possession of illegal game was in violation of the Federal Lacey Act. Being deputized as feds gave COs the authority to pursue them. Deputization was also supposed to enhance cooperation with the U.S. Fish and Wildlife Service, the federal agency Michigan's DNR was most likely to interface with. The implication for cooperation with and by the USFS, FBI, BATF, and an alphabet soup of other federal agencies remained a question mark. From experience he knew that major policy farts of this kind often required glacially calibrated clocks to gauge results, by which time the rules would no doubt change again.

Special Agent Monica reached into a black leather portfolio, pulled out a Temporary FBI ID card on a black lanyard, and set it on the table. "Wear this at all times around here. If you see somebody without one, make them show one to you, or put their face in the dirt—and yell for help. The only leaks out of this outfit will be the ones we choose to make for tactical reasons," she declared.

He looked at the identification badge. It was his photo. How did she get it so fast? The chief had left him with the impression that this was a chop-chop deal, but her having his photo suggested something very different, and he was suspicious.

"I'm sure you've got a lot of questions," she said, "but bear with me for a while, and for God's sake, drink a beer." She snapped off the cap for him and pushed the bottle closer. "Your father was a game warden," she said. "He was killed in the line of duty."

"He was a game warden who died while he was drunk on duty," Service said.

"But the state honored him as a hero," she countered.

He nodded. "He liked to stop and schmooze violets," he said. "The state didn't talk about that part."

"Violets?" she said with a puzzled look.

"Violators."

She smiled. "That's what all effective cops do," she said. "You don't drink with your . . . violets?" She seemed amused by the term.

"No," he said.

Agent Monica cocked her head slightly. "What did you think of your father?"

Service stiffened. "I didn't come here to have my head shrunk." First the shrinky-dink priest, now her. *Jesus.*

"I promise not to shrink it," she said. "But I do want to dig around in there—if you don't mind."

"I do mind," he said.

"In your place, I would too," she said sympathetically. "You've worked with Wisconsin warden Wayno Ficorelli."

Wayno. "Once."

"Your opinion of him?"

"Is he up for a federal job or something?"

"Just answer the question, okay?" Like most feds, Agent Monica was an adept interviewer, accomplished at deflecting and maintaining control.

"Wayno is smart, dedicated, and determined."

She raised an eyebrow. "When did you work with him?"

"Last fall." Time tended to lose meaning for game wardens, and the older he got, the worse the time dislocation seemed to get.

"Just that once?"

"Right."

"Contact since?"

"Now and then."

"About other cases?" she asked.

"It's none of your business," he said. There was a smugness—or something—in her attitude that was beginning to really rub him the wrong way.

*Hmmm,* her lips said.

He sensed she wouldn't let up. "He wanted a job in Michigan."

"Why?" she asked.

"Wisconsin wardens aren't fully empowered peace officers."

"Have you encouraged him?"

"No, and I haven't discouraged him either."

"Why not?"

"I don't take positions in hiring decisions unless I'm tasked to do background checks."

"What was your opinion of him?"

"Smart, dedicated, and determined," he said.

"You already told me that. Is there something else?"

"No."

"Let me add something," Monica said. "He's a pathological ass-man."

"If you say so." *What the hell was going on?* Service could feel the hairs standing up on his arms.

"I do say so, and by all reports, marital status hasn't ever been an issue for him."

"Why ask me?"

"Have you ever gotten mixed up with married women?"

"Only my wife," he said, "and that's none of your goddamn business." Why all these questions? She was beginning to really piss him off.

"That would be your ex, who died on 9/11 in Pennsylvania," she said. "I'm sorry for your loss."

"I bet," he said. Jesus, did she know his entire life history? *Then she must know about Nantz and Walter,* he thought. He felt his face flush and started to stand, but she reached out and grasped his arm.

"Wayno Ficorelli is dead," she said.

Service stared at her, trying to comprehend. "When?"

"A little more than forty-eight hours ago."

All the questions she had been asking were driving at something. "You think I know something about it?"

"Do you?"

"Don't be an asshole!" he snapped, standing up and telling himself if she shot off her mouth one more time, he was going to bury a fist in it.

"Have you ever lied to your violets?" Agent Monica asked.

What the hell was she trying to get at?

"When necessary," he said.

"Sit down," she said. "Please."

He sat. "How did Wayno die?"

She pondered this for a moment. "He was executed."

Service stared at her. Executed? "What the fuck does that mean?"

She said, "You have the reputation of being an extraordinarily skilled and aggressive officer."

"Do I?"

"Don't jerk me around. You're a loaded gun on bad guys. You've been wounded in the line of duty, both in the marines and as a game warden. Did Ficorelli mistreat prisoners and suspects?"

"Not that I saw," Service said.

"You and Ficorelli are a lot alike—except for a predilection for married women."

"Look," he said, trying to tamp down his rage, "I was ordered to come over here and cooperate. I didn't come here to get mind-fucked."

"Good," the agent said. "Just calm down and cooperate. I sense that you're not surprised someone killed him."

"I'm not happy about it, but I guess I'm not all that surprised. Wayno could push pretty hard."

"He stretched the envelope and made some enemies," she said.

"I worked with him just once, but I suspected he pissed off a whole lot of people."

"Which he surely did," she said. "Did you know that his second cousin is Wisconsin's attorney general?"

"No."

"Apparently Wayno talked to his cousin about you a lot. He said you were the best officer he'd ever worked with. He held you in the highest regard, Detective Service."

Service wasn't sure what to say.

"I want you to see something," she said. There was a video monitor on a table next to them, and she turned it on.

Service watched a series of digital photos, walked over to the door, and stepped outside, gasping for air. He had never seen anything so grotesque. The FBI agent was right on his heels as he fumbled to light a cigarette.

"You okay?" she asked.

"Fine."

"Have you ever seen anybody killed that way?"

He shook his head.

"Ever *hear* of anybody killed like that? In Vietnam, maybe?"

"No." Although the Viet Cong and North Vietnamese had done heinous things to people they got their hands on. He had seen too many instances of that, and had worked to erase the memories.

"You've got a reputation for locating hard-to-find people," she said.

"Most of the ones I find are dead by the time I get to them," he said.

"The nature of the search-and-rescue beast," she said softly. "Why don't you come back inside and sit down?"

"Are you going to tell me what this is all about?"

"I said I would."

Service took a slug of beer while she turned on a laptop computer and swiveled it toward him. "PowerPoint," she said. "Watch it all the way through and then we'll talk."

There was no narration. On many of the slides there were no photos, only names, dates, and locations. The first sequence ran from 1950 to 1970, followed by a gap of twelve years, then a new batch replete with crime scene photos, dates, names, and causes of death. The bodies in the second group since 2000 were mutilated like Ficorelli's. Until then the cause of death varied. The program ended with Wayno's death photo.

"What is this?" Service asked, looking away from the laptop with the photos of mutilated bodies.

"It's called a blood eagle. The Vikings used it on some of their . . . favored captives."

"Vikings."

"Yeah, Norsemen—Skandahoovians with attitude. They'd split open a captive's back to expose the spine. Then they'd hack through the back ribs, pull the lungs through, and drape them over his back. Some historians vehemently insist Vikings never did such things, that such reports were the creative inventions of Christian-centric chroniclers with political agendas, but the term 'blood eagle' exists in all the old Norse languages, and there are descriptions and drawings by Viking writers," said Agent Monica. "Some contend that exposing the lungs let the dead man's air flow out to be inhaled by those standing close to him, and if he had been especially valiant, his bravery would flow to them. Sometimes the exposed lungs flapped as they expelled air, and that's where the eagle part comes from. As far as we know, the Vikings didn't remove the eyes the way our guy has. Comments?"

"This is . . ." he started to say, but didn't finish.

"It's worse," she said. "It's said they usually did this while the victim was still alive, and sometimes they poured salt into the open wounds. Shall I proceed?"

Grady Service sucked in a deep breath and closed his eyes. Had Wayno been alive? He didn't want to think about it, and he didn't ask.

"The toll in the first go-round was twenty-seven game wardens in twenty-five states over twenty years—better than one a year."

"But it started again?" he said.

"After a hiatus of a dozen years, which we don't understand; but it's been steady since then, one a year, one in 2000, one in 2001, but two in '02, two in '03, and Wayno so far this year. The blood eagle has been the MO since 2000."

Service thought about the photos. "What about the eyes?"

"The killer started taking them in 2001—another change."

Two different killers—two separate groups of killings? "Copycat?" Service asked.

"That's one school of thought," Agent Monica answered, with a tone suggesting it wasn't her view. "Could be the killer was out of circulation during that time, out of the country, in a lockup or loony bin, or maybe he gave it up for Lent, but fell off the wagon. We just don't know," she said. "All we do know is that somebody has been killing game wardens all around the United States since 1950."

He couldn't believe what she was telling him. "I've never heard anything about this. How can game wardens be murdered around the country and nobody know about it? How can *game wardens* not know?"

"Because nobody detected a connection or saw the pattern until three years ago. Think about it. You kill one warden in a state at a rate of less than one a year, and each in a different way, and who would put it all together? Cops, like politicians, tend to think locally, and federal and state computers still don't talk to each other very effectively. Before 9/11 they didn't talk at all.

"In the latter part of the second group we had a common and spectacular MO, but the vicks in the first group were all done differently. The common denominator is that the victims are all game wardens, and it's been one per state, all of them found by water in relatively obscure but open areas," said the agent. "Obviously we recognized we had a serial with the second batch. An analyst was first to see the pattern and bring it forward. The same analyst then went back in time and found the first group. The method was different in most of the early murders, and the way they were spread out, there were no statistical or geographic clusters to work with. If the killer hadn't started up again, we never would have known about the first group."

"But now they're all the blood eagle," Service said. He did a quick mental calculation. "Twenty-seven in group one, twenty-one in the second batch."

"We thought it might be a copycat, but we've decided the blood eagle is just his latest method. Why? Who knows? Maybe he wants to make sure he gets credit. So many dead and nobody knowing about the first batch, and maybe now he wants everybody to know, so he changes his MO to provide an unmistakable signature for his work. There was no signature or consistent MO until 2000. Why a sudden need for recognition? Again, who knows? The key fact turns out to be that there has been one game warden killed in forty-eight states, and all that remains after Wayno Ficorelli are Missouri and Michigan."

"Are you thinking fifty is the magic number?" he asked, jumping to the obvious conclusion.

"Have you got a better take on it?"

He didn't. "A serial killer whacking game wardens," he said in disbelief.

"We prefer the term serial murderer. All the early murders were different, but we've learned that the crime sites were always by water, isolated, and probably the kills took place at night. We weren't sure about the last part until now because we never found a body that would enable forensics to unquestionably pinpoint time of death," the agent said. "The other constant is that all the vicks were professional hard-chargers, hard cases like your friend. Most were declared homicides, but not one of them in either group has ever been solved. In both sets the killer is highly organized, he's never communicated with law enforcement, clearly does his homework, understands how you people work, and finally, he seems to understand our weaknesses by changing venues and stringing out his killings over time, making it hard for a pattern to emerge."

"Suspects?" he asked.

"None," she said. "And getting the number of people we need to ratchet up the investigation has been a bitch since 9/11. Homeland Security and antiterrorism take priority and eat up a lot of resources. Add to this that state and local police units are all in terrible financial shape," she added. "We're lucky to be this far."

"Why am I here?" he asked. He could understand an unbalanced or pissed-off violet going after a game warden who'd bumped heads with him—but methodically killing game wardens all over the country? Never mind believability; it made no sense.

"You're a tracker; you're good at finding people, and you operate in the environment where all this goes down. The woods are your thing."

He shook his head. "I find *known* missing persons, not unknown, unidentified killers. That's for you people." He had inadvertently gotten involved in a number of homicides over the past three years and had been told repeatedly by his supervisers to keep to his own turf.

"Wisconsin's attorney general wants his cousin's killer caught, and he thought you might be able to assist. He called your governor, and here you are."

He cringed. Lorelei Timms: He blamed her for being bumped out of the Mosquito Wilderness to a detective job he neither wanted nor sought.

"I hear your governor's a big fan," Special Agent Monica said.

Service grimaced and wondered how many changes of clothes he had in his truck.

"It's not all bad news," she said.

"No?"

"I have to apologize," she said. "I'm sorry about your colleague, but this is the first body we've recovered in the golden window," she added. "I'm also sorry about your son and girlfriend. It's difficult to deal with so many losses so close together."

He shook his head. He was beginning to distinctly dislike Special Agent Monica. She seemed pretty straightforward, but there was something missing, something not quite right about her or the situation, and it was making him extremely uncomfortable. The golden window, he knew, was cop speak for the first forty-eight hours after death.

"Ficorelli was off duty and in this area to fish with a man named Thorkaldsson, who happens to be sheriff of Florence County. Thorkaldsson was supposed to meet Ficorelli, but he was late, and when he showed up, he found the body near their meeting place. He immediately secured the crime scene," she explained.

"Florence is small," she continued, "and the department is just Thorkaldsson and three deputies. The county doesn't even have its own lockup. They have to farm prisoners out to other counties. The sheriff may run a small-time cop shop, but he did one helluva job here, and we think his arrival was really close to the time of Wayno's death. Usually we find cold bodies dropped at locations different than the kill sites, so this case potentially gives us a leg up on gathering evidence and leads. We've never been able to locate an actual kill site, which means this could be the break we need. The body was still warm. It couldn't have been moved that far or that long before the sheriff arrived."

Service grunted acknowledgment, but he was still trying to process it all, and his gut was churning, never a good sign. "You think this dump site here is also the kill site?"

"No," she said, "but this is the soonest we've ever gotten to a victim. Want to take a look?"

## 11

# FLORENCE COUNTY, WISCONSIN
## MAY 20, 2004

They got into her Crown Victoria and headed down a slight grade. It took ten minutes to reach a place where a federal crime lab panel truck was parked, and a crime scene ribboned off. The area looked like a vehicle turn-around, and ahead Service saw four large, pale-gray boulders set back in white cedar trees beyond where a berm had been piled up by a dozer. Small yellow evidence pennants were stuck in the ground throughout the area. Service got out and Agent Monica showed him a gray plastic tub filled with green rubber swampers. She also held out a box of latex gloves.

"Soft ground?" he asked.

"We're just making sure that all of us wear a boot with the same tread. Any tracks that are different won't be from us."

They both tugged on boots and blue latex gloves. He noticed that while the old road seemed to end at the berm, a new trail had been created by four-wheeler traffic a few feet east of the boulders.

The FBI agent saw him looking and said, "There used to be a bridge, but it's long gone. The river's shallow here, with a hard bottom. People ride four-wheelers across."

She led him along the four-wheeler trail to a steadily moving stream.

"Pine River," she said, pointing. "You'd think people could've found something more original for a name."

A tarp had been constructed over an area along the north bank, and the area taped off. "The sheriff did a bang-up job here," Monica said. She showed him where to walk and pointed to the boulders, which had been marked to show where the body had been displayed. "There was blood, but not enough," she added. "Usually there isn't much at all where a body is found."

"Is that significant?" he asked, adding, "That he was laid out on the rocks?" If there wasn't much blood here, it probably wasn't the kill site. You didn't do the things this slimeball did without making a mess.

She said, "Certain kinds of serial murderers display their kills to send a message."

Certain *kinds?* "The body was right next to the four-wheeler trail, so he wanted it found, right?"

"Maybe," she said. "We can talk about that later."

Service began a methodical walk-around but saw nothing significant. The pictures of Wayno had left him shaken, but what bothered him more was the fact that the FBI was aware game wardens were being killed, and as far as he knew, the Bureau apparently had made no effort to warn anyone. This realization made it difficult to think clearly.

An hour later they were back at the command post on the hill.

"Anything pique your interest back there?" Agent Monica asked.

"What strikes me is what there *isn't.* This site looks like it was pretty well sanitized. Are you thinking the perp got disrupted?"

"We can't rule that out. We're thinking he hadn't been gone that long when Thorkaldsson arrived. The body was still warm, and that's a first."

"This is work for science types—crime scene techs," Service said.

"They're all over it," she said.

"Have you done DNA?"

"It's in process," she said. "The samples are in the lab now. In any case, vick DNA is redundant. Thorkaldsson was the man's friend, and he identified him."

Service was thinking that details counted in every line of police work. It was fine to have an ID, but until you had dentals *and* DNA, you were not done. "When will you release this to the public?"

She rolled her eyes and Service held up his hands. Special Agent Monica appeared to have very thin skin. "I'm not trying to do your job. Wayno lived with his mother," he added, "not far from Madison."

"We know," she said. "Do me a favor?"

"If I can."

"Someone from NCAVC is coming in tomorrow."

"Which is?" He loathed the acronym stew of the federal government.

"The National Center for the Analysis of Violent Crime."

He thought about it for a second. "The people who do the profiles?"

"Right. Do you know much about the process?"

"Only what I've seen in movies," he said.

"Yeah, like that's real," she said sarcastically. "Movies are mostly bullshit."

"You don't believe in it?" he countered.

"Profiling can be a useful tool when it's done right—not by itself, but coordinated with all the other specialties and tools. It's definitely not a crystal ball, and done wrong, it can take you down roads that can take you a long way from where you want to be," she said. "The media and Hollywood have made profiling out to be the magic crime-solving bullet, and in the public's mind, the greatest serial killer of all is probably Hannibal Lecter. Did you know that Lecter is loosely based on an actual killer named Albert Fish, who killed and ate children back in the twenties and thirties?"

"No," he said. He couldn't care less. He thought about Ficorelli and felt bad for him, maybe worse for his mother. "I don't think I'll be much use here," Service said grimly. "I'm just a woods cop, and fiction or not, this asshole's methods seem to approach Hannibal's."

"Understood," Monica said. "But just hang in here with the team for now and let us decide your role. Cool?"

"I guess," he said without enthusiasm. Orders were orders.

There were at least eight agents on site at all times, and sometimes as many as a dozen, plus various technicians and Wisconsin state troopers. No county personnel. The county didn't have people to share, even on a major case like this. Special Agents Bobbi Temple and Larry Gasparino looked no older than Walter, and seemed too young for this kind of heavy duty.

Special Agent Monica explained that normally they would set up a command post at the county sheriff's office in town, but Thorkaldsson's shop was too small, and they didn't want news of the Ficorelli killing getting out to the public yet. Until it got announced and they had milked the crime scene, they would remain in the woods. The land was state-owned, the timber concession leased to a paper company, which had installed the gate to prevent interference with their logging operations. Tatie Monica thought the isolated location and gate made this as secure a site as they could wish for. Service didn't argue, but he knew that the key feature of most isolated locations was the virtual impossibility of effective security, and in the North Country, most secrets didn't stay that way for long. Did the FBI not understand this? The woods were not a blanket to hide under.

Several large canvas wall tents were being erected as Service looked at a white bag of McDonald's burgers and Chicken McNuggets and turned up his nose. He also thought about the sign near the CP, a reminder that thoroughly securing this site was not going to happen.

"Mickey D's not up to your standards?" Special Agent Monica asked.

"Just not hungry," he lied.

She raised an eyebrow. "You're what, six-four, two twenty?"

"Close enough," he said.

"Eat," she said, sounding like a mother. He reluctantly took a piece of chicken and bit into it. It was like rubber, and just as bland.

"We've got sauces," Agent Temple said.

"I'm good," Service said.

Just before dark, he told the lead agent he wanted to look at the crime scene again.

Agent Monica looked at him. "Want company?"

"Alone," he said. She irked him. She bounced between officious and obsequious and seemed to almost hang on him.

"I can drive you," she offered.

"Rather walk," he said.

He took a penlight, stuck it in his shirt pocket, and headed out. He started making a mental list of questions to ask the FBI agent as he walked in the darkness.

Why did the killer leave bodies where they could be found? It would make more sense to leave them where he killed them. Also, were the missing eyes significant, and had any been recovered? Wasn't leaving the bodies where they could be found a form of communication—a kind of message? If so, what was the creep trying to say?

Below, through the trees, he could hear a generator and see the pink-orange glow of klieg lights at the crime scene.

Where had Wayno parked, and where was his vehicle now? Had he driven down here, or left his truck somewhere in the woods?

He skirted the crime scene, waded into the river, and moved upstream to look at the banks, moving slowly and turning on his penlight as he needed it. The military had discovered that green light was less disruptive than red to night vision. Many COs in the U.P. now carried the green lights.

The Pine River had the look and smell of good trout water. It felt cool on his legs, and several hundred yards west a feeder creek dumped in more cold water. The riffles in the main river would be saturated with oxygen in deep summer and serve as collecting points for fish that didn't flee up colder tributaries. Sweepers along the banks served as fish hotels as hydraulics forced current downward, excavating holes beneath the downed trees. He had taken only a cursory look at the water near the crime scene earlier and decided it was too shallow and not an area where Wayno would have lingered. He was more likely to fish further downstream, or upstream where there might be deeper water and more fish cover. So what had gotten him out of the water? And where? He wasn't a homicide expert, but he had seen countless animal kill sites and knew the difference between a butcher site, a resting place, and a cache. He had followed such trails thousands of times.

If Wayno had not been killed here, where did it happen? He assumed the feds had carefully covered the woods for blood and other signs, but did they understand that the river itself was a natural travel and transportation corridor? Europeans had discovered most Indians living along rivers for good reasons. Water could also wash away evidence.

After a couple of hours he decided it was pointless to continue scouting in the darkness and started back to the camp. Tomorrow at first light he would return and take a more careful look. The FBI had the crime scene covered; he would concentrate on the river and surrounding area. Someone might sanitize a crime scene, but it was unlikely they would be able to entirely eliminate all traces of their approach with the ground still relatively soft from spring rains and winter thaw, which made hiding tracks a lot more difficult. He was increasingly uneasy about the whole situation, especially his role.

He was deep in thought on the upslope when a voice startled him from the darkness. "Find anything?" It was Special Agent Monica.

"Jesus Christ!" he shouted. "Don't jump out at people like that."

The FBI agent stared at him. "I thought you people were used to being snuck up on."

He growled his displeasure, but said nothing more. He was unnerved that he hadn't heard or sensed her presence. Got to get your edge back, he chastised himself.

She was immediately on the defensive. "Okay, sorry. What did you see?"

"I'm thinking he was in the water and something got him out of the water and onto land."

"Why?" she asked.

"Maybe because he came to fish for trout and had the focus of a pit bull. Where's his vehicle?" What *would* have gotten Wayno out of the water?

"Across the river."

"Not on this side?"

"Nope, south side."

"Why?"

"We don't know."

"Where was the sheriff supposed to meet him?"

"About where we found the body," she said. "I think."

"Hmmm," Service said. Why the hell didn't she *know*, and why had the two men come in from different directions? Fishing pals usually rode together in one vehicle. Fewer vehicles left less impact on parking areas and less evidence for the uninitiated that an area was good fishing. Some secretive Yoopers would park a mile away from where they intended to fish or hunt, and walk in the direction opposite of their destination, before doubling back on ground where their trail would be difficult to follow. Why the two men came from different directions was an obvious question, and he started to get on her case but decided from her voice that she was dragging. *Her case, not yours*, he reminded himself. *Reel in before you get too much line out.*

"How long since you slept?" he asked.

"What year is it?" the agent said wearily.

"I looked around upstream. If I was going to fish and got here early, I'd go in upstream and fish my way back down to the meeting place—the water up that way looks pretty promising. Or I'd walk down and fish back up. If his partner was late or he was early, he probably wouldn't wait. He'd fish past and keep returning to the rendezvous point." That's what he and his friends would have done. "Get anything off his vehicle?"

"Not yet. It's being worked on. We haven't moved it yet."

There were swarms of mosquitoes in the air, and the FBI agent swatted at them continuously. "Are you impervious?" she asked, slapping the side of her face.

"Oblivious," he said.

"I'm glad you could get over here so quickly," she said.

"I'm not a homicide detective."

"No," she said, "but you hunt people. You and other woods cops regularly capture perps in the act of breaking laws. Most of us in law enforcement tend to be called in after the fact. Right?"

"I guess." He'd never considered his job in this light, but decided Agent Monica had a point, even though the significance of the distinction was not immediately apparent. In fact, nothing in this deal was apparent other than the fact the feds had not told the states what was happening. How many lives had this cost?

"You've already looked at the scene differently than any of us might have," she said. "The more perspectives we can get, the better off we are. Diversity gives us the multiple-view intellectual edge."

What the fuck was she babbling about? This was murder and she was spouting politically correct management theory? It still bothered him that the FBI had so much information on him, and he wanted to ask why, but once again decided to hold off.

Tatie Monica showed him to a tent. "Your crash pad," she said.

"Are you out of Chicago or Minneapolis?" Service asked.

"Milwaukee," she said. "I got a BS in psychology from Marquette, and then I did most of the work for a PhD in abnormal psychology. I still have to write my dissertation. Then I went to law school in Madison. Ficorelli's cousin and I were classmates at UW. I finished higher than he did," she added. "Then I worked in Milwaukee as an assistant prosecuting attorney for three years and found it pretty unsatisfying. It always felt like the prosecution was after all the real action, so I applied to the FBI and they took me. After the academy I did four years in LA. I liked it there, but I wanted to get back to the Midwest, so I asked for a transfer to Milwaukee. Some of my friends said it was a dumb move to a career backwater, but Wisconsin has had a couple of major serial murderers, and I liked the idea of being able to study records close to the scenes. This profiling thing gets overplayed and misrepresented in the media," she said.

"Okay," Service said. He had asked only if she was out of Chicago or Minneapolis and had gotten a professional life saga. Cops were taught active listening skills and to signal receipt of every statement without prejudice. The word "okay" was the most often employed. Service and Nantz had sometimes watched *Cops* on TV, and they would bet on the number of times the word would be used during a show. Monica had supplied so much information that he wondered if she was trying to sell herself, and if so, why? She was the team leader. What more authority did she need?

"Down the road I'd like to see profile training be mandatory for all law enforcement personnel, and for all of us to understand all the components," she went on. "We spend a lot of time trying to profile the killers, but geographic and victim profiling are equally important—all part of the total picture—and both underutilized."

Service didn't interrupt her. He was trying to size her up and not having a lot of success. She had an ego and seemed ambitious, but how competent was she? His make-talk question about her office had gotten him a detailed autobiography. Something was screwy here.

After a while he said good night, went into his tent, and eased onto a cot. He had just dozed off when he awoke to find her sitting on a cot across from him, a mug of hot coffee in hand. "Have you got something against sleep?" he asked.

"Talk to me about hunting," she said.

"It's a big subject."

"Hunting violets," she amended.

He rubbed the corners of his eyes and tried to clear his head. "Game is attracted to certain kinds of habitat at different times of year. Habitat equals food and cover: Where you find the most game, you find legal hunters—and violators. Some locations have better potential than others." He thought for a minute. "Bears, for example. In the fall when hunting them is legal, they're pigging out to put on weight for the winter sleep."

"You just camp out near their food," Special Agent Monica said.

"In the old days hunters would find their trails, put threads across runs to determine if they were in active use, and when they found one, they would track the animal. Nowadays a lot of hunters are too lazy or unknowledgeable to know what they're doing, so they put out piles of sweet baits and sit above them in tree stands. Other hunters use dogs to chase the bear up a tree."

"Dogs are *legal?*" she asked. "Is that fair?"

It never failed to surprise him how few people knew anything about hunting or the outdoors. "It's legal and there's nothing wrong with it. Hunting for most of our history has been about eating, not sport or fairness. If you go back in time, most hunting was done with dogs. In any event, some hunters have specially bred dogs for bears. Every night they drive the dirt and gravel roads and drag them clean with a metal bar or a mesh screen. First thing in the morning they load their dogs and cruise the roads looking for fresh tracks. The dog with the best nose sits outside in a basket welded to the grill. This is their strike dog. When the hunters find a track, they let the strike dog sniff it, and if it's hot, he'll take off. If he keeps going, the hunters release the pack to follow. Then they drive all over hell using radios to try to follow the dogs until the animal is treed."

"Interesting," she said. "The strike dog leads the parade?"

He stopped talking. "It was my understanding that my being here is a result of a pop-up request from the Wisconsin state attorney general, but you know too much about me for it to be that simple."

"Computers enable us to do a lot of things fast," she said.

"I thought the FBI was computer-challenged," he fired back.

"Since 9/11 we've been clawing our way into the new century. You were a sniper in Vietnam."

He wondered exactly how much she knew about what he had done during the war. "Actually the mission was long-range recon, but on occasion we did other things." He didn't want to get into details.

"Enemy military personnel?"

"Right. Sometimes we tried to decapitate certain units to disrupt and harass them."

"How did you find your targets?"

"It was all about the quality of our intelligence. Sometimes we got lucky and stumbled onto someone we wanted, but most often we sent out Kit Carson scouts—enemy soldiers who came over to our side and volunteered to work against the North Vietnamese. Most of them were reliable and good at what they did. The scout would be given a name and he'd slide off into the mountains for a week or two, and sometimes when he came back he'd have located the target and followed him long enough to discern a routine. Then we'd follow the scout and do our job."

"Any ethical concerns?"

He shook his head. "We targeted soldiers, not civilians."

"That's where you developed your tracking skills?"

"Honed them," he said, and guessing where she was going, he added, "but we always had a name and an identity, and usually a general location. We didn't just go out and wander around looking for someone. Hope is worthless in tracking." He listened to himself. Wouldn't this apply to this killer too? How did he find game wardens to kill?

She chuckled. "You're not very trusting."

"I prefer to think of it as an acute sense of situational awareness."

"I appreciate your candor," she said. "We have tried like hell to look at the victims to develop a suspect list, but the only suspects we've identified were local types who might have held a grudge against a particular murdered officer. Our perp is a bigger thinker, working on a much wider plane. You ever run into anyone like that among your violets?"

He didn't need to think long. "Not really," he said, leaving it at that.

"Bullshit," she snapped at him. "You helped take down an international poaching group last fall. You're like every other cop," she added.

She knew too much about him, and again he wondered why. "How's that?"

"It's called key fact hold-back, and that's not the name of a poker game, though cops act like it is. Cops don't willingly share with outsiders."

"What I ran into last year wasn't like this in any way," he countered.

She glared at him. "The person we're looking for has the ability and wherewithal to travel freely, and move around unimpeded. He's either independent, unemployed, or has a job that gives him the freedom he needs. The fact that he displays the bodies has us scratching our heads. Usually killers who display and arrange their victims are sexual predators, but there's no evidence of sex in these killings."

"But the guy *is* communicating," Service said.

"It's more like he's waving the medicus," she said.

"Medicus?"

"An antiquated English word for the middle finger."

The way she said it made it almost funny, but the memory of Wayno's mutilated body wiped away any humor.

## 12

## FLORENCE COUNTY, WISCONSIN

## MAY 21, 2004

Service's internal clock had him awake before first light. His first thought was of Newf. How could he have forgotten his animals? He was definitely not fully aware. Not a good condition to be in with a serial killer stalking the woods. He pulled on his wet boots and shirt and slipped outside the tent. He called and woke Candi McCants and asked her to check in on and feed Newf and Cat. He told her he wasn't sure when he'd be home.

He walked back into the tent and poked Monica's shoulder. "You coming?" he asked.

She snapped up and swung her feet off the cot. "Is the sun up?" she asked in a sandpapery voice.

"Soon," he said. He went outside, found an urn with fresh hot coffee, and filled two Styrofoam cups.

The FBI agent walked stiff-legged out of the tent, stretched, and dug a stick of gum out of her pocket. Her hair was molded to her head.

"You ready?" he asked, handing her a cup.

"Like the white chick said in *Dances with Wolves*, 'I go where you go.'"

"They were married," Service said.

"Don't nitpick," she shot back, sipping her coffee. "Do I need hip boots?" she asked.

"Only if you're afraid you'll melt," he said.

She shook her head and said, "Lead on, Natty Bumppo."

"Wouldn't it make more sense for the killer to leave the bodies where he killed them?"

"Most serials do. They kill, do their thing, and boogie."

"This guy wants you to find them."

"But not too easily or too fast," she said.

"What about the eyes?"

"We're clueless on that," she said. "One shrink talked to us about *mal occhio,* the evil eye, but that line of inquiry went nowhere. We had a serial in Texas who cut the eyes out of three victims. In some Arab countries they remove eyes as punishment for certain crimes. Because of the blood eagle we had a hard look at Viking practices and beliefs and drew a blank."

It occurred to him that maybe the eyes were irrelevant, but he was locked into another question. "Why did the Texas killer take the eyes?"

"So the victims wouldn't remember him."

He looked at her. "How could they if they were dead?"

"Exactly. He said he only intended to rape and release, but he ended up killing them. Then he gave us a line of bullshit about taking the eyes to confuse us."

He pondered this. Misdirection? In the natural world misdirection was something prey did, not predators. Or did they?

They crossed the river. The four-wheeler trail continued on the other side of the river, and to his right he saw the cement pilings of the old bridge.

"How far back is Wayno's truck?" Service asked as they splashed quietly across the cobble bottom.

"Maybe three hundred yards. The road's bermed on the south terminus to keep out civilian vehicles. He parked east along a two-track that sort of parallels the river over there," she said, pointing.

Tire marks showed that four-wheelers worked both sides of the river, and Service knew that Ficorelli, like any competent game warden, would never leave his vehicle where it would be obvious or easily found, even when he wasn't on duty.

"Thorkaldsson and Ficorelli were friends?"

"Long time, I gather. The sheriff says they came here to fish three times a year, spring, summer, and late September."

Service grimaced. Routine could be fatal to a game warden, even off duty. Ficorelli seemed to have possessed the self-protective paranoia that all good game wardens needed, but how many people knew about the fishing trips, and why did the two men park on opposite sides of the river?

Thick tag alders and cedar bordered the narrow road cut by four-wheelers. Tatie Monica triggered her handheld. "Julie, I'm coming up with a colleague."

"You're in our optics," a male voice squawked back over the radio.

"Julie?" Service said.

The agent smiled. "Julius White."

Another nondescript dark Crown Vick was parked sideways just behind the berm. Two agents met them. They were wearing blaze orange vests over navy blue polo shirts, with FBI in large black letters across the backs of the vests. "Anything?" she asked one of the men.

"We had a couple down here on a four-wheeler about midnight," he answered. "They drove down to the berm, stopped, stripped off their gear, and went at it on the seat." He pointed. "Right there."

"You talked to them?" she asked.

"Nope."

"What about Nelson?"

"He was makin' mud when they came racing by, but he radioed to us that they were coming."

"Did Nelson talk to them on the way out?" The annoyance in her voice was palpable.

"Yeah, he got their names and checked IDs. They told him they had a few too many. They live a few miles south. He said the woman was in tears. The guy she was with wasn't her husband."

"Who was he?"

"A playmate," the agent said, tongue in cheek. "Also a neighbor. She lives in Milwaukee and summers up here. Her old man only comes up weekends."

"They summered hard last night," the agent called Julie chirped.

Monica said menacingly, "Somebody needs to talk to them again. I want full statements. How often do they come down here? Did they see anything the night of the killing? We need to be thorough, milk every lead."

"Nelson's got their names, addresses, phone numbers. He took licenses and ran them. No wants or warrants. They both came back clean."

Service left her talking to the agents, and walked down the two-track, where he found Ficorelli's pickup backed into some white pines. It was roped off with crime scene tape, but no FBI personnel were around. Shouldn't there be security here?

Special Agent Monica caught up. "I think your guys enjoyed the show last night," he said.

"Julie's an FOA—First Office Agent," she snapped back. "Which is no excuse. He shouldn't have let the couple head back to Nelson once they got past him. They should have been detained and interviewed right there."

He agreed, and wondered if 9/11 was causing the FBI to ramp up manpower, and lower standards in the process. "This is where the truck was found?"

"As you see it."

The sun was beginning to illuminate the eastern sky with a band of low lavender and pink light.

"Your people check for foot tracks on the four-wheeler trail?"

"There are some matches with those on the other side, but that doesn't tell us much. We haven't found any that might be Ficorelli's by their size."

"Felt soles," Service said. "They keep you from slipping on rocky bottoms and leave a flat print like Bigfoot, but not distinct. Was Ficorelli wearing waders, and did his boots have calks?"

"He was naked. Calks . . . you mean, like metal spikes?"

"Not necessarily metal. Where are his boots, waders, vest?"

"We haven't found anything."

"Anything found from the previous victims?"

"Them either. Probably at the kill sites, but we haven't found one yet. What about calks?" she asked.

"They leave distinctive prints if they're not worn down." His own needed replacing, which he kept putting off. "We'll assume he moved directly downstream and fished back up to the meeting place. We ought to be able to find some sign of where he went down to the river and got out." It always amazed him that people with no outdoor interests had so little curiosity about it. In the U.P. even the least outdoorsy person knew a lot because the outdoor environment was everywhere around them and affected everyone who lived in it or near to it.

He moved slowly, using the increasing light to augment his penlight. He picked up on a trail not far from the black truck, but it looked more like a game trail than a fisherman's path. Still, he saw the muted prints of felt soles, and they were small enough to be Ficorelli's. No calks for sure. He marked two tracks with sticks, and thirty yards on, he found a pile of bear dung. The FBI agent didn't seem to notice and he didn't call it to her attention. It was a small pile, not particularly fresh.

The bank on the south side of the river was low, the water in front of it slow and skinny, not likely to hold fish. He saw no tracks or impressions in the gravel, and stood, looking across the river where the current was closer to the bank, where large rocks protruded and a lot of downed timber hung down in the water. "Let's angle down and across," he said.

They waded downstream until the bottom began to tail away, the water deepening into rapids with some energy. "The soft edges of this heavy water would be best for fish," Service said, thinking out loud. "But if he had to meet Thorkaldsson, he'd probably stop short and loop back upstream to meet him."

"Soft edges?" she asked.

He tugged some hairs on the back of his arm. "Prickly water looks like that," he said, showing her the arm.

"You can look at the river and tell what people would do?"

"I can guess what an experienced fisherman would be most likely to do. With an inexperienced one, all bets are off. With an experienced fisherman, every movement in the water is about finding and positioning to cast to fish."

They crossed seventy-five feet over to the north bank. "We'll stick close to the bank," he said. "Look for anything that seems out of place."

"People are out of place here," Special Agent Monica quipped, looking around.

"They are," he acknowledged.

She didn't complain about the slowness of his movement. Neither did she offer much in the way of observations, other than to volunteer that the current could tire somebody pretty quickly.

"It's more strenuous but safer going upstream," he said. "Downstream the water piles up behind your legs, and if you hit loose cobble, you'll lose your footing and float your hat. By the way, don't cross your legs when you wade. Move one foot, then the other."

"Float your hat: Does that mean, like, fall in?"

"Right."

"But we're going downstream."

"Be careful," he said.

He moved no more than ten feet at a time, scanning the shore. They waded for nearly forty minutes.

After a while he saw the silhouette of a straight line angled off a log. Morning light was beginning to form shafts in the trees. "See that?" he asked.

"See what?"

"Something that doesn't belong."

"No," she answered.

"Over there, a straight line," he said, pointing.

"That doesn't belong?"

"Nature rarely creates clean straight lines."

As he got closer he saw that a fly rod had been washed against a log and wedged in by the hydraulic pressure, the rod tip vibrating slightly.

He went over to it, but didn't pick it up. He could see the distinctive deep green color of the graphite and guessed it was an expensive Winston rod. He leaned his face down to the water. The reel was a pricey English-made Hardy.

"Ficorelli's?" the special agent asked, standing beside him.

"I don't know. Did you ask Thorkaldsson about Wayno's gear?"

"Not yet," she said.

Not yet? "That rod and reel are worth about fifteen hundred bucks new. A fly fisherman is more likely to risk breaking his leg or head than a good rod." Especially on a game warden's salary.

"But anyone could have dropped it."

"Right."

"You want me to get help?"

"Not yet. It could be the current carried it downstream."

"We keep moving downstream?" she said.

"Upstream. If the rod lodged here, it came down, not up, and he wouldn't be far from his rod if he had a choice."

He slowed, examining every log and rock along the shore until he looked past an overhanging tag alder and saw a metal Wheatley fly box on a log, its top open.

"I see it too," the agent said from behind him.

He moved up and studied the nearby shore, which was no more than three feet behind the log pile.

"Good place to sit and change a fly," he said, trying to visualize.

"And lose a rod?"

"Not necessarily; but if he dropped it or it fell in, he'd go get it," Service said. "Immediately."

"If he was able," she said.

"Uh-huh."

He saw a scrape on the log beside the fly box, fresh nicks in the bark where a few flakes had broken away. In the water below the log he saw a

fancy lanyard with forceps, a pocketknife, safety pins, floatant, and des-
sicant in special holders. The gear had sunk in soft water and was too heavy
to be moved downstream by the current.

The branch beyond the fly box had more scrapes. Service moved to the
end of the log, closer to the bank. He could see where the stalks of wildflow-
ers and thistle had been broken. "I'm climbing out," he said.

"You want help?"

"Just me."

He used a tag alder to pull himself up the grassy rise. Even from a distance of several feet he immediately saw dark spots on some blades of grass.
He found a stick and probed the ground. The end came out dark. Flies rose
and buzzed.

"You got something?" she said.

"Looks like," was all he said.

He saw signs of something heavy dragged west. He followed, and in
an opening just behind the tag alders, among crushed yellow birch saplings
and grass, he found the ground saturated with more blood and flies.

From there a drag trail led back to the water about twenty paces
upstream of where Ficorelli had come ashore. He slid back into the river
near Special Agent Monica. "How far from here to where the body was
found?" he asked her.

"About three quarters of a mile, maybe a mile," she said. "Why?"

"Did your people search down this far?"

"Not yet," she said, in a tone that suggested they had not planned to
come this far.

The distance was about what he had guesstimated. He turned to face
her. "I think this is your kill site. He got out for some reason and was killed
up there. The body was then dragged up the river to where it was found.
Dragging it through water dispersed evidence, helped drain the blood. The
killer probably gambled you would be more likely to concentrate upstream
because it would be easier to move the body down the river."

"Which means?"

"Our perp is strong to be able to move a body so far upstream."

"Not easy to drag dead weight against this current," she said.

"Exactly. It's not easy, but it's easier than you might think in the shallows, where the current isn't as persistent. Whoever did this is probably in pretty good shape." Ficorelli had not been a large man, but dead weight was dead weight.

"Did you find evidence of the body being dragged near where it was found?"

"Nothing; but as you saw, the site looked like it had been swept and cleaned."

"Makes sense. Ask your people to meet us at the dump site and we'll direct them down here. I think they can come in from landside." If the site had been sanitized, why had the perp left the rod, reel, and fly box here? And where were Wayno's vest and wading boots?

Service took one of the men downstream and told the others to parallel them inland. When they reached the new site, he showed the items in the water to the technician who had accompanied him, and talked the others down to the blood spots.

"Luminol?" Tatie Monica called out to one of the techs.

"Needs to be darker for good results," a female technician said.

"It's plenty dark under the trees," Service pointed out. Luminol was a chemical that glowed greenish-blue when it came in contact with blood, and it didn't take much to get a reading. He had seen it used a couple of times.

The crime scene techs and agents worked methodically while he remained in the river with Monica, watching them spray the two sites he had found.

"Luminol can react with some plant matter," she said while they waited. "But our people are trained to sort out and interpret what they find."

*Asinine comment,* Service thought. Was she trying to impress him, or the others? If so, it wasn't working for him.

Service saw a camera flash illuminate the woods under the trees. The flashes went off every few minutes, and he found himself flinching, not sure why.

"Drops indicate the body was dragged up to here, over to there, and back down to the river," a tech above said, pointing.

Service asked. "Footprints? There are no drag marks where I followed him up from the river, which means he crawled out under his own power. What about human blood?"

"What other kind of blood would be here?" the tech asked.

"There's old bear scat on the far bank and there are wolves in Wisconsin. The blood could be a fawn kill, or an adult deer."

"Scat? You mean bear shit?" Tatie Monica asked.

"It was between Ficorelli's truck and the river," he said.

"You didn't say anything."

"Didn't matter."

"I'd bet this is human," the tech said after conferring with colleagues. "There's a lot of it."

Tatie Monica announced, "Ficorelli was killed here, butchered, and dragged up to the other site by the old bridge."

*No shit.* "Somebody wanted to make sure the body was found," Service said. "Right by the four-wheeler track and all. Have all of them been left in open places?"

"I'd call them more obvious than open—if we discount the fact that they've all been off the grid, more or less. Let's go back and grab some more coffee and breakfast," she added. "The techs will call us if they need us."

"More Mickey D's?"

"We tried to get Emeril, but he charges too much for backwoods culinary camp calls."

This was a long cry from the backwoods. He called out to a technician, "Look for a vest, boots, shorts, maybe waders. He wasn't fishing in the buff."

They were within fifty yards of the command post when somebody yelled, "Crapoleon on the squawk box!"

Tatie Monica rubbed her eyes and walked over to the coffee urn. "Ninety seconds," she told the other agent. She rolled her eyes when Service gave her an inquisitive look. The next thing he knew they were standing under the tarp in the birch grove and a disembodied voice was saying, "Tatie?"

"Present—or accounted for," Special Agent Monica said sleepily into a black speaker phone.

"Get your team to Missouri," the voice said. "We have another prize."

"Where?" the FBI agent asked, pen and notebook in hand. She looked at Service and mouthed *Body*.

"South central part of the state in the Irish Wilderness Area, on the Eleven Point River. A bureau bird will pick you up in Iron Mountain and take you to the old Blytheville Air Force Base in Arkansas. There's more clutter and less visibility there. You could be dropped in Springfield, but you'll have better cover at the old base. It's all general aviation now, and also a major depot for picking up and delivering Guard and Reserve troops. You won't be noticed. I suggest you move with the utmost dispatch, Special Agent. We've got another golden window."

"On our way," Tatie Monica said, punching a button to break the telephone connection. She looked at the other FBI personnel. "You heard the man, people. Let's shake and bake."

"What about this site?" Agent Bobbi Temple asked.

"I'll talk to Thorkaldsson and his people can keep it secure. You're now the site commander."

"Is it possible that this guy has struck twice so soon?" Service asked.

"It doesn't fit the pattern for our guy, or for most serials. Usually there's a resting period between kills," Monica said. "But none of these blood eagle things match the earlier group of killings, so who knows?" The other agents stood blinking until Agent Monica clapped her hands and said, "We're burning daylight, people." This sent them scrambling, and she immediately turned to Service. "First we call Thorkaldsson. We'll grab breakfast on the way to Iron Mountain. You got fresh clothes?"

"For how long?" he asked.

"Never mind," she said dismissively. "You can draw from our stuff if you need it." She turned to walk away, and Service caught her by the arm. "Whoa," he said. "This train's moving a little fast for me. Care to fill me in?"

"That was Cranbrook P. Bonaparte on the speaker. He's the BAU—Behavioral Analysis Unit—acting ay-dick who was supposed to come here. We apparently have another body—in Missouri—and we're going down there now. You're coming along, and I'll explain more en route."

"Ay-dick?"

"Acting assistant director. I'll explain later."

*Later?* It seemed to Service that explanations from the FBI agent were always in abeyance, and when and if they came, tended to be pretty thin. But he also noticed that when she gave an order the others jumped into action.

"He said, 'you,'" Service said. "Not me."

"This is my decision." She put the back of her fist on his chest. "Have you got a problem with it?"

He shrugged. "I've got some fresh stuff in my truck."

"Larry and I will ride with you," she said. "Bobbi, you keep our vehicle."

The female agent nodded and trotted away.

Service got into his Tahoe, Gasparino got into the backseat, and Special Agent Monica jumped up into the passenger seat, buckled her seat belt, triggered her handheld radio, and told the Florence County sheriff to meet her at the interpretive center.

Sheriff Thorkaldsson was a bearded six-foot-nine giant with lavender-tinted wraparound sunglasses and a field of red moles on his forehead shaped like gumdrops. "Arnie," she said as they met between the vehicles, "this is Grady Service."

Thorkaldsson nodded. "Wayno told me about you," the sheriff said.

"We're leaving, Arnie," she said. "Agent Temple is in charge of the site; Bobbi has people to cover the gate and the roads. I have no idea when we'll get back. Soon, I hope. Meanwhile, I want to continue the embargo on the announcement of Ficorelli's death."

"People around here are already yammering," Thorkaldsson said. "The county rumor mill is churning. We're getting media calls."

"Just tell them there's no fucking story here!" she snapped, and quickly softened her voice. "Just keep the lid on it, and if things go funny, you have my cell phone number. Work with Bobbi."

"Yes, ma'am," the towering sheriff said.

Service asked, "How come Wayno parked on the other side of the river?"

"Always did," Thorkaldsson said. "Superstitious, maybe. We always did pretty good in that part of the river."

"You find his rod with the body?"

"No."

"What's he use?"

"Four-weight Winnie with a Hardy reel."

"We have it," Service said.

"And a probable kill site," Special Agent Monica added. "It's downstream about three-quarters of a mile from where you found him. The tech team is there now. They'll stay, but we'll have to widen the perimeter. That's why we need the Wispies." Members of the Wisconsin State Patrol were called Wispies.

The sheriff said, "Rather have people I know than strangers in on this. I've got an auxiliary."

She said, "It's Bobbi's call, but whatever she decides, keep it quiet."

Service thought the sheriff seemed a little possessive, which was not an uncommon reaction to the FBI's swooping in.

"Was Wayno's body wet when you found it?" Service asked.

"Yeah."

Service and the agents ate sticky cinnamon bear claws from a gas station on their way south. Tatie Monica inhaled three of them while Service was still working on his first one. "This is what you call breakfast?" he asked.

"You prefer the golden arches?" she countered.

"Crapoleon?"

She grinned. "FBI humor. His name is Cranbrook P. Bonaparte. Bonaparte equals Napoleon. Cranbrook P. gives us Crapoleon." She looked over at him. "Don't worry, it's an affectionate name. Cranbrook is about the most charming sonuvabitch you'll ever meet, a truly nice man, and very sincere."

Her words and tone didn't quite match. "Your boss?"

"No, he's *acting* head ay-dick of the Behavioral Analysis Unit in NCVAC, which for him is a temporary gig. He's been there forever. My boss is the special agent in charge of the Milwaukee field office, but I'm the lead investigator for the case. The analyst who put all this together called me to talk about what he'd found. I went to my boss, and he grabbed onto the case and got the Bureau to give me the lead."

"A career moment," he said.

"Yeah," she said. "Up or down. If I don't bring this one home, it'll be a big belly flop into Bumfuck." Her voice was matter-of-fact, resigned.

"Isn't that in Wisconsin?" Service asked with a straight face.

"Shove it," she said, grinning. "The Bureau is merciless about failure these days," she added.

"I keep wondering if it's possible that there could be two killings so close together."

"Certainly it's not what our boy's done in the past, but if Cranbrook says we have another, we have another."

She was respectful of the BAU man, Service thought, but he sensed an undercurrent of something else, a certain edge when she talked about him.

"Bonaparte's an expert on profiling?" Service asked as he drove.

"One of the pioneers," she said, looking over at him, "which puts him in a cast of dozens. Since profiling became popular with fiction writers and Hollywood, dozens of agents have stepped forward to claim they invented the concept."

"Him too?"

"No. Bonaparte's too nice and too smart to blatantly self-promote. His style is to quietly insinuate himself into those places and with those people he thinks can help him. He's got some theories that don't quite fit profiling coda."

"Is he good at what he does?"

"That's a loaded question. The naked fact is that no profiler has ever provided work product that allowed a field agent to capture a serial murderer. We think there are about one hundred of these killers active around the country at any given time, and the only way we ever get any of them is through a back door, or their fuckup—usually the latter. In practice, profiling helps us verify what we've got *after* we have a suspect or somebody in custody, and usually for reasons that don't relate to our primary interest. Historically, profiling hasn't enabled us to intervene."

"If Bonaparte's so good at the job and a pioneer, how come he's not director or permanent assistant director for BAU?"

"Fair question," she said. "When Louis Freeh left, there was an interim director before Mueller was named, and he quickly named his own people. Cranbrook didn't have time to suck up to Mueller, so he got passed over. Right now there's an opening, so he's filling in until the current powers can find their own man."

"Sore point with him?"

She paused to mull this over. "He probably wanted the job, but he seems more interested in his theories than in running the show."

"Theories?"

"I'll let him explain," she said. "Right, Larry?"

"Uh-huh," the child agent in the backseat mumbled. Gasparino was from the Bronx, less than nine months out of the academy.

There it was again, explanations lobbed into the future like fungoes. "You're a cop, right?" she said.

"Yeah."

"Then *drive* like one, for Christ's sake. Let's light up this jalopy and haul ass! Every minute we spend on the road is a minute we don't have at the next site."

# IRISH WILDERNESS AREA, MISSOURI
## MAY 22, 2004

They dozed on the plane and were taken in a dented, unmarked twelve-passenger van from the one-time military base in Arkansas north into Missouri and the Irish Wilderness Area in the southeastern part of the state. Their destination was the Eleven Point River, named either because it was eleven-point-some miles from something, or labeled tongue-in-cheek by early surveying crews who legend said had to stop eleven times in the first mile to change and record readings. Their driver said no one could recall the exact point of reference or the precise fraction; his own theory was that the name was an Anglicization of *Leve Pont,* which appeared on early French maps of the area.

The van hurtled along narrow, high-crested roads, up Highway 19, crossing numerous razorback ridges, and eventually descending into a deep, verdant valley. They drove into a crudely paved parking lot where four Missouri game wardens waited with canoes and johnboats at a cement step-down boat launch that looked like it had seen a lot of use. A wooden sign said GREER SPRINGS.

Tatie Monica had been extremely quiet during most of the drive, but en route made a point of explaining that Missouri's game wardens were called conservation agents, and properly addressed as agents.

One of the four men was sparsely bearded with wild gray eyes. He wore a gray shirt and green pants, the same as Michigan conservation officers. "Eddie Waco," the man said with a slight nod.

"Grady Service."

"Where's Bonaparte?" Special Agent Monica asked.

"Died a while back out on some island in the Atlantic, I heard," Eddie Waco said, deadpan, giving Service the once-over. "You handle a paddle?" he asked.

Service immediately felt a kinship in that they were both thrown in with feds and Waco seemed neither impressed nor intimidated. "Fat part or skinny part?" Service answered, earning a grin.

Agent Monica got into a johnboat with one of the other conservation agents. "Move out," she barked, her shoulders hunched forward.

Service's escort tapped a pack in the bottom of the canoe. "Got you'n's kit?" the man asked.

Service said, "Somewhere in the van."

"Best fetch hit right-quick an' jes git on in, sit up front, and let me do most of the work. Level's up some from spring rains, and the current's pert steady most of the way, so we don't have to grow us no wings," he added. Service grabbed his ruck and left the remainder of his gear in the van, assuming it would be brought downriver behind them, or be waiting in the vehicle when they came out tonight or tomorrow morning.

Larry Gasparino sat motionless in his craft, as if he had been nailed in place and was about to undertake the Bataan death float. Service wondered why some native New Yorkers seemed to disconnect when they were away from their concrete canyons.

The river was deep and slow as they pulled out of the narrow side channel where the launch was situated, and wide and slow for a while before suddenly narrowing, deepening, and speeding up, the water so clear Service could see huge rainbow trout suspended ten feet down in the deeper runs. Eddie Waco stroked almost casually, using his paddle over the left side both for propulsion and as a rudder. "There an overland way into where we're headed?" Service asked.

"More ways ta kill a dog thin chokin' 'im with buttern," the man said cryptically. "We been told no fuss and ta keep the button on this."

"Have you met Bonaparte?" Service asked.

Waco shot back, "What part you got in this bug-tussle?"

"I follow orders," Service said. He started to explain, but decided against it. The Feebs seemed obsessed with security, and like it or not, he was part of the federal team for now. Keeping quiet seemed the prudent course.

The Eleven Point River snaked around small wooded islands with thick stands of Ozark cane, and later split a multihued limestone and dolomite canyon, two hundred feet high, the sides clotted with dense stands of white oak, elm, hickory, sycamore, sassafras, and clumps of shortleaf pine and spruce. There was a heavy understory beneath the trees, almost black in the early afternoon sun. Towering rocky outcrops were yellow, black, and green in places, splotched by age and erosion. Service could see numerous small caves and openings in the rocks overhead, as well as the holes of bank swallows. Lily pads dotted side coves of gray-green frog water.

The four craft eventually reached a heavier riffle with protruding rocks. Eddie Waco guided their canoe expertly into the longest "V" and deftly slid them through the pinch-point. Service wasn't sure whether the man's silence was due to shyness or from his concentration on maneuvering.

When they floated into the head of another long eddy of quiet water, Service's guide said, "No easy way to hoof inta where we're a-goin', but hit's bin done."

Service thought more information might follow. It didn't.

Service and Waco had pushed off behind the other three craft, and Eddie Waco showed no urgency to catch up.

The Missouri conservation agent nosed the canoe onto a gravel bar with softball-size yellow and gray cobble and stepped out. "Got to see a man about a dawg," he said, stepping under the canopy of some sycamores that acted as an umbrella over the edge of the gravel. Service decided to avail himself of the stop, and when he'd finished and returned, Eddie Waco was sitting with one leg draped over a gunwale.

"You'n a part of this thing?"

"Michigan conversation officer," Service said. "I'm here to consult."

"Consult, eh?" Eddie Waco parroted. "What might that be?"

Service shrugged. "Beats me. You got any idea what we're doing?"

"A man's always got idees, but we been ordered ta walk the chalk," Waco said, offering a tin of Redman.

The man's words seemed a vague complaint, but Service shook his head, said "No thanks," and lit a cigarette. He had no idea what the man was talking about.

"Hear-tell you'n make a passel of cars up Michigan way." He wondered if the man's accent was real or put-on. The man seemed serious.

"That would be in Detroit," Service said, adding, "which many of us don't consider part of the state."

"Like St. Looey hereabouts," Eddie Waco said with a grin. "You not a city feller?"

"From the Upper Peninsula," Service said.

"Do tell," Waco said. "Heard you got some bears up thataway."

"Quite a few."

"We get us some mosey up from Arkansas time to time," the man said. "Couple years back I think a farmer up north a' here shot one a' them wolves a' your'n."

This was true. A young collared Michigan wolf had rambled more than five hundred miles from the Upper Peninsula into north central Missouri, where it had been shot by a farmboy, who had mistaken the animal for a coyote stalking his family's livestock. It had made the news throughout the Midwest. "I remember," Service said.

"Long walk ta go a-clicketing," Eddie Waco said, smirking.

A-clicketing? Strange word, but the meaning seemed clear and Service laughed. "Never say never." The young wolf probably had been seeking a mate to establish his own pack.

"I reckon."

"Shouldn't we be moving on?" Service asked. They had been sitting on the gravel bar for close to half an hour.

"Whatever them feds got downriver, I'm thinkin' the weathern's gon' turn a tetch bad."

Service looked at the man. "Meaning?"

"Storms comin' in—big ole front. Expect 'em in two . . . three hours, if'n we're lucky. Could bring some black-stem twisters, I reckon."

Tornadoes? Service wondered if Bonaparte and Tatie Monica knew this, and, if so, why they were all headed into a wilderness in canoes and johnboats, or headed there at all?

"I'm sure the feds have a plan," Service said.

"'Speck folks up New York–way couple years back might opine differ'nt."

Eddie Waco spit a bullet of tobacco juice, straddled the stern, nodded for Service to get in, pushed the canoe away from the gravel, and hop-stepped into the stern, digging his paddle into the bottom to ease them into the current.

Special Agent Monica was already waiting on a small gravel beach and prancing anxiously at the mouth of a steep trail. She motioned for him to follow her. Service nodded at his boat mate. "You coming?"

"Feds ain't give us the secret handshake," Eddie Waco said, shaking his head.

Service looked at the swirling yellow-gray sky and started up the steep, sandy trail. He could feel the pressure change in his ears and wondered what it meant.

Tatie Monica glared over her shoulder at him. "What the hell took you and Pa Kettle so long?"

The air was heavy, thick, making sweat pop. "Pit stop," Service explained. "People down here seem to move at their own pace." *A lot like people in the U.P.*, he thought, which he had always considered a good thing.

She muttered, "Bonaparte can be a dickhead about being late."

"Have you heard a weather forecast?" he asked. He didn't realize they had an ETA to meet.

She nodded. "Some rain. Bonaparte will have it covered. He's the detail man." Did she mean to imply that she wasn't? In his experience being an investigator was almost entirely about details.

"Agent Waco says there could be tornadoes."

She looked up and chewed her bottom lip. "Shit happens," she said.

There were sycamores and shortleaf pine, sassafras and other trees reaching over the narrow trail. "Not the greatest place to get caught in toothy weather," he said.

She said over her shoulder, "I thought you outdoor types thrived on this shit."

"You ever been in a twister?" he asked.

She shook her head. "You?"

"Once was enough." He'd been in a cyclone in Southeast Asia. It had wrecked a base camp and killed two marines and a Kit Carson scout named Minh. The only difference between there and here would be direction of cyclonic rotation.

When they finally reached the top of the bluff, they found an eight-person FBI crime scene team out of the St. Louis field office, and a four-wall, olive-drab green shelter with a generator humming outside. The FBI crime team members were dressed in white biohazard coveralls with hoods and face masks and looked like a NASA team getting ready for a launch. It struck him how a person could be alive and healthy one minute and dead and a health threat the next and this made him think of Nantz and Walter and made his stomach flip. The team's gear was scattered around helter-skelter. Service studied the area, thought it might have been a campground at one time. There were scars and scorched stones where there probably had been fire-pit rings.

Monica introduced herself and Service to the lead tech. "Where's Bonaparte?"

"Split," the crime scene tech said.

"When?"

"Three hours ago, maybe less. He said the weather was turning and he couldn't afford to get trapped out here. He said to tell you you're in command—you'd know what to do."

"*Did* he?" she said, her response clipped, her voice low and oily. "What do we have?"

The man led her to the shelter. "Refrigeration unit," he said. "Bonaparte said he wanted the site left untouched until you got here."

Untouched? How had they set up the shelter without fouling the site? Service wondered. The sheriff in Wisconsin had done a professional job—but this?

The man said, "Walk the green tape."

Service saw tape held to the limestone surface with small rocks.

The air inside the shelter was almost frigid, and while Service welcomed the cold at first, he quickly wished he had a jacket or a sweater. Dumb to leave his extra clothes in the van.

There was nude male body on the ground, mutilated in exactly the same manner as Wayno Ficorelli's. The man was huge, with red hair and a flaming red beard.

"What have we got?" Special Agent Monica asked.

"One very sick puppy," the tech said quietly.

"How long has the body been here?" she asked.

"By ambient air and body temperature, thirty-six hours, give or take. We can't be more accurate until we get the remains back to the lab."

She looked at the man. "How'd you get here?"

"Down the river, same as you."

"Did Bonaparte take a boat out?"

"Chopper," the man said with a disapproving grunt. "He seemed to be in a hurry."

"Who found the body?" Service asked.

"Don't know," the man said.

"You hear there's severe weather coming in?" Service asked.

"We heard, and if the winds pick up, this place will be toast. You got a plan?"

"Just keep doing what you're doing," Agent Monica said. "But do it fast."

"Mostly we've been waiting on you. We've done most everything we can do here. Bonaparte insisted we leave everything as is until you got a look."

"Not much blood," she said, leaning over the corpse. "Kill site?"

"Doubtful," the technician said, shaking his head.

The plastic walls began to snap and shake as the air turned blustery.

"Shit," the tech said. "That wind gets worse, it'll turn this thing into a parasail."

"You looked for alternate shelter?"

"No, ma'am. Our orders were to stand by, wait, and not talk to the locals."

Tatie Monica turned to Service. "We need a safe place to store the body—and us," she said.

"I'll tell the Missouri agents," he said, stepping out into the wind. He squinted as sand blasted his face. The storm was coming in fast. He felt a tug on his arm and found Larry Gasparino. "Weather's heading south; am I right, or what?"

"Way south," Service agreed, glancing at the swirling, dark clouds.

He bounced his way down the trail, found the watercraft tethered to chains at the end of nylon ropes on the beach. There was nobody with them. He sniffed smoke, looked at the pea gravel, saw impressions leading around a huge boulder on the downstream side, and followed them.

The prints and path led to an overhang six feet deep and high, and ten feet wide.

The four Missouri agents were squatting around a small Sterno fire. Eddie Waco looked up at him.

Service said, "Feels like the twisters are ahead of schedule."

"Always got they own minds," Waco said.

"We have a body up top and we need to get it under cover before the storm hits full force."

The conservation agents followed him at a jog to the top, without comment. Crime scene techs had already transferred the corpse into a black rubber bag. Service and the Missouri men labored down the steep trail as the wind suddenly stopped and everything became still.

Not even birds sang.

Service had one corner of the bag as it began to sprinkle. Eddie Waco said, "She be upon us, boys."

They dragged the bag under the overhang cave just as the rain started. It came down like marbles, a giant spigot opened wide, the rain coming in a steady roar. The eight techs, four Missouri agents, Larry Gasparino, and Tatie Monica pressed in with them, fifteen people and a corpse in a bag crammed into a tight space.

"What direction are we facing?" Service asked Waco. The trip down the twisting river with heavy overcast had pretty much obliterated his sense of direction. There was no sun to orient him.

"Southwest," Eddie Waco said. "More or less."

"Figures," Service said. A tornado would blow directly in on them. "We should find another place."

"Thet dog hain't a-gonna hunt," the conservation agent said. "Have to ride 'er out here."

Special Agent Monica got out her handheld radio and tried to get a chopper to evacuate the body, but was told through massive static there would be no flying until the storms passed.

Service thought she looked outwardly calm. He wondered what her real emotions were. He was on edge. Did she not realize what could happen? Could she be *that* clueless?

The steady rain turned to huge, loud drops that sounded like stones.

The drops changed to golf ball–size hailstones that clicked and ticked and ricocheted like bullets.

The temperature plummeted.

The wind started changing directions, intensified, and began to blast them with chips of chert, dust, and shards of bark. Everyone in the stone shelter covered their heads with their arms and turned their backs to the opening.

Service heard a roar he first thought was a helicopter, a thought he amended to a train a moment before his brain put it all together: *Tornado!* The afternoon sky was as night.

Large things began crashing and thumping against the side of the cliff.

"I'll be go to hell!" one of the techs cursed from his crouch.

"We all just might," another shaky voice said.

Wind suddenly ripped into the cave, toppling Service onto his side.

He immediately reached for the wall of the cave, looking for something to hold on to as the man beside him disappeared.

"Service!" Tatie Monica shrieked.

Service saw her arms splayed as she was yanked and spun outside by the wind. He jumped on her legs, trying to pin her with his weight, but they both kept sliding and skidded off a slippery ledge, and all he could think was, *Shit.*

The water was a shock, much colder than he expected.

He kicked his way to the surface, saw a boulder looming, and managed to use a hand to straight-arm it as he was propelled downstream, spinning. *Where was Tatie Monica?*

No idea how much time had passed, aware only that it was lighter, the rain still coming down in sheets, but there seemed to be more light and a little less wind. A tree crashed into the water ahead of him and raised a spout like a depth charge as objects began to splash all around him. At one point he saw a spotted fawn floating by, its neck bent at ninety degrees. He looked around, saw several people bobbing and splashing in the water, stretched out and swam to get speed, and when he had his stroke going, looked up, saw a gravel bar ahead, and swam onto it, scraping his chin as he beached himself.

A tech came by holding out a hand and Service got a wrist-lock and yanked him ashore. The man was bleeding from the mouth and nose. He helped a second man ashore and looked upstream but saw no more people. He assumed the others had found a way to safety or were somewhere downstream. The dead fawn was wedged between some rocks just below him.

He heard shouting, the rain drowning out most of the words.

"Body bag," a voice screamed. Service thought it was Tatie Monica, but he had no idea where she was.

Eddie Waco was soon crouched beside him. "I seen where hit went," he told Service, who nodded and said simply, "Let's go."

They eased into the water together and began to swim side by side.

The rising river carried them fifty yards through a narrow neck with a riffle before dumping them into a long frothy eddy. Service saw the bag floating ahead of him and got to it first. Eddie Waco joined him, and the two of them guided it, kicking their way into flatter water, pushing and pulling it toward the cliff wall with the most shoreline.

"I need a smoke," Service said, his chest heaving.

The Missouri man held out his snuff tin. "Why I carry this," he said.

Service shook his head. "We need to secure the body."

"Not down here," the man said. "This rain still a-goin', they'll be a crest rollin' downstream."

"How high?"

"Don't take much ta push 'er up six ta eight feet. I seen as much as twelve a couple times, and back in the nineties she once come way up over thirty."

Service scanned the rocks above them. "Another cave?" he asked.

"Plinty ta choose from, but we need ta get ta one up high enough."

The heavy rain reminded him of monsoons in Vietnam, but Waco had nylon rope and carabiners in his waist pack, and located a cubbyhole above them. Service climbed up while Waco secured the line to the body bag. With Service pulling and the other man climbing, and pushing and guiding, they got the body fifteen feet above the waterline and wedged into a space that was more scallop than cave.

"We ought to check on the others," Service said.

"They hain't safe, nothin' ta be done about hit."

Service stripped off his vest and turned it inside out. He always carried two packs of cigarettes sewn into a waterproof pouch inside the back of his bulletproof vest. He peeled off the vest cover and dug out a pack.

He reached into his pants pocket and fished out a sealed plastic container of wooden matches. "How long until it crests?"

"Cain't say, but she's a-risin' pert fast."

Service looked down and saw that it was true.

"The body's gonna be in bad shape," Service said.

"Dead's dead," Eddie Waco said.

Rain continued to fall unrelentingly, and an hour after they had snugged into their perch, they heard a voice shouting along the canyon wall. It was impossible to make out any words. Eddie Waco got outside and inched his way toward the sound, came back, and grabbed his pack.

"What?" Service asked.

"Got us a snakebite," the man said. "Water drives serpents ta cover, same as us."

Service lurched and looked around. He was not crazy about snakes. "*Poisonous* snakes?"

Eddie Waco said. "Like most folks, snakes don't bite less'n they's feelin' cornered."

"Great," Service said sardonically. One of the comforting things about the Upper Peninsula was the rarity of poisonous snakes.

The conservation agent put on his small pack and started along the rock wall. Service looked around, began imagining snakes in all the little crevices in the cave, and decided to go with Waco, invited or not.

It was a long, slippery, and clumsy crawl along the rock face through sheets of cold rain and powerful wind gusts before they reached another conservation agent. "Lady fed got herself bit," the man told them.

Service noted they were a little higher than where they had the body stashed.

Special Agent Tatie Monica was sitting in a hole sculpted from the limestone by nature and time. Her dark hair was mashed to her head like a helmet. Her eyes were rheumy, more from irritation than fear. A crime scene tech was sitting next to her. Every time he reached for her, she swatted his hand away.

"Tatie!" Service barked.

She glowered at him.

"What happened?"

"Snake," the tech beside her said.

"You get 'im?" Eddie Waco asked.

"She mashed its head with her pistol grip," the tech said, pointing.

The reddish-brown earth-tone serpent was piled up between some stones. Eddie Waco found a stick and prodded the reptile, which moved.

"Jesus, it's still alive!" the tech yipped, scrambling away from the FBI field agent.

Eddie Waco probed with the stick again and the snake pulled away. He kept poking it until he uncovered its tail, grabbed it, and snapped the snake backward like a whip. It cracked sharply in the heavy air and he dropped it on the ground, unsheathed a small knife, and cut off its head. "Copperhead," he announced. "Just a little feller. You'n got heart problems?" he asked Agent Monica.

"Field agents aren't authorized in the field if they have heart problems," she said defiantly.

"That's real good to know," Eddie Waco said. "How ya'll feelin'?"

"Stupid," the woman said.

"You got pain?"

"It burns."

"Where?" the conservation agent asked.

"Buttock," the tech said. "She won't let us look."

"Let's git thim trousers off," Eddie Waco said, but he found himself staring at the barrel of a 9-millimeter.

"You got antivenin?" Tatie Monica asked.

"No, ma'am."

"Snakebite kit?"

"No, ma'am."

"I don't want my ass carved," she said, her eyes rolling.

"The way it is," Eddie Waco said quietly, "copperheads don't kill many people except'n young 'uns and ole folks with heart problems. This 'un's not too big, which means not a lot of pizen, but even little fellers got enough ta kill flesh and muscle at the bite site. I reckon we need to get what pizen's in there out right quick afore it spreads."

She brandished the weapon. "*Nobody* touches my ass," she repeated.

Grady Service raised his left hand to deflect the barrel of her weapon up, and struck her hard on the chin with the heel of his right hand. The pistol came loose and she slumped to her left. He picked up the weapon, popped out the clip, and handed the weapon and magazine to Gasparino, who had joined them, his eyes bulging like jumbo egg yolks.

Eddie Waco rolled the stunned woman onto her stomach, cut her belt with his knife, and sliced open the fabric of her pants and underpants, skimpy black French cuts, which made Service think of Nantz and gulp.

The fang marks in her right buttock were small but distinct. The skin was already red, shiny, and swollen.

"You going to cut and suck?" Service asked.

"Cuttin' causes more damage less'n you'n a doctor man," the Missouri man said, "which I hain't." He put down his pack, reached into it, and took out a red bandanna, which he unfolded to reveal a flat, oval rock, white with brown speckles. He set the stone aside and took out a small, single-burner camp stove, connected the fuel canister, and handed a metal container to Gasparino. "Fill 'er with watern, quickety split." Eddie Waco lit the burner, which hissed.

Gasparino crawled clumsily down to the raging river, filled the cup, and passed it up. Waco took out another cup and filled it from a flask. He put the second cup on the burner, took some antibacterial soap out of his pack, washed the wound, and blotted away excess moisture.

Tatie Monica tried to roll over, but Service pressed her shoulder down. "Keep still," he said.

"Don't cut me," she muttered, with the side of her face pressed to the ground.

"Be no cuttin'," Eddie Waco said calmly.

When the liquid boiled he put the stone in it and let it bubble for a while. He took his Leatherman tool off his belt, opened it to form pliers, and extracted the rock, which had turned pure white from heat. Eddie Waco looked at Service, saying, "Bes' hold 'er down." Then to her, "This might could smart some."

He took the stone in his glove and pressed it to the wound, where it seared the flesh. Tatie Monica bucked and cursed, "Fuckers!"And passed out.

Service turned his head to avoid the smell. "What now?" Service asked. It was still pouring, but the wind had slackened.

"We wait," the Missouri agent said.

Service had no idea what was going on. "Is this for real?"

"I seen it done afore," he said. "You got a better idee, Michigan Man?" Service didn't.

Waco turned off the heat under the boiling liquid, picked up the flask, and handed it to Service. "For what ails you'n."

Service took a sip, swallowed, felt the fire bloom in his stomach. Eddie Waco also took a sip. "White mule yella corn," he said. "Best there is, aged some eight years." He held the flask out to Service again, who held up a hand.

"I'm good."

Service pointed to the stone on the FBI agent's right buttock. "What *is* that?"

"My great-granddaddy done shot him a white deer, found hit in the animal's belly, done passed hit down to my daddy, and Pa done passed hit on ta me. People down this way use such stones for the rabies."

"It works?"

"Sometimes, but hit's plenty good for snakebite, you git ta hit soon enough and there hain't too much pizen."

"What's it called?" Service asked.

"Madstone," the man said.

"You believe in witchcraft?" Service asked.

"I don't, but if'n I was in a pinch, I'd ask a witch for help, wouldn't you'n?"

Service nodded, knowing desperation was more the mother of invention than pedestrian need.

The tech left Service and Eddie Waco alone with Monica. "She'll live," Waco said. "Who be in the bag back yonder?" he asked.

"Don't know," Service said. "I just got a quick look when the storm blew in."

They sat for two hours, and when the stone fell off the agent's bare flesh, Eddie Waco reheated the stone in the alcohol, which turned green, and applied the madstone again.

"Maybe the stone cauterizes?" Service offered.

"I hain't much on science," Eddie Waco said.

After forty minutes, the stone came loose again. This time Eddie Waco repeated the process, but the alcohol remained clear and the stone wouldn't stick. He wiped it dry with the faded red bandanna, meticulously refolded it, and carefully put it in his pack. "Snake didn't get much inta her," he said. "She'll be fine, but we best git her outside to the hospital."

Service looked up at the sky, which was still roiling, but there were devil's smiles beginning to slice into the canyon, turning the water below them to quicksilver.

"How far to the get-out by boat?" Service asked.

"I reckon six mile," Eddie Waco said, "but with the watern up, they'll be a heap a' trees pilin' up in the narrers."

"The poison works on the heart, right?"

The Missouri man nodded.

"We gotta keep her still, limit exertion."

"Weather clears, we might can get a chopper in," Eddie Waco said. "Have ta mule her up top, but we got enough men for thet."

"No boats?"

"Too risky," the conservation agent said. "Would take too long."

The water looked like it had come up five feet and was still rising.

"She'll peak in two, three more hours, drop pert fast after thet."

Service found Monica's radio and gave it to the man. "Can you arrange pickup through your own contacts?"

"Not thim feds?"

"A fed left us here," Grady Service reminded him. "We can get the body and her out at the same time."

Eddie Waco nodded and started trying to radio for help.

Tatie Monica stirred beside them. "No cuts," she mumbled.

"No cuts," Service said. "Just a little brand for a keepsake."

She whined. "My ass."

"Think how good it'll feel when it stops," Service said. "Let's get some trousers from the others," he said to Eddie Waco.

"Just gon' cut 'em off when they get her inta the whirlybird," the man said.

"Looks like you get to moon the world," Service told her.

"My mother would just die," she mumbled.

"P'int is, ya'll don't," Eddie Waco said.

It took two hours to get the agent and the body bag on top of the bluff, and by then a Missouri Highway Patrol Huey was waiting with a medical team. Gasparino looked disoriented and Service couldn't blame him. The past few hours had been tough. Service sent two techs with the body. Tatie Monica was mostly awake, but far from alert, and offered no resistance.

They watched the helicopter rev its rotors, lift a swirl of debris, and lumber away.

"Missouri emblem on the chopper shows two bears," Service noted.

"They musta snuck up from Arkansas," the conservation agent said with a grin.

Service called over to the lead tech. "You recover photos?"

"Cameras are with our gear," he said, "if the wind didn't carry it all off to Kansas."

"Wind comin' from t'other direction," Eddie Waco pointed out.

The refrigerated shelter had been shredded. Pieces were pasted like confetti in trees, the metal frame posts twisted and bent. There was no sign of the generator. The crime scene techs' gear was scattered, but most of it had been blown inland. The tops of some trees upriver had been severed by wind shear. Eddie Waco surveyed the trees, said, "Twister jes sorta skipped over top like a flat rock."

The chopper had gotten in and out, but the leaden sky continued to threaten, and from time to time they heard thunder and saw flashes of lightning. It took the lead crime scene tech thirty minutes to find the plastic lockbox with the camera and digital crime scene photos. Why hadn't Tatie Monica brought the camera with her when they hauled the body down from the top of the bluff? Panic? Service and Eddie Waco sat on a downed tree and opened the box. The Missouri conservation agent studied the photographs and handed them back to Service without comment, his tanned skin looking a lot lighter.

"Somebody you know?"

"Agent Elray Spargo," Waco said with a sigh. "Elray was a card-carrying comminist lib'ral atheist, a by-God, down-to-the-bone secular humanist, which hereabouts is akin to bein' the devil. All that mattered to Elray was the law. That was his only religion, and he wrought legal hell on lawbreakers."

"He made enemies?"

"Most a' which he sent off to jail. After more'n twinny year, he purty well had control, an' ever-body knew it. Loan me one a thim cig'rettes a' your'n?"

Service held out a pack.

"I got me this feelin' they's more ta this thin just Elray," Eddie Waco said.

"Yeah?"

"You gonna say different, Michigan Man?"

Service shook his head. "It's a federal show."

"Way we see hit, kill one a' our kind makes hit our show."

Service understood and sympathized, but did not tell the man what he knew. "I hear you," he said.

"We best mosey," the Missouri game warden said.

"I thought we had to wait for the water to recede."

"I thought we'd take us a walk. Thim others can wait an' take the boats out."

Service called Gasparino over. "Agent Waco and I are walking out. Special Agent Gasparino, I guess that makes you in charge."

"Me?"

"Wait until the water level goes down and take the boats downstream." Service gave him Tatie Monica's handheld radio. "You'll probably have to wait for more boats to help haul everything out."

Gasparino nodded solemnly. "Where are you two going?"

"Things ta tend to," Eddie Waco said, standing up, putting on his pack, and offering no further explanation.

"What about more tornadoes?" the young FBI agent asked.

"Might be, might not," Waco said. "They come, you best find cover."

"What if somebody gets snakebit again?"

The Missouri game warden scratched his head. "Best hope hit ain't a big 'un."

# 14

## FOURTEEN, MISSOURI

## MAY 23, 2004

They had been walking in the darkness almost four hours, following military crests, occasionally dipping down to the uneven floors of steep ravines before climbing back up. The humidity was overwhelming in the valleys, but there was an occasional swirling breeze on top, and Grady Service found himself falling into the mindless trance that came with long-distance hiking.

Eddie Waco rarely stopped, and when he did it was usually for less than a minute before pushing on.

During one of their pauses in a canyon bottom, Waco said, "Y'all stay put," and moved into some stunted yellow-bark trees with intertwined trunks.

Service waited five minutes and looked for shade. He had taken a couple of steps when the bark of a hickory tree in front of him exploded by his head, clipping his shirt and face. He dropped to his belly as a second round took a chunk off a tree just behind him, the reports echoing through the canyon, their source impossible to pinpoint.

He had his hand on his SIG Sauer when he looked up and saw Eddie Waco grinning. "Stand down, Michigan Man," the Missouri warden said. "Thet's jes' thim ole Mahan boys a-barkin' on you'n."

Service got to his feet and brushed himself off.

"Whin I say stay, you best heed," Eddie Waco chastised him.

"Barking?" Service said.

"Thim Mahans got a still halfway up yonder ridge," he said, pointing ahead. "Anybody they don't know gits too close, they plink a few rounds inta the trees to discourage 'em. They don't shoot to hit nobody."

Waco cupped his hands and shouted, "Ikey, you and your brother put down them long guns. This here's Eddie Waco an' I'm just passin' through."

"We seen you hain't alone," a voice shouted down from some trees on the hill.

"He's the law, same as me. We hain't comin' yore way, boys, but you squeeze off another round, I reckon we gonna come up yonder, all ya'll hear?"

"We hear," the voice called back.

Waco looked at Service, nodded, and started walking.

"A still?" Service said.

"Don't got 'em up where you'n hail from?"

"Meth labs," Service said. "And marijuana plots in the state and national forests."

"We got us a dandy weed crop down this away too," Eddie Waco said. "I'd rather tussle with moonshiners."

Seven hours after they struck away from the Eleven Point River, they descended to a shallow, shale-bottom stream running down a steep canyon and walked into a clearing with a half-dozen dark stone buildings that looked like they had grown out of the ground. The dwellings were narrow, one-floor affairs, each with an oversize wooden porch under a steep roof. All of the wood needed paint. The roofs were covered with rich, yellowgreen moss. The houses looked like sturdier versions of old mining company houses in the Upper Peninsula's Copper Country.

"Where are we?" Service asked.

"Fourteen," Eddie Waco said.

"Fourteen what?"

"Jes Fourteen's how hit's called."

Service stopped, knelt, and splashed cool water on his neck and face. It had misted off and on during the hike, but the longer they walked the more the sun stayed out. Tendrils of steam rose off the rocks and ground. He stood up and looked: buildings but no people. "Ghost town?"

Eddie Waco grinned. "They's likely fifty sets a' eyes on us hain't ghosts, I 'speck. Long guns neither. The Spargo clan's partial ta goin'about armed."

"Elray Spargo lived here?"

"Lived up top, but he was a-born and reared down here. These here is his people and they need to know what's gone on."

"We should be moving," Service said, thinking of the FBI and his own ambiguous role in the undertaking.

"People got their own pace back this way," Waco said. "Do you good, stand down a bit, pay attention, listen, mebbe learn some."

A man in a rumpled brown suit appeared from the tree line and walked slowly toward them. He had a shotgun slung over his shoulder, the sling made of soiled gray rope. He wore a thin black tie, distressed high-top logging boots turned gray from use, and a dusty black porkpie hat cocked rakishly to the side and back of his head. Service realized the man had the hat pushed back to keep his eyes clear for possible shooting. He had done the same thing too many times to not recognize it for what it was.

"How do, Agent Waco," the man said, staring at Service. "Your'n partner be sippin' thet crick watern, he'll soon be havin' runs a-spurtin' outen 'is backside."

"You drink the watern?" Waco asked.

Service shook his head.

"Not too much trouble, we could use some sweetwater, Cotton," Waco said.

A young girl came out of the woods with a couple of quart jars and gave one to each of the two game wardens. Service noted that she kept her eyes down. She wore new white Asics tennis shoes with gaudy red and gold trim.

The water was cold and pure. Service looked at the girl and thanked her as she slunk back toward the trees.

"Sir, I done come ta talk," Waco told the old man.

The man in the brown suit walked over to them, gave Service the once-over, and squatted. Waco and Service squatted with him. "Cotton, I'm powerful sorry to tell you'n Elray got hisseff kilt."

With no emotion in his voice or face, the man said, "That what the ruckus over to the Leven Point was about?"

"Yessir, hit was."

"Did the boy die brave?" the man asked.

"He lived plenty brave; I expect he died the same," Eddie Waco said.

The man reached down and scooped up a handful of white dust, which he let play through his fingers. "Was a jimsonweed Christian," the man said. "The Lord never took hold with the boy."

"He was a lawman," Eddie Waco said.

"I reckon. You on your way to tell Fiannula?"

"Yessir."

The man nodded solemnly. "Reckon I'll jes mosey along with all y'all. You'n know how Fi kin git."

"Suit yerseff."

It occurred to Service that Waco was overly deferential to the old man.

"Fiannula packs 'at scattergun whin Elray's away," Cotton Spargo said.

"She knows me," Eddie Waco said.

"She frees thet wildcat, thet won't matter," Cotton said. "They gon' fetch my boy home?" the man asked.

"Thought I'd use the radio at Elray's to take care of it."

"Be good, we get the boy on his way to the Lord. How long since he done went?"

Waco looked at Service, who said, "About forty-eight hours."

"We ain't got much time left, this weather'n all," Cotton Spargo said.

The men stood up. No other people appeared. The man in the brown suit led the way with Waco and Service following. The man walked with remarkable grace at a brisk pace. Service guessed he was in his eighties.

"The body's legal evidence," Service whispered to the Missouri agent as they marched up a steep hill surrounded by a thick forest of gnarled pines.

"Things is differ'nt in these here hills," Eddie Waco said.

"Jimsonweed Christian?" Service whispered.

"Hush," Eddie Waco said softly. "Save your questions."

The house on the hill was built in a clearing with no trees closer than two hundred yards. The building was one story with rooms protruding at different angles. Something about it reminded Service of base camps in Vietnam, designed so that anyone approaching would have to cross a long stretch of open ground. Open space and the way rooms jutted out at ninety-degree angles suggested the place had been designed to create shooting lanes. It looked like a tidy fortress. Unlike the houses in the valley, this one was all wood and freshly painted, but in a brownish-gray color that made it difficult to see until you were actually in the clearing.

"Was Spargo ex-military?" he asked as they started across the clearing.

"Taught survival skills ta flyboys out ta Washington State," Eddie Waco said with a frown. "No more questions."

There was a small woman waiting on the porch. She had a sawed-off side-by-side shotgun in the crook of her right arm and a baby in the crook of her left. She had auburn hair in a severe bun and looked to be in her late thirties, her skin leathery from too much sun. She wore oversize bib overalls embroidered with colorful flowers, and yellow flip-flops. Service saw small faces in several windows. The woman's eyes were dark coals in red beds. She had been crying.

"Fiannula," the elder Spargo said.

Her eyes were locked on Eddie Waco and Service.

As they got closer Service smelled something sweet. The woman looked over her shoulder. "You young 'uns git away from them winders or I'll be cuttin' me a switch!" The faces disappeared instantly.

"Word done come about Elray," she said, turning back to her visitors. "I was jes about ta put on the black."

Service wondered how she knew, but Yoopers also had a grapevine that often surprised him in its speed and accuracy.

"They gon' fetch him home?" she asked

Cotton Spargo said, "Agent Waco here will see ta Elray, Fi."

"Obliged," the woman said with a faint nod to the conservation agent.

"Okay ta use the base radio?" Waco asked.

The woman nodded toward the house and made eye contact with Service. "Furriner," she said.

"Game warden from Michigan," Waco said. "Good man."

The woman sighed, said, "All y'all c'mon in the house," and shouted, "You kids fetch tea!" She had the bearing and demeanor of a drill instructor, Service thought.

The interior was neat and clean. There were bouquets of forget-me-nots in mason jars on every surface.

The woman led them into a large room with a long table and ten chairs around it. Everything appeared to be handmade, but there was nothing amateur about the work.

A boy of nine or ten brought a pitcher of tea and glasses.

They all sat down. "They best be gettin' my husband home right quick," she said. Service considered telling her that the authorities were slow to release bodies in cases of homicide, but this was Missouri, not Michigan, and he was a game warden, not a homicide detective. Curiously, the woman did not ask any of the normal questions about Elray's death, and he wondered how much she knew.

A couple of younger girls came into the room and crawled into Cotton Spargo's lap. Service drank his sweetened tea and kept quiet.

Eddie Waco came back and poured tea for himself. "Doug Hakes will make sure Elray gets brung up by helicopter, have him here at dayspring."

The woman nodded. "Them feds gon' raise a fuss?" she asked.

Service wondered how she knew about the feds.

"Sheriff's a-takin' care of hit," Eddie Waco said.

The woman's fingers tapped the trigger guard of the shotgun, which lay on the table. "Elray tell about his dream to you'n?" she asked her father-in-law.

The elder Spargo nodded. "I told him not to go see the man if'n he had the dream two nights in a row."

*What dream? What man?* Service wondered.

"I told 'im the Lord works in mysterious ways," the woman said. "But Elray, he laughed at me and said hit was my job in the family ta talk ta the Lord." She shook her head and flashed a wistful smile. "No way ta change thet man," she added. "You *Spargos.*"

The old man said, "My Liddy used to say stubbornness takes more men 'n pride."

The widow clucked her approval. "My Elray was a stubborn one."

Service wanted to ask questions, but Eddie Waco pressed a knee against him and Service got the message.

"You seen Cake?" Eddie Waco asked.

The woman stared at Waco, got up, and took the baby and shotgun away.

While the woman and her kids made dinner, Service and Waco sat on the porch in handmade wooden chairs. "What's going on?" Service asked.

Waco said, "I wanted to get over here and hear what got said. People hereabouts got they own ways."

"Nobody seems overly broken up about this," Service said. "What was Spargo's dream, how come his wife's not asking for details and knows about the feds, and how are you going to get the FBI to release the body?"

Waco grinned. "You'n listening real good, Michigan man. I done asked the sheriff and he'll take care of it. These people need to git Elray inta the ground. Feds want to exhume later, they can go through the courts. Old Doug Hakes will get 'im up here and the fun'ral will be tomorrow afternoon. You'll see plenty of sad then. Right now they's blinded by the git-evens."

"Like the start of a feud?" Service asked.

Eddie Waco chuckled. "You git thet from some ole Hatfield-McCoy movin' pitcher?"

Service felt like a fool, but the other man interrupted his embarrassment. "The real old days was sure 'nuff like thet, but it always got kept betwixt hill people. If an outsider done this, they got other ways. Widder will ask for a champeen."

Service didn't ask what this meant. "What's this about a cake?"

"Why we're here," Eddie Waco said. "Elray hardly went ta the privy without Cake Culkin skulkin' nearby."

"Culkin was an enemy?"

"More like a partner, though he don't wear a badge. Elray sent 'im off to jail a long time back and looked after his kin while he was away. Cake come out and they bin fast friends ever since. I'm thinkin' that whatever happened to Elray, Cake will know something."

"The wife already knew," Service said.

"Word moves fast in these hills," the Missouri game warden said. "The old man knew too, and I'm thinkin' hit was Cake brung word."

"Jimsonweed Christian?" Service asked.

Waco smiled. "Not a true believer," he said.

"There's a radio here?" Service asked.

Eddie Waco said, "Yup, but you don't need to be a talkin' at thet FBI woman. Word is she's in hospital down ta Wes Plains an' all drugged up."

"What happens now?" Service asked.

"We red up for supper," Eddie Waco said. "Then we eat, but don't be eatin' big on account we gon' be eatin' a whole heap till we git done here."

*Red up?* The local dialect and terms had Service befuddled, and suddenly he thought he knew what it was like to be a troll wandering into a village in the black spruce swamps of the Upper Peninsula for the first time. The people here, he decided, were a lot like Yoopers, and he found the thought comforting.

Service and Waco got a couple of sleeping bags out of the room in the house where the dead conservation agent kept his gear cache, took them out in the field, made a fire ring of stones, took wood from a pile near the house, kindled a fire, and settled into their bags to catch some sleep. Kids from the house brought them biscuits and ham and some kind of beans in runny red gravy.

Service was physically tired and sore, but couldn't sleep. Whenever the breeze let up, mosquitoes dropped on him en masse. He paid no attention to them. It seemed to him that people continuously filtered in and out of the house, most of them carrying food and other things the family might need. Two carpenters set up sawhorses just off the porch and hammered and sawed all night, making a simple coffin of white oak planks.

There were no stars and not much light from the house. Service could smell more rain in the air and wondered how long until it moved in. Sometimes the wind seemed to pick up, but then it would die away, which told him they were on the edge of a front rather than in the bull's-eye. If it stiffened and held, he knew the rain would quickly ride in on it.

His own cases back home sometimes had taken odd twists, but this was in a class of its own. How could somebody have been killing game wardens for so many years with impunity? As far as he was concerned, a bulletin should be sent immediately to all state fish and game agencies, wardens doubled up on patrols for safety, and all of them alerted to what was going on. But this had not happened, and probably wouldn't. One thing was certain: When he got back to Michigan he would make damn sure that Chief O'Driscoll heard what he had to say, even if he had to go over the chief's head to Governor Timms. Hell, *she* was the one who'd put him into this damn mess.

In his short time as a detective, he had learned that making a case required intense and continual attention to detail—and some luck. The greater the focus on details, the more likely you'd catch a break. So far he'd seen little in Tatie Monica's approach to create confidence. She was like an inexperienced angler in a major hatch, frantically chasing from fish to fish rather than focusing on one until it was caught, or stopped rising. Jumping around created movement, not direction, and movement for its own sake was not progress.

He was beginning to have serious doubts about the special agent's abilities to manage this case. Or maybe it was inexperience and he just couldn't see. But it seemed to him that the team should have remained in Wisconsin at the kill site to investigate it, rather than running down to Missouri to start all over. Something in the sequence and priorities just didn't set right.

The number of visitors seemed to increase well before sunrise. Eddie Waco led Service into the woods and downhill to a spring where they stripped off their shirts, rinsed with freezing spring water, and used their fingers to straighten their hair. They spent some time trying to knock the dust and dirt off their clothes and boots in order to achieve some semblance of presentability.

Cotton Spargo met them with a pot of coffee and two cups.

"Elray had a dream?" Eddie Waco asked.

"Said he done dreamt of this white light which he thought was the Lord Himself, but the Devil come out of it and grinned at him. Bothered the boy," Spargo said. "Would me too. Elray ain't been sharp since Sister Rosa went over to the Lord."

Cotton Spargo nodded politely, and stopped talking. Service followed Waco into the wood line.

They had heard the whine of a helicopter's turbines while they were at the spring, and by the time they got back to the house, the body had been carried inside and the chopper was sitting in the field, its rotors wobbling like a vulture's flight feathers in the variable breeze.

Waco introduced Oregon County sheriff Doug Hakes, who wore a chocolate-brown and blue-gray uniform shirt and a sweat-stained brown baseball cap. "Any trouble with the feds?" Waco asked.

"Snakebit fed's not able to make a fuss, and the young 'un's feelin' so much pressure he seems a bit tongue-tied," the sheriff said.

"What about Bonaparte?" Service asked.

The sheriff took off his hat and stroked his brush cut. "One which come out by whirlybird afore the storm? He's long gone."

Service wanted to ask where and when, but bit his tongue.

"They's fixin' ta clean Elray up," the sheriff said, leading them into the house. A young man came out of a room looking green and spewed vomit as he dashed for the outside.

Eddie Waco offered Service a small container of Vicks, and Service dabbed a little under each nostril.

"No call for thet," the sheriff growled. "He was 'frigerated and we brung him home in ice." He pushed open a door and held out his hand for them.

The room was white and stark. Service saw nail holes in the walls and knew that the room had been cleared. There was a table in the center. The dead man was unclothed, stretched out on his back, his skin gray. Damp white cloths lay on his hands. There were quarters where his eyes should have been. Service flinched at a *whump*, marking an explosion not that far from the house.

"Dirt up this way's thinner'n Maggie's drawers," Eddie Waco explained. "Hardpan and rock right up to a man's boot soles. Dynamite's quicker'n shovels."

Service understood. During the winter in the U.P., bodies were kept in storehouses until spring when the ground frost melted and holes could be dug for graves. What had to be done for and with the dead was not something most people gave much thought to until it was staring them in the face. Once he had arrested a poaching crew out of Champion. They used a body-storage facility to stash their take over winter. Standing among boxes of frozen human corpses and hanging deer carcasses, the lead poacher had looked at him and said, "Hell, dese folks don't mind, eh?"

Service studied the body. Elray Spargo looked even larger all spread out on his back than he had looked in the refrigerated tent on the Eleven Point River. Spargo had long red-gray hair, a thick neck, and broad shoulders. His beard had the texture of steel wool. His hands had protruding knuckles, and long thick fingers. What clothes had the man been wearing? More importantly, had Spargo intended to fish the night he'd been killed? There had been no mention of that so far. If fishing wasn't involved, did this mean another shift in pattern, another mistake, or had he misunderstood the pattern?

Service made a twisting motion with his hand, and Eddie Waco said to one of the men washing the body, "You don't mind, you fellers want ta help me roll ole Elray over on his belly?"

They did as they were asked. It was obvious they had handled bodies before.

The lungs had been removed, or put back into the body. The wounds that remained were horrific, and had been crudely stitched with what looked like coarse, braided black fishing line. Service was certain Tatie Monica and the FBI would go ballistic when they found out they no longer had the body. *Why did the killer remove the victims' eyes?* His mind kept going back to this and he wasn't sure why.

The law officers helped the men roll Elray Spargo onto his back again and went outside. Service lit a cigarette, Waco put a pinch in his cheek, and Doug Hakes took a cigar stump out of his shirt pocket and stuck it in his mouth without lighting it.

Thunder was buzzing intermittently to the southwest.

"Should hold off," the sheriff said, looking up. "What you make a' all this?" he added, glancing at Waco.

"Ain't no ord'nary man could git the edge on Elray."

"You hear anythin'?" the sheriff asked.

"You?" Eddie Waco answered, countering the question with a question, the sign of an experienced cop. Service hadn't known Waco long, but he was comfortable with him, and though Waco played the hick, and was a bit stingy with words, he seemed to have a sharp mind and a reason for the things he did.

"Think Cake was around?" Hakes asked.

"Have to see," Eddie Waco said, noncommittally.

At 10 a.m. people began to queue to view the body and pay their respects.

Hakes wandered off to talk to a plain woman in a navy blue frock. "Okay to ask questions yet?" Service asked.

"Not yet," Waco answered.

Service heard a lot of crying and wailing and caterwauling inside, but when people came out, they seemed composed and joined in normal conversations with others.

During the night sawhorses, doors, and planks had been used to make temporary tables outside the house. Around noon people began filtering to the tables and standing behind their chairs until Fiannula Spargo came out of the house with her eight children, all of them dressed in black. A small veil of black lace hung over her face. After the family was seated, the others sat down.

Platters of food were served: hams, turkeys, roasts, tubs of mashed potatoes, corn on the cob, string beans and black-eyed peas, huge pans of corn bread, endless pots of black coffee, and sweating pitchers of iced tea.

Eddie Waco snatched a cob of corn and began gnawing. Between bites he said, "This here's a real offmagandy. Local crop won't be in for two month. Somebody done toted this in from outside." Waco ate the corn without salt, pepper, or butter, shoveling ears into his mouth like logs on a conveyor belt. Because of his false teeth Service couldn't eat corn without cutting it off the cob, so he contented himself with other things, like the corn bread, which had onions and green peppers in it, and more than a dash of sugar to sweeten it.

People laughed and talked and gently scolded their kids like it was a church social. Service saw a man take two heaping plates, walk out to the wood line, and come back empty-handed a short while later. He nudged Eddie Waco, who said, "I seen," as he attacked another ear of corn.

After the meal was finished and table cleared, Service watched a sleek black horse pull a small trailer with rubber tires across the field toward the house. The horse was tall and wore a headdress of gaudy, tall, black plumes, which undulated as it moved. The air remained close and heavy. The open coffin was carried out by six men and slid onto the trailer. Elray Spargo was beginning to ripen. Service touched his upper lip and Waco gave him another dollop of Vicks.

The dead man's wife and children walked directly behind the horse-drawn trailer. Cotton Spargo and other relatives followed the widow. The rest of the mourners filed along behind. The shoes of two hundred people raised dust, leaving an opaque cloud hanging in the humid air. Thunder continued to rattle softly in the southwest like someone shaking cookie crumbs off a baking pan.

The grave had been blown out of a more or less flat spot by some boulders and several spiky white oak trees. The widow and her children gathered around as the coffin was placed on short logs beside the gaping hole. The six men worked ropes under the casket and stepped back.

The minister who stepped forward had a withered arm, and the twisted countenance of a demented chipmunk, but the crowd responded almost immediately, and in no time the preacher was slapping the sides of the casket and railing against sin and evil and demanding everyone live a righteous, God-fearing life.

Service tuned him out. The sermon, if that's what it was, went on interminably, but didn't dull the responsiveness of the mourners.

Cotton Spargo spoke. "Y'all know Elray done his duty twinny-four years. He done loved Fiannula and his kids and all his kin. Police respected him, lawbreakers a'feared him. Anybody needed help, Elray was there. All y'all know how he was. Couldn't bear to see people in bad times. . . . Bin a heap a' Spargos called home ta the Lord, but this time Lord—and preacher, I apologize for a-sayin' this—hit's too dadgum soon. I cain't explain God's ways, and neither can you'n, so we just accept and keep on livin', but I tell all y'all this . . ." He gulped, paused, and sobbed. "I loved that big ole boy a' mine, an' I'm gon' miss 'im ever day."

Grady Service choked up, remembering two boxes of ashes sitting in his cabin.

The crowd, led by the children, sang, "Will the Circle Be Unbroken." The young voices touched something inside Grady Service. He kept thinking about Walter, the son he had known nothing about until a year ago. At seventeen, Walter had left California alone to find his biological father. The boy had courage and determination beyond words. Service thought, *My life is out of order. Fathers should go before their kids.*

He remembered standing numbly at his own father's grave. There had been no children singing the day they buried his old man, only a bugle and rifle shots as snow wafted across the gray November landscape. There had been shock more than sadness, a sudden void where a partial void had been before, his father working most of the time and rising to legendary status.

The six men used the ropes to lower Elray Spargo's coffin into the grave. One of the men helped Cotton Spargo climb down, and handed him a screwdriver as he slid the lid in place and tightened the screws. When the dead man's father had finished, the men helped him out of the hole, and the preacher went into his ashes-to-ashes, dust-to-dust routine, and the crowd began to sing "Good-bye Until We Meet Again."

There was nothing rehearsed about any of this, nothing fake or forced, and Service felt himself enveloped in real community and family, and he found himself fighting back sobs with people he doubted he'd even recognize six hours from now. A steel-eyed Eddie Waco squeezed Service's arm.

The mourners dropped rocks and soil into the six-foot-deep hole until it was full. A wheelbarrow full of black dirt was dumped on top, and a dozen small children began tamping the dirt with their bare feet. Service looked at the pattern of footprints and saw young life walking on new death. He couldn't watch and turned away.

Fiannula Spargo watched her father-in-law hammer a small oak cross into a dirt mound and pile stones around it for support. She bent down, placed Elray's sweat-stained service cap on top, joined her hands, and straightened up. "All y'all come on back ta the house an' eat afore ev'thin' spoils."

What did a game warden's career reduce to? A lifetime of unending responsibity and duty, Service thought, then ashes to ashes, dirt to dirt, and all that remained was an old baseball cap perched on a rough-hewn cross, pounded into hard ground. He told himself he would rather be left where he fell to feed the wolves and coyotes and ravens and crows. It was too damned hard to put the living through this. His old man's funeral had been a circus, mourning a drunk run down by a drunk. But this was different. It had quiet, simple dignity, an acceptance of death as part of the cycle of life, even if it was sudden and from the hand of an animal. Maybe he had been selfish in not holding services for Maridly and Walter. It was an unsettling thought.

"Ready to work, Michigan Man?" Eddie Waco asked, interrupting Service's thoughts.

Service nodded and followed the Missouri conservation agent.

The man seated on the rock ten yards from the grave had a plaster cast on his lower left leg and a sling holding up his left arm. From a distance he was youthful-looking, with windblown, corn-colored hair. Up close he looked ancient and battered, with a ruddy complexion and crooked teeth that jutted out from lips grooved like licorice twists. There were two empty plates on the ground by the rock.

"We knew you'n was feelin' poorly, some of the boys woulda hepped draw you up closer, Cake," Eddie Waco said.

"I heared what got said," the man said. "Cain't face the widder and them young 'uns. You know was a time I took the fever, and Elray carried me home, and he and Fi and them kids done ministered ta me. They even got the Cherokee ta drive his buggy up and have a look. They had me in thet house goin' on a month—just like I was kin."

"You and Elray was close," Eddie Waco said supportively.

The man sighed. "I got the shame upon me."

Service heard the patter of raindrops on the oak leaves overhead and knew that if the rain came hard enough, it would leak through once the leaves were soaked.

"How's that, Cake?"

"What happened to Elray."

"Ya'll thinkin' hit's yore fault?"

The man nodded. "Shou'n'ta happened."

"You were with 'im, was you?"

"Made me stay back, but I seen what was done."

"You seen it happen?"

"I seen afterwards."

"After he met someone," Eddie Waco said.

"Yessir."

"You know who he met or what it was about?"

"I never seen the man and he wouldn't say. Jes said hit was official."

"Thim his words?"

"'Zackly how he done said."

"Did you hear anything?"

"Nossir. He done tole me stand tight for an hour less'n I heard a ruckus."

"And you waited."

"I always done what Elray asked."

"I know you did, Cake. Did you find him where you thought he'd be?"

"Said he'd be by the old bat cave camp, but he weren't."

"You found him at the abandoned Hurricane Creek Camp."

Waco pronounced the word *hur-a-cun,* and it took a second for Service to interpret.

"He was gone," Cake Culkin said, looking off in the distance. He took a deep breath. "I peeked quick and run," he said.

"Did you see anyone?"

"I just lit out and hit me a tree and whanged my shoulder and fell down a drop-off an' busted a bone in mah leg. Cracked it like a dry stick. Had to wait till first light to make me a splint and find a stick to hold on to, and then I come direckly here."

"When was this?"

Culkin looked up, like he was trying to recall. "Four days ago?"

"You hain't sure, Cake?"

"Like I said, I done hiked on over to Cotton's thet next day, an' me an' him done told Fi, and Cotton a'hauled me on over to the Cherokee's in his wagon, and the Cherokee popped my shoulder back in an' put that dang plaster on my leg. Ask Cotton when it was I come."

"You walked all that way on a broke bone?" Eddie Waco asked.

The man looked up at them. "Thet day I got out a jail, I went right out to my pap's and got me my twinny-two and went out and shot me a turkey to take over to my gal. I called a big ole Tom right in and put 'im down neat and quick. When I got over to thet bird, old Elray stepped out and grabbed a'holt a' my arm. He sit me down and lit up 'is pipe. Elray done said he was mighty perplexed about what to do with the likes a' me. He said he didn't want to send me back to jail since I'd just been gone six months. But he didn't feel like he could trust me, he said."

Cake Culkin paused. "Ole Elray finally says, 'Let's us do this with honor. Right here, right now, man to man. You c'n whup me, you go right on shootin' and fishin' whenever you a-want. I whup you and you'n never break the law again.'" Cake paused again, obviously reliving the moment. "Elray was a big ole boy with considerable grit, but I was on the wiry side myseff and I had me some nasty scraps and allus handled what got throwed my way. So I said, 'It's a deal.' We spit on our hands and shaked, fair and square. Then my head done exploded and I could feel I was goin' out and all I could see was Elray's eyes. I swear, he was *enjoyin'* whuppin' me near to death. Next thing I knew the Cherokee was a-tendin ta my face. He done sewed me up and Elray took me to my kin and give 'em thet turkey, too. For that man, I'd a' crawled to his kin with my head cut off."

"You become his pine shadow."

Cake Culkin nodded. "I never broke the law once, all them years—not that I weren't tempted time to time—but when I seen him dead like that, I run like a yella dog."

Eddie Waco patted the man's back. "You're no coward, Cake. You backed up ole Elray for twinny years, and the two of you'n barely got through some of them times. He was here now, he'd say you done right by 'im. You'n done what he asked and you'n cain't ask a shadow more'n thet."

"I cain't face the widder," Cake said.

"Sure you can," Eddie Waco said. "And soon as thet laig gets healed up, you gon' be my shadow; that sound okay by you, Cake?"

"I'll jes let you down," the man whispered, studying the ground.

"You'n do and I'll put a whuppin' on y'all make you'n think what Elray done give you'n was a schoolmarm's slap. You with me?"

"Sir, I reckon," the man said, nodding unenthusiastically.

The two game wardens helped the man walk to the house and set him down with the widow, who hugged him. They left them talking, with the kids gathered round. Service saw that the kids had great affection for Cake Culkin.

"State's never got money for enough agents," Waco explained. "Was Elray come up with the idee of shadows—unofficial helpers. Cake there was a young man when Elray took 'im on, poachin' since he was tin. Not a better man in the woods, and he never did break the law again—leastways not that Elray or any of the rest of us knew."

Michigan had used unarmed volunteer conservation officers—VCOs—for many years. They had twenty or so hours of training and worked for free. Last fall Chief Lorne O'Driscoll had canceled the program because the state's lawyers felt there were substantial liability issues. A lot of officers were still complaining about the decision. Two sets of eyes always beat one set, and two bodies at night served as a deterrent when violets turned frisky or vicious.

"The state knows about shadows?"

"Not officially, and ain't nothin' writ down on paper," Waco said, "but a body don't rise to top dog less'n he works his way up. It just don't get talked about . . . officially or unofficially. I believe Elray even done give some of his pay to Cake, but I hain't sure on thet. Wouldn't surprise me none, though."

The widow came over to them. It had been raining off and on since the funeral and the field was muddy. She carried two cups of coffee and handed them to the men.

"You'n not a G-man?" the woman said to Service.

"No, ma'am. I'm just along to see if I can help."

"You want to hep, find him which murdered my husband," she said. She held up a large cloth sack and Service looked inside. It was the horse headdress with the tall black plumes.

"Each a' them feathers rep'sents a Spargo done fell in service to his country. Most of 'em was durin' the wars—One, Two, Korea, Vietnam. Elray's the first lawman in the clan, and he deserves his feather, but I cain't put it in till we know justice's been done. You get things took care of, you bring 'em back, and I'll know."

Grady Service tried to return the bag to her, but she pushed it back at him. "Let it remind you what it is you got to do," she said.

Her sweet scent overwhelmed him, and all he could do was nod as she marched away to talk to others.

"What is that perfume?" Service asked.

"Plumgranny, not perfume," Eddie Waco said after a theatrical sniff. "Bin around as a sweet scent since the time a' Shakespeare, I hear."

"Does she actually think I can do something about finding her husband's killer?"

"Seems to me, you'n the one holdin' the bag," Eddie Waco said, grinning and looking down. "You done been made Elray Spargo's champeen, and thet hain't no little thing in these here parts."

Service rolled his eyes and muttered, "Just great."

## 15

## WEST PLAINS, MISSOURI

## MAY 26, 2004

The glassed-in lobby of the hospital in West Plains had the sharp angle of a ship's bow. Service found Special Agent Tatie Monica in a single room, in bed, flat on her stomach.

She craned to look over her shoulder and glared. "They stole our body."

"They?"

"Them, they, somebody. Our evidence is gone."

She was a very unhappy fed. He said, "You mean the man's family? They didn't steal him, they buried him."

"Some damn hillbilly sheriff carried it away in a helicopter," she said. "Without authorization, which is tampering with and impeding a federal investigation."

She wasn't listening. "He did it for the family, and relax—I know where he is."

"You know? You *know!* Jesus, why didn't you stop them?" she asked.

Service got a chair, pulled it around so she could see him, and sat down with the back of the chair against his chest. "They have some pretty firm convictions about how and when they bury their dead." He didn't reveal Agent Eddie Waco's role in what had happened.

She rolled her eyes and clenched her fists.

"You'll heal faster if you stay calm," Service said.

"I'm trying to find a murderer, some hillbilly sheriff ganks my evidence and . . . and *now* I'm getting health advice from a man who makes his living chasing people who chase *animals!*"

"Add fish, and that's a pretty good job description," he said.

The agent let loose a hiss of anguish. "I want *out* of this fucking place!"

"Who's stopping you?"

"They had to do surgery."

"I thought you said no cutting."

"Bite me," she shot at him.

"You brought it up."

She looked at him through tight eyes. "No bull, you *really* know where the body is?"

"I was at the funeral."

"I can't believe you didn't stop them," she keened.

"I also met a man who saw the body right after the killing."

Special Agent Monica sucked in a breath. "Don't shit me," she whispered, propping herself up on her elbows.

"Truth," he said. "He was the dead man's pine shadow."

She rolled her eyes again. "English, Service. What the *fuck* is a pine shadow?"

"Down here it's an unpaid volunteer partner to a conservation agent. Other places it's probably the darkness behind and below a tree when the sun shines on it."

She grimaced and switched on a professional tone. "This guy told you something?"

"Not yet." Cake Culkin had been in no shape for cogent thought, much less a penetrating interview.

"But he will?"

"That's the plan."

"Jesus," she complained. "Does the lead agent get to know this plan?"

"That's why I'm here," he said.

"Visitors are supposed to boost a patient's spirits and confidence."

"Real confidence comes from within," he said.

"Are you pathologically objective?"

"When I need to be."

"I don't like how this is playing out," Agent Monica said. "Two kills so close in time—that's never happened before."

"Maybe he's in a hurry."

"This guy doesn't make mistakes: He's unbelievable. We're taught that the average murderer makes at least two dozen mistakes. This guy hasn't made any so far . . . but it could be his psychosis is deepening," she said, almost to herself.

"We've got a potential witness here and the kill site in Wisconsin. Those're mistakes, and maybe there are more."

"And?" she said impatiently.

"Wayno's body was warm and wet. Thorkaldsson could have walked up on the killer, which means his timing was off, his source of information and calculations not what they've been, right? And he didn't bother to collect the fishing gear, which led us to the kill site. There's bound to be more if we look in the right place, and ask the right questions."

She looked at him for a long time before covering her eyes with a forearm and moaning loud enough to concern him. "You want me to call a nurse?"

Tatie Monica struggled to sit up and hissed, "I want *out* of here. I've been after this asshole for three years, and now that he's accelerating I am not going to lay here like of leg of ham."

"Lamb," Service said. "Leg of lamb, not ham."

"Lamb, Spam," she grumbled.

"Is that what happens in these cases—the killers speed up?"

"This one defies generalization," she said. "I've insisted all along that man is an imperfect animal. Locard's exchange principle tells us that when two things come in contact, each will leave something behind. There has to be *something* this guy is missing, *has* to be." She looked at him. "What's the plan?"

"Agent Waco is with the witness. When you're ready to leave, we'll go see them."

She pointed at a wall locker. "My clothes are in there."

"You were sorta short on clothes last time I saw you."

"My people brought more stuff."

He took out slacks, a blouse, and boots, and set them on the chair.

She managed to swing her legs down to the floor and sit up, but not without a lot of puffing and contorted faces. He pushed the chair down the side of the bed so that it was in front of her.

"You sure you want to do this?"

She said, "Stop gawking and get out."

He stepped outside the room to find Special Agent Larry Gasparino carrying two Styrofoam cups. Service blocked the door. "She's getting dressed."

"They're kicking her loose?" the young agent asked.

"In a manner of speaking. You got off the river okay?"

"We had to use chain saws and axes all the way down. How is she?"

"Testy," Service said.

"Normal, then."

"She thinks things are falling apart."

Gasparino stared at him. "Optimism isn't part of her genetic wiring."

"Perfectionist?"

"Tendencies, but usually she knows when she goes too far."

"Pressure's getting to her," Service said.

"The list is her safety valve," the agent said.

List? "We all gotta believe in something," Service said, "and a list is as good as anything." What was Gasparino inadvertently disclosing?

"So far," Gasparino said. "Not that it's put us ahead of the game."

A *list of what?* He knew he couldn't ask directly. Gasparino had let something slip and didn't seem to realize it. "Been with her long?"

"January," the man said. "Fucking Wisconsin winters. We got people in our office who pray for thirty below for Packer games, and I'm talking, like, *out-fucking-doors!* They paint their man-boobs in Packer green and go to the frigging games *shirtless.* Is that supposed to be normal, or what?" The man shook his head.

"Monica good to work for?"

"Better than I thought she'd be," Gasparino said.

Service saw a flash of panic in the man's eyes. Rule one for feds: Never talk outside school.

He backed off and told himself he needed to know more about the list but didn't want to spook the young agent.

"You talk to the agent holding down the site in Wisconsin?"

"Bobbi?" He shook his head again. "I've been too busy securing what we brought down the river. Then I slept like a dead man. I thought chain saws were supposed to make wood cutting fast and easy."

Service nodded sympathetically. Were any of the agents focused on the big picture in this case? "That storm was bad."

"I was in the city on 9/11," Gasparino said. "Not near Ground Zero, but it was scary enough. This was worse."

The disaster in New York City had become the standard for measuring the magnitude and meaning of all disasters and atrocities, Service thought. People who survived natural disasters had similar respect in the aftermath. Gasparino was young and seemed earnest, but he was also green. He had mentioned the list on the unwarranted assumption that Service was in the loop, and his gut told him he'd better quickly find a way into it.

Tatie Monica limped gingerly out of her room and started down the hall with the two men flanking her. "This turns out to be bullshit . . . ," she muttered, not finishing her statement.

## 16

# LEFT SHOULDER RIDGE, MISSOURI

## MAY 26, 2004

Gasparino had a fairly new black Ford Expedition, and he helped Monica into the backseat so she could stretch out her legs. Service sat up front to navigate. Eddie Waco had shown him the road to Cake Culkin's place during the trip to West Plains to drop him off. He told Gasparino to turn north along the border between Oregon and Ripley counties.

"Jesus, are we there yet?" Monica asked repeatedly, the first time less than two minutes outside the West Plains city limits.

"Chill," Service said the first time she complained. "It's about forty miles—and there's no interstate."

Gasparino reacted by speeding up, but when he fishtailed around a curve, Service told him to slow down. "We don't want to end up in a ditch with the snakes," he said. This reminded him that Nantz would have easily negotiated these roads, which were a lot more difficult than M-35. *Not an accident,* he told himself for the umpteenth time. What did he need to move the Troops off their conclusion and to reopen the investigation? More importantly, who would want to run her off the road?

"Goddammit, Larry, *listen* to the man!" Tatie Monica squawked from the backseat.

Cake Culkin lived about five miles from the Spargos' place, in the rocky saddle and shadow of a razorback ridge called Left Shoulder. They parked on the main gravel road, and Service led them on foot down the edge of a rutted dirt-and-gravel track that served as the man's driveway. The cabin was small and tidy, with a rickety carport and an older-model black Chevy pickup in front, the truck Eddie Waco had used to take him to West Plains.

Service left the agents in the woods while he went to the house. The hood of the truck was cold. He stood to the side of the door, knocked, waited.

Eddie Waco answered the door, looked up, and nodded. "Back quicker'n I figgered," he said, opening it. "Them feds lurkin' out yonder?"

"Two of them."

"Best fetch 'em on in."

Service looked back and waved.

Waco led them into a small kitchen. Cake Culkin was sitting at a small round table, his hands folded in front of him, his leg up on a chair.

"Cake, these folks want ta talk at ya'll some," Waco said.

The man didn't look up. "They feds?"

"Two of 'em," Eddie Waco said.

"You can wait outside," Tatie Monica said dismissively to the Missouri conservation agent.

"We both stay," Service said.

The FBI agent glared.

"Waco saved your ass," Service said. "Literally."

Monica shrugged with resignation and rolled her eyes. She couldn't communicate without facial punctuation, a lousy habit for a cop or a poker player. The more he saw, the greater his concern about her competence. He couldn't put his finger on it, but there were moments when she seemed almost desperate.

"You found Agent Spargo," she began, a statement, not a question. Right to the point, no empathy for the man's potential discomfort or anxieties.

"I reckon I seen 'im," Cake said. "And run." His voice cracked as he sucked in a breath.

The FBI agent seemed to realize something was wrong and she suddenly switched gears. "Your name's Cake, right? I'm Tatie." Off a beat and too late, Service thought. The man was going to turtle. Was it lack of skills on her part, or impatience?

Cake Culkin gave a pleading look to Eddie Waco, whose face remained impassive.

"Let's start again," Tatie Monica said. "I'm Tatie, Cake. You want anything?"

Too late, Service thought. Her initial directness had put the man on his heels, left him tight and withdrawn.

"I hain't sick," Culkin said.

"Cake," Eddie Waco said, "these folks want to find who done Elray like thet."

"I'll talk ta you'n," the man said. "And him," he added with a nod to Service, "but I already done took all y'all through this afore."

Service brushed Monica's sleeve to let her know she should keep quiet. Apparently she got the hint.

"Memories kin be a might slippery sometimes," Eddie Waco said. "'Member back whin you'n an' Elray an' me done chased thet ole boy kilt his wife over ta White Briar? Me an' Elray was sure it were a blue truck, but it weren't. Was black, jes like you said."

"Had dirt all over it," Cake Culkin said. "Coulda bin blue."

"But it weren't, and been just Elray and me, we'd a' missed that ole boy, but havin' you along made the case. That's what we got here, Cake. More heads we got, better off we are, okay? We need to go over what you seen again."

"Shoot," Culkin said with a grin. "You been ta college and you got you a steel-trap mind."

"The trap sometimes gets a mite rusty," Waco said with a smile.

Service could feel Tatie Monica fidgeting and bumped her to settle her down.

"Seein' Elray that way spooked us all," Waco added.

"You boys din't run," Culkin said, running his hands through his hair and sucking in a deep breath. "Who you think wanna do somethin' like that ta Elray?"

"Don't know yet," Waco said. "But you can help us ta help Fi and them young 'uns."

Cake Culkin nodded emphatically. "I done said what I seen."

"He had a meeting?" Waco asked.

Culkin nodded.

"Who did he meet, Cake?"

"Elray didn't say."

"You and him went way back. You *knew* him."

"Nobody knew Elray. Well, mebbe Fi. He was differ'nt to differ'nt folks. Always told me he was a *thespeen*. What's that mean?"

"Actor," Service said.

Culkin grinned. "That was ole Elray."

"You cain't work all them years with a man and not know him," Eddie Waco said.

"You agents is all the same. Nobody knows all y'all."

Eddie Waco said, "I take yore pint, Cake, but the way it is, you don't give us somethin', we gon' be plumb outta luck."

"You mind if I ask a question, Cake?" Service asked.

"'Speck not."

"You got good trout fishing around here?"

"Passable, I reckon."

"You fish?"

The man said, "Whin I git the chance."

"How do you know when the bite's on?" Service asked.

Cake Culkin rolled his tongue inside his cheek. "I jes keep my eyes open."

"Weather, maybe?"

"Wind tells a man a lot. Warm rain fallin'. An' I kick the grass with my boots, see what might skitter about."

"Spiderwebs under bridges?" Service asked.

Culkin grinned and raised an eyebrow. "I reckon you done some fishin' yoreseff."

"Some," Service allowed. "What we have here, Cake, is an empty web, and we're not kickin anything up in the grass. Did you and Elray plan to fish that night?"

"Nossir."

A *change*, Service thought. Had the other dead officers been fishing, or were they just found near water? This wasn't clear and it bothered him not to know. "Was Agent Spargo's meeting with a man?"

Culkin's face darkened. "Not proper a married-up man meet private-like with a womarn not his'n."

"Unless he had official business with her and needed to keep it private," Eddie Waco interjected, picking up on Service's comment.

"Thet's so," Culkin said. "But were a man got met."

"You're certain?" Service asked softly.

Culkin chewed his lip and spoke haltingly. "I ast, all ya'll 'll tell Fi and them young 'uns it were a man?"

"We'd do that," Eddie Waco said. "Sometimes ole Elray, he asked you to keep things in confidence."

"Was how it were."

"And if that was the case here, you'd keep that confidence no matter what. You'd not be able to say it."

"A man's word's his word," Culkin said.

"You understand how important this is," Eddie Waco said.

"Yessir, I truly do."

"It's good you keep your word, Cake. How about we bend this saplin' another direction?"

Culkin looked skeptical, but shrugged and said, "I reckon."

"Just for now, let's jes say a man is a one and a womarn is a two. You with me?"

Culkin nodded.

"If a man's one and a womarn's two, what was the sum of the people at thet meetin' ole Elray had?"

"Four," Culkin said without hesitation.

"Now, Cake, it cain't be four," Eddie Waco said. "Gotta be two or three."

"Were four," Culkin insisted through clenched teeth.

Service intervened: "One plus one, *plus* two?"

Culkin nodded. "Thet's four."

"At the same time?" Service added.

"Reckon not," Culkin said.

"You saw one of them, Cake?"

"Could be."

Waco took over again. "Let me guess. You seen a two, but not a one, on account Elray done made you think the meeting was with a one, only you seen a two and mebbe now you're a'wonderin if'n there was a one a'tall."

Tatie Monica moaned and Service dug his heel into her instep, making her recoil.

Cake Culkin was sweaty and deathly still.

"You'n recognized the two," Eddie Waco said.

"Reckon you'n would, too," Culkin said quickly, "her wearin' a badge an' all."

"Y'all seen a badge?"

"Not thet day."

"But you know who this two is, am I right?"

"Rigmutton, I 'speck, not the sort you see at weekly meetin's."

"This be a badge a body might see round the courthouse?" Waco asked.

"Could be," Culkin said. "Hear tell there's a place on the Warm Fork, west end of Millstone Holler."

"West of Koshkonong?"

"I just heard they's a place over thet way is all."

"How long after you saw the two did you find Elray?" Service asked.

"Not long after the lightnin' done spit."

"Lightnin' spit?" Waco asked.

"Seen the flash, never heard the boom."

"When?"

"A while after Elray done went on by hisseff," the man said, his hands shifting to palms up. Service suspected they'd heard all they were going to hear.

Service asked, "You didn't find Elray where he said he was going to meet?"

"Nossir. Found him over to the Hurricane."

"How?" Eddie Waco asked.

"Blood trail," Culkin said, hanging his head.

Service said, "You said the sum was four, but Elray and the woman make three. Are you counting yourself?"

Culkin shook his head. "I reckon they was another."

"You saw another man?" Waco asked.

"Jes a peek."

"When?"

"Jes afore I come upon Elray at the Hurricane."

"Did you see the two?" Waco asked.

"Nossir, but Elray said he was meetin' her."

Service intervened. "You actually saw just the man."

"I reckon she was there somewheres."

Eddie Waco walked Service and the feds outside. "A setup. I'm thinking she arranged for Elray ta meet someone."

"Jesus," Tatie Monica said. "Who the fuck are we talking about? Ones and twos? *Hello!* Jesus, is this *Earth?*"

"Laglenda Owens, deputy with Oregon County. Hired from Jeff City 'bout a year back. She calls us both with stuff she sees out on road patrol."

Deputies in the U.P. did the same for Service. "They were friends, Deputy Owens and Spargo?"

"I reckon thet's all they was. Once Elray met Fi, that was hit for other womern."

"How can you be sure she's the right woman?" Service asked.

"Only one female totin' a badge in the county, and I know where she lives, 'zackly the place Cake was talkin' on. Want, we can run on over there."

Tatie Monica said, "Okay, Opie and Gomer, can we fucking do this now, or do we have to have a chaw and spee-it fest first?"

Eddie Waco held out a tin of Redman. "'Backy?"

Even Tatie Monica laughed.

Service found it odd that they had just learned the location of another possible kill site and she wasn't asking questions. How far was it to the Hurricane camp from where Spargo was supposed to meet the deputy—*if* he met her? He thought about Elray Spargo. It was one thing to drag the diminutive Wayno Ficorelli up a river. It was a whole different challenge for one man to drag a giant like Spargo over rough ground through brush tangles. And if Spargo had no intention of fishing that night, wasn't that a break in the pattern? Where were his clothes? Grady Service had endless questions, but Tatie Monica seemed to have none. He didn't know if her lack of interest made him angry or worried.

## 17

## WARM FORK, MISSOURI

## MAY 26, 2004

As soon as they got into the Expedition, Tatie Monica again demanded to know how long the drive would take.

Service said, "Let's wait for Agent Waco."

The conservation agent drove his truck out to the gravel road, parked in front of them, and walked back. "I jes talked at Sheriff Hakes. Owens has herself four days off and Doug thinks she mighta run up to Jeff City ta see kin. I called out ta her place, but all I got was a dadblame machine."

"We need to take a look," Tatie Monica said. "How far is it?"

"Good sixty mile from where we sit now," Eddie Waco said, "Twinny mile t'other side of Alton."

Special Agent Monica leaned her head back and muttered, "Shit."

Eddie Waco nodded Service toward his truck. "Join me?"

Service told Gasparino he was going to ride with Waco, and the two vehicles pulled out.

Waco drove at a steady, almost leisurely pace and Service wondered if it was intentional. He looked back and imagined he could see Monica fidgeting in the backseat. "Who actually reported findin' Elray?" Eddie Waco asked.

Service said, "You don't *know?* I assume it was Cotton Spargo. Cake Culkin went to him first, right?"

"Nope. I done talked to 'im, and he only tol' family. But Cotton hain't one to spit it all out. Could be he called Doug Hakes and Doug called the state."

"Which agency got the official notification? We got our call from Bonaparte."

"Where'd that ole boy get off to, anyways?" Eddie Waco asked.

"Beats me. You met him at the river site."

"Never set eyes on the man," Waco said. "Heard from the boys he's a nice-enough feller, not strung tight like your typical fed. You gettin' a feel for what's a-goin' on?"

On the contrary; it seemed like every few hours the case seemed to tumble into a flat spin. "I wish."

"I can tell you this: Somebody got the jump on Elray, they's somethin' special."

"Or they had help," Service said. He'd seen Spargo's size. Even he would have a hard time in a scrap with a man that large. Maybe there was more than one attacker? No evidence for this, just a thought—but it took hold.

Eddie Waco looked over at Service. "Hit don't play, Laglenda Owens bein' in the middle of this. She's a solid deputy. She mixed up in this, I'm thinkin' she got herseff blutterbunged."

"Blutterbunged?" Service repeated. "What language is this down here?"

"Means tricked, some say. The language ya'll hear some claim is close ta what got spoke in Shakespeare's day." Eddie Waco winked. "It prolly done changed a tetch . . ."

"There or here?" Service said.

Both men laughed. "Both," Eddie Waco said.

Service said, "If the Owens woman is out of town, we can still call her, right?"

"Doug's people don't leave town without leavin' a contact number," Eddie Waco said. "Doug Hakes may be a country boy, but he runs his ship tight as a tick on a blade a' long June grass."

"What's the Owens woman's background?"

"People in these parts don't put much stock in the past what was somewhere else. What matters is what a body does now."

"Cake implied the deputy was . . ."

"Cake's a prude," Waco said. "But she's a young 'un with fire in 'er belly."

"You and Elray share Oregon County?"

"Mostly his. I got Ripley, and sometimes we worked together."

Waco looked in the rearview mirror and smiled. "They close 'nuff to lick our bumper."

Service looked back, saw Gasparino tailgating only a few feet behind them. Tatie Monica was gesticulating wildly from the backseat.

"The thing about breakin' in a mule," Eddie Waco said, maintaining his speed, "you jes gotta baffound 'im."


The Warm Fork of the Spring River, like the Eleven Point, flowed in a southeasterly direction, starting as Howell Creek in the town of West Plains. The water was cloudy with a grayish-green cast to it, and a rocky bottom. More limestone, Service thought, or clay. The flow was steady, down small steps into skinny-water pools, the banks heavily wooded near the deputy's small house.

They left the vehicles two hundred yards up the road from the house and moved down through scrub brush, tall Ozark cane, and small, tightly packed trees. The one-story house was small and narrow, facing the river, which flowed less than thirty feet from the back stoop. The main entrance was on the south side. Eddie Waco volunteered to go up to the house because he knew the deputy. Service watched the back of the place. Monica and Gasparino each took a side.

A grim-faced Eddie Waco stepped onto the back porch and waved Service in. Service smelled the odor before he got to the door, and accepted Vicks from the Missouri agent.

The woman was unclothed on the bed, a large hole in the peak of her head, the pillow, sheets, and backboard stained with brain tissue and blood. No defensive wounds. The only entry wound was under the chin. Had she known the killer? Her clothes were ripped and scattered around the room. Eddie Waco showed Service the body and shook his head. There were flies in the room, and a computer in the corner.

"Gunshot," Service said. No weapon in sight. "Homicide."

Waco nodded, and Service went out and summoned the FBI agents.

Tatie Monica took a deep breath and said, "Okay, first we isolate the house. Call the county to provide perimeter security—but *only* the FBI comes down the road this far. Second, get the crime scene team back from St. Louis." She looked at the computer in the dining room. "Third, tell them to send someone from cyberforensics, Larry. Got it?" Gasparino nodded and dashed outside.

"Not my business," Eddie Waco said, "but Doug Hakes ain't gonna sit second banana with one a' his deputies a-layin' here dead. This here's his deputy and hit's *his* county."

"You're right," Tatie Monica said. "It's *not* your business, and who the fuck is Doug Hakes?"

"Sheriff."

"This connects to a federal case," she said. "You send this Hakes to me when he gets here."

"Won't have to send 'im," Waco said. When Monica went outside to find out if Gasparino had gotten through to the St. Louis field office, Eddie Waco said, "Don't you jes love jurisdictional harmony."

Sheriff Hakes arrived on the scene twenty minutes after the word went out. He came in talking and puffing, his face red with an adrenaline surge. "Okay, I got people settin' up a perimeter, and the state's got a crime scene team rolling," he announced.

"That won't be necessary," Tatie Monica said.

"I guess I'll be decidin' what's necessary," the sheriff shot back.

They were nose to nose, their voices low, words clipped.

Service said, "Comforts one to see how 9/11's got law enforcement agencies operating as one team."

"Sound as sweet as buzznack," Eddie Waco said under his breath.

Tatie Monica attacked. "There's no debate here, Sheriff! The death of Deputy Owens is related to the Spargo case."

"Says who?"

"A witness places her at the crime scene at or about the TOD."

"Mebbe I ain't buyin' what you'n sellin', and we'll jes see what the county prosecutor has to say 'bout this."

She brandished her forefinger like a sword. "You tampered with a federal investigation, you sonuvabitch, and you removed evidence without authorization. When you talk to the county prosecutor, make sure he knows there'll be a federal warrant coming down with *your* name on it. He can file it under 'A' for asshole."

Service watched Hakes take a half-step backward. His jaw was still rigid, but he had just retreated and given up ground. "You hain't heard the last word on this," the sheriff said.

"I have from you, Ernest T. Bass. Just make sure your people keep the goddamned road closed off." She turned to Gasparino. "St. Louis?"

"Chopper in the air in thirty," he said. "Cyberforensics is sending Pappas."

Tatie Monica stepped outside and looked up the road and pointed. "The chopper can put down over there. Tell them." Gasparino took his handheld and stepped away. Monica muttered, "Glory Drophat, that airhead bimbo."

Why was Tatie Monica directing the helicopter landing site and not examining the crime scene? "Where's Bonaparte?" Service asked.

Tatie Monica looked at him and tilted her head. "Don't tell me how to do my job," she said, turning away.

Service caught her by the arm. "I'm not trying to tell you *anything*. I'm trying to figure out what *I'm* supposed to be doing here."

Her attitude softened. "You're doing fine. Just stay close to me, and if you see something you think I should know, tell me."

"What about Bonaparte?" he repeated.

"*My* case," she said. "Not his."

When she tried to turn away again, Service stepped in her path. "Who reported Spargo's body? Bonaparte called us and we came, but who told him and put all this into action?" He wasn't sure when the thought implanted, but his mind kept swinging back to Bonaparte, his role, his movement, his absence.

She looked at him and smiled. "Now *that's* the kind of question I like to hear asked." Statement made, she walked away and, as usual, no answer was forthcoming.

Service studied the dead woman's body and wondered if there had been consensual sex, a rape, or no sex at all.

"Somethin' weighin' y'all down?" Eddie Waco asked.

Grady Service walked to Waco's truck and pulled latex gloves out of a box he has seen there. He returned to the house and leaned over the body. "You got a magnifying glass?" he asked.

"Got some cheaters I use ta tie on itsy-bitsy flies."

"Mind if I borrow them?"

Waco brought them back and Service hovered over the dead woman's face for nearly two minutes, stood up, and handed the magnifiers back to Waco. "Did Cake actually see the woman that day, or did Elray just tell him about her?"

"Thet still hain't real clear in my mind neither," the game warden said. "You see somethin'?"

"Not sure," Service said. In fact, her eyes looked normal, an observation that strangely disappointed him. Why did the blood eagle killer take his victims' eyes?

They found the sheriff sulking up the road.

"Who gave you the word on Spargo?" Service asked.

"The highway patrol got a call from the feds and they called me."

"You didn't talk to Cotton Spargo or Cake Culkin?"

"Jes at the fun'ral."

Service and Waco looked at each other, but said nothing. *What feds?* How had the FBI learned about the body before local law enforcement? In previous cases, had anyone called the FBI directly, or had information about new killings come up through other law enforcement agencies? The longer this thing went on, the more questions he had, the less direction there seemed to be, and the more irritated he was getting.

The cyberforensics expert arrived with the crime scene team, floated into the house without greeting or acknowledging anyone, sat down at the wooden chair in front of the dead deputy's computer, and tapped a key to turn it on. She looked up at Gasparino and said, "I need the full name, place, and date of birth, names of vick's parents and siblings, and a photo album."

Glory Drophat was well over six feet with a thick mane of corn-yellow hair and a figure that would make men gape and women roll their eyes. Service thought she also had the slightly distant stare of someone in need of a new contact lens prescription. Her fingernails were chewed to the quick.

Gasparino looked at Tatie Monica, who nodded assent and approached the computer expert. "You're supposed to check in with the lead agent, Glory."

"Don't start," the blonde said wearily, "and *don't* call me that. LA is history. I'd say bury the hatchet, but this is the twenty-first century. You ought to think about joining it."

A less-than-harmonious history between the women, Service surmised.

Ten minutes after Gasparino gave her the things she asked for, the statuesque agent reported, "I'm in," adding, "E-mail's through AOL, same passwords for everything." She clucked disapproval and mumbled, "People are so predictably stupid." Having invaded the dead woman's electronic domain, she turned to Special Agent Monica. "What am I looking for?"

"We're not sure; maybe a string of notes, an invitation to meet, something."

"Hoping for luck to strike again?" the woman said, turning her back to Monica and tapping keys.

"Just do your job," Tatie Monica said.

"Not a problem when you're competent," the woman countered.

Service nudged Gasparino. "What's all this about?"

The two men stepped into the next room. "Word has it that Pappas and Monica were part of a high-profile investigation out of the LA field office. They have a history."

"Pappas?"

"Glory Drophat is what Tatie calls her. Her name's Alona Pappas. The way I heard it, Pappas boffed somebody above Monica to get the team lead on that case, but after she got it, the investigation went into free fall. Monica never bought what Pappas was selling and went her own way and broke the case. Pappas moved over to cyber and Monica ended up in Milwaukee. Last we heard Pappas was in New York, on loan to Homeland Security. We didn't know she was in St. Louis."

Service inferred that both women had been disciplined. "What kind of case in LA?" Special Agent Monica had told him Milwaukee was her choice.

"Multiple homicide: four people sliced and diced the same night in an upscale Brentwood apartment building. Pappas was sure it was an inside job, but Monica thought it was too much like an unsolved in Houston. Pappas pushed for the arrest of a simp, the twenty-something-year-old son of one of the vics. Monica insisted the simp might do one out of passion, but not four. There was no apparent motive or weapon, and nothing in the man's background to indicate serial murder personality traits, like sadistic tendencies. Monica learned that one of the suspects from the Houston case had moved to LA, and she hunted him down and found the weapon stashed at a house where he worked as a gardener."

It sounded to Service like good police work. "Why Drophat?"

"Tatie claims Pappas will boink anybody, anytime, anywhere, to get ahead—like, at the drop of a hat?"

"Okay," Service said. Not only did he not understand yet why he was here or what exactly they expected from him, but now it appeared he would also have to contend with internecine warfare. Of all the agencies he had

worked with over the years, the FBI was, hands down, the most uncooperative, secretive, and parochial, and, from what he was hearing, 9/11 hadn't
improved either their attitudes or their performance. If anything, the FBI
was imperious, looking at itself as the penultimate professionals of law
enforcement and all other agencies as rank amateurs. Wink Rector, the FBI
man who covered the U.P. out of Marquette, was a good guy, but even Wink
pretty much towed the agency's line, and Service had learned the hard way
to be wary.

Service walked outside and found Eddie Waco perched on a rock by the
river. "How all y'all doin' in 'ere?"

"Whole lot of thunder and no lightning," Service said.

"Any word from thet Bonaparte feller?"

"I'd be the last to know," Service said. He still hadn't even met the man.

Eddie Waco propelled a stream of tobacco juice onto the ground.
"Make y'all wonder a-why they done brung you to the hoedown?"

"It's crossed my mind," Service admitted, knowing it was time to nail
Special Agent Monica's ass to a record. How many days had he been gone? It
seemed like a month, and he had not called the captain, the chief, or O'Brien.
The captain and chief would both understand. Grant would explain to the
priest he was out of state and on a case and didn't have time. "Your man
Cake be okay?" Service asked.

"Cake's Cake. He be lookin' like a sick dawg with a thorn in his foot fer
now, but he'll get on, I reckon."

## ALTON, MISSOURI

### MAY 27, 2004

Service waited until they had checked into a sleep-cheap in Alton for the night before calling Tatie Monica out to the parking lot. "Pappas get anything?"

"Not yet. She'll take the hard drive to St. Louis, see what she can recover. Don't bother crossing your fingers."

"Then what?"

"St. Louis will send more agents and we'll canvas friends and associates of both vicks and see what we get. It would've been too easy if the computer gave us a trail," she lamented.

"As slick as this guy seems to be, you'd think he'd be stupid enough to use a computer?" he asked.

"We'll have to check it out to rule it out."

Slogans made Service cringe.

"You can do without me. I think I'm going to head for home," Service announced. He doubted that talking to hill people would give the FBI much more than they had. It was a tight society not open to outsiders unless they got vouched in by someone like Eddie Waco. He had work to do back home. Nantz's killer was on the loose. He was wasting his time here. Also, if a serial killer planned to knock off a Michigan CO to fill his scorecard, Service had no business being out here. People needed to be warned.

The FBI agent looked at him through squinty eyes. "Leaving on whose authority?"

"My own," he said. "I'm not in the homicide business."

"I already explained your value to the team and effort," she countered, looking like she wanted to scream at him. After a pause and a glance at the night sky, she added, "How about waiting for Bonaparte? Will you do that?" She sounded like she was choking on her words.

"When?" Service asked.

"Soon," she said.

"Not good enough," he shot back. "I ask questions and the check is always in the mail. When will he be here?"

"Not here," she said. "Wisconsin."

"When?" Service pressed.

"First, we have to get things squared away here," she said, clumsily negotiating for time."

"Dammit, Tatie, *when?*"

"He's supposed to be there tomorrow."

"Good. Get me on a plane tonight."

"I don't have that kind of muscle."

"I'm out of here, one way or another."

He thought she was on the verge of a tantrum, but she toggled her handheld and said calmly, "Larry, call Wes and tell him we need a bird to transport Detective Service back to Iron Mountain."

Gasparino asked, "Now?"

"*Right* now," she said emphatically.

"Wes?" Service asked.

"My boss in Milwaukee."

The two of them stood in the parking lot not saying anything. A red Jeep Liberty pulled into a parking spot and a couple got out, laughing. When they started groping each other Tatie Monica growled, "Take that shit inside!" The startled couple fled.

"Drives me crazy," she said to Service, "us up to our asses in gore and people carrying on like the world is normal."

"It is normal," Service said. "At least, it's our job to make it seem that way."

Gasparino came outside. "Bonaparte's here," he said breathlessly.

"Here?" Monica asked, unable to hide her surprise.

"He walked into the hotel ten minutes ago and wants a sit-down, ASAP."

Tatie Monica looked confused, then concerned. She turned to Service. "I guess you won't need that plane."

"We'll see," he said.

Cranbrook P. Bonaparte was a nondescript man with a receding hairline, pasty skin, and the benign, almost grandfatherly countenance of the legendary basketball coach, John Wooden. His eyes were pale green and he had a number-three pencil poised in his right hand. A half-dozen more pencils were on the coffee table atop a pocket protector, making it look like a raft. He also had a notepad, a cell phone, and a handheld radio in front of him. His squint suggested contacts or weak eyes. Service guessed his age as late fifties, give or take. A cane was hooked on the edge of the desk.

When Service walked in with Monica and Gasparino, Bonaparte brightened and, looking at Service, stood, extended his hand, and said, "I don't believe we've been introduced."

The man's voice was friendly and welcoming, his handshake neither too soft, nor too emphatic. Nothing about him suggested FBI. His shirt was wrinkled and he had a smudge above his shirt pocket.

Tatie Monica said, "Detective Grady Service, Michigan Department of Natural Resources."

Bonaparte studied him. "Yes, of course."

"I thought he might add a unique perspective to the investigation, and he has already helped locate the kill site in Wisconsin by thinking like a trout fisherman."

Service picked up on her words. *She* thought? Hadn't his involvement been the Wisconsin AG's idea?

"Excellent," Bonaparte said. "Creative initiative, Special Agent Monica, invariably yields results."

They all sat down and Tatie Monica took Bonaparte through the Wisconsin killing, then the Missouri murder, adding, "Detective Service identified a witness who accompanied the dead man. The witness saw a woman he knew near the kill site. We later found her body. She was murdered in her home. She was a local deputy county sheriff."

"*May* have accompanied the vick," Service corrected her. "And we haven't found the actual kill site, but Culkin told us approximately where to look."

Tatie Monica looked over at him. "Culkin said Spargo met the woman, and with the storm coming in, we can't be sure of the kill site, though the body was found not that far from where the witness thought the meeting took place."

When did she learn this? Service said, "That's not what I heard Culkin say. Deputy Owens may have been at that scene, or she may have just set up a meet for Spargo—or neither."

"I heard what the man said," Special Agent Monica said too forcefully.

"We should wait for the autopsy to determine her TOD," Service said.

"Is that your *professional* opinion?" the FBI woman shot back.

"Common sense."

Service expected Bonaparte to intervene, but he continued to scribble notes.

"Sorry to interrupt," Service said.

Tatie Monica resumed her report, explaining the theft and subsequent burial of the dead conservation agent's body. Service thought he detected a twinkle in Bonaparte's eye. Either he was enjoying Monica's anguish, or he was just an agreeable sort, which seemed to fit his demeanor.

When Tatie Monica finished, Bonaparte looked at Service. "Any other observations or constructive criticism you would care to share, Detective?"

Jesus Christ, was the man inviting him to pile on? Was Bonaparte trying to irritate Monica? Service considered questioning his own role in the boondoggle, but decided this wasn't the right time. He wanted clarification and direction, not more conflict and confusion. Monica allegedly had responded to the Wisconsin attorney general's request to bring him into this, and he still didn't fully understand why. Had she lied? "I've seen some things, but it would be useful to see all the case reports and wait for the autopsy on the Owens woman."

"All before these last two are in the computer," Tatie Monica said. "We'll get you a password."

"I'm not comfortable with the electronic world," Service said. "I like the feel of paper in my hands."

"A man of traditional values," Bonaparte said pleasantly, "a view I wholeheartedly share."

Service smiled and tried to get back to the point. "When can I get hard copies?"

Monica looked at Gasparino, who left the room. Service quickly excused himself and followed the man out, leaving Tatie Monica and Bonaparte alone. "Larry, the case reports will include the list, right?" He tried to keep it light, a friendly afterthought.

"Tatie's the only one who issues copies of the list. It's her baby."

"I lost mine," Service lied. "Any chance to get another copy?"

Gasparino paused before answering. "Sorry, it's her rule; only she makes copies," the young agent insisted.

*Shit,* Service thought. "How about a quick look at yours? I just need to refresh my memory on something before I dig into the case reports."

Gasparino paused again, but shrugged and said, "Okay, man. When I get the other stuff—cool?"

"Thanks," Service said, and let himself back into the meeting room where a tight-lipped Tatie Monica passed him on her way out.

"Ah," Bonaparte said as Service sat down. "Your timing is propitious. I wanted some time alone with you, and let me say at the outset that I must apologize for Special Agent Monica's impetuosity. She sometimes lets enthusiasm turn to zeal, which tends to overpower all reason. For example, I had no idea she would call in a favor from Wisconsin's attorney general."

"What favor?"

"To have you seconded to the investigative team."

"I'm not following this," Service said, but he was. *Seconded?*

"Your governor was asked to send you here so that Agent Monica could look after you. Your governor, of course, was not fully informed, and it's a questionable judgment—albeit grounded in the best of intentions. This sort of knee-jerk reaction has marked her career."

*What the hell was going on?* Bonaparte had just taken a crap on the case's lead agent.

"Why would she want to 'look after' me?" He didn't know whether to laugh out loud or let Bonaparte keep talking.

"I have tried to convince her that we are in pursuit of the perfect killer," Bonaparte said, "a killer who makes no mistakes—or if he does, cleanses them, the net result being perfection."

"Nobody's perfect," Service said.

Bonaparte said enthusiastically, "It comes down to faith, you see? Mankind accepts perfection in God by whatever name, and we are taught we are all made in the image of a creator, and while the vast majority fall short, statistical probability alone tells us there will be the occasional perfect human being."

Mother Teresa, Service could buy—maybe—but not a murderer. "What does any of this have to do with my being looked after?"

"Precisely," Bonaparte said, fluttering his eyebrows. "It's not at all clear to me that a professional of your caliber needs protection, but she has developed the list, and that seems to be driving all of her decisions and tactics."

"List?" he asked.

"Yes," Bonaparte said wearily. "I'm surprised she hasn't filled you in. When our analyst informed us of his findings, she immediately queried the states and asked them to rate their top officers in terms of effectiveness, aggressiveness, and so forth. God knows why, much less what all she threw into the stew," Bonaparte said. "It's ludicrous and presumptuous to think she could so easily develop a predictive instrument—or even attempt it—but that's our Tatie, both decisive and intuitive, even when she's wrong."

Ranking game wardens? Service nearly laughed until it suddenly dawned on him that his name must be on her list. Why else would she have singled him out? Gus Turnage was the best CO he knew, and he could think of at least ten men and women in the state who deserved to be on such a list, and why the hell was Lansing even giving out such bullshit information?

"The point is," Bonaparte continued, "the killer simply switches targets, which folds opportunity cost into the equation. If Special Agent Monica mobilizes to protect A, he strikes B. This flexibility is part of his brilliance."

"B?"

"Look at the situation in Missouri. The top-rated man on her list is an Agent Waco, but it was number two who got killed."

"Elray Spargo," Service said, feeling his pulse quicken. "Are you telling me that my being here puts somebody else at risk back in my state?"

"I'm speculating, but I would think there is an extremely high probability," Bonaparte said solemnly. "The killer seems to have well-established goals."

"Are you suggesting that the best course for me is to retreat to my own turf and wait?"

"I wouldn't call it a retreat."

Service felt a bolt of ice in his heart. "Has he attacked families?"

"Not yet; but given his adaptability, we can't rule it out, can we? He's creative, and if the analysis is correct, Michigan appears to be the final task in his mission."

"Monica brought me here to protect me," Service said, still not taking the thought fully on board.

"Good intentions, but poorly thought out," Bonaparte said. "He could go after you anywhere. But on your own territory, presumably you would have the advantage."

"Has he killed a warden outside the warden's state?"

"No, but he's both dedicated and creative. Most serial murderers are psychotic and essentially unstable. This one appears to be neither. A sociopath perhaps, but for whatever reason he seems to have set this mission for himself, and when it's completed by the rules he's set for himself, he'll stop."

"That's what your profile predicts?"

"A profile is a work in progress until the killer is captured or killed."

"But he's already gone off his pattern," Service said, "with two kills so close together, and perhaps the Owens woman as well. That's a change. Tatie thinks he's feeling pressure."

Bonaparte countered. "Special Agent Monica has a tendency to engage in wishful thinking. It's more likely that this has been part of his plan from the start."

"The guy's got to be a wacko," Service said.

"Why?" Bonaparte asked, leaning forward.

"Look what he does to the bodies, how he tears them up."

Bonaparte studied him for several seconds. "Is what he does to a body any worse than what a bomb does?"

"Bombs aren't aimed at individuals."

"No? As I seem to recall, it was exactly such intent that got the the most recent war rolling in Iraq, and if the bomb doesn't hit the intended target, is the destruction of others less gruesome?"

Before Service could respond, Bonaparte said, "May I call you Grady?"

Service nodded. Bonaparte was one of the strangest people he had ever met, yet he felt comfortable with the man.

"Tell me, Grady, do you really think that the ability to kill requires one to be insane; for example, a mother defending her child in self-defense, or an executioner following a sentence prescribed by law? Ah," he said. "What enables any soldier to kill in combat?"

Again before Service could answer, the FBI man added, "Thanks to Special Agent Monica, we're aware of your record: You've killed."

"In a war."

"Do you remember the faces of the men you killed?"

"No." He remembered the emotions needed for killing, the intensity and desperate rage, but not the individuals.

"Do you think you're the *only* person who can kill and not be affected? Here you are, a contributing member of society, an effective law enforcement professional in a difficult and underappreciated field. Individuals are individuals, Grady. Some serials remember faces, others do not. Everything we think we know about these people we have to unlearn and start over. Some people can kill as easily as they urinate. Some can't do it at all, no matter the stakes. Judeo-Christian morality proclaims, 'Thou Shalt Not Murder,' and cultures built on this turn right around and support their soldiers in war, imploring God to assist them by making a distinction between murder and killing for society's benefit. Some states and nations have capital punishment, others don't. We're a fragmented and splintered world, Grady. We can't really decide *what* we think about the taking of human life. And as for those who carry out government policy, they kill because they possess the necessary aptitude. Some people can jump four feet straight up. Some can't get their soles off the ground. Each of us is born with certain capabilities and potential. Did it ever occur to you that what you did as a marine with your country's blessing was sanctioned serial murder?"

The man was making outrageous statements, yet they seemed almost rational. One thing seemed certain: the man believed what he was saying. It was time to cut this off.

Service stood up and stared down at the Behavioral Analysis Unit veteran, who announced, "I think we shall review the Wisconsin case in more detail and as a team."

"You can inform Special Agent Monica that I'm returning to where I belong."

"A sound decision, Grady," Bonaparte proclaimed. "I'll tender your regrets, but I wish we had more time to get to know each other better."

Service made eye contact with the man for several seconds before turning away. He fetched his gear from his room and found Eddie Waco in the lobby. "I'm going back to Michigan," he told Waco.

"How?"

"Closest commercial airport?"

"Springfield," Waco said, answering the question about an airport. "I've got my rig," he added.

Special Agent Larry Gasparino caught up to them in the parking lot and handed a large envelope to Service. "The reports you wanted."

"The list too?"

"I made you a copy. Don't tell Tatie."

"No problem—and thanks, Larry."

"You bugging out?"

"Taking care of some loose threads," Service lied.

Service felt duped by Tatie Monica, but he wasn't angry at her. He could sense her desperation to catch the killer, and in her shoes he might have made the same choices, but one thing was for sure: With only Michigan remaining, the COs at home were entitled to know what was going on. He told Eddie Waco the whole story about the killings and the list. They were twenty miles down the road when Service's cell phone rang.

"Good news," biologist Buster Beal greeted him. "It's definitely not what we feared."

"Is that the lab's conclusion?"

"Nope, mine," Beal said, "but I sent slides and tissue samples to confirm. I found the deer's problem. The poor bastard had pneumonia and was blind."

"You're sure?"

"Certain to four nines." Service knew this was techie talk for 99.99 percent. "I sent both eyes to the lab to confirm, but I'm telling you I'm sure."

"Blind," Service said. This would explain some of the animal's bizarre behavior.

"It happens. It also looks like his nose was injured, which compounded things—no sight, no smell, all he had were his ears, and they aren't much good for finding food. Think what that would do to you."

Service felt relieved. Buster was a damn good biologist, and if he was certain this wasn't CWD, chances were it wasn't. "Okay, thanks. Anything else?"

"Yeah, it looks to me like the deer's eyes were burned."

"How does an animal burn its eyes?"

"That's an answer I *don't* have, but if I had to characterize it, I'd say the animal was exposed to some source of concentrated heat or light. Maybe he got mixed up with a downed power line or something. Deer aren't the brightest bulbs in the woods."

"That's pretty hard to swallow."

"So is a deer eating fish," Beal said.

The biologist had once observed a small buck walking the shallows of a river, its snout in the water. Beal took several photographs of minnows hanging out of the animal's mouth. Nobody could explain it, but it had happened, just as Service had once watched a thirteen-stripe chipmunk eating another of its kind, which had been struck by a vehicle. According to biologists, such creatures fed exclusively on seeds, nuts, and the occasional insect, not the flesh of other mammals, especially their own kind. "I hear you," Service said. "Thanks, Chewy."

"I'm just glad it was a false alarm," the biologist said.

Service closed the cell phone and lay it on the dash.

It immediately rang again. "Grady, Gus. Where the hell are you?"

"On assignment."

Gus Turnage chuckled. "The shadowy world of secret squirrels." This was what COs sometimes called their detectives. "Listen, I thought you'd want to know that the word is out that Honeypat Allerdyce was seen in L'Anse."

"When?"

"About a month ago."

Service made a quick calculation. Honeypat was Limpy's daughter-in-law, and she had once tried to usurp power in the clan and nearly killed Limpy in the effort. Limpy was the sort to tackle problems head-on. Honeypat was something entirely different, and dangerous. "Source?"

"I heard it from the magistrate here in Houghton. He heard it from a Baraga County judge named Kryder."

"The judge saw her?"

"That I can't say for sure."

"Can you pin it down for me?"

"Can try, if it's important."

"It could be." Honeypat Allerdyce had cleared out, no doubt with a serious grudge against him. He knew she was capable of attacking Nantz and Walter for revenge. His heart began to race.

"Everything going okay?" Gus asked.

"Jury's out on that," Service said, hanging up.

"Home front?" Eddie Waco asked.

"Yeah." He no longer had a home front, but he kept this to himself.

"Whin families and wardens find out what has gone on, they all gon' be one unhappy bunch," Eddie Waco said. "I can't believe game wardens bin gettin' kilt and nobody got told," Waco added as they drove along.

"I had a hard time believing it too, but you saw Elray's body, and he's not the first one. There are all those others."

Service had shared Bonaparte's theory of the killer. Waco looked over and said, "You'n ever meet a perfect lawbreaker?"

"Excluding politicians?" Service responded, which got them both laughing.

Waco grimaced. "What thet ole boy tole you'n, how I was the big dawg here, thet ain't true."

"Bonaparte said Special Agent Monica got your name from your department."

"Our honchos are a secretive bunch. You git on thet Internet thing just to get the name a' yer local agent, and you won't be a-findin' hit there. They hain't no way the feds gonna get a list worth coon pie from our people. I'm tellin' you'n, Elray Spargo was *the* man and has been for years."

Which meant the killer had not killed anyone except the top person on the list, Service concluded. Why did Bonaparte tell him differently, and why was he suddenly in a rush to get home if he was the target and not Gus or another officer? He found himself lost in his thoughts as the truck's headlights bored a hole in the darkness. *Honeypat back in the U.P.?* This needed to be confirmed. If true, maybe it would provide the leverage he needed to get the Troops to go back and take another look at Nantz's accident scene. His mind was swimming with images, but the one that kept coming back was the freaky light he had seen at Mormon Creek; at the time he didn't think much about it. There also was a blind deer with burnt eyes, and maybe there was sort of a thread, but he couldn't see it. Cake Culkin also claimed to have seen something he seemed to think was lightning without thunder, and the killer who inflicted his victims with the blood eagle had removed their eyes. Service looked over at Eddie Waco. "Is there a television station near here?"

"Closest is West Plains."

"Let's talk to Cake again and go visit the weatherman," Service said.

Eddie Waco said, "I hear grit in 'at voice," he said. "I believe you'n and Elray would've got along good."

## LEFT SHOULDER RIDGE, MISSOURI

### MAY 28, 2004

Cake Culkin came to the door looking antsy. "Where's them feds at?" he asked, craning to look into the night past the two game wardens.

"Hit's jes us, Cake," Eddie Waco said. "We found Laglenda Owens dead."

The blood ran out of Culkin's face.

Service jumped in. "Cake, did you actually see Deputy Owens that night?"

"Nossir. I told all y'all I didn't see her badge thet night."

"And not her without the badge, out of uniform?"

"Nope; Elray done tole me he was gonna meet her and another feller."

"He say what about?" Waco asked.

"Nossir."

"Remember telling us you saw a flash of light?" Service asked.

"Lightnin'."

"But you never heard thunder."

"Right."

"You sure it was lightnin', Cake?"

"Was bright enough, I reckon. What else might it be?"

Service asked, "Was Elray acting normal before this happened?" He knew from experience that even when you thought your mood was hidden, others could often read it—especially a partner or a lover.

Cake chewed his lip. "He weren't quite right since his baby sister Rosa done got called ta her reward. They was close, them two."

"When was that, Cake?" Service asked.

"Couple fortnights back, I reckon, give or take."

"How'd she die?"

"Her car rolled over," Agent Waco said.

"Anything unusual about the crash?"

Waco said, "Only that she was a good driver and the weather was good."

He had seen no cars in Fourteen, and no roads. "She didn't live with the family?"

"She lived over ta West Plains with her husband and young 'uns."

"Huh," Grady Service said. Spargo's sister and Nantz and Walter had died about the same time and in a similar manner. It was a weird coincidence.

Service looked at Cake Culkin. "You followed a blood trail and found Elray's body?"

"I said."

"Big blood trail?"

"Like a deer got drug."

"Can you show Agent Waco where you picked up the trail?"

"Rained since then, won't be no p'int."

"Still like ta," Waco chimed in. "Kin we get us a four-wheeler back thet far?"

"I reckon," Culkin said.

"Back tomorrow, Cake," Eddie Waco said.

Service wanted to be sure what he had heard. "Elray said he was meeting Deputy Owens and another man. You never saw her, but you got a glimpse of a man, is that right, Cake?"

Culkin nodded. "That's how it were."

## WEST PLAINS, MISSOURI
### MAY 28, 2004

The meteorologist at the television station was middle-aged and overweight with gray-blond hair in a pompadour.

"You got records for the weather goin' back a spell?" Eddie Waco asked.

"That depends on how one defines spell," the man said. "A spell of love can last seconds or a lifetime, a spell of weather somewhere in between."

Service gave him the date.

"Clear night," the weatherman said. "Could see smiles in the stars."

"You can remember what the weather was back then?"

"What they pay me for. We've also got records to corroborate."

"No lightning?" Service asked.

"Nothin' closer than western Kansas, and if you boys are seeking Oz, you don't have to travel that far afield."

Back in Waco's truck Service said, "What lightning was Cake talking about?"

"He's a bit addled. Is it important?"

"I don't know." He was having trouble sorting out the things he had seen and heard, and he was tired.

## CABOOL, MISSOURI

### MAY 29, 2004

Service didn't want to answer his vibrating cell phone. It was Special Agent Tatie Monica. "Service, you are not leaving until we talk."

"I've had enough talk," Service said.

"Please," the special agent said. "Where are you?"

Service looked over at Eddie Waco. "Where are we?"

"Short spit down the road from Cabool," Waco said.

"Near Cabool," Service told the FBI agent.

"Afghanistan?" she asked.

Service looked at Waco. "She wants to know where that is."

"Texas County," the Missouri man said. "North a' her."

Service passed the word.

"They got an airport?" she asked.

"Airport?" Service said.

"Size of a three-cent stamp," Waco said.

"Little one," Service told her.

"I'll meet you at airport security in two hours," she said. "And I'll arrange for a plane to take you to where you want to go. Just wait for me, okay?"

"Don't waste my time," Service said.

"I'll be there."

He closed the cell phone and cut her off.

"Change in plans?" Eddie Waco asked.

"The feds want a meet."

"And you agreed?"

"She said please."

"I reckon that changes everything," Waco said.

They drove past darkened fields and, on the outskirts of town, farm-implement dealer lots filled with huge, brightly colored machines illuminated by garish neon lights. They pulled into the parking lot of an orange building called The Fish-Walker. The interior was dark, with a century-old stand-up bar, vases filled with peacock feathers, and dusty stuffed fish on the walls, mostly trout.

The waitress had long straight hair and a gaunt face. She stood with her legs apart like a linebacker waiting to make a tackle.

"How'd this place get its name?" Service asked.

"Town's posed to be named for some Indian. The place is named for the owner. Why is anybody's guess. He's a lawyer over St. Looey way, a bit in his own world, all twisty-headed about trout. They ain't no fish on the menu today, gents. What'll it be?"

Waco ordered fried pork steaks for both of them, and Service settled in with the reports.

While Service tried to read, patrons tentatively approached Agent Waco, each of them using the same opener: "Hey, got a question for you." Every game warden in the world had heard this so many times that it was an inside joke.

The commonalities in the cases were few: Every victim had been a game warden; no collateral fatalities had been discovered, unless Deputy Owens counted; the most recent victims had been killed and displayed in the same way, their eyes removed. All the bodies had been found unclothed near water. No kill sites had been discovered until Ficorelli's. Culkin would show Waco another possible kill site, but in the wake of the storm, it was unlikely there would be much evidence there. But these were only the second batch. What about records for the first set of killings?

He saved Monica's list until last. His name was listed for Michigan, Eddie Waco for Missouri, and Wayno Ficorelli for Wisconsin. His name didn't freak him out as much as make his face turn red with anger.

A waitress brought the steaks, said to Waco, "You need anything more, you give a wave, okay, hon?"

"You're top of the list," Service said.

Eddie Waco glanced at him. "Thet list hain't right."

"Any way to find out who sent the information from your higher-ups to the feds, and to whom?"

"I reckon, but I'm thinking weren't nothin' sent."

"How long have you been a warden?" Service asked.

"Twenty year."

"You been ta college," Service said, mimicking Cake Culkin.

Waco nodded. "Mizzou."

Service raised an eyebrow: University of Missouri. "Studying what?"

"Biology and forestry."

Service said, "I thought you said you don't know science."

"Learned enough ta slide through. All I ever wanted was to be a game warden."

"I guess you turned out to be a pretty good one."

Waco's eyes narrowed. "Elray was the best I seen. You think the feds are going to waste your time again?"

"Our time," Service said. "The way I figure it, we both have a stake in this fiasco, and if I'm in, you're in. The feds have had this thing closed up in a box for too damn long. It needs air and light."

After eating, they waited in darkness at the airport. The unlit field was tiny, with only three small planes parked in the open air.

"Where's Security?" Monica asked when she pulled up.

"I reckon we're it," Waco said.

"Let's go inside," she said.

"We're outdoor guys," Service said. "And there isn't an inside unless you want to sit in the truck."

Eddie Waco grinned.

Monica handed him a large envelope. "Larry only gave you the records from the second group. I thought you might want these."

"You lied to me," Service said. "You put the bite on your old classmate. It wasn't his idea to contact Governor Timms. It was yours."

She held up her hands. "*Nolo contendere,*" she said. "I wanted you close."

"To protect me," Service said.

"The killer hasn't struck an officer outside his home state. If you were with us, I figured you'd be clear until we could get this damn thing figured out. I swear it was in your interest."

"Bonaparte says you're a zealot."

She said, "I'm also damn good."

"Which is why you got dumped in Milwaukee."

"That's bullshit. I broke the case in LA and I *asked* for Milwaukee."

"Your colleagues say differently."

"Gasparino?" she said. "Larry's green, still susceptible to the most outrageous gossip. There's always gossip when a woman gets the job done. You want, call my boss in Milwaukee. He'll confirm it."

Service looked over at Eddie Waco, who shrugged.

"You have had a chance to look at the reports?" she asked.

"We looked."

"And?"

"Not much there."

"That's the truth."

Service said, "But it seems to me we have a few things. Bonaparte insists this guy is the perfect serial murderer, but he hit Elray Spargo, when Agent Waco is the top man on the list for Missouri. He also may have killed Deputy Owens, and the fact that he may have brought her in as a third party to arrange a meeting suggests he's changed his ways, or is unsure of himself. Something is changing. He was also close to getting confronted in Wisconsin by the sheriff. This guy may be good, but he's not flawless—if your list means a damn thing. The real key is what do all the victims on the list have in common—other than the obvious?"

She scratched the corner of her mouth. "That's one of the things I wanted to talk to you about—the list."

"We're listening," Service said.

"The analyst who discovered the pattern also suggested the list. I mean, who were the victims? Were they targets of opportunity, the best guys, or unlucky foul-ups? The list was intended to help us pinpoint more of a pattern."

"Which it did."

"It became pretty clear that only the top people were being targeted."

"But Spargo died, not Waco."

"You have to understand, we were getting a little desperate. We have to fight like hell for resources nowadays and we were getting big pressure to produce. We thought the list would be a way of assessing patterns, and then it started to have predictive value, so I decided to rig a control, hoping I could speed up things."

Service thought he misheard. "You *switched* Spargo for Waco?"

"It was strictly an alphabetical choice. They were both on the Missouri list."

"Which got Elray killed," a tense Eddie Waco said. Service wondered if he should move the federal agent away from him.

Tatie Monica shook her head and sucked in a deep breath. "Maybe, but the fact that the killer went for Agent Spargo tells us a couple of things."

Service said, "One, he makes mistakes."

"Hit also says he's wired into the dadblame list," Eddie Waco interjected.

"Which has very limited distribution," Monica said.

"I managed to get a copy," Service said, "which doesn't say much for your security."

"I know, I know, but I wanted you to have the list, and you would have gotten it, but you duped Larry before I could get to it."

"It wasn't difficult."

"He came to me and told me what he'd done. His instincts are good."

"The killer has thet list," Eddie Waco repeated.

"Only he fucked up," Service said.

"Not in *his* mind," Monica said. "As far as the killer's concerned, and according to the control, he took out the top man in Missouri. In his mind, he's still perfect, and it's what's in *his* mind that matters to us."

"Bonaparte said the man's flexible and creative."

"Both of which may be true, but he still took the wrong man. Bonaparte says I'm a zealot, but he won't give up his bullshit perfect-killer theory."

"Who called the FBI about Spargo?" Service asked.

"The call came into the St. Louis office," she said.

"Recorded?"

"Yes, but the audio people say the caller used a pay phone and a masking device. They haven't been able to filter it yet, and they probably won't."

"Pay phone where?"

"St. Louis," she said.

"How did Bonaparte get involved?"

"He was in St. Louis when the call came in. I had talked to him about joining us in Wisconsin, but this broke before he could get there."

"And he went to the site here and left before we came in?" Service asked.

She nodded.

"Does he go to all the crime scenes?"

"Not all, but it's fairly standard procedure for BAU people, especially in a major case."

"Even for an acting assistant director?"

"He's been a profiler for a long time, and his management gig is short-term."

"He really believes his theory?"

"Absolutely," she said.

"Supporters?" Service asked.

"These killings are certainly earning him some. Look," she said, "if you want to go home, it's your call. I'm sorry I pulled you into this the way I did."

"We might have met with my lungs pulled through my ribs."

"I know," she said. "I was desperate, and I'm sorry."

"Officers have a right to know all about this," Service said, looking to Eddie Waco, who nodded. "Do the states' fish and game division law enforcement people know this is going on?"

"No," she said.

"*Unacceptable!*" Service said, nearly shouting.

"We thought we could get the guy without making a big public case."

"All ya'll were wrong," Eddie Waco said. "That puts some of the body count on all ya'll's heads."

"I hear what you guys're saying, and in your position I might be feeling the same thing, but we can't call back the past. There's no do-overs in this, so all we can do is move on."

"How many people are privy to the list?" Service asked.

"Two dozen max."

"Two dozen like Larry?" Service shot back.

"I hope not," Tatie Monica said.

"This don't give a soul a heap of confidence," Eddie Waco chimed in.

"Look, I admit I've made mistakes. But now you know, and it's up to you to decide where you go from here."

Service studied her. "You remember when you asked me about hunting?"

"I remember."

"I forgot to say it's not a group activity," he said. "I'm thinking Agent Waco and I need to talk, and then we'll get back to you."

"Are you going to stay?" she asked.

"Did you order a plane?"

"Be here soon."

"Good. I'm going to go back to Michigan."

"Home?"

"I haven't decided that yet," Service said.

Special Agent Monica looked at Eddie Waco. "You?"

"Like the man says, we'll get back at you'n," the conservation agent said.

"Any chance the killer has both the original list and the control?"

"Looks that way, but I don't see how," Tatie Monica said. "Only the analyst and I had the list with the control."

"Did the killings that took place before the list conform to the list?"

"Yes," she said.

"But those states that already had lost a man wouldn't be on the list."

"We went only to the states that had not lost someone."

"What about the states that had already lost people?"

"We had names of victims, and went directly to each state to get a sense of the victim's value."

"They *all* valuable," Eddie Waco growled.

"I didn't mean it like that," the federal agent said. "Some of the states said the victim was their top performer, or *a* top performer."

"But the killer has focused on *the* top warden in each state."

"What are you getting at?" she asked.

"How did the killer identify victims before the list?"

She looked at Service for a long moment. "We don't know."

Service said, "You can't just wander into the woods and hope to bump into the top warden—or any warden, for that matter. Most of us aren't predictable in our patterns. And, if you want to target the top people, it takes time to find them in order to do what you're gonna do. Who supplied evaluations to you?"

"The top law enforcement official in each state."

"How long to get back to you?"

"A day or two at the most."

"States don't keep such lists," Eddie Waco said, "an' the top law dog is the attorney general."

Service said, "Safari Club gives an award every year to the outstanding law enforcement officer in Michigan. Probably other states, too. The turkey federation also gives an award. Probably Ducks Unlimited too."

"You ever win any of those?" Tatie Monica asked.

Service shook his head.

"Then they're irrelevant," she said.

"This list thing isn't helping," Service said. "The killer has to have a way of picking targets, a connection between the violets other than their jobs. We just have to figure out what it is. Where's that plane?" he asked.

"I said I ordered it."

Service looked at her and frowned. "It's coming here?"

"Destination?" she asked.

"Iron Mountain. I need my truck."

She went to her vehicle, got on the radio, scribbled some notes, and came back. "Here's fine. One hour."

"You'd better call someone and get the lights on here." Obviously she had not ordered the plane, or was holding it back, hoping she could convince him to stay.

"I really think it would be better if you remained with the team," she said.

"No chance," he answered. He still couldn't figure her out, but he had too many doubts about her motivation and competence to keep doing what she wanted.

"You'll be in touch?" she asked.

"If I have reason."

When she was gone Service looked over at the Missouri agent. "You can go too. I've got plenty of reading to keep me occupied."

"Pass me some a' them files, partner."

"Don't you have something to do?"

"I *am* doing it," the man said.

After reading by flashlight for a while, Waco said, "If the same feller did all these folks, he musta got started whin he was the size of a popcorn fart."

Service looked over at the man. "I've had similar thoughts."

"Hard as it is ta find the likes of us, could be more'n one perp, I 'speck." Waco added, "I'm thinking you want a well, you best be willin' to dig all the way down ta water, and if this ole boy's the perfectionist them feds claim and he's never got hisself caught, how come he'd switch to a new way? Way I read history, ole Babe Ruth never stopped swingin' for fences even if he struck out more times thin he smacked homers. And Old Ty Cobb never stopped slidin' with 'is spikes up."

The plane arrived and pulled in, Service walked across the apron, verified his credentials, loaded his gear, and walked back to the Missouri agent.

"Good huntin'," Waco said, extending his hand.

"What makes you think I'm going to hunt?"

Waco grinned. "You got the look. You think you get you a scent, call me and we'll make it a pack hunt." Waco handed him a card with several phone numbers and an e-mail address. "Me'n Cake will look at the site in the morning."

Service watched the conservation agent standing expressionless in front of his pickup as the plane taxied into position for takeoff.

## PART II
## MICHISSIPPI

*Prendre le chemin des écoliers*
To take the schoolboy's route

## 23

## WISCONSIN REDUX

## MAY 30, 2004

Grady Service found himself beset with jumbled thoughts. The killer had not struck every year in either group. Why? Waco had suggested there was a group at work, and although possible, this didn't seem likely. Still, a group would better explain how the killer might track his targets. More than one killer could explain how someone could get the better of the imposing Elray Spargo, much less drag his huge body alone. Most COs didn't have easy or predictable routines for an outsider to key in on, and often they didn't know from one moment to the next where they would be or what they would be doing.

He knew that successful long-term fish and game violators tended to be fairly well organized, and often the shooters were not the same ones who located the targets. It could also apply to humans. That's what their Kit Carson scouts had done for them in Vietnam.

But if a crew had been operating over so many years, the odds were that one of them, or somebody who knew one of them, would have snitched. And why had there been a gap of a dozen years between the groups? Had "helpers" outlived their usefulness? The death of the Missouri deputy was definitely something the FBI ought to be taking a long, hard look at, but would they? They had known about the killings for three years and not informed game wardens around the country. Jesus. They were running around with a lot of people, and what seemed to him more velocity than direction. What the hell was Special Agent T. R. Monica really thinking? There were moments when she seemed to be on top of things, and others when she seemed almost clueless. Whatever she was, his gut said not to trust her. As he thought about it, he even wondered if she was somehow involved. Why else would the investigation seem so cockamamie and have so many holes? He wondered if he could check her whereabouts against the killings and timing to see if there was a pattern, but decided this was a reach. Sometimes in an investigation you could have some strange notions. It paid to recognize them for what they were and move on. It would take one imposing person or two to take down Spargo, and Monica had been with him in Wisconsin, which eliminated her from involvement. Right?

Early on she had seemed most interested in his tracking abilities. Why? What trail was he supposed to follow? He was on the list. Okay, but what else? He didn't know if he was tracking a chimpanzee or a chickadee. He had a record of finding people who were *known* to be lost. And he had a good record of intervening in outdoor crime because he had experience and pretty good instincts about where things might happen. Wanting to protect him seemed ludicrous, but she had used political connections to pull him in, and she had admitted it to him. Maybe she believed having him close was the right thing to do.

Whatever her reasoning, he decided there was only one trail, and that was in Wisconsin. He knew from experience that when you lost a trail, you often had to double back to where you'd lost it—all the way to the beginning, if necessary.

He was still in the parking lot of Ford Airport in Iron Mountain when he decided he would not head home. He drove toward Florence, deep in thought.

Why would the man who had killed so invisibly in so many different ways in the first group, and most of the second, suddenly switch to the blood eagle, which was impossible to hide? He had tried not to think about the gruesome details of the most recent killings, but he had a curious thought that such butchering required a fair amount of knowledge about the human anatomy, and some cutting skill. How the hell could someone just jump into killing like that unless they'd first tried it out? Could forensics see a difference in the technique of the mutilations from killing to killing? Was the killer getting better, or worse; was he changing his cutting methods . . . anything? There was no analysis of techniques in the reports. He knew from experience that gutting and butchering a large animal was not something you did perfectly the first time. The more you did it, the more efficient you got.

The fact that he'd never heard of the blood eagle didn't mean it had not been used somewhere; maybe not the whole thing, but part of it. If the killer was truly a perfectionist, as Bonaparte insisted, and he wanted to get it right, he'd do all kinds of homework about game warden habits and movement patterns. Wouldn't he also do the same in creating the blood eagle? So why had his timing been off in Wisconsin?

Only Monica and her analyst knew about the control. Significance? He wasn't sure. Why didn't Bonaparte know? Had she intentionally withheld it from him and other agents? And if so, why?

And what was it that Bonaparte had said to him that struck an odd chord? He couldn't remember the specific thing, only that it had jarred him momentarily.

Something Eddie Waco said had stayed with him: "Babe Ruth never stopped swinging for the fences." In hockey when you tried to score a goal on every shot, you were bound to score some, miss some, and have some blocked or saved. So why didn't this killer ever miss?

This thing was way out of his league, he decided, but he had to do something, and he knew he needed help.

Special Agent Temple met him when he parked at the command post on the hill above the Pine River. Her hair was mussed, her clothes dusty, her shirt soaked with sweat. The temperature was in the low nineties, the humidity unbearable, especially for those who lived this far north. Yoopers would walk about on a sunny thirty-below-zero day talking about the nice weather, and carp incessantly when the temperature got above eighty in summer.

She said. "Tatie called me about what you found in Missouri."

He nodded. "Anything new here?"

"Not a lot. The techs don't think the vick got it in the water. No drag marks up to the kill site, just down that other bank. Something or someone got him to get out."

The techs *thought?* "That's it?" Service said, mulling over the information. This wasn't new. Dammit, he'd read the signs himself, pointed them out to Tatie Monica.

"I swear this asshole could clean my apartment," Temple added. "He's a neat freak."

If so, why hadn't the neat freak picked up Ficorelli's fishing gear in order to mask the kill site? He felt like blowing up, but took a deep breath. This wasn't Temple's fault. "Where's the vick's vehicle now?"

"Impounded in town."

"Has it been announced yet?"

"If it had, I'm sure you would have heard about it," she said. "We've been able to sit on it so far."

Given where he'd been the last few days, he might have missed the opening of World War III. "Does his mother know?"

"She died last month."

Service sucked in a breath. "She died?"

"Car wreck."

*Another car wreck?* Service said, "This needs to be announced. If the media finds out you've been sitting on this for so long, they may jump on you and play the story in a bigger way than they might have."

"You're singing to the choir. Special Agent Monica has her own mind and ways of doing things. Her orders are to sit on it."

Service said, "If it's made public, we might get some people coming forward, maybe find someone who saw something that could help us." This tactic had worked with fish and game violations and had led to the conviction of illegal wolf and bear killers.

"More likely to pull in cranks and nutcases," she said.

"Some of the things cranks and nut jobs see are real," he reminded her. What had Bonaparte said—that the perp had never tried to communicate with law enforcement? Would an announcement stimulate that? Maybe, maybe not. "What else have you got?" he asked. "Did those people seen down by the river that night get interviewed?"

"Transcripts for you," she said, pulling a clipboard out of her vehicle and handing him some stapled pages.

"You mind if I look around the site?" Service asked.

"You know the drill," she said.

The only change he saw at the kill site was an orange-string grid and several marker flags inside a yellow-ribbon perimeter. Other pennants had been placed where he had found the rod and fly box. Service thought himself through what he'd seen previously, and retraced the discovery of the kill site. After an hour he moved over to the riverbank and sat on a cedar blowdown to read the transcripts. The man and woman both had been interviewed. Neither had been shown a photograph of Ficorelli. All the questions had been about movements on the road on the other side of the river, and questions about any suspicious activity they might have observed. What the hell was the FBI thinking? They'd missed the point.

Service tapped the pages. They had not just missed a potential trail, but also ignored the possibility of another angle. He corrected himself: They had no way of knowing firsthand about Wayno's predilections, so he couldn't fairly hang an oversight on them. But not announcing the killing to the public could have played into the law of unintended consequences, and he had a hunch. Not exactly a hunch; more like elevated curiosity. Monica knew Wayno couldn't keep it in his pants, but it was doubtful she knew the extent of his philandering.

Service didn't let Special Agent Temple know his real intentions, but asked permission to take his truck through the river at the four-wheeler ford. When he asked her for a photograph of Ficorelli, she hemmed and hawed before providing one.

According to transcripts, the woman's name was Sondra Andreesen, married fifteen years to Monte, who owned Super-Saver Appliances & Electronics, a chain headquartered in Milwaukee, with stores stretching from northern Illinois up to St. Paul, Minnesota. She was forty-four, her husband, forty. The man the FBI had caught her with was Jinks Schwarz, thirty-nine, a house painter and year-round resident of the area; no criminal record, not even a traffic citation.

He saw no point in talking to Schwarz until he met the woman.

The Andreesen house was five miles south of the river. It looked new and out of place, a three-story glass-and-steel-beam monstrosity that towered over a grove of five-year-old aspens like a botanical goiter. A driveway curved about a hundred yards from the road to the house. The road to the river was invisible from the house.

When he arrived, a woman was standing on the porch. She wore a yellow sundress draped to her ankles, and stringy gold sandals with soles as thin as vellum. She had a deep, unseasonal tan, no jewelry or makeup, but reddish polish on several fingernails. It looked like she had been interrupted. He could smell fresh nail polish.

"Mrs. Sondra Andreesen?" He showed his FBI ID. "Do you have an electronic security system?" Service asked.

"Why do you ask?"

"It looks to me like you were out on the porch waiting for me."

"I was just on my way out to run some errands."

Service said, "I thought maybe your system alerted you I was coming in."

"It's an eye or something," she said, blinking furiously. "I don't really pay attention to it."

"You didn't finish your nails."

She instinctively curled her fingertips to hide them.

"Can I have a few minutes of your time?" Service asked.

"I have some errands," she said. "Really."

"This won't take long," Service said. She was uptight.

"I already talked to the other agents," she said, adding, "and I'm ashamed. Are you people ever going to leave me alone? I don't even know what the point of this is."

He could sense she wanted to let loose her indignation, but was holding back. Her eyes were wide, her posture tense. She was nervous as hell about something.

"If you give me a few minutes, maybe I can clarify the situation," Service said.

She reluctantly opened the door and led him into a great room with one wall of windows and half a roof of sloping skylights. The place was shades of white, totally sterile, no sign of children. "Plenty of room," Service said, looking around.

"This house was Monte's idea," she said. "I wanted a little cabin in the woods and of course he wanted an investment. With Monte everything is about money."

A less-than-blissful union, Service observed.

She didn't offer a seat or refreshments. "What's this about?" she wanted to know.

Service handed her a five-by-seven photograph of Wayno Ficorelli.

She lurched visibly, but tried to recover her poise.

"Do you know this man?"

She answered, "With Monte's business we meet so many people."

"His name is Wayno Ficorelli," Service said.

"I just don't remember," she said, avoiding his eyes. "Is it important?"

Service considered his options. The woman had been caught in *flagrante dilecto* with one man, and there had to be a reason other than fishing for Ficorelli to keep coming back to this area. It was a long shot that felt right. "He's been murdered, Mrs. Andreesen."

Blood ran out of the woman's face and she started to wobble. Service caught her by the arm and guided her down into a chair. She shook her head listlessly and stared at the floor, her breath coming fast. "When?" she asked.

Service told her the date and she began to gasp for air.

"Nothing . . . in . . . news," she mumbled, her voice cracking.

"There are reasons for that," Service said, not amplifying. "I'm sorry to be the one to tell you, but we need help finding his killer."

She responded with an almost imperceptible nod.

"You knew him," Service said, a declarative statement, not a question.

"Yes."

"When did you see him last?"

"That same day," she said. "He got here late morning and left to meet Arnie Thorkaldsson to fish."

"You know the sheriff?"

"For a long time."

"Did Wayno act different in any way on that day?"

She rolled her eyes and managed a smile. "God, he was the poster boy for different."

"But that day specifically?"

"He wasn't himself," she said with resignation. "He was really hurting over his mom's death. He never talked about work. I want work talk, Monte has more than enough."

"What time did Wayno leave here?"

"Four, maybe a little after. He usually left about the same time. He and Arnie always bet a beer on the most fish, and he liked to get there first. But that day he was reluctant to leave, said he wasn't in the mood, and I told him to go," she said, stifling a sob.

"This is not your fault," he said, trying to keep her calm and talking. "Did you see Wayno often?"

"Whenever he came to see Arnie."

"Three times a year?"

"Yes," she mumbled, her eyes wide with disbelief, obviously disturbed that he knew the frequency.

"Does Arnie know about you and Wayno?"

"Nobody knows," she said. "*Knew.*"

"Where'd you two meet?"

"Monte's company sponsors youth outdoor education programs, and sometimes we have Wisconsin wardens come in to talk to the kids. Wayno was a guest speaker at a meeting near Fond du Lac."

"How long ago was this?"

"Seven years."

"And you've been seeing him ever since?"

"It was flingy," she said. "You know, not serious. Wayno had a wild, bad-boy side and Monte has none, and doesn't know anything about having fun unless he's making money."

"Seven years seems like a long fling," he said.

"Like I already said, Wayno was Wayno, and what it was, was all it ever was going to be," she said.

"How'd you arrange your meetings and times?"

"We set them a year ahead," she said.

"And he never missed?"

"He said he controlled his own schedule," she said. "Did he suffer?"

"No," Service said, knowing this was what she wanted to hear. "Did you vary the dates?" he asked.

"No, it was pretty much the same three days every year. You know, because of the fishing, something to do with certain insects."

"I appreciate your cooperation," Service said, knowing now that fishing was not Wayno's only reason for coming to Florence County.

"Who told you about us?" she asked.

"That's confidential, and you also need to keep this quiet. We won't be talking to your husband."

She rolled her eyes. "Like *I'm* going to talk about it?" she said. "I feel stupid and I feel bad about all of this. Wayno was . . ." Tears were welling in her eyes.

"I can let myself out," Service told her. He turned around at the door. "You said Wayno was really bothered by his mom's death?"

"Devastated. He couldn't understand how it happened."

When he got to the truck he sat for a while. Wayno's mother, Elray Spargo's sister, Maridly Nantz. Two murdered game wardens and another on the alleged target list, and all with sudden losses of people they were close to. This defied coincidence. He had seen Wayno in action. He had been an aggressive warden. And because of his mother's death Wayno may not have been on his game.

Now he also knew that Wayno wasn't as unpredictable as he should have been. Three times a year, same place, parking in the same spot—these were things a killer could work with, and they probably had cost him his life. What it didn't do was explain why Ficorelli was chosen by the killer, or how. Killer or killers, he reminded himself. The list? Maybe, maybe not. *Keep an open mind,* he cautioned himself, as he drove back down to the river, showed his temporary ID to the security agents on duty. He parked where Wayno's vehicle had been, got out his waders, and walked down the path into the river and up toward the kill site, trying to sort out his thoughts.

The killer had missed Ficorelli's gear. Had he planned to dump the body and come back? Had Thorkdalsson's arrival been too close a call and spooked him? What else had he missed?

## 24

# FLORENCE COUNTY, WISCONSIN
## MAY 30, 2004

What would get a fisherman out of the water? Correction: not just a fisherman, but a game warden. If he had been on duty, it might have been to help someone, or to watch or stop something, but Wayno had been off duty, and fishing. Service sat on the log where he had found the rod and the fly box, which had been submerged but open. Had Wayno been changing flies? If so, was it because he wanted a new pattern, or because he'd lost one in the trees or foliage? The greenery was certainly dense enough along the bank to eat flies.

Service tried to read the water. There was a pool with smooth water about thirty yards upstream, and a riffle nearer to him—less a riffle than pocket water. The best run was close to the bank, and that's where the trout were most likely to be—unless a hatch was happening in low light, in which case the trout would be inclined to move more toward the middle to feed, which could have put Ficorelli's backcast in jeopardy. But if the rises had been along the seam by the bank, Wayno would have been in the middle casting toward shore, with little chance of getting hung up high behind him. The old rule was that if you weren't occasionally getting hung in the low wood, you weren't fishing aggressively enough. Rising trout stuck close to cover, which meant casts had to be no more than an inch or two off the target. His attention kept shifting from the coincidental deaths to Wayno's fishing. He needed to focus. He sat down, lit a cigarette, and let his eyes begin to sweep the foliage along the banks. Looking for a fly in a tree was worse than looking for a needle in haystack.

Grady Service was studying the trees when Special Agent Temple showed up.

"Bird-watching?" she joked from above him.

"Something like that."

What would be hatching now? Not sulfurs at night, and it was too early for hex. Drakes probably, brown or gray. Drakes would mate and spin down over the riffle. Drakes were good-size flies, 10s or 12s. If Ficorelli had lost a fly, was it because he snagged a leaf or a woodpile, or because of a bad knot? Bad knots combined with poor casts took more flies than anything else. He guessed Ficorelli was a pretty good caster, but everyone tied bad knots, either because they were in a hurry, or because the tippet was old or frayed.

"Geez," he said out loud.

"What?" Temple asked.

"Where's the evidence recovered from the river—the victim's rod and the fly box?"

"Locked up back at camp."

"Let's go take a look."

"Are you going to tell me what this is about?" she wanted to know.

"Tree fish," he said, not bothering to expand.

When they got to the evidence locker, he put on latex gloves and got out the rod with the reel still attached. He looked at the tippet, the end-portion of the leader, and saw a telltale curlicue, which suggested a bad knot or weak tippet. The leader was segmented with different diameters of monofilament, hand-tied. The closest knot to the end of the tippet was about four inches up. Obviously some tippet had come off with the fly. "Okay then," he said.

"Okay what?" the federal agent asked.

"I'm pretty sure it's a tree fish," he said. He handed her the rod, peeled off the gloves, and started back to the river.

He tried to use the late sun to his advantage. If tippet was still attached to the fly, the monofilament might catch and reflect some light. He eased slowly along the bank, using a long stick to part leaves and branches. It took fifteen minutes to find what he was looking for: about six inches of mono wrapped around a tag alder branch, impossible to reach unless you got onto land and came down the other side of the trees.

The body had been found just above here. If this is when the attack came, he reasoned, Wayno would never have reached the fly, and considering that other evidence had not been picked up by the killer, the fly might still be there.

He considered getting onto land, but studied the mono for several minutes. Years of fishing had taught him that the sorts of angles and tangles that could beset a line would confound all known laws of physics. The key to recovering a fly on a light tippet was to work the line slowly and gently, not to jerk it. There was sunken timber in front of him, just below the broken tippet. He moved over close, bent down, and began to run his hand along the back of a small log behind a larger one. It didn't take long to feel the fly stuck in the wood. He put on another pair of latex gloves, knelt on the larger of the logs, leaned close, and wiggled the fly loose. There was a curlicue of monofilament hanging off the fly. He now thought he understood. A fish had been rising near the wood, and Wayne's cast had gone into the tags and hooked the wood, but when he tried to pull it loose, it had broken. Not being able to see anything but the monofilament, Ficorelli probably had gotten out of the water to see if he could retrieve it from landside.

Why the hell would he retrieve a fly if he had fish rising? Most fishermen would just tie on another fly, cast again, and hope the fish kept coming up. But by getting out and coming in from the land, he would not have had to wade through the run and put down rising trout. This made sense. When you fished for trout, you did everything in your power not to disturb what was happening. It was in your own self-interest.

Okay, he thought. The scenario makes sense. Rising fish, stuck fly, retrieve it, don't disturb the risers. Service stared at the fly. It looked vaguely like a brown drake, but in a dressing and style he had never seen before. As he handled it, the hook itself fell apart and dropped into the water, leaving him with only the upper part of the fly.

He put the evidence in his pocket, sat down, and lit another cigarette. The scene was forming in his mind. Wayno had gotten out of the water to recover a lost fly and was attacked. Was it the only one of that kind that he had? Possibly. He probably never saw the attack coming, which suggested the assailant had been shadowing him along the bank. Because he had a pretty good idea where Ficorelli had gotten into the river and crossed to this side, he had a pretty good idea where the shadowing began. He got out of the river and walked downstream along the bank, keeping the same distance from the water as the attack site had been.

Eventually he came to a downed oak, one that had rotted and probably come down under the weight of winter snow. There was a partial track in between some branches near the ground. The track was treadless. Felt soles? Service guessed that the assailant had stopped here and watched Ficorelli come across the river and begin fishing upstream. Eventually the hung fly offered opportunity.

Service took some tissue paper out of his pocket, broke off a stick, pushed it in the ground, and attached the tissue to it like a small flag. He continued backtracking across a cedar swamp, past an old bear-bait site, and up a gentle slope to a two-track turnaround. The whole area was covered with thigh-deep ferns, but he moved cautiously and used a stick to part the ferns until he saw something near where some vehicles had turned around. Wading boots, shorts, a vest, and a nylon shirt were on the ground beneath the ferns, and from what he could see, there was no obvious blood. He used sticks to mark the spot and tried to estimate how far from the kill site he was. Maybe another half-mile, which meant he was close to a mile and a half from the dump site, and close to two miles from the FBI camp. Had the feds checked the two-track in front of him, and if not, *why* not?

He hiked back through the lengthening shadows of the cedar swamp and started toward the camp, and along the way met Bobbi Temple coming toward him. Service nodded for her to follow, led her to the print and explained his theory, and then took her through the swamp and showed her the clothing.

"Did your people check out this road?"

"Have to ask Tatie," she said. "I spent most of my time at the dump site."

She was on the radio as he approached the old bear bait.

He heard Agent Temple's voice behind him, asking, "Where do you think you're going?"

He didn't bother to answer her. The FBI reeked of incompetence. He had no time or desire to slow down and pull the feds along with him.


Sheriff Arnie Thorkaldsson was in his cramped office with his long legs and huge boots propped up on a desk glider. "Monica back too?" the sheriff asked.

"Just me."

"We ought to be announcing this thing," the sheriff said. "This delay is outrageous."

"It's the FBI's case," Service said.

"You must have your own opinion . . . or have they brainwashed you?"

"I've got one, but it carries the same weight as yours."

"The feds make us locals feel like tits on a boar."

"They do the same to state types," Service said. "Do you mind if we run through the timelines of that night?"

"Be my guest," Thorkaldsson said. "I can't get it out of my mind."

"What time were you supposed to meet?"

"Nineish. The hatches don't get started till closer to dark, but I got held up on a traffic deal and I was a little late."

"How late?"

"Forty-five minutes or so."

"Were you always late and him always early?"

"No, he was usually the late one." Service made a mental note.

"Why'd you go to the old bridge ford?"

"We always met there," Thorkaldsson said. "Like I told you earlier, he always came up from the south and parked across the river. Probably superstitious. We always had good luck there, and you know how luck and fishing get joined at the hip."

*No doubt,* Service thought. If Thorkaldsson suspected anything about Ficorelli's dalliances with the Andreesen woman, he wasn't letting on.

"Good a reason to park there as any," Service said.

"Only reason, ask me. Easier to get to the river from my side, and we could close the gate behind us." The sheriff stared at Service. "This thing's bigger'n Wayno, isn't it?"

"I can't say," Service said, feeling guilty. It was wrong to hide information from other police agencies.

"How long are you gonna hang with this boondoggle?"

"That's what I'm trying to figure out," Service said.

"You need anything, just sing out. We don't have much manpower here—and not much need for it—but I swear I'd personally give Madison an enema with a fire hose to help find Wayno's killer."

"Okay if I tie up one of your phones?"

Thorkaldsson stood up and stretched. "Use mine. Dial eight to get an outside line," he said from the doorway. "I'm gonna go up the street and grab supper at the Puddin-Et-Pi. My sister-in-law owns the place."

The phone in a Detroit law office was answered on the first ring. "Grady Service calling. Is Shamekia available?"

"I'll see if she is, sir."

Shamekia Cilyopus-Woofswshecom was an ex-FBI special agent turned attorney, her last name so strange as to be unpronounceable by earthlings. Why the hell she didn't change it, Service didn't know, but people were kind of strange about their names, and what did it really matter? Most people who knew her didn't attempt her last name, simply calling her Shamekia.

His friend Tree had introduced him to her, and she had helped him solve a couple of complex cases.

"Ah, the intrepid woods cop," she greeted him. "How's life in Michissippi, Grady?"

A black Detroit politician had labeled the U.P. this way because of its sparse population and heavy unemployment. "Been better."

"What have you got going this time?"

He took her through the case, ending with the possibility of some sort of trial-run killings.

"Lord Almighty," the attorney said. "VICAP didn't spit out anything?"

VICAP was the FBI's Violent Criminal Apprehension Program. All police agencies were supposed to enter their local violent-crime data so all the information could be searched by any police officer anywhere. He wondered if the DNR filed its data in the system, and if so, who handled it.

"I don't know, and I don't know exactly what they did or how or when; I'm just wondering if there's something that was missed."

"You know," she said, "some cops call it VICRAP for a reason."

"Really?"

"Yeah, it's a monster, and it's easy to miss something; or are you coming at this from a different angle than the Bureau?"

"Case myopia," he said.

She clucked. "Uh-huh. Linkage blindness happens to all of us at one time or another. You let yourself get going on certain leads or angles and you can't let loose even when it's obvious you're not getting anywhere."

"Something like that," he said.

"What exactly are you looking for?"

"If I knew exactly, this wouldn't be so hard. Several questions come to mind: Has this blood eagle thing been used anywhere at any time? Or have there been killings with edged weapons that are sort of bizarre and ritualistic? And not just game warden victims, any cases."

"Anywhere in the whole country?"

"Hell, anywhere in the solar system."

"Some sort of geographic starting point, at least; location of the first killing or something along that line?"

He tried to remember the state where the first murder had taken place, but he couldn't. "Let me call you back on that."

"Never mind," she said. "There's enough in the way of unique factors here to get me rolling. I'll be back at you if I find something. You got your cell phone with you?" She paused and added, "You understand that the system has flaws? Some local agencies, especially in cities, don't enter all their current cases, and a lot of them don't have the funding or enough trained people to go back and log the old cases. The program started up in 1985, and most agencies have lagged behind since the beginning. VICAP is a great tool when it works, but win or lose, it's always a crapshoot."

"Thanks, Shamekia."

She laughed and said, "Stay safe," before breaking the connection.

Service called Chief Lorne O'Driscoll, who answered his own phone.

"Service."

"Are you still in Wisconsin?"

"Just back from Missouri," Service said.

"What the heck is going on?"

Service described the cases and imagined he could hear the chief's blood pressure rising.

"Forty-nine officers?"

"Yessir."

"Grady, I don't know what crap they're shoveling at you, but no such list came out of here, certainly not without my knowing. I'm telling you I would *never* release such a list unless the FBI director himself was standing here in my office holding a gun to my head—and even then the chances would be fifty-fifty."

"My name is on the list, Chief."

*"Dammit!"* Lorne O'Driscoll exploded.

"Sir, I'm thinking we ought to at least alert our people."

"You let me worry about that," the chief said.

"And sir, it was the FBI who asked the Wisconsin secretary of state to request me from Governor Timms. You want me to stay?"

"Why did the FBI do this?"

"Partly to protect me, but beyond that I'm not sure." There was something else, his gut told him, but so far he couldn't get a nail into it.

"Do what you think you have to do, Detective. List, my ass," O'Driscoll muttered with disgust before hanging up.

Service walked over to the main drag to join the sheriff at the Puddin-Et-Pi.

Thorkaldsson greeted him as he sat down, "You've got the look of a man with fresh dog shit on the soles of his brand-new church shoes."

"Did you call the FBI when you found Wayno?"

"No reason to call the feds out of the gate," Thorkaldsson said. "I got my people in to secure the site and called the Wispies. We rarely get homicides in this county, but when we do, I call the state first."

"You don't know who contacted the feds?" Service asked.

"Not me is all I know. I assume it was the state," said Thorkaldsson.

"When did the feds come in?"

"Monica was about an hour behind the Wispies, and her people swooped in an hour after that and took over," said Thorkaldsson. "The Wispies musta known the FBI was coming because they just stood around and waited with their thumbs up their keesters."

Service asked, "Special Agent Monica strike you as competent?"

The sheriff shook his head slowly and said, "Define competent."

Service drove back to the encampment near the crime scene, hoping Shamekia would come up with some answers. Had the feds missed something? This was more than possible, he knew; the Bureau was the same outfit that knew some jerkwads from the Middle East were taking flight lessons with more interest in takeoffs than in landings, and did nothing about it. Shit happened in bureaucracyland; investigators blinded themselves with their own assumptions, and it didn't hurt to question everything, even with an agency with more assets than God.

In his experience the FBI and other government agencies tended to reach for an ICBM when a bottle rocket might better do the job. Maybe they had handled this just fine, but he needed to know, and so far what he was seeing was way below his own standards. Back at the camp he walked into a clearing, opened his cell phone, got three bars, and punched in Father O'Brien's number.

"OB here," the priest answered.

"Service."

"I gather you're okay," O'Brien said.

"I guess I deserve that," Service said. "But I got called out of state on a case and I haven't been back yet. Call my captain."

"I already did," the priest said. "I wasn't being sarcastic."

"Do you remember a psychology student from your days at Marquette?"

"Does she have a name?"

"Last name is Monica."

"Ah," the priest said. "The indomitable Tatie. Sure, I knew her."

"What can you tell me about her?"

"Why do you ask?"

"I can't say."

"Pretty good student, hardworking, strictly out for herself, which is normal for students seeking higher degrees. What's she doing now?"

"She's an FBI agent."

"That doesn't surprise me," O'Brien said. "She had a strong interest in abnormal psychology and did a couple of insightful papers on serial killers." There was a pause. "Is *this* about a serial killer?"

"I can't say."

O'Brien remembered her. Good student. He felt disappointed, wanted to hear something else, only he wasn't sure what. "Aren't most students in PhD programs supposed to be more than pretty good?"

Long pause. "She was superb at memorizing facts but less strong at analysis."

"In what way?"

"She'd get a notion into her head and not let go, even when her approach was clearly wrong."

"Yet she got her doctorate."

"She qualified. I was sure she'd never make it in a practice, but in the context of the FBI or a large organization, she'd do okay."

"She did papers on serial killers?"

"Borderline obsession for her."

"You remember which ones?"

"Sorry; it's been a long time, and I had a lot of students. My memory isn't so good anymore."

"Anything else you can tell me about her?"

"I remember that she had a tendency to rely more on instinct than empirical data, and sometimes she tried to stretch miminal data beyond its inherent value to support her position."

"That's it?"

"Martin Grolosch," O'Brien said. "He was a killer in Wisconsin in the 1920s. He got caught by some people up near Hurley and they hung him before the authorities could intervene."

"She was interested in Grolosch?"

"Like I said, it was close to an obsession."

"Any idea why?"

"Sorry. Something about a minister in Rhinelander who hung himself."

"I don't get it," Service said.

"Me either," the priest said.

"So . . . ," Tatie Monica said from the trees. "The prodigal son."

Service stepped toward her. "I talked to my chief. He says there's never been a Michigan list and he sure as hell didn't talk to you."

"Semantics," she said. "There are lots of roads to the same destination."

"You want me here for something more than protecting me," he said.

"We'll talk about it."

"When—after my lungs are pulled out my back?"

He was not surprised when she didn't follow him.

The eastern sky was hinting azure when Service stepped into Tatie Monica's tent with two cups of coffee from the camp urn. She was asleep, an arm draped over her face, snoring a steady buzz.

He sat down beside her. "Wake up."

She answered with a snort.

"Coffee," he said.

She removed her arm and looked up at him. "I hate this outdoor shit," she said.

"You're not outdoors. You're in a tent."

Tatie Monica winced as she swung her legs off the cot and pushed herself up. She was wearing running shorts and rumpled gray T-shirt. Service held out a cup.

"What?" she asked.

"Too many question marks," he said. "The only constant in this thing has been inconsistency."

"You see what I've been living with for three years," she said. "Consistency is the hobgoblin of small minds. I don't remember who said that."

"From where I stand you look like the vector of inconsistency."

"I said I've made mistakes. You haven't?"

"I try to fix mine."

"Must be nice to have a job that lets you," she countered.

"Where did the list come from?"

"I had our field agents talk to game wardens."

"That's not exactly a scientific sample."

"Fuck science," she said. "It's vastly overrated."

"Did you even try to approach state agencies?"

"A few, but they stonewalled me."

"So you gathered the names based on gossip."

"Don't give me any shit," she said. "How many of you in Michigan?"

"One eighty or so in the field, two forty overall."

"In an operation that size, everybody knows who the go-to guy is. All cops keep track; you know that: who's good, who's a liability. Walk into a New York or Detroit police precinct and every officer can tell you who their top cop is, so don't preach to me about science. The point is that the killer has validated the list by his actions. He's hitting only the top people."

"Except in Missouri."

"Spargo was the control. The conclusion stands."

"You let a man die."

"Your long-term 'violets' don't know how to use the system against you? This guy sure seems to know ours. He crosses jurisdictions and uses time and geography to his advantage. The fact that we even found the first group is close to a miracle. The biggest problem we have sometimes is getting local agencies to cooperate with us. They want to hold on to their cases, can't see beyond what they've got. I suppose you've never held things back from other agencies?"

"It's a two-lane road. You're not telling them more, so they go with what they know."

"Bullshit. The real problem is elected law enforcement personnel. They all want merit badges for their next election."

He agreed, but this was off the point. He needed for her to focus. "How did you find the pattern in the first group?"

"VICAP," she said.

"You mean VICRAP?" he countered. "I'm told it's not particularly useful in cases before 1985, and the older the case, the greater the crapshoot."

Monica paused before responding. "That's partially true," she said. "But rural areas are pretty good about loading their cases. It's mostly the cities that seem to lag, and where have our killings taken place? Not in cities. VICAP has its weaknesses and its critics, but it did the job this time."

"Who actually found the first group?"

She took a sip of coffee before answering. "Micah Yoder."

"A Milwaukee buddy?"

"Why are you asking this? You going to redo all of our work, check on us twice, like Santy Claus?"

"Your idea for me to ask questions."

"Micah's not just a computer geek, he's an analyst, and VICAP was only one source. There are half a dozen other national databases. Do you think I made this up?" Her voice was rising.

"I'm trying to focus and get up to speed. You brought me in blind and the light hasn't been fast in coming."

"Okay," she said. "Let me back up. Micah *is* a computer nerd, but he's also more than that . . . a lot more. I've known him for ten years, and he can always find what I can't."

"Like tying your Houston killer to LA?"

"Know how we learned he was in LA?"

Service didn't answer.

"The Houston killer took credit cards but never used them. We assumed he threw them away. But a Houston vick's card popped up in LA, and Micah was the only one who caught it. We checked all the suspects for the date and all but one had an alibi, and that one couldn't be found in Houston anymore. He'd blown town. I took the suspect's photo to the store that processed the card, the clerk made a positive ID, and the LAPD helped us take it from there."

"Quite a story," Service said. He didn't point out that if Houston agents had been keeping close tabs on all their serious suspects, they would have known the man was gone. Still, it was pretty good police work.

"In our business, networking supports luck," she said. "You find good people and maintain relationships. They help you, you help them."

"Any chance I can talk to Yoder?"

"Why?"

"Maybe I can use him for my network," he said sarcastically.

"You really can be an asshole when you set your mind to it."

"I haven't even tried yet," he said. "I just want to understand how he did this."

"Micah's pretty hard to see."

"He works, right?"

"Not regular hours."

"The FBI allows this for its staff people?"

"I never said he worked *for* the Bureau. I said he's an analyst and he's out of Detroit."

"Has Yoder worked with Bonaparte?"

"Micah works alone."

"You mean he freelances for you. The Bureau allows agents to use outside analysts?"

"You're suddenly an expert on Bureau culture and procedures?"

"The woman your boys talked to about being with the guy on the four-wheeler by the river that night?"

"What about her?"

"She and Ficorelli had a thing."

"A thing?"

"A seven-year thing."

"Jesus," she said, "how did you learn that?"

"I talked to her, showed her Ficorelli's photo."

"And she just spit it out?"

"More or less. Your people talked to her, but it was just about seeing strangers on the road or in the area. Ficorelli wasn't a stranger. He left her place at 4 p.m. the day he was killed. She didn't want to talk, but I convinced her, and I told her that her husband didn't need to know."

"How did you suspect?"

"You said it the night I got here—that Ficorelli was a pathological ass-man with a penchant for married women. He's been coming here for years, same time every year, parking in the same spot. There was a chance there was more to it than fishing. The real question is why you didn't think of the possible connection and see to it that your people showed the woman his photograph."

"That's damn impressive investigative work," she said.

"Martin Grolosch," he said.

Tatie Monica looked at him and blinked. "What did you say?"

"Martin Grolosch and Rhinelander."

"What about him?"

"You tell me."

She drained her coffee, obviously trying to collect her thoughts. "Grolosch was from Rhinelander. My grandfather went off to the war in 1941. My grandmother hung herself while he was gone. He didn't know until after the war because he was a POW. When he came back and found out, he hung himself in the same tree."

"Sad story," Service said. "Why did your grandmother kill herself?"

"Martin Grolosch was her son by her first husband. She and my grandfather never believed Martin was a killer. But Grandmother started to do some renovations in their house and discovered a cache of papers—things Martin had written about what he had done. He killed fourteen women before he got caught. Grandmother couldn't live with what her son had done."

"Your interest in Grolosch is personal."

"Personal and professional," she said quickly. "My brother Lance hung himself at fifteen, and afterward my parents discovered he had been torturing small animals. This is a typical finding in the background of a serial. It was really sick, and I started wondering if there's a genetic component to serial murder; you know, if it runs in families."

"You wondered if your brother would have become a monster."

"Yes," she said.

This cinched it for him: Tatie Monica was damaged goods and had no business running the team. "I've done about everything I can do here," Service said. "I'm heading home."

"There's a target on your back," she said as he started to get up.

He turned and looked down at her. "No, I'm the strike dog," he said.

"Who's the pack backing you?" she asked.

"I wonder the same thing," he said. "But don't bother coming to the U.P. to protect me."

"There are forty-nine dead game wardens," she said, "some of them the best in their state, and they couldn't avoid it. What makes you different?"

"I know the asshole's out there," he said. "And if some of those dead men had known, this might have put an end to this shit a long time ago."

He walked out. He was done listening to her. He had a high quotient for bullshit, but some of what she said was right. Networking was key, and he had his own to tap into.

It was time to go home, sort things out there, and get ready. Tatie Monica was chasing personal demons. He was going to hunt a killer who did not yet know he was the prey.

## 25

## FOSTER CITY, MICHIGAN
## MAY 31, 2004

For one of the few times in his life Grady Service found himself at a loss for exactly what to do—both professionally and personally. How many times had he reached for the cell phone to talk to Nantz, only to remember she was no longer there? Where was home, and *what* was it? Him, a giant dog, and a surly cat?

He pulled into the lot of the Mill Town Inn. He needed caffeine and time to think. The inn was a converted house about forty-five miles west of Escanaba. Swedish pancakes were the specialty, the atmosphere quiet, and it was run by an ex-marine and retired Saginaw homicide detective named Barratt, who was called Toe Tag by most of his cop friends.

Gaudy white and yellow flowers bloomed in beds below the front porch; others climbed vines on a green trellis. The scents of lilac and Russian olive perfumed the small yard.

There were two narrow dining rooms in the old house, single white flowers in small red bud vases, and the work of local landscape painters framed on the walls. Barratt Adams saw him and immediately brought coffee. "Haven't seen much of you recently."

"I've been here and there," Service said.

"Got a big brown last night at dusk on a brown drake. You gonna ask where?"

"A man needs to keep some secrets," Service said.

"Semper Fi. Yell when you're ready for chow."

Service was staring at his cup when he felt someone watching and looked up to see a small, wiry man in a blue blazer, white shirt, and narrow red tie. He stared at the man for a moment before it dawned on him. "Allerdyce?"

"I seen youse sittin' dere makin' eye-holes in dat coffee. Youse got tea leaves or chicken guts in dere, sonny?"

Limpy eased his scrawny frame into a chair and grinned.

Service had never seen him with teeth before. "Suit, teeth, clean-shaven, no ponytail. Very spiffy."

The old poacher cackled. "Hunt turkey, youse gotta wear camo, am I right, sonny?"

Allerdyce was prone to strange pronouncements that seemed like bizarre non sequiturs, but the old man rarely spoke without intending to convey a message. His crude ways made him seem stupid and ignorant to a lot of people, but Service knew better.

Allerdyce nodded toward the cash register. Service saw an attractive woman, fortyish, in shorts, platform sandals, and a turquoise tank top. "I'm poppin' dat," the old poacher croaked, making a fist.

She looked well groomed and light years away from Limpy's class. "Is she blind?" Service asked, making the old man scowl. Limpy's prodigious sexual appetite and reputation were legendary, but this woman? Not possible.

"I got what she wants," Allerdyce said. "Youse an' me got no more bullshit between us, eh."

"Where are you living?"

"Where I always been," the man said.

The woman came over to the table and stood beside the poacher with her hand on his shoulder. "Introductions, Andrew?"

"Dis here's DNR Detective Service."

*Andrew?* Service stifled a grin. Even the man's rap sheet listed him as Limpy.

The woman extended her hand. "*You're* the one. I'm Joan Pillars." She had a soft voice and a firm handshake. "Andrew has told me a lot about you."

"She's a schoolteacher up da college," Limpy added.

"Visiting professor from North Carolina–Wilmington," she said by way of amplification. "I've been at Northern since the first of May. It's a one-year appointment." Her accent was from the Northeast, maybe Maine, Service thought.

"Writin' her a book," Limpy said with a toothy grin that unnerved Service.

"About over-the-hill poachers or broke-down paroled felons?" Service said.

Limpy protested. "I'm retired, not over no bloody hill."

"But still a paroled felon," Service said.

"Actually, the subject is rural crime and the public's widespread lack of recognition," the woman interjected. "Perhaps you would have some time to talk to me," she added. She slid a business card onto the table, took out a ballpoint pen, and wrote something on the back.

Service ignored it. "I'm kind of busy," he said.

"Told youse," Allerdyce said. "Da boy ain't much on makin' social da way 'is ole man was."

The woman started for the door and Limpy got up and leaned over. "She's a screamer, dat one. Be seein' youse, sonny."

"Whatever you say, *Andrew*. You hear Honeypat's back in the U.P.?" Gus had not yet confirmed this for him, but Service wanted to see the old man's reaction.

Allerdyce stared at him. "Where?"

Service shrugged. "Just a rumor. If I confirm it, I'll get in touch."

Allerdyce frowned as he followed the woman out the door, turned around, and came back. "I'm real sorry about your gal."

Barratt came over to the table. "You decided?"

"Stack of Swedes. Keweenaw lingonberry jam?"

"You bet, but Dottie put back some chokecherry jelly last fall."

"Make it Dottie's," Service said. Dottie was Toe Tag's wife, a local girl, the chef for the restaurant, and manager of the two-room guesthouse. Toe Tag provided the capital and did odd jobs for her between fishing trips.

"I'll tell 'er."

"Grab a cup and join me."

The retired cop came back with a cup and two giant apple fritters. "Some habits don't break easy," he said sheepishly, offering the plate to Service, who held up a hand.

"Who's the woman with Limpy?"

"Professor of some kind. They've been in a couple of times. He tell you he's getting that?"

"He says that about every woman," Service said.

"I don't buy it with this one. Gotta say, though, she sure cleaned him up good." Allerdyce was well known for his less than enthusiastic or consistent personal hygiene.

"He says he's living back at the compound."

"Maybe he rebuilt," Barratt said. "His bunch isn't exactly the sort to broadcast their news."

"The clan scattered after the compound burned."

"Not that far, I'd think. That old man's got an eerie hold on them, like a black hole always pulling the rest of his universe toward him."

"His hold on Honeypat didn't seem too firm," Service said. Honeypat was the daughter-in-law who had tried to take over the clan.

Barratt grinned. "Exceptions to every rule. The hell of it is, I kind of like old Limpy. I imagine you might have a different take."

Service didn't reply. The truth was that with all of Allerdyce's disgusting ways, he sometimes got a perverse kick out of the old man. He just didn't understand or trust him. "How long were you in homicide?"

"Fourteen years," Barratt said. "It took about fifteen minutes to adjust to retirement. I saw enough dead bodies for several people, let alone one worn-out old cop."

"Did your department use VICAP?"

"Ate from it more than we fed it. The entry process wasn't that easy, and we never had enough people or money to spend the time."

"But a good tool?"

"Better now than then. They've simplified data entry over the years. Nowadays if you have a hot case, they have the staff at NCAVC jump on it quick. It will get better, but it works now."

"Did you ever catch any serial murder cases?"

Barratt smirked. "Hey, we had druggies whacking homeboy competitors like they were cockroaches on their mama's birthday cake, but these weren't the sort of serials the Feebs got off on. Most of our body count was domestic or drug-related. Our dealers were small fish on the fantail of the Chicago-Detroit-Flint supply ship. Why the interest?"

"We're never too old to learn."

Barratt laughed. "You and Allerdyce: Neither of you ask questions without purpose. You hear the president's coming?"

"Which one?"

"Dubya," the retired cop said. "Marquette, next month. He'll be the first sitting president in the U.P. since Taft in 1911."

The president coming to Marquette? So what? It wouldn't have any effect on him.

After breakfast he dropped the woman's card in the trash by the register but found another one under his windshield wiper. The woman had scribbled, "I'm very persistent!" She had added a smiley face. He loathed smiley faces.

He looked at the card. It read: Joan Pillars, PhD, Professor of Criminology, University of North Carolina at Wilmington. He stuck the card under the sun visor, opened his cell phone, and called the Marquette office.

Captain Grant's formidable door guard, Fern LeBlanc, answered. "It's Grady. Is he in?"

"One moment, please."

"Detective," the captain greeted him. "The chief has briefed me."

"Has the word gone out?"

"Not yet. The chief and I want to meet with you."

"The word needs to get out yesterday, Cap'n. What this guy does to people is not pretty."

"Tomorrow afternoon in my office, sixteen hundred hours?"

"The chief will be *here* tomorrow?"

"He'll be here for a security meeting at noon."

"The Bush visit?"

Heavy silence from Grant. "Where did you hear that? It's not been announced yet, and the trip is only tentative."

"Toe Tag Barratt."

The captain said in his faint southern drawl, "The Secret Service is going to have its hands full up here."

U.P. residents didn't like being fenced in or herded by the government, even one they had elected.

"Tomorrow at four, Cap'n."


He started driving east on M-69 toward Escanaba, checked his cell phone for a signal, and called Gus Turnage.

"Were you able to confirm that thing with Honeypat?"

"The judge saw her at the casino in Baraga. She was wearing a wig, but he's sure it was her. He had her in his court a couple of times. He tried to talk to her but she pretended to be someone else. I talked to the captain right after he got off the phone with you, and he's going to put out a BOLO to all of our people."

"Thanks, Gus."

"Where are you?"

"Heading for home."

"You got something working?"

"I'll talk to you later."

Honeypat would have a reason to hurt him through Nantz and Walter, but Ficorelli and Spargo also had close relatives killed in auto accidents not long before they died. Was Honeypat Allerdyce the only possibility? If it was her, it had nothing to do with the serial killings. Or did it? Her reappearance only complicated things.

## 26

## SLIPPERY CREEK, MICHIGAN

## MAY 31, 2004

He dropped his gear and bags inside the front door, surveyed his cabin, and saw it for what it was: a wooden shell, not a house—and certainly not a home. But he couldn't think how he could change it, or why he should bother. It had always been adequate, and would be again.

He gathered his clothes and took them to the laundry in a small room off the back porch and mudroom. He loaded the washer, poured in some detergent, set the dials, and started the load. He looked around for Cat and Newf but couldn't find them. Eventually he found a note on his refrigerator from McCants, saying she had taken them to her place. He had been gone longer than he had expected. He hadn't really thought about the logistics of McCants coming by each day, twice a day, to let Newf out. He should have suggested she take them in the first place. He wasn't thinking things through.

He considered calling McCants and picking up his animals but decided not to. The animals were safe and that's all that mattered. What else was he overlooking?

A serial killer was out there, and he was the next victim on the list. For a fleeting moment he thought of locking the cabin door. It would have been ridiculous. He never had before and he wouldn't begin now. The killer would be waiting for him in the woods. That's how he worked. And Service would be ready for him.

## 27

## MARQUETTE, MICHIGAN

### JUNE 1, 2004

If the best part of being a detective was not wearing a uniform every day, the worst was spending time in a cookie-cutter cubicle in the DNR's regional office. Most Wildlife Resources Protection unit detectives operated out of home offices, but Captain Grant insisted on Service putting in a regular appearance in Marquette, probably because the captain wanted to keep track of him. As a CO, Service had for years operated out of his truck and Slippery Creek Camp, and had been accountable primarily to sergeants, who largely had left him alone. He had never been one to need or welcome a lot of direction and supervision.

He waved at Fern LeBlanc on the way to his cubicle, stopped, and pulled his mail out of his box. He went to the copier room, made copies of the FBI reports, and went back to his office and turned on his computer. While it was booting up, he checked his voice-mail messages. One was from Joan Pillars. *Who the hell?* Then he remembered: Limpy's alleged squeeze. She had left a card and note in the restaurant, stuck another under his windshield wiper, and now, here was a phone call. She said she was persistent and it appeared she was true to her word. He decided he'd call her back if he had time—just to get her off his back.

Fern LeBlanc appeared in his cubicle. "They're ready for you."

Service checked his watch: 3 p.m. "The meeting's not until four."

"Things change," she said. "They're waiting."

"Sounds like I'm in trouble," he joked.

"Familiar terrain for you," she said, but her tone suggested she was joking. *Weird,* he thought. The woman had never liked him. But even Fern was treating him differently since the accident. *Not an accident!* He quickly corrected himself.

"On my way," he said, gathering his folders.

Captain Ware Grant and Chief Lorne O'Driscoll were sitting in the captain's office, which looked out on distant Lake Superior. The lake was lit by the sun, and a gentle breeze made it look like it was pocked with diamonds.

The captain pointed to a chair at the table with the chief and remained behind his desk. Service gave one set of records to the chief and the other to the captain. "Coffee?"

"Buzz Fern," the captain said, opening his folder.

"I'll get it," Service said.

"I could have done that," Fern said as he filled three cups in the canteen. "You don't need to do my job for me."

"Sorry," he said. So much for joking. Nothing he did, it seemed, met with Fern's approval. She scowled and walked away.

The chief looked up when he returned. "Ficorelli's death was announced last night," he said. "No details, no date, and only an approximate location. It's being called a homicide. Why such a long delay?"

"The Feebs found their first kill site there. They wanted to protect it. I argued for a release to encourage tips." He didn't tell the captain or chief he had been the one to find the kill site.

Captain Grant said, "The bureau loathes media attention unless they want to tell a story that will benefit them."

The chief glared at one of the photos of the mutilated wardens, tapped it on the table, and shook his head. No words came out and Service understood. The photos were enough to turn the stomach of the most callous lawman.

The three men sat in lugubrious silence. Service sensed they were as much at a loss of where to start as he was. Finally, Chief O'Driscoll spoke. "Do you believe the FBI arranged to have you in Wisconsin to shield you?"

"They admitted as much," Service said.

The captain asked, "If you had been the victim, would they have brought Ficorelli or the other man in to protect them?"

Service hadn't considered this angle, and wondered why the captain had asked it, and if he was trying to make a point. "I don't know," he said. Elray Spargo was their control, which had doomed him. "It's down to one state now." Why Spargo and not him or Ficorelli as the control? Pure luck, he guessed.

"I called Director Mueller in Washington," Chief O'Driscoll said. "He is somewhat familiar with the case, but I believe he knows nothing about the list or the Missouri control angle. I told him we'll request assistance if we need it to protect our own, but it's our intent to handle this ourselves."

"He agreed?"

"He said they have to bring a team here as an adjunct of the presidential security detail, so they'll be available. I think that's his way of telling us to expect them to be around."

*Great,* Service thought.

"The Bureau has resources we don't," the captain said, playing devil's advocate.

"Which have gotten them nowhere," the chief said. "This is our problem." O'Driscoll looked into Service's eyes. "We have to assume you're the target, but I intend to brief all officers. Captains will brief lieutenants and sergeants, and together they will meet with all personnel in each district."

"What about leaks?" Service asked.

"There will be no leaks," the chief said. "I will tell our people about the killings and what we know, but you will not be identified as the possible target. We want all officers on their toes, and all officers up here will be asked to exercise extreme caution in riverine environments. We'll continue solo patrols, but backup is to be called in if any officer encounters *anything* that seems unusually suspicious or out of place."

Service wondered how many officers would take the chief's advice to heart. Most of them tended to be self-reliant, stubborn, and not easily intimidated. "Will you show them a photo? Asking for caution is one thing; seeing the reality is a whole other thing."

The chief looked over at the captain, who nodded agreement.

"How do you propose to handle your situation?" the chief asked. "Are you pulling yourself off the FBI team?"

Did he have that option? "I haven't thought it through yet. I called a contact in Detroit. She's using her sources to go through the VICAP data. Agent Waco, the warden I worked with in Missouri, thinks it's possible that there's more than one perp—that even in targeting specific individuals, wardens are difficult to track. Considerable preparation would be essential."

"Why VICAP?"

"Two groups of killings. The MO varies throughout the first group. But the blood eagle is a constant in only the most recent killings in the second group, and the location near water is the same for both groups. There was a method change in the last few, and the feds don't understand why, or what it means. Given the complexity of the blood eagle, I think it's possible the perp gave the method a test run—maybe on civilians. The Feebs claim VICAP led them to both groups. I thought I should go back and see exactly what it gave them." He said nothing about Tatie Monica's non-FBI analyst.

"VICAP should have turned up something," the chief said.

"You'd think," Service said. "I didn't know much about VICAP before this, and what I've learned so far is that it has more wrinkles than a cheap suit. It's not unreasonable to expect that something has been missed, something small but significant."

"We're not going to lecture you on caution," the chief said.

"I hear you," Service replied. "Everybody's going to be uptight about this. I want to keep working my sources. This guy is methodical, and method implies routine, which suggests predictability. There's got to be something we're not seeing."

Service thought about sharing information about the fly he had found, and the coincidental deaths that might or might not be linked to the killings, but he decided he didn't have enough information to make sense and kept quiet. Besides, he had stuck the fly in his pocket and forgotten to turn it over to the FBI for evidence.

After O'Driscoll departed for Lansing, Captain Grant said, "The FBI pulled you under their wings for more than protection. They were buying time to get their act together. Understood?"

"It's occurred to me that they want me to be their bait," Service said.

"Where's the ideal spot to place bait?"

"Where the predator expects to find it."

"Does such a place come to mind?" the captain asked.

"Several."

"Good. When you're ready, let me know."

"I'm thinking the more sources I reach out to, the better off we are."

"I agree," the captain said. "I'll do the same."

"Do you want me to check in with O'Brien?"

"Not necessary," the captain said. "He's a good man and will help you only if you need it. You *are* all right, yes?"

"I'm good to go, Captain." But he wasn't convinced, himself. "Cap'n," he added, "You talked to Gus about Honeypat Allerdyce?"

The captain nodded. "I put out a BOLO. Are you thinking there is a connection between the woman's return and Nantz's death?"

"You know her background. We can't rule it out, and there's another reason for revisiting the accident." He explained about Ficorelli's mother, Spargo's sister, and the timing.

The captain made notes, looked up, and pointed with his pen. "I'll follow up with the Troops. You make sure to keep your mind on *you*."

Wayno Ficorelli's memorial was held in an old firehouse-turned-community-meeting-room in Jefferson, the town where he'd lived with his mother. While the service had involved mostly family members, Service and three Wisconsin wardens were included.

The way Wayno died had left everyone pensive. It was one thing to be killed in the performance of duty and another to be slaughtered like a pig. The public had not been told about the mutilations, but the family of the victim and his fellow wardens knew.

There was a reception at the Ficorelli house, a mile north of Jefferson, after the burial. Marge Ciucci, Ficorelli's aunt, was in charge. She had obviously been cooking for several days. She was effusive and friendly, circulating like a dervish, making sure her guests were overfed and comfortable. At one point she came over to Grady Service: "You're staying tonight, yes?"

"Thought I'd head back to Michigan."

"Nonsense," she said. "You're staying. We need to talk, you and me."

Service thought she had the voice of an angel and the eyes of hangman.

When the last guests were gone, Marge Ciucci took him to a small out-building. It was filled with fly-fishing equipment and tying materials. The walls held more than a dozen impressive brook trout mounts.

"It was Wayno's plan when he retired to open a fly shop up north," she said. Over the years he and my sister bought several fine properties on good rivers." She paused and took a deep breath. "He would have wanted you to have some of his gear," she said. "He'd want the sheriff to have his rods. I'm giving you all his flies; there are boxes and boxes of them."

"I can't do that," Service said.

"Plus the gear the FBI has," she added. "When they release that, I'll send it to you. He thought you were the best," the dead man's aunt said, "and he had a high opinion of himself, that boy."

Service sensed the woman fighting to hold back her emotions.

"So you take all this stuff and load it in your truck; use it in good health and enjoy. Life is too short."

"I don't know what to say," Grady Service said.

"Say you'll get who did this," the old woman said.

It was more than clear in the woman's tone that she was not referring to simply bringing the killer to justice, but something more final.

"The justice system will take care of it," he said.

"The system?" Marge Ciucci said. "*Non me rompere le palle!* In the old country they have other ways to take care of animals like this." Her face tightened into a mask and she hissed, "*Nessuno me lo ficca in culo!*"

Service understood her anger, but not her specific words "I'll do my best."

The old woman reached up, pinched his face, and nodded. "Compari to settle the stomach before we go to bed?"

It was not a question.

In the morning she had coffee waiting and fried three eggs for him. "I'm sorry about last night," she said. "You don't speak Italian and I lost my temper, but you and Wayno are men of the world, and you have a right to know what I said. First, I told you not to break my balls. Then I said *nobody* fucks me up the ass! You catch the *animale* who did this to my nephew and you cut off his balls, *si?*" She made a violent slicing gesture with the side of her hand.

*Definitely not someone he would want to cross,* he thought as he loaded Wayno's boxes of flies into his vehicle.

## 29

## ALLERDYCE COMPOUND,
## SOUTHWEST MARQUETTE COUNTY, MICHIGAN
## JUNE 9, 2004

On the way back to Michigan, Service called the cell phone number that Joan Pillars had left for him. The phone rang interminably and he was about to hang up when she finally answered. "Hello?"

"This is Grady Service."

"*Yes,*" she said, her voice brightening. "The detective. Andrew's friend."

Limpy's friend? He almost laughed out loud. "You said you wanted to talk."

"Not over the phone," she said.

"I'm free this afternoon."

"Oh," she said. "Well, I'm at Andrew's camp today, and tomorrow I'm leaving for North Carolina for a few days."

It was difficult to picture the chic professor in Allerdyce's crude camp in southwest Marquette County. "I'll be there in about three hours, give or take."

There was a two-track off a U.S. Forest Service road down to the compound's parking area, then a half-mile walk along a twisting trail from there into the camp itself. The surrounding area was dense with black spruce, cedars, hemlocks, and tamaracks. He parked and began to make his way along the dark trail on foot.

It was normal to not see a soul en route to or in the compound, but today there were people everywhere in the camp, and Allerdyce himself was seated at a picnic table, freshly shaved, teeth in, grinning. It irked him that neither he nor the old poacher had their real teeth.

"Sonny," he said, "Joanie told me youse was dropping by, but I din't believe her, eh." The old man winked. "She got the gift for sure."

Service had no idea what gift Allerdyce was referring to and didn't care.

Pillars walked out of the old man's cabin, drying her hands on a dish-towel. "Good afternoon, Detective."

Pillars invited him to sit at the table, turned to Allerdyce, and said, "Shoo, Andrew! This is business." Allerdyce laughed his wheezing laugh, got up, and walked through the camp as people came up to him and engulfed him with questions.

The cabin was new, identical to the old one that had burned, though this version had a new metal roof. Other buildings in the compound were under construction, but there were no construction company trucks.

"Andrew's family is doing all the work," Pillars said. "They can do anything."

She was obviously impressed. Service wasn't. "You wanted to talk."

"Yes. I'm writing a book about woods crime. It started out as rural crime, but as I got into the subject I realized that what goes on in the deep woods is a lot more interesting and complex, and I shifted my focus. My publisher doesn't understand how I can find enough to fill a book on the subject, but I could write several if I wanted to. At this point I've talked to a lot of people around the country, but now I want to start shifting gears and get the views of law enforcement."

One of Limpy's grandchildren brought iced tea in tall glasses. The boy wore a Packer chook pulled down over his ears, and a Pistons jersey and shorts that reached almost to his beat-up high-top sneakers, a rural thug in training.

The professor took a sip. "I've interviewed many criminals around the country, but I have to tell you, Andrew is by far the most interesting of them . . . and near as I can tell, he's also been one of the most successful."

"If you don't count his stint in Jackson," Service said.

"Yes, Andrew told me about that. He said it was an accident that you got shot. He still feels bad about that."

Service knew better. Limpy Allerdyce had no conscience.

"Andrew genuinely cares about you," the woman said. "You'll never hear it from him, but it's true. He's very old school about not emoting."

Service wanted to say that this was because the only emotions the man had were evil, but he kept this to himself.

"I believe Andrew has changed," Pillars said. "He readily admits to his violent past and says that since he nearly died, he has reevaluated and changed his ways."

Service wanted to laugh out loud. Among his many skills, Limpy was at heart a world-class con man.

"Ah," the professor said. "I can see in your eyes you don't agree. When we undertake to change ourselves drastically from what we once were, people are understandably skeptical."

"Words are cheap and only actions speak, but the truth is that he and his family are no longer poaching or breaking laws," she added. "He has seen the light, and has inculcated the others."

*Bullshit.* Limpy hated the light. He was a creature of darkness, secretive in nature, evil in intent. He and his tribe were cedar swamp savages. "Right," Service said, his voice dripping sarcasm.

"The interesting thing about Andrew is that although he's not formally educated, he is extremely intelligent, and even more than that, he's very clever. He has made a great deal of money in his endeavors, but he has spent only what he's needed for his operations. He chooses to live quite frugally. Do you know that he owns a warehouse in Marquette that's being converted to condos with a view of the city harbor? He's the majority shareholder in the development, and the condos are a thousand square feet and going at a million dollars each. The project was fully subscribed before construction even began," Pillars said.

*Allerdyce in real estate?* Nantz had shown him the development over-looking the old iron dock in Marquette, insisting that the city would be the state's next Traverse City. She claimed that people would flock to the area from California and Texas to buy lake properties, and that in ten years Marquette would be a far different place than it had been. Her prediction had turned his stomach, but she had wealth she never talked about and seemed to understand money at a level he couldn't imagine.

"He owns a great deal of prime property," the professor added.

"He claims."

"Yes, of course, but he authorized me to talk to his accountant, and I have seen proof. Andrew is a man of considerable wealth, which is likely to keep increasing as he moves deeper into development."

There was a picture: Poacher turned developer! Service tried not to laugh. It was just a different facet of the same business, driven by the same values. "What can I do for you?" he asked. The last thing he wanted to do was listen to some professor sing the praises of the worst poacher in the state.

"He really has changed," Pillars repeated. "In fact, if you check with your RAP people, you will find that they have gotten a number of anonymous tips over the past sixty days, and all of them have led to arrests and convictions." RAP (Report All Poaching) was the 800 line to Lansing where people called in infractions. She put a piece of notebook paper on the table. "All the times of the calls are there. Check them out and you'll see. Instead of breaking laws, Andrew's people are helping you and your colleagues enforce them. Who better to help than someone who is an expert on the other end of the process?"

Service shoved the paper into his pocket.

"Crimes vary in their severity," she said. "And criminals vary in the degrees and extents to which they are involved. How do you see the criminals you engage?"

He couldn't believe he was having this conversation, but he was here and he wanted to get it over with. "Most fish and game violations grow out of unchecked common emotions, not evil intent," Service began.

"That's a remarkably enlightened view," the professor said.

"All I can tell you about is my own experience. Some churchgoing, Boy Scout–leading wrench-twister from Flat Rock sees not one, but two eight-point bucks, and before he can sort out his emotions, *bang-bang,* two dead deer and only one permit. Accidental violator."

He plowed on, "Or a woman from Oscoda gets a weekend pass from her old man. She's on the East Branch of the Black River catching trout, nice ones, big ones, eager ones. One, three, five, limit reached—but God, are they ever biting. Geez, I can't quit now. Might never ever have another day like this in my life, and the hubby won't believe me if he doesn't see the evidence. Just this once, I'll take them home, all twenty-two of them, when the limit is five and no more than three over fifteen inches. Out steps the game warden and uh-oh, accidental violator. The fine will be ten bucks for every fish over the limit, and she has a big fine to remind her to follow the law in the future. Most folks are sorry about it and won't do it again. Sometimes we warn them, and sometimes we cite them, but these people are not the ones that cause the real problems."

"But Andrew is different," said Pillars.

"Limpy and his people are in it for one thing—money—and the way to that is wholesale slaughter by whatever method works best. They take jobs for people who want trophies, or they take huge quantities of meat and fish for black-market sales. They will do whatever it takes to get what they want, and they won't stop on their own."

"You're saying they're professionals," she said.

"Right, but there's also another class: the career violators who do it because they like the game between us and them, and like the feeling of getting away with something. Sometimes these people turn violent, but mostly it's just a game, and they take their tickets and pay their fines or do their time and eventually go back to doing what they did before. They're like those folks who pirate cable lines from the neighbor's house, or break the speed limit with radar detectors. They like to see how far they can push the envelope."

"What about subsistence poaching?"

"That goes on," Service said. "But we usually know which people are in need—even the proud ones who won't admit to it. If I catch one of these folks, I usually warn him and let him keep what he has, but I also tell him not to do it again. Later I make sure that when we confiscate game from violators, I deliver it to people who need it."

"But some people would starve without such things."

"Some yes, and some I'm not sure about. A lot of people who need the meat also have the most modern weapons, new trucks, snowmobiles, boats and motors, ATVs, all the toys. The fact is that their per-pound cost is higher for the game they take without licenses or without regard to limits than if they bought it at the local IGA. A lot of people try to pass themselves off as subsistence poachers when really they're in that see-what-we-can-get-away-with group."

The professor was making occasional notes in a small notebook, but mostly checking a small tape recorder sitting on the table. "Are you seeing changes in the kinds and frequency of crimes?"

"It used to be the woods were full of jacklighters and people shooting deer out of season. We don't see as much of that anymore. We see more drugs and timber theft than we used to—probably because lumber costs so much now. The patterns change, but there's usually some fairly apparent reason for it. One of the reasons for decreasing frequencies is that fewer people are hunting and fishing. Not as many kids grow up in the woods anymore, and they never learn how to do it legally, much less consider illegal methods. If they can't do it on a couch with a remote, they aren't interested." His son Walter had loved the outdoors.

"Are you saying the woods are getting more peaceful?" Pillars asked.

"No, the patterns are just changing. Now we see more boozers and druggies lugging around weapons, some legal, some not. More domestic abuse, assault, the same stuff other cops see."

"Do you really believe that people don't change, or that they can't?"

"I hear people claiming to change, but I don't see the actual changes. People will tell a cop what they think a cop wants to hear."

"That's an exceptionally pessimistic view of the human condition," she said.

"Pessimism for a college professor is reality for a woods cop."

"On that uplifting note," she said, turning off the tape recorder.

As he talked to Pillars, Service carefully watched what was going on in the camp. Interview completed, he stood up and stretched. "You claim Limpy has changed," he said, pointing to one of the cabins. "But there's a rifle leaning against that cabin wall, and he's on parole and cannot possess or be around anyone with a firearm. And that red Honda four-wheeler over here doesn't have a registration. If I walked through this camp I could write at least a dozen violations. Limpy claims he's changing? Great. That would be good, but I deal with evidence, not hot air, and maybe you shouldn't either."

Allerdyce came back as they were preparing to leave. "You stayin' for supper, sonny?"

"Gotta move on," Service said.

"Fresh brook trout," the old poacher said, smacking his lips

"And if I looked in your freezer, all you'd have is the daily possession limit, right?"

"Cross my heart," Allerdyce said with a cackle. "Changed my ways, boy."

Service nodded for Limpy to follow, and as they walked away from Pillars he said to the old man, "Honeypat was in Baraga at the casino a while back."

"She's gone," Allerdyce said, his eyes gleaming.

"Gone?" Service asked.

"Moved on; won't never be back."

"You saw her?"

Allerdyce said, "Tell me dis, sonny. How a woman who can fly an airplane crack up a pickup down below Palmer on dry road, eh?"

"The state ruled it an accident."

Allerdyce shook his head.

Service left Limpy and turned back to Pillars. "Tell him the things I pointed out."

Service was certain the poacher would always be out for himself. You could paint a skunk red and call it a fox, but it was still a skunk under the paint job, and he did not like Limpy's tone when he said Honeypat was never coming back, or his question abut Nantz's death.

Back at his car, Service turned his attention to his own concerns. He read the accident report. Then he drove to the regional state police post in Negaunee and talked to a sergeant named Chastain. He had known Chastain casually for many years, but had never worked with the man, who had the reputation of a laid-back straight shooter. "Hey, Chas," Service greeted him after he showed his credentials and was admitted to the operations area.

"Geez, Grady, everybody feels really bad."

"Thanks." Service placed the accident report on the sergeant's desk. "The Troop who handled this, his name is Villemure?"

"Yeah, Fritz. He grew up in Herman."

"He on road patrol today?"

Chastain stood up and looked down into another cubicle. "Hey, Tonia, is Villemure on?"

A female voice said, "Yeah; we show him out by Diorite."

Chastain looked down at Service. "You heard?"

"I'd like to talk to him. Can you ask him to meet me at the Circle in Humboldt?"

"What's your call sign?"

"Twenty Five Fourteen. Say, thirty minutes, if that works for him."

"Tonia, ask Villemure to meet DNR Twenty Five Fourteen at the Circle in Humboldt in thirty minutes."

The Circle was a local stop-and-rob that sold live bait, snacks, deli sandwiches, ammunition, and camping gear. The state police cruiser was already parked in the lot when Service pulled up and went inside.

"Villemure?"

"Twenty Five Fourteen?"

"Grady Service." The two men shook hands. Service bought two coffees from the owner's twenty-something daughter.

"Service," Villemure said. "Geez, that wreck was terrible. I'm sorry."

"Thanks. I wanted to talk to you about it."

"Is there a problem?"

No defensiveness. The kid was straight and all-business, and Service liked him immediately. "Nope; curiosity, mostly. You were first on the scene."

"Yeah. A passerby called the station and Dispatch sent me. I was ten minutes away."

"A passerby; did he stop at the wreck?"

"No. All he said was that a vehicle might be in the ditch."

"It was a man?"

"Yeah."

"Did Dispatch get a tape?"

"I think they tape everything, but I don't know how long they keep the stuff. You'd have to ask. What's up?"

"What was your first impression when you pulled up?"

"It looked bad, and I took my handheld and called for help as I went down the embankment to the truck—is that what you mean?"

"I'm not sure. At some point did you just stand and take in the scene and try to picture what happened in your mind?"

"Yeah, later, after the EMS come."

"And?"

"I don't know."

"This isn't a test, Officer."

"Call me Fritz. Yeah, I don't know. I mean, I looked, and I thought, How the heck did she lose control there? The road was dry and it's banked and it's been resurfaced and it's smooth. I mean, it's not a place generally where people might lose control."

"Did you take that impression and go with it?"

The young Troop looked perplexed. "No witnesses, no survivors; where could I take it?"

"Did you ask about the call-in?"

"Yeah—anonymous, no name."

"Who took the call?"

"Tonia Tonte. She's on Dispatch right now, the one who called me to meet you."

"Thanks, Fritz."

"Is there a problem?"

Most young Troops worried about mistakes and the repercussions of follow-ups.

"No, no problem. Thanks for indulging me."

Service looked over the counter at Tonia Tonte. She had ebony hair with streaks of gray, wore little makeup and small dangling earrings that sparkled in the artificial lighting of the control center. "I'm Service," he said. "About a month back you dispatched Officer Villemure to a wreck down by Palmer. You got a call from a passerby."

"I'm on break in ten minutes," she said. "It's kind of crazy right now. Meet in the break room?"

He agreed, and passed the time by talking to a couple of Troops he knew in the back room, one of them a female undercover from the integrated county drug team.

Tonia Tonte came into the room and poured a cup of coffee from the urn. "You smoke?" she asked. "I can't seem to quit, and by the time breaks roll around, I'm climbing the walls."

They stepped outside. She opened her small purse and took out a pack of Salems. He lit her cigarette for her.

"That night," she began, "I never said the caller was a passerby, and he never said it, but you know how things get started."

"You have caller ID?"

"Right; the ID showed Colorado, which means it was probably a pre-paid telephone card."

"It was a man?"

"Yeah, definitely a guy."

"Anything special about the voice?"

"Young; you know, the dude type. He said, 'Hey dude. I think there's a red pickup truck in the ditch.'"

"He said dude and red pickup?"

"Yes. Most people don't notice details like that."

"Do you still have the tape?"

"No. Case closed, tape gets erased. But I kept a transcript. I always keep transcripts of anonymous call-ins—just in case."

"How long have you been on the job?"

"Six years. My husband died of leukemia seven years ago, and I had to go back to work. I moved here from the Soo to live with my sister and I got this job. Lucky for me. You want a copy of the transcript?"

"Is it more extensive than what you told me?"

"No. It was short and to the point." She looked at him. "Service? It was your girlfriend and son in the truck that night, right?"

He nodded.

"That's rough," she said. "I've been there."

# MARQUETTE, MICHIGAN
## JULY 13, 2004

There had been an off-and-on rain all morning under a fuliginous sky. "Goya on acid," a college girl standing near Grady Service said as she looked up. She had long hair, purple and electric green, and wore a white T-shirt with a solid black triangle on it, and the words THE ONLY BUSH I TRUST IS MY OWN.

Grady Service was amused and tried not to smile. He was in uniform outside the Yooperdome in Marquette, waiting for President Bush to arrive; around him were dozens of demonstrators, each with a personal ax to grind. Three beer-guts in frayed camo hats wore new red T-shirts that pronounced LABORERS FOR KERRY. A man wore a blue T-shirt that read ILLINOIS IS A WAR ZONE. What the hell? Two men in camos and old jungle boots carried identical signs: HOT DAMN VIETNAM—DEJA VU. Another of them carried a huge sign that said DUBYA DUCKED: OTHERS GOT FUCKED.

As he observed, he mulled over Nantz's accident. The cop Villemure couldn't understand how it had happened. The dispatcher, Tonia Tonte, had had an anonymous caller, a male. Did that rule out Honeypat? Was he confusing two things? Not an accident. That was all he knew for sure. *Let the captain do his job and you do yours,* he told himself. *Whatever the fuck it is.* Why am I here at this circus?

The parade of signs was endless: KEEP DA U.P. WILD, EH! was followed by a bearded man carrying one that read NATIVE AMERICANS' RIGHTS ARE WAY TO THE LEFT. Another wore a T-shirt that proclaimed U.P. DUBYA DIGIT UNEMPLOYMENT. A dumpy woman in earth shoes and an ankle-length dress carried a sign: JUMP YOUR BONES FOR FOOD (OR DOPE). Service recognized her as an undercover from Escanaba.

Decades of causes, hurts, and policy non sequiturs were bubbling out, but for the most part, the demonstrators were quiet and nearly lethargic in humidity dense enough to slice like cudighi. A skinny woman in short-shorts wore a shirt that said MY BODY IS NOT PUBLIC PROPERTY. Service knew her, and if her body wasn't exactly public, it was frequently and freely shared at closing times in several local watering holes.

A college girl in a sweatshirt (representing Wildcat Women for Kerry) was telling a group of friends how she had dutifully waited in line three hours for a ticket to get inside the Yooperdome, only to be refused because she was a registered Democrat. "They're, like, *totally* fascist?" the girl said. "Too bad some of the young dudes are so hot, eh?"

"You can get a tax deduction for fucking Republicans," a girl in her entourage said. "But you can't dance with them, eh."

"Shuuut up . . ." the first girl said, giggling.

Historically the U.P. had voted Democrat and pro union, and though this was changing, it still tended toward its historical inclinations, and the Bush people were doing their best to pack the hall with vetted true believers. With Democrat Lori Timms as the state's new governor, Michigan was being viewed as a swing state, and Bush's minders were determined not to cede to the Democrats a single electoral vote. Thus, Republican legions had descended upon Marquette and a lot of locals, while honored by the leader of the land being there, were equally pissed off at the costs being imposed by the presidential visit.

It was a fine circus, and Service was there with several other officers from various agencies, all in uniform with no particular role to play other than to stand around and look official. Captain Grant had been in several meetings with the Secret Service, but in the end, DNR law enforcement personnel were deployed primarily along the twenty-mile motorcade route from Sawyer to Marquette. Service told himself he would have been happy standing out in the boonies watching the presidential vehicles fly by at seventy-five miles per hour, but the captain had asked him to join him in Marquette, so here he was among the other outsiders. He had been in Vietnam during the antiwar demonstrations in the U.S., and he figured this was about as close to such displays as he would ever get. More than a few of the protesters were of his generation, graying peace-bangers desperately fishing for another cause.

The people headed into the Yooperdome were well dressed, slicked down, and orderly, carrying red, white, and blue balloons, and wearing patriotic party hats. There were even a few signs: JUGULATE A TERRORIST FOR JESUS and AMMO SPECIAL FOR BIN LADEN: DUBYA-OUGHT BUCK! The town's year-round population was about 20,000, but the crowd at the dome was expected to be more than half of that, the vast majority from places other than Marquette, buses coming in from all over the U.P., Wisconsin, and from below the bridge to pack the house with conservative pedigrees and cheering voices for George Bush.

The captain caught Service's attention and motioned for him to follow him.

They went to a parking lot away from the protesters. "'Buckshot' is going to arrive here," the captain said as a Secret Service agent in a black suit approached them. The agent wasn't tall, but he was built like an iron-pumper, and wore dark shades despite the total absence of sun.

The captain shook hands with the man. "This is Detective Service."

The agent gave him the once-over and said, "Follow me, please."

Grady Service looked at his captain's impassive face. *Now what the hell was this?* He followed the agent to a loading dock and stopped when the man put out his arm like a railway crossing. "We'll wait here."

"For what?"

No explanation was offered.

Soon he heard sirens and saw a shiny black Cadillac limo come racing into the lot toward the dock. It was followed by several black SUVs, which stopped and unloaded Secret Service agents before anyone opened the limo doors.

The president got out and lifted his chin to stretch his neck.

Several people were talking to him and he was nodding, but appeared not to be paying a whole lot of attention to any of the voices. After a few moments, the president of the United States started walking toward the loading dock entrance. He was wearing a black suit that looked like it had cost a fortune, shiny black oxfords, a blue button-down shirt, and a pale blue tie that gave off a sort of lavender sheen in the low light.

As the president neared, the Secret Service agent stepped out and George Bush stopped, looked at Service, and as if prompted, reached out his hand. "This is Michigan Department of Natural Resources Detective Service," the Secret Service agent announced.

The president's hair was mussed some and it was much grayer than Service had expected. He was tall, maybe six feet.

"Gordy, I been hearin' good things about you," the president said with a one-sided smile that looked like a smirk.

Service blinked. *What the hell?* Before he knew it, he was saying, "It's Grady, Mr. President, not Gordy."

Flashlights were popping and Bush laughed. "Heh-heh, I meet a lot of folks, and names sort of run off on me like untamed colts, big guy. From what I hear, you got the big *cojones,* son. Your country needs men a' your caliber, so keep up the good work, and maybe there'll be a role for you in Homeland Security. Ya gotta unnerstand, that's important work, big fella."

Service looked into the president's eyes, but they were dancing around, searching for other visual stimulation. "Sir, I don't think our shaking hands out here in public is such a good idea."

Bush looked confused and giggled again. "You ain't one-a them Dem'crats, are ya, big guy?"

"Sir, have you been briefed that somebody is gunning for me, and that at this moment you could be in extreme danger?" Service couldn't help himself.

George Bush's hand dropped and he said, "Uh, heh-heh, uh . . ." and looked around with the wide eyes of a deer caught in the headlights of an oncoming eighteen-wheeler. "Uh, well, ah gotta git on inside and dew mah speech, son. Kin I count on yore vote come November?" And then he was gone inside with Service's escort and an entourage of stern-faced men.

Minutes later Service rejoined the captain. "Sir, *what* is going on?"

"Don't know for sure," Captain Ware Grant said with a grin. "The request came directly from the director of the FBI."

Service was at a loss for words.

"What was the point?"

"He likes being photographed with law enforcement and first-responder types. His handlers think it makes him look like a man of the people."

"Seeing him shaking hands with a game warden won't win him a lot of votes up here," Service said.

"Maybe that's why the chief agreed to the FBI's request," the captain said, breaking a rare smile.

Service watched a woman walk by with a sign: HOW DO YOU CONFUSE A TEXAS POLITICIAN? PUT THREE SHOVELS AGAINST A WALL AND ASK HIM TO TAKE HIS PICK.

He went downtown to Snowbound Books after the rally, looking for something to read. He saw a woman with a sweatshirt that said MOTHER EARTH PRAYS FOR YOU. He was about to turn back to a bookshelf when he recognized the woman in the sweatshirt as one of Tatie Monica's agents.

"Bobbi?" he said, stepping toward her.

The woman tried to twist away, but he caught her sleeve. "Tell Special Agent Monica I don't need a bunch of amateur babysitters." The woman fled the store.

He was pissed beyond words, threw up his hands, and walked out of the store.

Service found the captain in his office at the regional office. "There's Feeb surveillance all over me," he griped.

The captain looked at him, saying only, "A good game warden knows how to throw people off his trail."

# 32

## SLIPPERY CREEK, MICHIGAN

### JULY 15, 2004

Service had called Shark on his way to Limpy's to tell him about Wayno Ficorelli's fly collection. Shark had called back and announced that he and Limey would be bringing dinner over that night. Grady Service didn't want company. McCants had dropped off his animals that day, and they were about all the companionship he could handle.

He had maps and charts pinned up all around the main room of the cabin. He had taken locations of killings from FBI reports and tried to convert them to points on the maps so that he could see what sort of patterns might appear. He didn't want to be interrupted, but Shark was a force and would be there soon.

The results of his efforts so far seemed negligible. Most of the bodies had been found near rivers and streams—water. But those in Rhode Island, Louisiana, and Florida were on the ocean or one of its brackish bays. Given the disparity, how the hell had Monica's analyst found a pattern? He sure as hell didn't see it. All by water. Big deal.

Newf tipped her water bowl, a signal that it was empty and she was thirsty. As he filled the bowl, some of it slopped over the side and soaked his bare foot. It struck him: moving water. Rivers and streams moved, and oceans moved; they had tides. The link wasn't simply water, but *moving* water, and the way the killer moved Ficorelli's body suggested why. But what about Spargo? He had been killed two hundred feet *above* the Eleven Point.

It was an alarming realization. How many other obvious things was he missing?

He wanted to keep working, but suddenly the cabin door flew open, Newf started barking and charged Shark, who collided with the dog. Limey came in behind her husband, caught Service's eye, and shook her head. Yalmer Wetelainen was an old friend from Houghton who managed a motel and worked only to finance his hunting and fishing obsessions. He was bald, thin, short, and partial to beer, especially homemade, which he made and drank in copious quantities, mostly because it was cheap. Service and Gus Turnage had once administered a preliminary breathalyzer test to their friend during an all-night nickel-and-dime poker game. The unique Finn drank a case of beer and shots of straight vodka in a fairly short time, but never registered legally drunk. Neither CO could figure it out. Yalmer drank like a fish and ate like a pig, yet there was not even a hint of fat on his body.

They decided that their friend didn't fit any known human physiological profile, and because of his unique metabolism, they nicknamed him Shark, and the name stuck. Limey Pyykkonen was a homicide detective for Houghton County. A strapping, angular woman with a small round face, Limey had close-cropped blonde hair and thin lips. She had once had a brief fling with Wayno Ficorelli, but for some time now, she and Shark had been married and were a rock-solid couple.

Limey hugged Service while Newf and Shark wrestled. "I was really sorry to hear about Wayno," she said. "The feds got any leads?"

"Don't know," Service said as Shark came bouncing over with a gallon jug of bright red wine. "Last year's chokecherries," Shark announced, plopping it down on the kitchen table. "Kicks like a ten gauge. Where the heck are the new flies?"

They went over to the area in the main room where Service kept his fishing gear. Wetelainen was like a kid at Christmas, ripping through the fly boxes. He shouted, "Hey woman, fetch your man some wine!"

Pyykkonen yelled back, "You break a leg?"

Service said, "I'll get it," and heard Pyykkonen mumble, "Why do men revert to adolescence when they get new toys?"

"That hurts," Service said, pouring three glasses of wine and putting one in front of her. Limey rolled her eyes.

When Service got back to Shark, he found his friend holding a fly and looking perplexed. "Somebody steal one of your patterns?"

"You know what this is?" Shark asked, holding up a fly.

Service looked at it. "Some kind of brown drake?"

Shark shook his head. "Right, brown drake, but what *kind* of brown drake?"

"Dun?"

"Holy Wah! You gotta stop working so bloody much and fish more. It's a booger brown drake."

"Is that supposed to mean something to me?"

"Booger flies," Shark said. "*Look* at it."

Service took the fly and examined it. "It's got a rubber body. Should float good, right?"

"Float *good?* Hell, they float the *best,* and they aren't made of rubber."

"Some kind of plastic?"

"Nobody knows *what* it is. A guy from Curran ties these things, or he used to. I don't know if he's still alive. Crazy old fart; he always claimed they were made from nasal mucus."

Service dropped the fly on his desk and grimaced.

Wetelainen picked it up and touched the tip of his tongue to it. "Got a faint flavor. This is the real deal, not a knockoff."

"Boogers?" Service said disgustedly.

"Could be," Shark said obliviously. "Man, you do *not* see booger flies in the boxes of weekend warriors. Only serious trout-chasers know about them, much less use them. Hell, they were three bucks a copy back when I bought them—and that's a good fifteen years ago."

"*You* bought flies tied by somebody else?"

Shark got defensive. "Just a couple. I wanted to see if I could replicate the body material, but I couldn't. The way these flies are made, they ride right in the film. Sweet! And they'll float all night. Only drawback: One good bite and they're usually shot. I thought I could come up with something more durable. I managed the durable part, but I couldn't get mine to float low like the originals."

Wetelainen suddenly looked around the room. "You putting together a national compendium of trout spots?"

"Right," Service said. "Trout in the ocean," he said sarcastically.

Shark looked at his friend. "Sure."

"Bullshit."

"Not bullshit, science."

"Trout in Florida and Louisiana?" asked Service.

"*Cynoscion nebulosus,*" Wetelainen said. "Spotted sea trout."

"An actual trout?"

"The rednecks are a little loose in their definitions. They look a lot like trout, though, and they eat good. Sometimes they even call them specks, like Funnelheads call brookies. Only their specks got a couple of big fangs, like this," his friend said, using his fingers to simulate protruding fangs.

Wetelainen walked over to the maps and tapped the northeastern states where there were marks along the oceans. "I don't think *Cynoscion nebulosus* is that far north. When they talk about sea trout up there, they'd probably mean salmonids that migrate into the oceans and return to rivers to spawn. You get up into Maine and eastern Canada, and they have both rainbows and brookies that do this. In the other states, it's pretty much browns."

"I've never heard of such a thing."

"Because you live in your own world. In New England the boys who chase sea-run browns are more secretive than morel-chasers up here. Hell, the fish and game departments in those states can't even get an accurate estimate on the populations because the guys who catch the most fish never report them, and some people think because there's no data, there're no fish."

Service sipped his wine. In his current state of mind, drinking too much invited disaster, and Shark's chokecherry wine was known for its potency—far above commercially available wine in alcohol content. "You're telling me that all of those marks on the maps are places where trout are caught?"

"What's the question?" Wetelainen countered. "'Course you can catch trout in all those locations."

Service pointed at the other maps. "What about the other states?"

"Hell, it's like Michigan. Some will be warm-water fisheries, some cold-water. Each state's DNR would have to tell you what's what."

*Great,* Service thought. *More information to chase.* He nudged the fly on his desk with a pencil. "Booger fly, huh?"

"You betcha. The old guy's name, I think it was Main. The old man, he was a strange duck, always going on about astronomy and physics. His shop was like something out of a Hollywood back lot, shit everywhere. But the man was a genius when it came to inventing flies. Had him a whole line of booger flies: brown drakes, gray drakes, green drakes, Hexagenia, even a white-gloved howdy."

"In Curran—south of Alpena?"

"Yeah, that general area."

"You've been there?"

"Once. I'd been striper fishing down in Kentucky, and I was on my way back to the U.P. I'd heard about this guy, so I stopped in. He and I had one helluva discussion about flies and their histories."

"You bought the flies then?"

"Nah, I needed what dough I had for gas to get back to Houghton. He gave me a cheap mimeographed catalog, and when I got back I wrote him a letter and placed my order. See, his shop isn't listed officially as a shop. It's in his house. There's nothing about it in the Yellow Pages. If you asked around Curran, everybody would play dumb because he was a foul-tempered old coot and he let his neighbors know the only way people could find out about the place was through word of mouth from other trout fanatics. To know about the place, you had to hear about it and get directions from somebody who had been there. Talk about brilliant marketing! The old man didn't even have a phone. I've heard about guys who drove a thousand miles to see him, and when they got there he was gone fishing. I doubt the old bastard cared about missed sales. The flies were just something he did when he wasn't chasing trout."

"Have you still got the catalog?"

"Somewhere, but it's, like, ancient."

Shark's place was a virtual graveyard for old fishing supplies, but he was generally organized.

"Give a call when you get home and give me the address, okay?"

Shark Wetelainen shrugged. "Yah, sure."

"Let's eat, boys," Limey announced.

Shark said with a grunt, "Man, it's about time! You know, if I remember right, New Mexico tried to plant sea trout in mountain streams about fifteen years back."

"Ocean-runs or spotted?" Service said.

"Holy Wah!" Shark snorted. "What's wrong with your head? Ain't no place to run *from* into New Mexico, boy. It was spotteds, I think."

The thing about Shark was that once somebody flipped his switch, it was hard to shut off. As they sat down to eat, he said, "Zane Grey claimed ocean-run browns were the kings of the trout world, toughest fighters by far."

Limey Pyykkonen said, "*Yalmer,*" and he was immediately silent.

Service looked at his friends and knew that Shark Wetelainen was head-over-heels for the cop who stood a good six inches taller than him.

He also realized that it had been a booger fly he had recovered from the Ficorelli kill site, and his gut was telling him this was important. If it was as rare and valuable as Shark said, it helped explain why Wayno got out of the river to try to recover it. There was one other realization: The bodies were found not just near water, but moving water, and according to Shark, it was probably all trout water. This was the funny thing about investigations. They could stall for eons and suddenly vault forward on some seemingly insignificant fact that all at once became significant. Nantz would really appreciate this. She'd be running around the room right now, pumping her arms in triumph.

"Grady," Limey Pykkonnen said. "Are you coming back soon?"

He looked at the woman and said, "I'm back," picked up his fork, and began eating. All the while he ate, he saw Nantz sitting next to Limey, the two women yakking away at each other. He knew she wasn't really there, but it felt right to imagine she was.

## 33

## MARQUETTE, MICHIGAN
## JULY 16, 2004

"I might have something for you to work with," Shamekia said. The former FBI agent tended to get right to the point. Service was sitting in his cubicle, planning to spend the morning contacting state fishery agencies to verify if the places where murdered game wardens had been found held trout. Looking at a map wasn't enough, because over many generations, most state agencies had finagled with natural orders, planting all sorts of species in places where nature had never put them, and they couldn't and didn't survive, including Shark's odd story about sea trout being planted in New Mexico. In many states fishery people were torn between planting rubber fish from hatcheries and managing the rivers to create naturally reproducing wild stocks. Michigan was moving steadily toward the latter strategy.

Shamekia added, "I'm sending everything I have via messenger, there tonight. Want it at your house or office?"

"House," he said, then gave her the Slippery Rock address and told her the messenger should leave the package and not wait for him to be there to sign for it.

She said, "Okay, it's going out the door now, but here's the short version."

She continued, "June 1970, the Mexican federal police arrested a U.S. citizen in Ciudad Juárez—that's across the river from El Paso. A woman reported her husband being assaulted by an Americano in a black El Dorado. About the same time, a couple of local cops stopped the same guy in town, probably to shake him down, and he resisted. There was a fight and they put the cuffs on him. Turns out he was driving a black Cadillac. Had a woman and a boy with him. The locals found blood all over the trunk of the Cadillac, and the assaulted man identified the adult male as his assailant.

The locals called the *federales* to brag themselves up some, and the *federales* immediately swooped in and intervened. They took the vehicle and the prisoner. Turns out that there had been three brutal killings in Nogales, Mexicali, and Matamoros, all male victims with mutilations along their spines. A black Cadillac had been reported near two of the killings."

"This was 1970? Near El Paso?"

"Mid-June."

Service immediately checked the list of killings he had gotten from the FBI. The body of a New Mexico game warden had been found in late June 1970. He looked quickly at the atlas he kept on his desk and saw that El Paso, Texas, was not that far from New Mexico. Geographic coincidence? "What did the federal police do?"

"My sources say they interrogated the man with great vigor."

"Car batteries and wires?" Service interjected.

"The Mexicans believe in going right at the bad guys—unless, of course, they have some political clout and can get back at them. But this was just some asshole gringo, so they probably did a number on him. Only he wouldn't crack. He insisted he'd done nothing and, according to the reports, remained silent, no matter what they did. They tried him in 1972, found him guilty of three homicides and one attempted, sentenced him to death, and packed him off to some shithole prison in the south of the country to await execution. But before they could carry out the sentence, the American was murdered by a prison guard. This was just before Christmas 1974," said Shamekia.

"There a name for this guy?"

"Wellington Ney from Pigeon River, Indiana."

He'd never heard of a town called Pigeon River. There was a river by that name in northern Indiana, close to the Michigan border, but not a town. "What about his wife and kid?" asked Service.

"It's not clear it was his wife or his kid. The reports say simply a woman in her thirties, and a boy of fifteen or sixteen. The locals kicked them after they pinched the guy. They split after the arrest and were never seen again. The *federales* called in the Bureau, but the town name was bogus, and there was nobody named Ney anywhere in Indiana."

"False name?"

"Maybe. The Mexicans weren't that competent in those days, and it was easy enough to hide your identity, even in this country," said Shamekia.

"Did you get the names of the Bureau agents who worked the case on this side of the border?"

"Lead man was Special Agent Philip L. Orbet. He retired in 1976 and died ten years later."

"Others on the case?"

"Just Orbet after a while. Apparently he was obsessed with the case, thought there was something more to it, and kept looking into it after he retired, but he died before he got anywhere with it. You know how cold cases go," she added.

He did. "But this wasn't a U.S. case," Service said.

"Right, but Orbet was one of those old-time G-men who felt that if this guy had been a serial killer in Mexico, he probably did it up here too."

"Where did Orbet live?" Service heard the lawyer leafing through paperwork.

"Toledo, Ohio."

"You think this fits?" he asked.

"You tell me: The victims had an ax taken to their ribs along the spine," she said.

"Hmmm," Service said. "Photos in the paperwork you're sending?"

"There are. Photos of the victims and of the man Ney."

"Can you get me an address for Orbet in Toledo, names of his survivors, all that?"

"It's in the package. You thinking he left behind his case notes?"

"Could be," Service thought.

"Okay," Shamekia said, "write this down."

||||||||||||||||||||||||||||||||||||||||||||||||||||||||||||||||||||||||||||||||||||||||||||||||||||||||||||||||||||||||||||||||||||||||||

34

CLIFF'S RIDGE,

SOUTH OF MARQUETTE, MICHIGAN

JULY 16, 2004

He was still deeply troubled about Nantz's accident being something else, but the list of follow-up items in the federal case was mounting, and Service had begun to assemble notes to himself about things that needed to be checked out. He had not seen any further surveillance since Bobbi Temple had ducked out of Snowbound Books, but he had not moved around that much, and despite his mind being preoccupied with Nantz and Walter, he had come to the realization that he needed to reach some sort of accommodation with Special Agent T. R. Monica.

Wink Rector was the lone FBI agent in the Upper Peninsula and a pretty good guy, but also savvy enough to toe the bureau line when he needed to. Rector was rarely in his office in Marquette, and Service was surprised when he answered his phone.

"Federal Bureau of Investigation, Marquette Regional Office, Special Agent Rector."

"It's Grady Service, Wink."

"Hey, was that you I saw on the tube with the president?" Rector greeted him.

"Did you know about that beforehand?"

Rector laughed. "Hey, I'm only the resident agent up here. That sort of crap is way above my pay grade."

Bitterness or resignation? "You got time to talk?"

"Phone or in person?"

"Not on the phone," Service said. "Cliff's Ridge. The old gravel pit. About an hour?"

"Sounds mysterious. I'll be there with coffee."

The Carp River was a narrow bedrock river that squeezed through a spot the locals referred to as the Gorge, which was only about forty feet deep. Marquette Mountain ski hill rose immediately to the southwest of the area, and in summer the ski lifts looked like flensed bones sticking out of the landscape. Decades before, the ski area had been known as Cliff's Ridge, but the name had changed, and only those with a long history in the area would remember it by the old name.

Rector was there before Service. A huge thermos and two cups sat on the hood of his Crown Victoria.

"Black like your heart?" Rector said, holding up the thermos.

Service nodded and got to the point. "You know a special agent out of Milwaukee named T. R. Monica?"

"Heard about her, and I might have met her once somewhere along the road."

"She a pretty good agent?"

Rector took a breath to buy time to think. "Kinda depends on who you talk to. I think she's probably competent enough, but a real pain in the ass. Why?"

"Are you aware that she and her people are running surveillance on me?"

The FBI agent blinked. "On *you?*"

"You heard about the game warden murdered in Wisconsin?"

"It was on the news and I got a bulletin, but there wasn't much detail."

"I knew the guy."

"No shit?"

"He's not the only game warden to die." Service went back to his truck, got out an envelope, and gave it to Rector, who opened it and gawked at the photographs.

"Holy cow," was all he managed to say.

"Twenty-seven game wardens in twenty-five states, killed between 1950 and 1970. No common MO and no suspect."

"Suspect, singular?"

"Until three years ago, nobody saw a connection. The kills were spread out over twenty years. In 1982 the killings started again. Most recently Ficorelli was killed in Wisconsin, and a few days later another warden bought it in Missouri. The kills in the second group were by an assortment of methods until 2000. Then they all took the same MO." Service tapped the photographs. "All just like that. Monica is the one who identified the pattern, and she's lead agent on the case."

"Onward and upward," Rector said.

"Not if she fails."

Rector nodded. "True; the Bureau's got a low tolerance for public failure nowadays."

"Your people think the perp is targeting me," Service said, pausing to let the information sink in.

Rector grinned. "This is a put-on, right?"

"It's real, Wink."

"You don't seem all that broken up. If Special Agent Monica has a team up here dogging you, she must think it's credible."

"Bingo. Give the man a Kewpie doll."

"Give me cash instead," the agent said. "I've got a basement full of crappy gewgaws."

"Aren't you surprised to be out of the loop on any of this?"

"I guess not," Wink Rector said. "Since 9/11 everyone's gotten more secretive than before. We've got more compartments than a printer's table these days."

"Now you know," Service said. "Monica's got to be here somewhere, and I want to have a sit-down with her."

"Pick up the telephone."

"No. I want this on my terms, on my turf."

"I suppose you want me to arrange it."

"I figure you've got a stake in this too."

"Like that would matter," Rector said bitterly. "When and where?"

"End of the Mulligan Creek road, where it crosses the creek."

"North of Ishpeming?"

"There's only one road in from the south, which means it will be fairly secure."

"Okay, when?"

"Soon as. She can pick the time."

Rector took a sip of coffee. "I'll get on it today and give you a call when it's set."

"Thanks, Wink."

"You realize that bringing me into this is going to piss her off, and some others above her as well."

"Never had a doubt, but I also felt pretty sure you'd want to know what was going down in your own backyard. I would." This was an allusion to a wolf-killing case Service had been involved in three years before, a time when Rector had held back information from him, and the FBI had impeded his investigation.

"You were right to tell me," Rector said. "I've put in my papers, and I'm hanging it up December 31. Everything's set. I'm waiting now for my replacement to show so I can bring them up to speed on what's going on up here."

"This fits the category of what's going on up here," Service said.

Rector's reply was a muffled grunt as he picked up his thermos and cups and got into his vehicle.

Service loaded his Honda ATV into the bed of his personal truck, stowed the portable ramp beneath the four-wheeler, and started north on County Road 550 toward Big Bay. He thought he spotted a tail near the Northern Michigan Campus, cut north, and lost the follower by going off-road to the west up a power line where only a high-centered four-wheel-drive vehicle could get through. He continued west, until he hit County Road 510 and turned north, for the Triple A Road, more than twenty miles north.

He had received the package of information from Shamekia. The photos of the victims were nothing like those of the blood eagle killings, but they were gruesome all the same.

Halfway across the Yellow Dog Plains on the Triple A, he hid the truck, offloaded his Honda, and rode the ATV south across the Yellow Dog River into the southern fringe of the Huron Mountains. Eventually the trail connected to the road that ended at Mulligan Creek. This route required a great deal of extra time, but he wanted to make a point with the FBI. The meeting was set for first light and he was in place nearly an hour early. He hid the Honda a quarter-mile away, on the north side of the creek, crossed the makeshift one-lane snowmobile bridge the DNR had built a few years back, and found a place to wait in the popples on the lip of a rise just above where the road from the south dead-ended in the shadows of steep rock bluffs.

On the sandy two-track to the west he saw a gray wolf trot northwest, nervously glancing over its shoulder in his direction as it passed. Then he heard vehicle tires swishing through soft sand on the two-track above the creek. The wolf had been spooked by the vehicle, not him.

Wink Rector drove his own vehicle to the edge of the creek, backed up twenty yards, parked, and got out. It was getting lighter, but the sun itself remained hidden by ridges to the east.

"Where the hell is he?" Tatie Monica asked when she got out.

Rector got out his thermos and poured coffee. "Game wardens don't announce themselves."

"What's that supposed to mean?"

"You see fresh tire tracks on the way in?"

"No. So he's behind us?"

"My guess is that he's already here."

"Games," she said.

"It's not a game," Wink Rector corrected her. "This is how these people live. If he asked us to meet him here fifty times, he wouldn't come in the same way twice."

"We're not the enemy," Tatie Monica said.

Wink Rector remained silent.

"I don't know why the hell he got you involved," she complained.

"Things work differently up here," Rector said. "The Bureau is just one more law enforcement outfit and we all have to cooperate to graduate."

"You've never had to keep things close?"

"I was ordered to stonewall him once, but never again. Once you earn trust up here, you do *not* want to lose it."

Service saw the woman check her watch impatiently, pick up her radio, and make a call. He couldn't make out what was being said, but he was pretty sure she had left a rear guard south on the two-track.

"Trust me, he won't come in from behind us," Rector said.

Service eased out of the tags to the side of Rector's Crown Vic and waited until Special Agent Monica turned away to step out beside Rector, who immediately spilled his coffee. "For Pete's sake!"

Tatie Monica turned around and glared at him.

Service said, "Special Agent Rector knows all about what's going on, so there's no need to play cute this morning."

"You had no right," she said. "*Either* of you."

"I've got my retirement date," Rector said. "I plan to live here. That give you a hint where my priorities are?"

She ignored Rector and stared at Service. "What the hell is this about?"

"To bring you up to speed," he said. He then laid out the situation in Mexico and watched for a reaction to see if any of it was familiar to her. It didn't appear to be.

"Why didn't you call me with this as soon as you had it?"

"I knew you were here somewhere. I saw Bobbi the day Bush was here, and that's when it dawned on me that you had a team dogging my ass."

She didn't deny it. "You're wasting my time. I could have been following up on Special Agent Orbet."

"You could have, and whatever you learned would still leave me in the dark." He did not mention what he had learned about the sites where the bodies had been found, or Shark's identification of the booger fly. One thing he had learned as a detective was that you had to keep a few cards back, not play them until they mattered most.

"What are you suggesting?" Monica asked.

"We do some of this my way."

"You have no experience with this sort of thing. You told me that yourself."

Service said, "Don't underestimate the value of someone who doesn't share your experiences and prejudices."

Wink Rector kept out of it.

"Okay," Tatie Monica said, "spell out what you want."

"First, I think we should go together to find Orbet's survivors and see if he left any records."

"Everything would have been turned over to the Bureau," she countered.

Service nodded to Wink Rector. "Is that how it is?"

"Officially he would have turned over all his paperwork when he retired, but if the case stuck in his craw, he'd have copies at home, and if he continued to investigate, there'd be paper for that too, I guess," Rector added.

"Which means there could be notes, or something."

"If his family didn't pitch the whole lot," Rector said.

"Okay," Tatie Monica said. "What else?"

"Call off your surveillance."

"It's for *your* protection," she said.

"It's also an arrow pointing right at me, not to mention a waste of time and manpower," he said. "If I want to become invisible, I can, and there's no way you can follow me."

"You're pretty sure of yourself," she said.

"There's a whole lot I'm not so good at," he said, "but finding my way around in the woods without being detected isn't one of them. This is where I live, who I am."

"Is that it?"

"I need to revisit Elray Spargo's widow."

"Why?"

"I'll explain later."

"How about now?"

"Later. That's how you usually answer me, only later never seems to arrive. I also want to meet your analyst."

"You're asking for the whole ball of wax," Monica said.

"If your theory's right, that I'm the final target, the whole ball of wax reduces to me. Either you get this guy this time, or—"

"Point taken," she said, cutting him off.

"Are we agreed on this or not?"

"We'll get in touch with Orbet's family to see what they have, and if they have something, and if they're agreeable, you and I can go visit them. I'll also go with you to Missouri. As for surveillance, I don't want to call it off, but I'll agree to it—with the stipulation I can turn it on again if I think we need it."

Service said, "What about your analyst?"

"He may not want to talk to you," she said.

"If we go to Toledo, Detroit is right on the way."

"I never said Micah Yoder lived in Detroit. I said he operated out of there."

"What the hell does that mean?"

"This is the electronic age, Service. With a computer, cell phone, and modem, you can work from anywhere."

"Meaning he doesn't live in Detroit?"

"I don't really know where he lives."

*Holy Christ*, he thought. "That doesn't bother you?"

"It's the twenty-first century," she said.

"Either you and I meet him, or I go my own way and you go yours, and we'll see if we intersect somewhere down the line."

"How did you find out about Orbet and Mexico?"

Service grinned. "That information came right out of the Bureau." This was not technically correct, but he knew Shamekia retained sources in Washington, D.C., which she seemed to be able to use at her pleasure.

"Bullshit," Tatie Monica said. "If the Bureau had this information, I would have known."

"Not if you didn't ask the right questions," Service said.

"What else?"

Service said, "If I think of something, I'll let you know."

"All right," she said. "I'll get my team moving on the Orbet thing, and I'll talk to my guy and see if the family's amenable to a sit-down."

"And you'll call off the minders?"

"For now," she said, offering her hand.

"And Wink here joins your team," he added, causing her to drop her hand momentarily.

She looked at Rector. "You sure you want to do this?"

"Hey," he said, "what can they do to me? Pack me off to the Upper Peninsula of Michigan and forget about me? Oh, wait—they already did that. Yeah, I'm sure."

Monica asked "Your source sent you records?"

"They're in the mail," he said, lying. "You know how the post office can be."

"I'll get back to you," she said.

"Wink, did you see the wolf tracks up the road?"

Rector shook his head.

"Crossed two minutes before you guys drove in."

"Wolf?" Tatie Monica said, her eyes wide.

"Don't worry," Grady Service said. "Little Red Riding Hood was just a fairy tale."

## 36

## BABOQUIVARI WELLS, ARIZONA

## JULY 23, 2004

Grady Service found the gate unlocked, lifted it, drove through, got out of his rental, and closed the gate behind him. He wiped the dust off his sweaty forehead, took a long pull from a $5.00 bottle of water, and lit a cigarette. The thermometer in the rental car said 108. The ground through his shoes felt fifty degrees hotter. His shirt and trousers were soaked with sweat and stuck to him, and he was tired from traveling. He had spent the previous day on commercial flights, Marquette to Green Bay to Minneapolis, where he had spent the night sleeping in an airport lounge, and this morning from Minneapolis to Phoenix to Tucson, where he rented the vehicle.

He had not asked for approval of the trip from his captain, and had not told Special Agent Tatie Monica he was leaving town.

Another call from Shamekia had put him on the move. "Grady, I've found another source for you. His name is Eduardo Perez. He was with the *federales* during the Ney investigation. He's since moved to the States and become a U.S. citizen. He works for the Border Patrol as an undercover agent, moving back and forth across the border in the Sonoran Desert. It was a fluke that I found him. He's due to go undercover again in three days, but if you can get down to Arizona, he'll talk to you. I get the feeling he is not all that anxious to talk about the Ney case." She gave him instructions for finding the place, which was near Fresnal Canyon in the south central Baboquivari Mountains, about eighty miles southwest of Tucson.

He had quickly weighed his options and decided to go. There was no time to touch base with anyone, and as he and Tree had learned in the marines, it was often easier to ask for forgiveness than permission.

A rough sand road led from a macadam state highway toward Fresnal Canyon to the east; eight miles after the turnoff he found the gate on the south side of the powdery dirt road.

He finished his cigarette, mashed the butt into the ground, got in, and drove another nine miles south to where the road ended. There was a World War II jeep parked near a stand of saguaro cacti, which cast almost human shadows.

The colors of the landscape ranged from black to orange and ochre. He got out and walked over to the jeep. There were no prints. Around him there were creosote bushes, and more saguaros, these with multiple bullet holes, and several stunted Joshua trees.

The ground was caliche, baked sand that seemed to absorb and radiate the sun. Service sat with his legs out of the car, kicked off his shoes, and switched to his boots. He got his pack, water supply, his compass, and started walking. To the northeast he saw a shimmering line of mountains and in the middle, a peak that looked like a large white nipple. Immediately ahead of him there was a small rise with pale yellow boulders and between two of them, what appeared to be a game trail. What sort of animals could endure such heat? On a rock near the boulders he saw the tail of a snake flick as it escaped into the shadows of a small crevice. The game trail continued eastward and, reaching the crest of the second steep hill, he looked down into a valley with hundreds of saguaro.

The trail led into the middle of the giant plants, where he saw a structure of crude slats with a flat thatched roof. The slats looked like gray bones; the structure was vaguely reminiscent of a rib cage. A man sat cross-legged on a blanket in the shade of the shelter and looked up at him.

Service batted dust off his clothes.

The man was thin, with a reddish-mahogany complexion, smooth skin, and ragged black salt-and-pepper hair. He looked freshly shaved.

"Perez?" he greeted the man. "Service."

The man looked up, pointed to a blanket across a small cook fire. There was a pot hanging over the fire, which made almost no smoke. The man lifted the red earthenware vessel beside him and poured its contents into clay mugs.

"You got your bona fides?" the man asked in a sonorous voice.

Service showed his state badge and ID. "You?"

The man took a gold shield out of his pocket and hung it around his neck. It read CBP BORDER PATROL, PATROL AGENT PEREZ.

Service wanted to start asking questions, but decided they needed to sit for a few minutes, get used to each other. The worst thing you could do with a reluctant interviewee was to push too hard too soon, especially when the heat was beyond belief. "Been with the border patrol long?"

"Drink," the man said. He had delicate hands and moved slowly.

Service sipped the reddish liquid. It was slightly sweet, slightly fermented. "Ten years," the man said. "This is called *nuwait*. You?"

"Twenty plus," Service said. "You talked to Shamekia?"

"Yes, the lady lawyer from Detroit with the impossible last name. She said you want to talk about the Ney case."

"Affirmative. She also said you seemed reluctant."

The man smiled. "Occupational lockjaw. This job, it sometimes pulls our lips tight, yes? Too much time alone, perhaps."

Service understood.

The man said. "Silence is often a better weapon than a gun."

Perez had no accent. "You were with the Mexican Federal Police."

"Yes. I grew up in Nogales. My father was a judge. I came to the States for college, law enforcement administration at Arizona State in Tempe. After I graduated I went home. My father was a wise and moral man who hoped that U.S.-style training for *federales* would lead to a less corrupt, more effective force, but what difference can one man make?" the man said with a shrug. "I spent three years on the Yucatán and rose to the rank of special inspector. This earned me a transfer to the north and a unit called Special Crimes, those involving foreign nationals."

"That's how you got on to Ney."

"I was visiting my parents in Nogales when Ney was detained in Juárez. It was I who picked out the detail of the Cadillac and convinced my superior to take the team there to investigate. The locals, of course, resisted, but the boss called in authority from above and we took custody of the suspect."

"Ney never talked," Service said.

"He talked quite a lot and he was pleasant, but he never admitted to the crime. All he would say was that his work was complete."

"Meaning?"

Perez shrugged and held out his hands. "We had no idea, but he was convicted and sentenced to die."

"And killed while in custody.'

"Not in the way you may think. He convinced a guard at the prison to kill him, in exchange for ten thousand U.S. dollars, for which he provided a letter of credit at a bank in the Cayman Islands. When the guard contacted the bank, they denied his letter."

"Ney was dead by then."

"Of course. To a naive, simple man, ten thousand American dollars is a treasure. There was a great deal of anger over the death. The FBI sent a scathing and critical letter to the head of our national police, but there was nothing to be done. Ney was dead, the case finished. We tried to clean up the aftermath, did an autopsy, and punished the guard, who admitted his foolishness."

"An autopsy?"

"The rules are the same there as here for any violent or unexpected death. The pathologist found the man filled with cancer, which had metastasized. He had only weeks or months to live, and the death would certainly have been agonizing. The care in our prisons was less than humane. Faced with such an end, any man might consider a similar solution."

"But you could not positively identify him."

"It was the FBI who had that responsibility and no, they failed."

"The reports said a woman and a boy were with him."

"Indeed, when he was stopped in Juárez, but of course he was stopped there because the locals wished only *mordida,* you understand?" Perez rubbed his fingers together. "The man resisted and they arrested him. They let the woman and the boy go before we arrived. We never saw them."

Service tried to process the information, which didn't seem to amount to much.

"I have told you what I know," Perez said. "May I ask your interest?"

Service explained about the murders of game wardens, and the blood eagle MO. "We thought that the man might have tested the method. Shamekia found the Ney cases in Mexico. Interestingly, a game warden was killed in New Mexico about ten days after Ney was arrested."

"I see," Perez said. "But of course, this Ney could not have killed the man in New Mexico."

"I realize that," Service said.

"Was this killing in New Mexico one of mutilation?" Perez asked.

"No, the man there was strangled."

"Do you have other questions for me?"

"Not right now."

Perez got two bowls from a soft pack beside him and scooped something from the pot over the fire. "Mesquite beans, barley, corn, cholla buds, and hot peppers," he said. "The peppers heat you inside to reduce the difference with the heat outside."

The soup was thick and distinctive. Nantz and Walter would have loved it.

When their soup was gone the man gave him a pancake-like thing, which had been sitting on a rock in the sun. Onto this he poured a viscous orange substance. "I don't know the name of this food in English," he said. "It is something I have made and enjoyed since I was a child. The syrup is taken from the fruit of the saguaro."

The syrup was a vague blend of fig and strawberry flavors, sweet but not overpowering.

"You are here at a propitious time," Perez said. "The saguaro are giving us their fruit and my people are making foods from them, including
the wine."

The man took another pull on his wine and refilled his glass. "The idea
is to fill our bodies with wine so that God will fill the earth with rain and
everything that depends on it can live another year."

"Your people?" Service asked, taking another drink of wine.

"Tohono O'odham—Papagos," the man said. "Desert People. We are
among the few native tribes to never have been removed from our reserva-
tions. Long ago the Apache were our traditional enemies and we helped the
American army bring Geronimo to justice."

Service was confused. "I thought you were Mexican."

"We were once called Pima, and we lived on both sides of the line which
divided Mexico from America under the Gadsden Purchase. In Mexico they
call us *Frijolero*—bean people. Traditionally we have lived among ourselves
in the Sonora, but my father was unique. He was educated in Mexico City,
Spain, and the United States. Being a *Frijolero* among *federales* was a position of low odds. I decided to come to America. Now I am employed to look
for and interdict coyotes; you understand?"

Coyotes were illegal immigrants. Service nodded.

"I spend weeks alone in the field and return to my home in Tucson
from time to time. Before I go back into the field, I come here to harden
myself for life the old way and to readjust to the air, the heat, and the hard-
ships of the caliche. My people have never mixed well with whites, and the
Sonora is a prime area for coyotes, so I can move among them freely and
not arouse suspicion."

The solitude of the man's job reminded Service of his own.

"When I was first hired, the Border Service believed that my people
were involved in coyote trafficking. I knew this to be untrue, so I agreed to
take the position. It is well established now that their premise was wrong.
I never thought I would come to love such a way of life, but I have. I am

happiest here, alone, and dependent solely upon myself. I have friends who are game wardens. We live a similar life, you and I."

Service nodded.

"This man, Ney. I talked to him many times. He was a pleasant and gentle fellow."

"And a killer."

Perez shrugged. "Perhaps."

"You think he was innocent?"

"The man is dead. We will never know."

"But you suspect something."

"It is only that he repeatedly asked only about his son. He showed no interest in the woman."

"He called him his son?"

"Yes, but never by name. Always it was 'my boy, my creation.'"

"My *creation?*" Odd.

"Yes, his exact words."

"And the woman?"

"He never mentioned her, never once inquired about her fate."

"Maybe she wasn't his wife," Service said.

"I would agree with that," Perez said, refilling their mugs. "Take off your shoes, my friend."

Service stared at the man. "Why?"

"I will show you something special."

Service took off his shoes and socks and wiggled his toes. There was no breeze, but the thatched roof gave shade and made the temperature almost manageable.

Perez went off into the rocks and came back with a bowl of red powder, which he mixed with water until it was a deep vermillion paste. He handed the bowl to Service. "Paint the bottom of your feet with this."

Service laughed, but did as the man asked.

The substance dried almost immediately.

"We get drunk to appease God," Perez said, "but we paint our feet for our women."

Service shook his head. "Listen . . ."

"Do not be alarmed, my friend. I am not *berdache*—a man who sleeps with other men. You have left a woman behind?"

"No." Service could hardly get the word out.

"It doesn't matter. We will paint our feet to honor the women who gave us life, and we will fill our bodies with *nuwait* for I'itoi, the creator of all souls. If we drink enough, our women will dream of us tonight. I'itoi lives on the mountain behind us," Perez said. "I think he is too busy to come to visit tonight, so we will sleep drunk and tomorrow we will rise with thick heads and leave for our missions: you to find the killer of men who protect animals, I to find those who would steal the souls of the desperate."

The two men went at the wine with serious intent.

In the morning Eduardo Perez looked fresh and was already shaved. Service felt like hell and could hardly stand up. The man gave him two of the red earthenware jugs. "These vessels are called *olla*. The large one holds *nuwait*. The smaller one contains powder. If you want a particular woman to love you, paint your feet and drink *nuwait* with her and she will be engulfed by great desire for you."

Service laughed. "Isn't that date rape?"

Perez held up a finger. "Don't wait too long to use the power of *nuwait*, my friend or it will turn to vinegar, just as love sours when it is not nurtured."

The man put on his pack. He wore long black trousers, a loose, light-colored shirt, and ankle-high moccasins. He took a step out of the shelter and turned back. "Hunt with your brain, *compadre*, not your heart."

Service watched him lope away into the cool morning air and lay back with a pounding head.

When he got back to his rental he found the doors unlocked and two mason jars of *nuwait* on the front seat with a note: *Service, one of these is for you and a woman you choose. The other I would ask that you deliver for me.*

*When you get on the hard road north to Sells, go two miles and you will see
a cemetery off to the east. Park and go through the fence. Look for the grave
with purple flowers and leave the other jar there. Via con dios, compadre.
Eduardo.*

The cemetery was in a white sand area. There were hundreds of markers and crosses, all of the graves decorated with gaudy flowers and plastic statues of everyone from Jesus Christ to Darth Vader. The grave with purple flowers was in the back, closest to the purple mountains in the distance. Service looked at the name carved into a crude wooden cross: ROSALITA PEREZ, 1950–2003.

Perez was a widower and alone.

They had more than their jobs in common.

## 37

## FOURTEEN, MISSOURI

## JULY 24, 2004

He could not get Eduardo Perez out of his mind. The man had lost his wife a year ago and was burying himself in work. Had this contributed to his wife's death? Or was it a result of it? As soon as he got to the airport in Tucson he changed his ticket to Missouri.

When he had left Michigan he had begun to feel the distance, which made his sense of loss heavier, and he chastised himself for allowing his feelings to disturb his concentration.

He got some questions in security about his mason jars and *olla,* but when he showed his identification and surrendered his sidearm, they allowed him to board.

It was afternoon by the time he reached Springfield, rented a vehicle, called Eddie Waco's cell phone, and got his voice mail. "It's Service. I'm just leaving Springfield, heading for Elray Spargo's house. Meet me there if you can."

When he reached the house there were three kids on the front porch, and as he got out of the rental he heard one of them yell, "Mama, that Michigan man done just pulled up."

Fiannula Spargo stepped onto the porch wearing an apron and dripping flour. "Agent Waco called, said he'll be along soon. You'n bring me news, Michigan Man?"

"No ma'am, not yet."

"What brings ye?"

"Was your husband a trout fisherman?"

She cracked a smile. "I reckon thet and the law was the only religions my man ever took to: trout on the fly. I guess we all done took to hit. Or by hit, I hain't sure which."

"I know it sounds strange, but would you mind if I took a look at his flies?"

She raised an eyebrow. "I reckon they's better times ta fish the hill cricks thin now."

"I didn't come to fish."

She nodded and pushed open the door for him.

Spargo kept his flies in the room that served as his home office. Fiannula stood beside Service as he surveyed the room and saw a Renzetti fly-tying vise. "Elray tied his own?"

"Was a disease," she said. "That man would hardly go to town, exceptin' ta drag me inta craft stores and the Wal-Mart, lookin' for beads and feathers and such. Said trout get used ta somethin', got to change up offerin's ta catch 'em by surprise." She opened a corner cabinet. "Hits all in thim drawers," she said, pointing.

"What about his fly boxes?"

She opened a closet. The boxes were stacked on a shelf above and on the floor in cardboard cartons. "You need anything, or can I get back at my bakin'?"

"Thanks, I'm good." He pulled a chair over to the closet, sat down, and began going through the fly boxes one by one. They weren't labeled and they weren't organized like his boxes, which he put together by month, based on the hatches that would be coming off. Elray's were organized by type: mayflies in one box, caddis in another, stoneflies in yet another, nymphs, streamers. He made a mental note, estimated fifty boxes to go through, and settled back.

"You'n got us a good lead?" a familiar voice asked.

Eddie Waco slid into the room and handed him a glass of iced tea.

"More like a real thin hunch," Service said.

"Hunches work," Waco said. "They bubble up from thet part a' the brain where we don't think. Acts like a computer, sendin' along an unexpected e-mail from time to time."

"I hope this one's not spam," Service said. Both men laughed. "Elray have a system for his fly boxes?"

"Had a differ'nt system ever time we fished," Waco said. "Only thing in his life he couldn't never make up his mind on."

Service understood. The monthly boxes were only the latest iteration of his own system, which changed frequently. "He tie all his own?"

"Thing was, ole Elray was of a frugal nature, couldn't abide buyin' what he could make for himseff."

Service pushed a carton over to Waco. "We're looking for brown drakes," he said.

"Little late for them," the Missouri agent quipped.

It took them more than thirty minutes to go through the inventory. They found brown drakes and hex, but not the pattern he had hoped for.

"You'n not findin' somethin'?" Waco asked.

"Are these all of his flies?"

"All save them which bin retired."

"Retired?"

"Elray caught him a hawg, he released the fish, and retired the fly."

"What's a hawg around here?"

"Tin pound at least."

"You've got ten-pound browns here?"

"Mosey cross the border to the White River 'round Mountain Home and they catch 'em a heap bigger, fish for 'em outen inner tubes at night."

"Where are his retired flies?"

"Have to ask Fi thet."

She was in the kitchen taking pies out of the oven, the aroma overwhelming the room. "Fi," Waco said, "Sorry to git in yore way, but where'd ole Elray keep them flies he bragged on so much?"

The woman turned and looked at the men, her face contorted. "Lord, I know I done seen them things. He kept 'em in a red tin box." After a moment she stepped into the hallway and shouted, "You kids git on down here this minute."

The children trooped into the hall beside the kitchen. "Which one a' you floor monkeys seen yore daddy's red box?"

"Wasn't my idea," a little girl said. "Was hers." She pointed to another child who looked like a twin.

"Now y-you d-done got me in trouble," the second girl whined with indignation.

"Did not. Was you'n took Daddy's red box."

"Hush," Fiannula said gently. "Just fetch it now, hear?"

"We in trouble, Mama?" the first girl asked.

Spargo's widow patted the girl's head affectionately. "I don't blame you for looking at Daddy's special things, but you'n got to put 'em back so's the others can look too."

The girl looked relieved when the second girl produced the red box and handed it to Grady Service.

"Thanks," he told the girl, who giggled and nudged her sister.

"You men want pie?" Fiannula asked. "I got a couple coolin' down on the winder ledge and still warm."

"Yes, ma'am," Waco said.

One of the twins said, "Can we have pie, Mama?"

Fiannula Spargo smiled. "'Course you can, you and your sister. Others will have ta wait for supper."

The five of them sat in the dining area. Service opened the box. Each fly was hooked to a piece of paper with a Polaroid photo of the fish, its size, the date, and location where it had been caught. Each paper also gave the time, wind, light, and water conditions.

Service found what he was looking for near the bottom of the pile and held it up for Waco to see. "You recognize this?"

Waco said, "Yep, thet's his booger fly. Never seen him use it, but that's what hit is, I reckon."

"He didn't tie this himself."

"Nope. He done heard about booger flies from some old boy he done met down on the Eleven Point. Man was from Illinois, if memory serves me right, and Elray give 'im a warning for too many fish, and the fella give 'im the address of the man what tied them booger flies—up your way, I think."

Service looked at the date below the photo: 2003—last year.

Fiannula put large pieces of pie in front of each of them. Service held up the paper with the fly and photo. "You remember when Elray ordered this fly?"

The widow laughed. "I told him he was crazy orderin' such expensive things—especially them made a' boogers."

The little girls giggled.

"You girls hush," their mother warned them. "You come in here ta eat pie or make a show of yourseffs?"

"Eat pie," the girls said in unison.

Service asked, "You wouldn't happen to know how he paid for this, would you?"

"I reckon they's records about. The man couldn't throw away anything." She looked over at Service. "This important?"

Service nodded.

"I'll find it. He didn't send away for much, and whin he did, he paid by check."

While she was gone, Service said to Waco, "There were game wardens killed in Kansas and Illinois. When I get back, I'll send you their names and personal information. Think you could call their families and find out if they were fly fishermen, and if so, did they use flies like this, bought from Michigan?"

"You send the information, I'll take care of 'er," Waco said.

"How's Cake?" Service asked.

"Up and stumpin' aroun' on crutches. Cain't wait ta get started as my pine shadow. You think this fly thing gonna take us somewhere?"

"I hope," Service said.

The widow came back, looking perplexed. "I cain't seem ta find thim boxes with the taxes and checks," she said. "You reckon I could send 'em along whin I find 'em?"

"Give them to Eddie and he'll get in touch," Service said.

"All y'all better get at thim pies afore they cool too much," she said.

"Mama," one of the twins said, "I think she got a bigger piece thin me."

"Did not," the other girl snapped with a big grin.

"Kids," Fiannula Spargo said with a big grin. "Little kids, little problems; big kids, big problems. I expect hit never ends for parents."

Service thought: *Something I'll never know.*

## 38

## SLIPPERY CREEK, MICHIGAN
## JULY 25, 2004

It was just before 11 p.m. when the flight landed at the Marquette County Airport, twenty miles south of town. The airfield had once been K. I. Sawyer Air Force Base, a combined Strategic and Air Defense Command base. The B-52s from Sawyer had dropped thousands of bombs on Vietnam when he and Tree were there. Service found Tatie Monica waiting near his truck.

"How were Arizona and Missouri?" she greeted him, adding, "Maybe we can't follow you out in the damn woods, but the rest of the goddamn country is *our* turf."

"It was okay," he said.

"I've made arrangements for the Toledo trip."

"Now?"

"If not now, when?" she said.

"What about your analyst?"

"I'm working on it."

"No deal," Service said.

"I'm keeping my end of the bargain," she argued.

"Selectively," he said.

"You are operating without authorization," she said.

"You talked to Orbet's family?"

"His son and widow. They say he left a couple of boxes of papers and we can make copies, but they want to keep the originals."

"Did he get anywhere in his investigation?"

"The wife says no. The son says his father hinted at having something," Monica said.

"Maybe you'd better check it out."

"Not you?"

"I need to get home and take care of my animals." McCants had come to the rescue again. He was going to owe her.

She said, "Don't go running off on me."

"Wouldn't think of it," he said.

"Bullshit."

Newf greeted him with huge slurps and followed him to where he looked up the site names of the dead game wardens in Illinois and Kansas, and called Eddie Waco to pass along the information.

"Fi found thet cancelled check. Hit's made out to Booger Baits, Curran, Michigan."

"Date?"

"March a' this year."

"I had the impression it was older."

"Fi's thinkin' Elray reordered."

"There an address on the check?"

Waco gave him the number on DeJarlais Road.

Newf sat with her massive head on Service's leg while he toggled his 800 megahertz radio. "Station Twenty, Twenty Five Fourteen. Who's the officer in Curran?"

"Denninger," the dispatcher in Lansing reported. "Seven, Two Twenty Two."

"Denninger on tonight?"

"Affirmative, Station Twenty clear."

Service switched to District Seven's channel on the 800. "Seven, Two Twenty Two, Twenty Five Fourteen."

"Go, Twenty Five Fourteen."

"You know an outfit called Booger Baits?"

"That's affirmative."

"An old man named Main still run the business?"

"Son's in charge now. The old man's still around though."

"They have a history with the department?"

"Negative, but they aren't real friendly."

"If I drive down there, can we meet?"

"Affirmative; where and when?"

"Tomorrow, early afternoon. How much longer you on?"

"Couple hours. I'm really sorry about Nantz. She and I knew each other."

"Thanks. I'll bump you when I get close tomorrow."

"Seven, Two Twenty Two clear."

Newf had paced all night and gotten into a scrap with Cat. Service had not slept well and called McCants in the morning. She agreed to watch the animals until he got back, and said she would pick them up around noon.

"You made good time," Denninger said. She was about five-eight or -nine and slender, with long brown hair knotted in a thick French braid, long legs. "Heard a lot about you," she said, extending her hand.

He left his truck and rode with Denninger.

"Booger Baits," he said quickly, trying to get them focused on the job.

"It was started by the old man, Charley Main Jr. He moved up here fifty years ago. Now his son Charley Main the third runs the show. Locally he's known as Charley the Turd."

"You get along with him?"

"I've made a lot of people unhappy since I got here," the young officer confessed. "My FTO told me the locals were going to piss and moan, complain and hate me no matter what I did, so I might as well bring the hammer down early and let them know how it was going to be.

"The Mains don't like anybody. People in parts of this county think they make their own laws. It's either rich dicks in their fancy clubs, or mullet-heads who can't read cereal boxes."

Service thought the woman sounded pretty negative for so early in her career.

"Charley the Turd?"

"Treats everyone like shit. Their house looks like a garbage dump, but don't be fooled. They've made a bunch of dough off their business. How, I have no idea. What's this about?" she asked, looking over at Service.

"Got a case where we've found booger flies and we're thinking they might connect to something important. We need to get them to let us look at their mailing lists."

Denninger laughed out loud. "Never happen."

Service said, "If I have to, I can bring in the Feebs with subpoenas."

"Must be something big," Denninger said.

"Important," Service said. "Any suggestions how to play this?"

"Get in his face. The man's a bully and he's got clout in the county, and in Lansing. You've got to get him back on his heels."

Booger Baits was a few miles south of Curran. There was no sign identifying a commercial operation of any kind. The grass was overgrown and there were boats and trailers all over the yard, sawhorses with small motors, several dogs on chains, and a six-by-six elk rack over an open garage, which was packed with so much junk it looked like there was no opening inside. The whole area reeked of refuse and dog shit.

Denninger walked up to the house with him. Service tried ringing the bell, but it didn't work. Several dogs in the yard began to bark. He knocked on the door several times, but there was no answer. "No car in the driveway," he said. "Maybe they're not here."

"They park behind the house," Denninger said. "They're here."

The young officer stood in front of the door, boots spread apart, and pounded the doorjamb loud enough to get all the dogs going.

The door swung open to reveal a man who towered over Service and the other officer, and had to weigh close to four hundred pounds. He was wearing a sleeveless mesh Detroit Lions jersey and shorts.

"Open the door, Main."

"You," he said to Denninger.

"I'm not going to ask again," she said.

"Dad's taking a nap." The man looked at Service, ignoring Denninger.

She said, "You've got no licenses for all those dogs, Main, and you're running a business on property zoned residential. You want trouble, I can arrange *beaucoup*."

The man exhaled and shook his head. "Don't let your mouth make threats your body can't back up, little girl," he said, looking amused.

Service felt Denninger tense, but her voice remained calm. "Open the door *now*, Charley."

The man opened the door. "See how sugar gets you more than vinegar," he said.

"We want to talk to you about your business," Service said.

The man's face turned red. "The county zoning commission give us an exception. Dickless Tracy there *knows* that."

"Call her that again and I'll put your head through the drywall," Service said with a menacing growl. "It's not about zoning," he added. "It's about your mail-order business."

"That's between me, the postal service, and the IRS."

Service was beginning to understand why Main was known as Charley the Turd. Service said, "We need help, and like it or not, you're it."

"You want flies, we got 'em. But we ain't no help desk for fish dicks."

Service made sure he got direct eye contact. "We're here to ask politely. You cop an attitude, I'll pass this to the FBI, and let them handle it their way."

This got the man's attention, causing him to step back. "I guess we can work something out," he said, moving aside.

The living room was stacked with old newspapers and candy wrappers. Clots of dog hair were everywhere, there were layers of dust on the furniture, and the carpet was soiled and smelled of dog urine. The man stopped them in the living room and crossed his arms. "So what's this about?"

"Your customers. We need to look at your catalog mailing lists."

"There ain't no catalog," the man said. "Dad used to send one, but it cost too much. We do all our business by word of mouth."

"Your customer list, not your catalog list," Service said.

"No fucking chance," the man snapped. "You don't got no legal right to our books."

"I'm not interested in your accounting practices," Service said. "We just want names going back as far as you have them."

"IRS says we only gotta keep records seven years."

"We're not trying to jack you around, Mr. Main. We need help with an important case and we're hoping you can provide us with information to let us take the case forward."

"You want me to narc?"

"No," Service said. "You're not under suspicion of anything." Before the man could answer, Service added, "Is there something here we *should* be suspicious of?"

"No," the man said. "We run a clean business."

"That's what we've been told. And as a legitimate businessman, we're hoping you can help us."

"What do I get out of it?"

Denninger said, "The satisfaction of helping law enforcement."

"Like I give a whoop-shit," he said.

Service was annoyed. "Okay, here's the deal. We want to see your customer list. We've asked politely, but here's the bottom line: If we need to get subpoenas, we'll get them, and sit right here until the FBI shows up with the paper. Might be a few hours, might be all night, so it's your call. We're not leaving without that list."

"Lists are confidential," the man said, stammering. "It's like the federal government monitoring books people check out of the public library."

"Are you sending out something you shouldn't, Mr. Main?"

"No."

The answer suggested to Service the man was telling the truth, and his resistance was not a matter of hiding something, but being a jerk in the face of authority. It was a familiar attitude in the Upper Peninsula.

Denninger said, "If the FBI comes into this thing they're also gonna bring the IRS. They'll rip the house apart and take *everything* they think could possibly help the case. We're just asking for a list. The FBI will get subpoenas that will let them cast a much wider net, and you won't get your stuff back for a long, long time. Once the FBI comes in, all your local contacts will back off because they won't want the entanglement with the feds. You're on your own, Charley."

"They can't jack around a businessman like that," the man protested.

"They can," Service said. "And they will. I guarantee it."

"You got any idea how many customers we have?"

"No," Service said.

"Over seven years, gotta be close to twenty thousand people—all over the world."

"Just burn the list onto a disk," Denninger offered.

"We aren't into computers," the man said. "We do everything by hand. We like doing business the old way."

"So what *do* you have?"

"Files," he said. "Fifty boxes, maybe sixty; hell, I ain't never counted them."

"Then we'll take the boxes, make copies, and bring them back."

The man's eyes darkened and his cheeks puffed out. "Them files ain't leaving this house," he said. "What happens if you have an accident or something?"

"Okay," Service said, "how about we try this: You show us your files and we'll sit down and make a list from them—the old way."

"My dad won't like it," the man said.

"I thought you were running the business now," Denninger challenged him.

"I do, but I got feelings for my dad, you know."

"Main, we can take those boxes if we call in the FBI. We understand your concern about losing them, but we've offered a compromise. So how do you want to play this? The options are on the table. Pick one."

The man covered his mouth with his hand and mumbled, "You can make your list, but you gotta be done by tonight."

Grady Service was tired and beyond annoyed. "Main, we'll take as long as we need. Now show us to the damn boxes—all of them."

The number of boxes was more than a hundred, and they were dusty, falling apart, and stacked all over a musty basement with no overhead light.

"You going to tell me what this is about?" Denninger asked as they settled in.

"Have you been briefed on the game warden murders?"

Her eyes widened and she nodded. "This is about that?"

"Let's hope," he said.

Charley the Turd brought a couple of battery-powered lanterns and left without comment.

Service looked at his watch. It was going on 11 p.m. when he sensed there was someone standing in the doorway. "You folks get something to eat?"

The man was ancient, with white hair and a wrinkled face. There were veins showing in his nose and cheeks and he looked like the mere act of standing exhausted him. "You Charley Junior?" Service asked.

"I am."

"Your booger flies work great," Service said.

"You've used 'em?"

"Friends have."

"The secret is, you gotta let the snot dry," the man said.

Denninger looked up with her mouth agape.

"Don't give me that look," the old man said. "You wanted to know the secret, right?"

"Not really," Service said. "But how'd you get the idea?"

"Come to me one day when I was fishing—came to me like a gift from God. Finally got around to making a fly. Showed it to my daddy and he beat my butt red, called it disgusting. But it caught fish, right from the start."

"Dad," Charley the Turd said from behind the old man. "You're not supposed to be up."

"Man's gotta have bowel movements," the old man said, turning and wobbling past his son.

"He tell you how he come up with the booger fly," Charley the Turd asked. "The 'gift from God' crap?"

"Said he was out fishing."

"He's told that lie so long he believes it. He didn't invent anything. Was his uncle give him the idea, back in Pigeon River."

Service perked up. "The town of Pigeon River?"

"Name's Mongo now, but it used to be Pigeon River. The old man started making and selling the flies. His uncle wanted credit and royalties, but the old man, he don't know the meaning of share, so he moved up here and has been here ever since."

Service knew Mongo. He had a case a couple of years back involving a fishing camp on the river, near an Indiana state fish hatchery. "You ever hear of a man named Ney?"

"Can't say I have," Charley the Turd said.

"What about your old man?"

"Have to ask him yourself."

Just as Service walked into the other room, the old man entered the bathroom and closed the door behind him. "Mr. Main?"

"I'd say I'd be out in a minute, but at my age the bowels move at their own speed, which ain't much to speak of. Best talk at me right through the door."

"You grew up in Pigeon River?"

"Changed the name since then," the old man answered. Service heard him wheezing and grunting.

"Did you ever hear of a man or a family named Ney?"

"Nope," the old man said.

Service went back to the boxes and returned to work.

It was nearly 3 a.m. before the list was complete.

Charley the Turd was snoring in an easy chair in the living room.

They were at the front door when they heard the old man shuffling behind them. "Weren't no Neys in town," he said. "Was a whole mob of Peys, though. My uncle married one of 'em who later run off with an Army Air Corps flight engineer during the big war. Them Peys bred like rabbits, maybe 'cause they was Frogs."

"Any of them have trouble with the law?"

The old man chuckled. "Hell, they all had troubles with the law, when the law had nerve enough to bring it up, which mostly they didn't."

"What kind of troubles?"

"You name it. Anybody pissed one of 'em off, the whole clan would be on 'em."

"Any of them disappear?"

"Lots of 'em. They'd beat it out of town until the heat let up some."

"You think they're still there?"

"They ain't the kind to do much movin' around. I expect there's still plenty of Peys down there, but I ain't been back since I left, and I ain't had no interest in doin' so."

"You ever sell any of your booger flies to the Peys?"

"Had one steal some from me once, but they weren't the sporting folk the Mains was. The Peys was strictly out for meat."

"Thanks for your help," Service said. "Tell your son we appreciate his cooperation."

"My son don't know sunshine from a shoe shine," the old man said disgustedly.

"What was that all about?" Denninger asked when he got out to the truck.

"The old man told me about growing up in Indiana."

She rolled her eyes as she turned the key and started the engine.

As she dropped him off at his truck, she offered, "You want, you can bunk at my place tonight," she offered. "I live near Glennie."

"I'll sleep here, but thanks."

"You sure?" Denninger asked Service.

"I've got to get an early start."

The young woman shrugged. "You want me to type up what we have?" During the night they had realized it was too difficult to look for CO names and had instead written down all Michigan customers. Service had seen Shark's name, but that was the only one he recognized.

"Yep, that would be good, and thanks again."

He took two blankets out of the truck and spread them on the grass. He had a hard time getting to sleep. Indiana, Pey, Ney. Maybe he finally had something to grab onto. In the morning he would head south.

## 40

## MONGO, INDIANA

## JULY 27, 2004

Service dug around in his emergency food pack but all he could find was a crumbled Moon Pie of indeterminate age. Normally he took pride in eating good food, but since the loss of Nantz and Walter, he found little pleasure in food. He ate only for sustenance, mainly junk food, and after a determined start, he was not getting the workouts he needed. He could feel a little paunch forming. *You're falling apart,* he told himself.

Just north of St. Johns he looked up the Woodpecker's cell phone number and wrote it down. Murphy Shanahan, aka the Woodpecker, was a longtime officer with bright red hair that came to a dramatic point over his forehead, and a prominent, thin nose. He had once served in the U.P. in Keweenaw County but had married a woman from Below The Bridge, and had transferred to St. Joseph County on the Indiana border. Murph was also a federal deputy, and he'd know his Indiana counterpart.

He called Shanahan on the cell but got no answer, and switched to Channel 12 on his 800 megahertz as he approached Marshall. "Twelve, Three Ten, you got TX? This is Twenty Five Fourteen."

"Affirmative TX. I had it off."

"I'm in Marshall and headed your way. I need your help with something."

"Where do you want to meet?"

"You pick."

"Sturgis at the cop house. See you when you get here."

"I need to go down to Mongo to meet the CO down there."

"I'll set it up," the Woodpecker said.

Murphy Shanahan was in top shape. He grinned when he shook hands. "What's going down?"

"You get briefed on the game warden murders?"

"Creeped us all out. This about that?"

"I'm helping the Feebs with some background interviews."

"I bumped Westy Karkowski down in LaGrange County. He'll meet us there. Indiana hasn't told their people about the killings, but I passed it on to Westy. He's a good warden, been around twenty-five years and still charging."

Westy Karkowski looked like he'd have a hard time getting off a couch, much less charging forward in his job, but he was interested, and had a quick mind. He wore the dark green short-sleeved shirt and dark green pants of an Indiana game warden, the shirt covered with gaudy state patches. The three trucks were snugged into a turnoff, next to the Pigeon River, just west of the village of Mongo.

"Indeed, there's a heap of Peys in the county, and I've had contact with more than a few of them, but the guy who knows 'em best is Arlo Danielson. He spent forty years as the warden here, and retired after I took over. Getting on now, but he's still sharp and in pretty good shape. He lives about five miles east of here on the river and spends most of his time fishing."

It seemed to Service that being a detective was more about patience and stamina than anything else. He seemed to spend all of his time trying to find somebody who knew somebody, who had heard something about somebody, and sometimes persistence paid off. It could also be a waste of time, but he knew that every lead not followed could be the one that would have paid off. As an old hockey player, he knew the essence of that game was to keep your feet moving, finish your checks, push the puck up to the guy in a better position, take every shot chance you got, and always, always follow the puck until there was a whistle. Being a detective was similar.

They found Danielson sitting on a patio, under a striped awning on a wooden deck, overlooking the river. He was a small man with a flat face and scars near his left ear that left a gap in his hair.

Karkowski made the introductions and the retired game warden said, "So many badges in one place, I thought mebbe you all thought I was pinching state fish."

Service asked about the Pey family, and Danielson made a sour face. "Pips, that bunch. Worst was Big Ben. He's ninety-two now and still got his hair, his hearing, and his eyesight. I arrested him so many times that even when he was behaving, which he did from time to time, he'd drop by and tell me about some other family member who was running afoul of the law. Wasn't that Ben got a shot of righteousness from doing it; he just didn't like the others out on the harvest when he couldn't be."

Grady Service wasn't sure how much to reveal, but it seemed to him there was a whole lot of history on hand here, and if he failed to take advantage, he might be sorry later. He laid out the killings of the game wardens, the Mexican incident, booger flies, the whole thing.

"The man arrested in Mexico had a woman and a boy with him. The local police cut them loose and they disappeared. The man gave his name as Ney, but the FBI couldn't find any Neys in Pigeon River, or even in Indiana."

"Big Ben might could know something," Danielson said. "Let's walk over and talk to him."

"He lives nearby?"

"Right smack across the river. We got to be friends and our kids built us a footbridge so we could visit back and forth. He's bit as hard for trout as me, and he isn't the wild thing he once was." Danielson chuckled and added, "None of us are."

Big Ben Pey was no more than five feet tall, with a full head of only slightly gray hair, mottled skin, and black moles all over his hands. He was wearing overalls, no shirt, and workboots that looked to be as old as him.

Danielson said, "Ben, this is Grady Service. He's a game warden up in the Upper Peninsula, down here trying to get some information."

The old man stared at Service. "Used ta hunt up that way with my boys some, but game wardens up there didn't seem too partial to outsiders. Had an old chum up there, name of Allerdyce."

"Limpy," Service said. It figured. The big poachers all seemed to know each other.

I heard he took bad-sick a while back."

"He recovered." The thought of the Indiana poacher and retired warden being buddy-buddy stuck in his craw. It would not happen with Limpy and him.

"Never met a man knew the woods like Allerdyce," Big Ben Pey said.

"Or game wardens," Service added.

Pey laughed. "Sure enough. He used ta tell me only one of you boys ever got the best of him, but he died a long time ago."

Service was sure that this had been his father, but said nothing.

"So what's this question you're burnin' ta ask?" the old man said.

He told the story again and concluded, "I just learned that Pigeon River is Mongo, and that there are a lot of your kin around here. Did you know a Frankie Ney or Pey?"

"Prob'ly Francois Ney Pey. His people come down from Québec a long time back, and they was always hung up over that French stuff. Name was François, but he went by Frankie."

"He had a son?"

"Not that I heard. Unlike the rest of the family, Frankie went off to college, got him a dandy job. Lived in Detroit a spell, I think, but he was all over tarnation and made good dough."

"He come back here often?"

"Used to be sweet on a woman named Greenleaf, lived on the river in town. Folks used to say he slipped back in to town from time to time to slip it to her, if you know what I mean, but I never seen him. I don't think he cared much for his kin."

"This woman still around?"

"Name's Esther, but ev'body called her Essie. She was peculiar, that's for sure. She lives with her daughter up in Sturgis now, in one of them Polack neighborhoods. She's got to be in her seventies now, maybe even eighty. My mind ain't so good anymore."

"What's her daughter's name?"

The old man thought for a minute. "Let me call my son." He went back into the house and came back five minutes later. "Daughter's name is Ruth Zalinske, with an "e," not an "i." Zalinskes claim to be Ukrainians, but Ukes're just another flavor of Polack."

Service asked, "Do you remember who Frankie worked for?"

Big Ben lifted his eyes toward the sky. "I think it was Sears Roebuck, or maybe Monkey Ward, one a' them big outfits. His job was to go into stores and check their bookkeeping or some such numbers thing. Frankie was real smart."

"What did Frankie look like?"

"I think I got a pitcher somewhere in the house. You want me to look?"

"If you wouldn't mind."

"Exercise do me good." Big Ben looked over at Danielson. "Got two dandy trout after you went in last night."

"I hope they were legal," the retired game warden said.

The old man laughed and disappeared into the house again. He came out carrying a faded photograph in small square format, like something from an old Brownie Hawkeye. There were marks on the corner of the photo where it had obviously been affixed to an album.

Service studied the photo. There was a vague resemblance to the Mexican photo, but he couldn't be sure if it was real or wishful thinking. "How old was he in this?"

"Oh, he woulda been eighteen or nineteen, just before he went off ta college."

"Where was that?"

"Up your way in Marquette."

Northern? "When?"

"I'd say 1932. Moved to Detroit after college and signed up for the navy after Pearl Harbor, spent the war out in the Pacific somewheres, and never come back to Pigeon River."

Eighteen or nineteen in 1932 would have made Pey thirty-eight years older when the Mexicans arrested him. Service made a mental note.

"What kind of a boy was he?"

"Just a boy, I guess, 'cept he liked school, which most Peys didn't. Hunted and fished a lot, and he run a trapline in winter. Sold furs to buy him a Chevy. That boy liked to move around."

"Liked to move around?"

"Used to drive over to Montreal every summer. Relatives there, I guess."

"What relation to you is he?"

Big Ben stared at the ceiling. "They all sort of run together. I guess I'd be a nephew. His mother was Pauline, who was my half sister."

"Is Pauline still alive?"

"Died the year Frankie went off to college."

"Died how?"

"Got murdered."

"Did they catch the killer?"

"Nossir. Somebody cut her throat. She was married, but she and her husband, Jacques, both run around on each other. Some say it was one of her boyfriends did her in, but it never got solved."

"Can I borrow this photo?" Service asked.

"If it'll help, sure," said Big Ben.

Service thanked the man and was silent as he followed Shanahan back to Sturgis. Frankie Pey was a trapper and a hunter, which meant he knew how to skin animals. And his mother had been found with her throat cut, the murder never solved. He went to college and never came back. Up in Marquette? Was this possible? This was beginning to have the feel of something almost solid, but there remained plenty of holes and gaps.

## 41

## STURGIS, MICHIGAN
### JULY 27, 2004

By late afternoon they were in Sturgis in a neighborhood of small houses well past their prime and only marginally kept up. Someone had put a hand-painted sign in a yard that read POLISH ACRES. Service knocked on the door and a woman answered. "I'm looking for Esther Greenleaf."

"I'm her daughter," the woman said.

Service explained who he was and showed his badge. "Is she here?"

"She's not well," the woman said.

"It's important that we talk," Service said.

"Can you keep it brief?" the woman asked. She opened the door tentatively and let him in.

The old woman was watching television. "I always watch *Jeopardy*," she announced. "This one's a rerun, but tonight the reg'lar show's on."

The daughter said, "Mom, this police officer would like to talk to you."

"There's no category for police on *Jeopardy*," the woman said. "There was, I'd know. I seen every show ever made."

Service sat down on a couch beside the recliner where the old woman sat. The daughter stood beside her mother. "Mrs. Greenleaf, I'd like to ask you some questions about Frankie Pey."

The old woman looked up at her daughter and dismissed her with a wave of the hand. "Ruthie, you just scoot on out of here now."

The daughter obeyed without protest.

"I don't want to bring up any bad things from your past," Service began. "But you knew Frankie Pey."

The woman looked at him for the first time and scowled. "What is the definition of 'knew'?"

Service said, "You know—a friend or something like that?"

"No, it's the game! You must put it in question form, 'What was the name of the man who used to be sweet on Essie Greenleaf?'"

*Oh boy,* Service thought. The circuits in the old lady's brain were a little frayed and she was seeing the world through the prism of *Jeopardy.* "What was the name of the man who used to be sweet on Essie Greenleaf?"

"Who is Frankie Pey?" the old woman said, pressing her hands together.

Service had only taken a cursory glance at *Jeopardy* over the years, in fact, rarely watched television, and had to rack his brain for the right words.

"Okay," he said. "The category is Frankie Pey."

"I never seen that on the show," she said.

"It's coming up on a future one," he said.

"Oh good, I'll be ready."

"First answer," Service said. "Mexico."

"What is Frankie's final resting place?"

"Right," Service said. "Essie."

"What is his last lover's name?" the woman said.

"Their son's name?" Service asked.

The woman looked agitated. "Can't answer no trick question. They didn't have no son."

"The name of the boy who traveled with them?"

"Who is Marcel?" she said.

"Where is Marcel now?" he asked.

The woman lurched in her chair. "Improper question. I have to confer with the judges." She looked at the wall, whispered animatedly, and turned back to him.

"What Frankie was doing in Mexico when he was arrested?" Service said.

"What is completing his life's work?" she said, clapping her hands together. "Did I get the Daily Double?"

What the fuck was a daily double? "Sure," he said.

"No," she said, her eyes narrowing. "You're not Alex and this isn't *Jeopardy*. You don't even know the rules. I won't play with nobody who don't know the rules. It ruins everything. Ruthie!" she screamed. "Ruthie! *Ruthie!*"

The daughter rushed into the room.

"He's a fake. I need my medicine. I don't play with no fakes."

The daughter walked outside with Service, her lips quivering.

"Look," he said. "I had no intention of upsetting your mother. She's difficult to talk to, but it's clear that she may possess some information that will be important to the authorities. I'm leaving, but you can expect the FBI to come to see her."

"Oh my God. The FBI! She doesn't know what she's talking about," the daughter said. "She's trapped inside the television."

"Maybe so," Service said, but he suspected she wasn't in there alone.

iii

## 42

## SLIPPERY CREEK, MICHIGAN

## JULY 28, 2004

Service checked his e-mail and phone messages as he drove north. His in-box was empty except for routine notices from division HQ in Lansing. It was getting late.

Captain Grant had called, wondering where he was, and, as usual, the captain's voice was controlled, neutral, and impossible to read.

Special Agent Monica left a one-word voice-mail message: "Asshole."

Service stopped at the Windmill truck stop south of Lansing, ordered coffee, got out a pad of paper, and tried to make notes about the case. It wasn't long before his mind was consumed and he paid no attention to anything going on around him.

1) First batch of killings: 1950–1970 [27 dead]. Killer inactive, 1970–1982. Second batch: 1982–present (2004) [22 dead]. Ney murdered in prison just before Xmas, 1974. Never confessed.

2) Suspect in Mexico gave name as Ney; FBI had failed to identify Pigeon River as Mongo, unable to find any Neys anywhere in state of Indiana. Per Big Ben, Pey; François Pey, aka Frankie Ney. Was this the Mexico Ney? Former girlfriend Essie Greenleaf says he is/was.

3) Boy involved, named Marcel, relationship and last name unknown. Estimated age 15–16 in 1970, which would make him approx. 48–49 now.

4) A New Mexico game warden killed two weeks after Ney arrested in Mexico. The killer's work, someone else, coincidence? Definitely not Ney. (Pey?)

5) Ney cut Mexican victims along the spine. Precursor of blood eagle? Frankie Pey was trapper as a kid—has skinning knowledge, comfortable with a cutting edge. Also liked to move around. Montreal, relatives?

6) Ficorelli and Spargo both used booger flies mail-ordered from Booger Baits in Curran. What about the other victims? [Waco checking Illinois, Kansas] The list has to be carefully analyzed. FACT: List only goes back seven years; no apparent way to connect flies to the first batch of killings. If Mains use no computers, how could killer access list? Need F/U by Denninger? C. Main III nervous about government oversight. Why? All of this seems to point to something, but what?

7) Give photo from Big Ben Pey to FBI to compare with the Mexican photo.

8) Per Big Ben: Frankie Pey may have gone to college "up in Marquette"; from same source, Frankie served in the navy in the Pacific during World War II. Did he graduate? Are there college and/or navy records on the man? Check NMU, DOD.

9) Pey might have worked for Sears or Monkey Ward. [FBI F/U] According to Big Ben: Frankie Pey a sort of roving bookkeeper or auditor. [NOTE: Seems to fit the kind of job and freedom Monica theorizes for the serial murderer.] Way to track his movements over the years and coordinate those with killings? Expense, trip, or sales reports? Anything? How long do companies keep such records, if at all?

10) Frankie's mother murdered the year he went to college, estim. 1932. Throat cut. Speculation: probably a boyfriend. No arrests. Frankie comfortable with cutting edges. Who investigated the case? Were there suspects? Was Frankie ever one of them? [FBI F/U]

11) When will Monica have notes of deceased agent in Toledo? If so, any new leads, information in the dead agent's files and notes?

12) Where is Monica's analyst? Why so difficult to arrange a meeting? What's her reluctance? Is she holding back, and if so, why?

13) Can forensic pathologist/medical examiner look at wounds in Mexico vicks, and those in the blood eagle killings, see a connection or a progression? Something?

14) Initial victims in the second group = no blood eagle. Why the sudden shift in MO. Why change? Something different in killer's state of mind?

15) Nantz, Mama Ficorelli, Spargo's sister: all killed in freak auto accidents: Coincidence, or what? How do these fit, if at all? Ptacek from U.P. Autobody says paint flecks on bumper lining should not be there, indicative of PIT? Need second opinion on evidence. [NOTE: Nantz not an accident. Others misread in WI, MO?]

16) FACT: I'm not on Booger Baits list. Never used the flies, never even heard of them until now. If killer finds victims via fly orders, how would he use list to find me? As of last night, no MI COs on Booger Baits lists—only Shark. Denninger will type Michigan list, double-check.

Most predators in the animal kingdom, he knew, were born efficient, and tended to single out a specific victim, either because it was outside the group or perceived to be weaker than the others. Then it slow-hunted, narrowing the victim's options until it was either trapped or panicked. Prey panic? The phrase stuck in his mind. Were human predators different?

"You writin' a juicy love letter, hon?"

Service looked up, felt confused. *Nantz?* A waitress with huge eyes was bending down over him. He immediately turned over the pad and she stepped back.

"Dude," she said icily, "I wasn't snooping. You want a refill or not?"

He gave the girl his thermos and asked her to fill it with the leaded stuff.

He paid for his coffee and continued north. At eighty miles an hour it would take him roughly three-and-a-half hours to reach the bridge and another ninety minutes to get back to the cabin. *Watch for deer,* he warned himself, as he went around Lansing on the I-69 bypass and headed north. He tightened his seat belt and tried to put the case out of his mind. Stay in the moment, watch for deer, and don't forget elk after Gaylord. *Damn, it's dark.*

Vince Vilardo's Chrysler minivan was parked at the cabin. Service got out stiff-legged, and found the retired medical examiner for Delta County asleep on the footlocker bed; a stranger was asleep in his old upholstered chair. Both of them were snoring.

"Vince," Service said gruffly.

Vilardo stirred. "Two minutes, Rose."

"It's Grady, not your wife. What the hell are you doing here, Vince?"

Vilardo sat up like a spring had been unwound. "Huh . . . What?" He rubbed his eyes and shook his head. "Grady?"

"What are you doing here, Vince? Do you know what time it is?"

"What time it is?"

"It's midnight. Stop repeating what I say and wake up."

Vilardo shuffled over to the sink and splashed water on his face.

"Boy, I was zonked." He looked at Service, who was looking at the stranger. "That's Charles Marschke, Esquire. He went to the Gladstone house and nobody was there. He asked the county for help and they called me and I brought him out. He claims he's one of Maridly's lawyers."

*One* of them?

"Hey," Service said, nudging the sleeping man's foot. "Wake up."

The man opened his eyes and stared up, the sleep falling off like a coverlet. He reached into his shirt pocket and took out a business card. "Charles Marschke—Maridly was my client. I'm sorry for your loss."

"You were her lawyer?"

"She had several, but I was her personal affairs lawyer, family friend, and financial manager. I'll miss her. She never mentioned my name?"

"She didn't talk about money."

The man smiled. "That was Maridly. May I ask why you never married her?"

Service kept asking himself the same question. "That's none of your business."

The man held up his hands. "You're absolutely right, and it's irrelevant. Married or not, she named you her sole heir. It will take a while to transfer everything, but it will be done in six to ten months. Do you have a financial consultant I can confer with?"

Service was confused and tired. "Hell, I haven't balanced my checkbook in I don't know how long."

The man smiled. "If you need a consultant, I'd be pleased to be of assistance."

"I don't need a consultant. I work for the state."

"But you do," the man said. "You do."

"I don't want to inherit anything from Nantz," Grady Service said.

"You're getting everything: all her assets, the house in Gladstone, her aircraft, her investments. Those alone come to about eighty, eighty-five."

"Eighty thousand?"

The man laughed. "*Million,* Mr. Service, and growing daily. She was a very, very wealthy woman, and now you are going to be a wealthy man."

Service felt his legs go soft.

Marschke took papers out of his briefcase and took them to a table, spreading them out. "There's a sticky tag in each place where you need to sign."

"What if I don't sign?"

"You'll still get it all. It will just take longer. This is what you call a done deal. Go with the flow."

"Sign," Vince Vilardo yipped. "*Sign!*"

"Shut up, Vince."

Service signed the papers and watched the man fold them and put them back into his briefcase. He walked out to Vince's car with the men and told Vince, "You keep your mouth shut about this."

When they were gone he sat down on his steps and stared into the darkness. What the fuck was he going to do with eighty million dollars? *If Nantz was here now, he'd strangle her,* he told himself. Go ahead and laugh, Mar. This is not funny!

At 6 a.m. and with virtually no sleep, he telephoned Special Agent Monica. "Tatie, this is Service. Just wake up and listen. When I was in Arizona, I talked to a CBP agent who was part of the *federales* team that arrested Ney. He said Ney's murder in prison was not what it seemed. Ney scammed a guard to kill him because he was dying of cancer and he had only weeks or months to live. He also said that all Ney would tell the *federales* was that he had completed his life's work. Nobody knew what that meant."

He kept talking, couldn't stop. "After Ficorelli's funeral, his aunt gave me his fishing gear, including his fly collection. A friend of mine came down from Houghton to look at the flies and he found a unique one called a booger fly. It's made in only one place, by an old guy down in Curran, Michigan, which is about thirty miles south of Alpena," he said. "I found the same kind of fly at the kill site. I think Ficorelli got out of the river to retrieve the fly and was killed."

Tatie Monica perked up. "You *found* evidence and didn't tell me?"

"Shut up, Tatie. I also went back to Elray Spargo's place. He had booger flies in his collection. I drove down to Curran and talked to the man who makes the flies. The old guy grew up in Mongo, in northern Indiana, and invented the fly there, but he moved up to Michigan and has been here fifty years. I plotted all the body sites on maps to see if I could pick up a trend.

What threw me is that some were by the ocean. It took a while to remember tides—moving water. Your analyst understood that. I began to wonder if what our victims had in common was that they were all trout fishermen and they used flies—specifically booger flies. The business up in Curran has records only for seven years, but we convinced them to let us compile a list. It's run by a man called Charles Main Jr. and his son, Charles Main the third. The locals call the younger one Charley the Turd." Service picked up his notepad and looked at it. "I know it's a long shot," he concluded.

"What have you been smoking, Service?" the FBI agent asked.

"You need to listen, and we need to get on the same page. You need to get your people to go through the list, to find out how many of our victims bought booger flies by mail," he said. "I've got an agent in Missouri checking on the Illinois and Kansas victims."

"One of my agents?"

"No, Missouri conservation agent Eddie Waco—the guy with the beard? We can't look at the first batch of victims, but we can sure as hell compare the customer list to the second group and see what comes up. If it turns out they were all using booger flies, then we have a potential intersect, a way for the killer to identify certain game wardens. Maybe this is how he picked them, I don't know. Maybe it was a coincidence that victims were also some of the best in each state. You have the resources to do this; I don't," he said.

"How would the killer get their list?" she asked.

This stopped him momentarily. "I don't know yet. Now listen to this: Mongo was once called Pigeon River. It's built on the Pigeon River. The name was changed. The fly tier, whose name is Main, never heard of a family named Ney, but he said there was a large family named Pey in Pigeon River."

Service let her digest the information. "I went to Mongo, where I met the current game warden, and a retired warden. The retired warden introduced us to an old man named Big Ben Pey. The old man told us he had a distant relative named Francois *Ney* Pey, and that this man went by the name of Frankie. Frankie Pey worked for Sears or Montgomery Ward out of Chicago. He went to college in Marquette, and served in the navy during World War Two. No idea if he graduated, but it's a starting place, *and* he was some sort of traveling auditor for his employer and moved all over the country. Apparently he came back to Mongo only to see a girlfriend, who was married to somebody else," said Service.

"The woman now lives with her daughter just up the road in Sturgis, Michigan," Service continued. "Her name is Greenleaf, Essie Greenleaf. I talked to her and she's batty, but she also let me know in a strange and roundabout way that she had a thing with Frankie Pey. She said Pey died in Mexico. When I asked her what he was doing down there, she told me, 'Completing his life's work.' She also confirmed there was a boy with them, but said he was neither his son—nor hers. She said the kid's name was Marcel. He was about fifteen or sixteen at the time. It can't be a coincidence that she used the same words the border agent used. Big Ben Pey gave me a photo. He says it's Frankie just before he left for college, which made him eighteen or nineteen in 1932. I think I can see some similarity to the photo I got from the *federales,* but you people have specialists and software to take this and age it and see if there's a potential match, right?"

The FBI agent said, "Jesus . . . This is unbelievable."

"I know," he said. "Where is your asshole consultant? We need to talk to him."

He heard her scratching on paper. "Eighteen or nineteen in 1932; that makes this guy in his mid fifties by 1970."

"Is that significant?"

"Ballpark age for a lot of serial murderers."

There was a long pause before she spoke again. "It can't be this easy," she lamented.

"It's not, but it's beginning to look like we've got some meat to grab, and we need to move on it. Are you awake?"

"Okay, okay," was all she could say. "I'll get dressed and head out to your shack."

"I want to talk to your analyst."

"Why?" she asked, her voice rising.

"I want to find out how he picked up on this whole deal, what his thinking was, how he got one plus one to equal a shitpot more. I'm also wondering why the hell this second batch begins with a variety of MOs and suddenly shifts to the blood eagle? Does this signify some sort of psychological shift? Or do we have a different killer?"

Tatie Monica said, "Why in hell is somebody with your ability wasting himself in the backwoods?"

Service said, "When do I meet your analyst?"

"You won't," she said.

He waited for an explanation.

Finally, in exasperation, she said, "I can't find him, and he won't respond to my messages."

Service could hardly contain his rage. "You have got to be *shitting* me! You'd better get your people dogging his sorry ass, and I mean *right now*. Maybe this is nothing, but I don't like this guy pointing us at all this and then taking a sudden hike into Neverland."

"I've already got people on it," she said. "I'll be there with Larry and Bobbi in an hour. I take it you're not off the case."

"Let me put something else on the table: Ficorelli's mother and Spargo's sister died in car wrecks within a month of their killings. My girlfriend and son died in the same way not long ago, dry pavement, no apparent reason. I talked to a guy up here who found something that suggests my girlfriend got run off the road, and the more I think about it, the more it makes sense. The state police ruled it an accident, despite evidence to the contrary. She was a great pilot. There had to be a reason for the wreck. You ever hear of prey-induced panic?"

"No," she said.

"I'll explain it when you get here. Also, Frankie Pey was a trapper as a kid, and the year he left for college his mother was found murdered, with her throat cut. The case was never solved. I'm in this sonuvabitch to the end," he said.

"I'm running out the door now," Monica said.

Service lay on his footlocker bed and tried to sleep. The case was no longer in his mind. He had exorcised that. Now all he could think about was what the hell he should do with eighty million dollars that he had no right to. Couldn't he somehow trade it all back for Nantz and Walter?

## PART III
## GREEN BEAR ISLAND

*Omnes una manet nox*
The same night awaits us all.
—*Horace*

While he waited for Tatie Monica, Service made fresh coffee and started making more notes, mostly questions. If the killer had access to Main's customer list, how had he gotten it, and when? Was it possible that Charley the Turd and/or his father were involved? Had the list been used for both groups of killings? Pey died in 1974 in prison in Mexico. Where did Marcel go? Was Marcel a killer? *The* killer?

"Too many holes," he said out loud, crumpling the notes and bouncing them off the wall.

He awoke on the floor to find Tatie Monica standing over him. She had the crumpled notes in hand and was trying to read them. "How long since you've slept?" she asked.

"Not sure."

"An exhausted investigator fucks up. Go to bed."

"I don't have a bed," he said.

She gave him a quizzical look and he pointed to the footlockers. "Sweet Jesus," she said. "Give me all your notes and I'll take them back to Marquette with us. You sleep. That's an order."

"I don't report to you."

"Think of me as your mother."

"She died in childbirth."

"Probably lucky for her." Special Agent Monica stormed out the door and Service lay down to try and sleep.

His mind refused to shut off. He got up and grabbed his handheld and called Officer Denninger. "I need your help again."

"Whatever you need," she said.

"If the Mains aren't computerized, how could somebody get their list? Did they ever report a theft? Talk to the county and the state, and then talk to the old man alone. Charley the Turd will just try to stonewall you again."

"I'll get back to you."

Service called Eddie Waco. "Anything on the men in Kansas and Illinois?"

"I'm in Illinois now. The officer's name here was Retucci. He was a fly-fishing nut and he had booger flies. I'm headed to Kansas next. I'd call ahead to the family, but it's better to show up in person. Gives it more weight."

"I agree. Thanks."

"I'll be back to you'n quick as I can. You gettin' close?"

"Maybe."

"Count me in for the finish."

"Your supervision will approve that?"

"You let me worry about that, Michigan Man. You'n call, I'll haul. Heck, I might even get to see me a bear."

Grady Service liked Eddie Waco. But were they really beginning to get close to something? He wasn't sure. This was like hunting blind. He dozed off thinking about hunting and bears, and he slept through the rest of the day and night.

## MARQUETTE, MICHIGAN
### JULY 29, 2004

Most of the regional HQ was dark when Service parked in the lot south of the building, but there was a light on in the captain's office. The fog this morning had been thick, the driving slow.

The captain had already made coffee. Service poured a cup for himself and made his way to Grant's office.

"You look perplexed."

Service took him through the case, omitting nothing and emphasizing the accidents of Ficorelli's and Spargo's relatives. As was his way, the captain listened and made notes before asking questions.

"The analyst aspect is disturbing," the captain said.

"It's a major loose end," Service said.

"You know the preferred tactic for weathering a shit storm?"

Service looked up. His captain never used such language.

"You sit under a good strong roof until it's done falling," Grant said.

"Are you telling me you're going to chain me to my desk?"

"You know better than that. If Nantz and Walter were killed intentionally, the killer is trying to rattle you. I'm going to insist that the state lab people go over the wreck again. What you do is keep pushing and prodding."

"Eventually there's going to be a collision," Service said.

"I have no doubt," the captain said, "but when it happens, let it be you who determines the location and rules of engagement."

"I've already had that thought."

"I was certain you had," Captain Grant said with a nod.

When Service got back to his cubicle, there was tapping on his outside window. He looked out to see Limpy Allerdyce standing there. Service knew Allerdyce would not come into the building. He got a cup of coffee for the old poacher and went outside to meet him.

"Proud of you," Service joked. "You actually touched the building."

Allerdyce squinted. "Youse tink more about youse's gal?"

Service suddenly picked up on the old man's rage, which he was struggling to contain. He pointed a finger at Allerdyce. "I don't need your help, thank you very much."

"Up here we take care of each udder, sonny."

"What're you gonna do, take my back?"

The old man grinned and said nothing.

"You get caught with anything that even faintly can be construed as a weapon and you'll be in violation of your parole, and you will go back inside. You want to ruin your image with your girlfriend?"

Allerdyce drank his coffee, scowled, and looked out toward Lake Superior, which was beginning to lighten in the rising sun. "My day," he said, "I never t'ought twice 'bout shootin' dogs, runnin' deers an' such. Dere's some t'ings a man don't turn 'is cheek to."

"Stay out of it, Allerdyce. Go blow more smoke up your professor's behind."

The old poacher cackled. "Not a joke, sonny. I changed, and my people, they changin' too. How it was ain't how it gonna be. Go ahead, youse make fun of me, but youse'll see."

"Stay out of my business," Service said emphatically, splashing his coffee on the grass as he went back inside. Being around the old man always gave him the creeps, and right now he didn't need any more distractions. Limpy was capable of just about anything. What had the professor said—to check with the RAP people? Where was that goddamn list she'd given him? He found it in a folder and picked up his phone.

"Station Twenty, Twenty Five Fourteen. I've got a list of times alleged RAP tips from informants came in to the RAP line. Can you verify receipt and disposal?" He read off the dates and times.

The RAP dispatcher in Lansing came back on the radio after ten minutes. "They all check out, Twenty Five Fourteen. There were sixteen calls, and all of them resulted in citations. All callers were anonymous."

"Twenty Five Fourteen clear." Jesus Christ, what was going on? There was no way Limpy could change. The only possible explanation was that he was up to something.

Fern LeBlanc passed his cubicle, looked in, and said, "Nice to see you could grace us with your presence." She came back five minutes later with a handful of pink callback slips. "Your adoring public," she said, dropping them on his desk.

He had just started looking through the notes when LeBlanc came back and said, "I'm going to transfer a call to you." This usually meant there was someone or something she didn't want to handle, because she was experienced and talented enough to deal with just about anything that came through the door or over the phone.

He saw the line light blink and picked up the phone. "Detective Service."

"I ast for DNR, not reg'lar cops," a male voice complained.

"This is the DNR," Service reassured him. In the minds of Yoopers, game wardens were not cops.

"When youse get deteckatives?"

"It's been awhile," Service said. He hated calls like this.

"No kiddin' . . . Well, I got me a dead calf out here. Wolf come in and kilt 'im. Somebody gonna come out and take a look? I wanta file me one of dem claims."

Service rocked back in his chair. An alleged wolf depredation call was one of the most contentious complaints to deal with.

"You're sure it was a wolf?"

"Yeah, sure, and I coulda shot da bot' a' dem, but I figgered youse guys would get yore skivvies all in a yank, so's I din't shoot, and now I'm callin' youse. Youse comin' or not?"

"Give me your address," Service said and wrote it down.

McFarland was about forty miles south, and there was no direct route. "I'll be there in thirty, forty minutes."

"What I do, them bloody wolfs come skulkin' back?"

"Secure the carcass and don't shoot them."

"Damn tings all over da place nowadays," the man said, and hung up. Service had not even gotten his name.

He told LeBlanc where he was headed and drove south on US 41.

# 45

## McFARLAND, MICHIGAN

## JULY 29, 2004

The farm was typical of many that lay on the plateau south of Marquette, toward Rapid River: several ancient apple trees, a few acres of potatoes, a small field of stunted corn, some multicolored chickens running loose to provide free-range snacks for local coyotes, three sway-back dairy cows, a half-dozen beefs, and a small flock of dusty sheep; all in all, a virtual walk-up cafe for wolves and other predators. The house was low with multiple roofs to help reduce winter snow loads, the fences hadn't been painted since soldiers wore brown boots, and there were two rusted-out tractors in a rock-strewn field serving as hotels for various birds and rodents.

The farmer was sixtyish, gaunt, dressed in all his agrestic glory: a flannel shirt with missing buttons, unlaced muddy, green, high-top Converse All Stars, a Budweiser can in hand.

"Took youse long enough," the man greeted him.

Service looked at his watch: thirty-two minutes had elapsed since he'd left the regional office lot. When you were part of the DNR in the U.P., there were myriad ways to disappoint locals, and few ways to make them happy. This was not going to be a happy interaction. Many Yoopers welcomed the return of wolves to the area, but there were few farmers in the pro-wolf forces, and Service was fairly certain that more than a few wolves were being quietly shot and disposed of. The state had a reparations program for animals lost to wolves, but in most instances the predation was done by wild dogs or coyotes, not wolves. No matter; some farmers blamed wolves for virtually all the ills of the northern part of the state, including seasonal cycles in deer populations.

The man led him to a ramshackle shed tilted precariously to the east, and showed him the dead calf. Service looked at two sets of footprints in the mud and dust in the area around the building. They were too small for wolves: coyotes or wild dogs, he guessed. He could see where they had approached, not in single file like wolves, but apart.

"Not wolves," Service told the man.

"Youse telling me I don't know a bloody wolf when it come sniffing around?"

"I'm just telling you that these tracks and signs indicate coyotes or dogs, not wolves."

"You buckos always got answers," the man complained. "Tink the rest of us a buncha emptyheads?"

There was no point arguing. "Tell me what you saw."

"Da she-wolf, she was up to da side a' da shed over dere, and she looked back, and a smaller one come up behind her."

"You saw them go inside?"

"Seen 'em on da doorstep. Din't see no coyotes."

"But you didn't actually see wolves on the kill?"

"Din't have to."

Service looked at the carcass. "How do you know it was a *female* wolf?" he asked.

"Big one and a little one."

"Twenty pounds—fifty, eighty?"

"I din't weigh 'em, eh."

"What position was the tail?"

The man looked confused. "I wasn't watchin' no damn tails!"

Service asked the man to look at the carcass. He explained, "Wolves have a fairly regular pattern of eating. They start by stripping the rump and organs. They don't hit the legs and other musculature until the bigger portions are consumed. This calf's legs have barely been chewed. Two wolves would have done a lot more damage."

"I don't know why 'n hell dey tell us ta call da state when all youse do is stonewall us."

"If you call the biologist from Marquette, he'll tell you the same thing I'm telling you."

"Bloody DNR, da whole worthless bunchayas."

"I'll call for you." Service gave the man one of his business cards and wrote down the name of a biologist in the Marquette regional office. "His name is Herndon. I'll try to get him out here today."

"I see dem critters again, I'm gonna shoot first," the farmer said.

"I wouldn't advise that," Service said, trying to retain his composure and be polite. There were so many crank calls about wolves and other things that it was easy to write callers off, but his job was to find out what happened, not discourage citizens.

As far as he knew, confirmed U.P.-wide wolf predation over the past two years had amounted to a dozen dogs, eighteen cows, a dozen chickens, and a few sheep. Since the 1990s the state had paid less than $20,000 in reparations to farmers, who claimed the DNR was purposely misidentifying predators in order to not pay them for their losses.

Leaving the farm, he had no interest in going back to the office. He called Paulie Herndon, told him what to expect, and headed south into northern Delta County to look around and think. Parking near the Escanaba River, he called Buster Beal. The visit to the farmer had started some unformed notions rolling around in his head.

"Chewy, Grady. You know much about wolf behavior?"

"Some. When you manage deer, you learn about wolves. Deer herd is like Mickey D's to a wolf pack."

"The adults in the packs bring food to the pups, right?"

"While they're in the denning area. When the pups get to about twenty pounds, the pack moves to a rendezvous area for the summer and remains fairly stationary as the pack teaches the young ones to hunt. By September pups are thirty to forty pounds and strong enough to get in on the chase, but in summer the wolves are more likely to be eating beaver than deer. They'd rather wait until deep snow in winter for their venison. Kills come a lot easier then."

"The mothers teach the pups to hunt?"

"Roles aren't that clearly delineated. Adult males and females all take part in the hunt, and the pups follow along and mimic what they see the other pack members doing. Hey, it's not a lot different than the men in the family taking a kid out to deer camp and his dad, grandpa, uncles, and older brothers all teaching him how it's done."

"Do wolves ever kill individually?"

"Beaver sometimes, but not larger ungulates. Too risky. With wolves, eating and killing are group activities."

"Single wolf and a pup kill a calf?"

"Could," the biologist said, "but usually it's only the adults doing the killing and the pups just jumping in for their share of the grub."

"Thanks, Chewy."

"That help you?"

"Maybe," Service said. The wolf incident got him thinking about Frankie Pey, Essie Greenleaf, and the boy called Marcel. He wasn't sure why. The border patrol agent said that the prisoner Ney had called the boy his creation.

He was beginning to formulate a thought, but it remained vague and he couldn't quite pull it together. Not yet.

## 46

## SLIPPERY CREEK, MICHIGAN
## JULY 29, 2004

It was dark when Grady Service got home. McCants still had Newf and Cat and he thought about fetching them, but decided to wait until the next day.

Two Crown Vics were parked at the cabin. It looked like Gasparino beside one of the vehicles. Tatie Monica was on the porch. He invited her in and made a fresh pot of coffee. Her face was splotched with something that looked like hives, and there was a vein sticking out of her temple. She wore a black business pantsuit, black pumps with low heels, her hair in a bun, her face masked with heavy makeup. She looked like she was dressed for a vampire's coming-out party.

"What's the deal?

"I've been summoned to the Bureau to eat a shit sandwich," she said.

"Ketchup or mustard?"

"It's not a joke! I may soon be off the case, in which case they'll send a yessiroid to replace me."

She looked and sounded broken, but he couldn't summon much sympathy.

"I'm ex officio, not part of the team," he reminded her.

"If they pull me out, you're probably not going to have a choice, and you've gotten to places alone that we never got to."

"Meaning?"

"I can make sure they pull you in and sit on you."

"Control to the end," he said.

"You don't know what you're dealing with," she said.

"And you do?"

Tatie Monica held up her hands. "I'm not here to fight or threaten," she said quietly. "My analyst was not authorized by the Bureau. My career was in the incognito Batwoman mode, like going nowhere, and Check Six popped up and set the case on my platter. I hadn't heard anything from him since LA, and he was righteous that time. What would you have done?"

"Check Six?"

"Shut up and listen. You need to understand the context. The Bureau has been trying for years to claw its way out of the interregnum of Hoover and bring computers into the main culture. Freeh started a project called Trilogy, which was supposed to provide us with online connectivity and shareware built around something called the Virtual Case File. But Freeh retired after the debacle in New York. Pickard came in as interim director, and then Mueller was named to be Freeh's permanent replacement. Mueller has balls: He served in Vietnam with distinction, but now he's caught dodging political hacky sacks filled with C4. With the creation of Homeland Security, he's been dealt out of the top power loop. The bottom line is that Trilogy doesn't work and it's not going to work. The Bureau's spent close to six hundred mil and we have bupkiss. I'm guessing that within a year you'll hear that the custom-designed program will be junked for off-the-shelf technology. Meanwhile, those of us who need to share and search information haven't had shit to work with. This guy came to me and I jumped on it."

"Which your bosses didn't approve."

"Right. Do you know any computer geeks?" She didn't wait for a response. "This guy is your classic prototypical hactivist, believes the Bureau's inker mindset threatens national security. How he got into our records, I have no idea, but he did, and he found this and I took it and away we went."

"And bodies kept piling up."

She nodded almost imperceptibly. "I don't even know his real name. I lied to you about that. Check Six is one of his handles. Another is Rud Hud, and our relationship is what geeks in Electronland call h4xxOr, which means illegal. He's not supposed to be in the data he's in, and I'm not supposed to employ anyone who hasn't been vetted through Bureau security."

There was a tone in her voice that suggested an undecipherable smugness. "My out is that I haven't actually employed him in the sense of paying for his services. Officially he's like an unpaid informant, a patriotic citizen willing to help."

"You think your bosses will buy that?" asked Service.

"You don't understand how they can circle the wagons to protect the Bureau's rep. I've seen some major fuckups and messes swept quietly away because the Bureau decided the guilty ones didn't intend to do anything technically illegal or immoral, and were simply trying to work their cases. The Bureau likes initiative. If I can give them a reason to let me keep going, I'm hoping they'll take it. With all the criticisms after 9/11, they don't want more, especially in the area of domestic law enforcement. The meta-logic is: Okay, we kinda, sorta, maybe fucked up a skosh on 9/11, but we're still the country's top cops, and since the seventies the crown jewel in the agency's reputation has been our record with serial murderers. Never mind that most of them were caught by accident, by local agencies, or in the backwash of their own fuckups; the Bureau has used serial murder and profiling as a sexy publicity engine for showing the public how great we are. They've milked it in ways you cannot even begin to imagine," said Monica.

"What does this have to do with me?"

"You remember the shit with Hanssen?"

"The agent who sold information to the Russians?"

"He was like a total head case. What most people don't understand is just how badly the agency screwed the pooch. They had been tipped about him by another agent four years *before* Hanssen was arrested, and it was only after the fact that they learned he was mucking around in databases where he didn't belong, asking questions he wasn't authorized to ask, not to mention leading a private life with more red flags than a Chinese picnic. Nobody had bothered to look at his electronic trail, or his personal life. You think any of us in the trenches were surprised by the 9/11 meltdown? You can't ever acknowledge a potential personal mistake or weakness because it could point upward. Hell, we are all selected for the Bureau. If we fail, the Bureau fails, and the Bureau won't allow that. That's the culture Hoover nurtured," she said. "What I'm telling you is that your sources may be able to quietly take a look and see if they can find a trail for Rud Hud. I don't begin to understand the minutiae of the cyberworld, but the truth is, I can't find him, and the only possible way is through his tracks in our files."

"This is way outside my expertise," he said. "Are you thinking this guy is more than a public-minded bird dog?"

"I don't know what I'm thinking, but you want to talk to him, and I want to talk to him, and I can't find him, and I know you have some sort of back door into the Bureau. I've seen the results."

"Your people will stay off my ass?"

"That's *our* deal, but if they replace me, that deal is off."

"How much contact did you have with this Check Six, Rud Hud?"

She reached into a portfolio and pulled out a neat stack of papers under a clip. "I printed this for you. I'm gonna be incomputerado for awhile."

When she drove away from the cabin, Gasparino came to the porch, begged a cigarette, and lit it clumsily. "She's freaking out, am I right?" the young agent asked.

"She thinks she's gonna be pulled off the case," Service said. "She's headed back to Washington."

"Oh shit. Professional Instant Death Syndrome."

*Whatever that was.* More and more he was finding that people around him were using vocabularies that eluded him.

"Fuck," Gasparino said. "If she goes down, that could mean East Jesus for me."

"East Jesus?"

"Yeah, sixty miles past Bumfuck. Nobody comes back from East Jesus, hear what I'm sayin'?"

Service invited the young agent inside for coffee. It was disconcerting how important careers were to federal officers.

"For real, you think she's out?" Gasparino said.

"She said it's possible."

"Squared shit."

"Does it matter?" Service asked.

"Hey, she's got tunnel vision and she pisses off a lot of people, but she's a pretty good leader, ya know? I trust her with my six," the young agent said.

To trust someone with your six was to entrust your life to them. This was the first positive thing Service had heard about Tatie Monica. But Gasparino was green and didn't have enough experience to understand how few people you could truly trust.

Her sudden contrition had no currency. His gut said she was a game-playing screwup with major personal issues who would never have been able to lead an investigation had it not been for the luck/courtesy of Check Six/Rud Hud. The major question now was, Who is he, and what the hell is his angle?

Gasparino departed with a sad face and Service wrote down the name *Rud Hud* several times, underlining each iteration.

He thought about sleeping, but there was too much loose detail in his mind. Even with the list, how did the killer actually *find* game wardens in the field, much less get the better of one? This case had all sorts of threads of varying lengths, like wires someone had randomly chopped. How did you reassemble spaghetti?

The phone rang several times before the sound registered, and when he picked it up, there was nobody there. What the hell?

He lit a cigarette, stripped to his undershorts, and called Candi McCants. "It's Grady. I'm sorry to call so late."

"They're fine," she said. "Don't worry."

"I don't know when I can pick them up."

"Really, Grady, they're just fine. Newf loves everyone and Cat—well, she's Cat."

Service was groping for words when headlights flashed in front of the cabin. *Jesus,* he thought. "Candi, I gotta go."

Karylanne Pengelly, his late son's girlfriend, stormed into the cabin without knocking. Service scrambled for his trousers but she walked over to him, put her arms around him, put her head on his chest, held tight, and began to sob. He tried to pry her loose but couldn't break her grip; he had to stand helpless, feeling her body convulse.

Eventually the sobs relented. He led her to a chair at the card table, sat her down, gave her a box of tissues and a glass of water, tugged on his trousers, and joined her at the table.

She wiped her nose and glared at him, saying nothing. One minute she was clinging to him and now her eyes looked like they could kill.

After a long pause she said, "How *could* you? What kind of monster are you?"

Before he could say anything she shouted, "You didn't even bury them, you selfish bastard!"

He decided to keep quiet and weather the storm.

"Do you have any herbal tea?" she asked, wiping her nose again.

"Coffee."

"I can't have caffeine."

"A little won't hurt," he offered.

He lit a cigarette and she slapped the table angrily and screamed, "Put that out!"

"It's my house."

"Secondhand smoke is dangerous for the baby!"

Grady Service looked across the table at her. Baby?

She glared at him. "That's right," she said slowly. "I'm pregnant, and you're gonna be the grandpa, but there isn't going to be a father." The sobbing started all over again.

He had no idea what to say. And so it went: periods of sobbing followed by increasingly longer periods of rationality, and bit by bit she told him how she had been on the pill, but it wasn't 100 percent, and Walter died not even knowing. She had learned a few days before he died and never got to tell him. She had her heart set on finishing school, but she wanted the baby more than anything. She did not want to go home to her parents in Canada.

Service had learned from Maridly Nantz that women sometimes simply wanted to vent to a sympathetic ear. They were not looking for male problem solving, and this seemed like one of those times. *Grandfather? Geez . . .* He'd barely had time to adjust to being a father. But a grandfather? Christ, he was too damn young to be a grandfather!

"I wasn't going to tell anybody about this," she said, "but when I saw you I couldn't keep it inside. Do you ever get the feeling that God is a mean sonuvabitch?"

"Sometimes."

She looked up at the ceiling and shook a fist. "You can kick my ass, but you can't break me." She looked back at Service. "I guess I'll have a little coffee. Have you got cream?"

He nodded dumbly, poured coffee for her, added powdered cream, and stepped outside to have a smoke.

"Hey," she called out, "come back inside. I was out of line. This is your house. You can smoke in here—it's okay. Really," she added, "I just panicked a little. I mean, it's only been two months; it could be a false alarm."

Two months?

"Have you been to a doctor?"

"No. I used an over-the-counter test and it was positive, but I also know they have false positives. Nothing is ever a hundred percent, right?"

He flicked the cigarette away, stepped back into the cabin, sat down, and looked at her. She reached out a hand. "Can I have a cigarette?"

Grady Service pushed her hand away. "Not a chance."

She shrugged and looked at one of the notepads on the table.

"Are you into Gaelic punk?" she called out.

She had pulled him into a vortex of non sequiturs and illogic, and he was having a hard time keeping up. "Huh?"

"Rud," she said, pointing to his notepad. "Are you interested in Mill a h-Uile Rud?"

He said, "I have no idea what you're talking about."

"It's a punk band from the Seattle area. I think the name means something like 'destroy everything,' or something like that."

"Gaelic?"

"Yeah, Scotland, Ireland, even Wales, I guess. It all derives from Celtic," said Karylanne.

"How do you know that?"

"Some of Walter's teammates were big into punk. There's a retired prof in Houghton who knows all about Gaelic punk. He taught at U of M in Ann Arbor I think."

"What's his name?"

"Flaherty. He was an English professor and he's a computer nerd, but most of all he's a hockey freak. He skates with the boys sometimes, eh. He's in his sixties, but he moves around pretty good, and Walter said he's slick with the puck. He has an over-thirty team called the Galloping Gothinks."

"Gothics?"

"Go-*thinks*. It's a play on words."

"Flaherty?"

"Yeah, but all the boys call him Knickknack. He has team dinners at his house once a month during the season, and the place is filled with all sorts of weird and cool stuff—suits of armor, things like that. He's got one of Tony Esposito's old Tech sweaters in a frame on the wall."

Esposito was a Michigan Tech alum and an NHL Hall of Fame goalie. "What do you mean he's a computer nerd?"

"One of the guys on the team told Walter that Flaherty's a big-time hacker. His specialty is getting into closed university collections."

"To do what?'

"Read and learn, what else?"

"I thought hackers screwed around with things."

"Mr. Service, you really ought to find a way into this century. Hackers exploit holes in software to help make it better. Crackers are the ones who inflict damage."

"Flaherty, a hacker who knows Gaelic," he said.

"I'm not supposed to know about his computer life. See, by accessing closed collections, he saves money and time he'd have to spend traveling, and after he's seen what he needs, he lets the collection keepers know he was in and how he got there. He's like ancient, but a way-cool dude."

"Do you know him?"

"Sure, I used to go to the dinners with Walter and the team."

"Where are you staying?" he asked Karylanne.

"I had a place in Houghton with Walter."

*With* Walter. "You two were living together?"

"Yeah," she said. "Maridly knew."

"She did, did she?"

Walter had been living with this girl and he hadn't known. What else had he missed in his son's life, and why hadn't he paid more attention?

"She used to drive over and have dinner with us." Nantz hadn't told him.

"Do you know where Walter and Nantz were going when they crashed?" he asked her, already knowing what she'd say.

"I wish I did," she said. "Maybe she was taking him shopping. She sometimes did that for us." There was a lot Nantz hadn't told him. But if he'd been less thickheaded, he might have seen things himself.

"You drove here tonight from Houghton?"

"Yeah, I have to go back to Canada. I sort of ran out of money, and the landlord sort of kicked me out."

She was acting tough, but he saw fear in her eyes. "You're not going to Canada tonight," he said.

"I don't want to impose."

"If you're pregnant, Karylanne, I'd say that makes us related, and I don't turn family away." Not that he'd ever had any family before Nantz and Walter. For the longest time there had been just him and the old man. He didn't count his ex-wife.

He pointed to the footlockers. "The only bed I have."

"No offense, but that's *not* a bed, eh. I've got my sleeping bag in my car. The floor and my air mattress will be fine."

While she was getting her sleeping bag, Grady Service sat down and tried to focus on something, *anything.* Grandfather? Holy shit! Nantz would have been sky-high. He wasn't sure *how* he felt about it. He felt oddly grateful to Karylanne for being pregnant with Walter's child. This baby would be his only link to Walter, however tenuous.

Denninger called at 6 a.m.

"Where are you?" he asked.

"Home. What a day and night. Charley the Turd lost his cool yesterday and jumped me. I had to whack him behind the leg with my baton. I swear the earth shook when he hit the ground, and then he started complaining of chest pains so I had to call EMS and haul his worthless ass to the hospital. I took his father with me and it turns out he's eccentric, but pretty decent. He said they were computerized until this summer, but somebody got into their program and poached their lists."

"Did they report the theft?" Service asked.

"No. Charley the Turd just dumped the program and went back to the old way."

"Any idea who it was?"

"No clue, but the old man thinks it had to be one of their customers. They had a rudimentary Web site, and the guy must've come in through e-mail."

"What about Charley the Turd?"

"Not a heart attack. Turned out to be gallstones. The doctor says he may wish it was his heart in the long run."

"Can you write this up for me?"

"Planned to."

"Don't send it electronically."

"Why not?"

"I don't know," he said. "Maybe I'm old-fashioned like the Mains." Or he was suddenly feeling very insecure about the security of the cyberworld. He gave her his Slippery Creek address and she promised to send the report. He knew his apprehension about computers was turning into paranoia.

"Great job, Denninger."

"My name's Dani."

"Great job, Dani."

## 47

## HOUGHTON, MICHIGAN
### JULY 30, 2004

Karylanne called the retired professor in the morning and rode to Houghton with Service. The house on Seventh Avenue was multi-gabled and painted several shades of black and blue. A sign on the lawn said HOUSE OF DARK LIGHT.

"Did I mention he's Goth?" Karylanne asked.

Service had to think for a few seconds. "You mean, the name of his hockey team?"

"No, his lifestyle."

Another pause. "The freak-jobs who dress in black and paint their faces white?"

"Pretty much."

They parked in the street in front of the house and went up to the porch, where they were greeted by a young woman in a tight, slinky black outfit and black Mary Janes. Stiff red ribbons stuck out of her glistening black hair like stalagmites. She wore a see-through black blouse and some sort of vinyl gismo underneath.

"Ice-jock girl," she greeted Karylanne. "S'up with the turkey bacon?"

"A friend."

The girl smiled at him, said, "S'up," in a cutesy voice, and slithered past them.

"You know her?"

"She's an instructor in computer engineering."

"Turkey bacon?" Service asked.

"Technically it means security guard, but more generally, any police officer."

"I'm not in uniform," he said.

She laughed. "Yeah, like *that* fools anyone."

Flaherty looked almost normal. He was average height with white hair in a buzz cut, and one tiny gold stud in his right nostril. "Service?"

"Grady."

"I'm sorry about your son. He was a great kid, and he was going to be an outstanding player. Heard you were a player too."

"Pleistocene age," Service said.

They were seated in an old-fashioned parlor. There was a suit of armor on a pedestal in one corner and a broad-blade ax with a six-foot handle on one wall.

"Is that real?" Service asked, pointing to the weapon.

"It's a replica of a Viking battle-ax," Flaherty said.

"How could anybody use that thing?" Service wondered out loud.

"Teamwork," Flaherty said. "Something to drink? Beer, soda—name your poison."

Service wasn't thirsty, and by the looks of the place, he didn't have a lot of faith in what might be served. "I'm sorry to drop in like this," he began, "but I'm working on an investigation of a hacker who calls himself Rud Hud, or Check Six. We're trying to identify him."

Flaherty said, "I thought the police had unlimited cyber assets."

"Not the DNR," Service said, not bothering to amplify. "Is it possible to find someone's real name based on a screen name?"

Flaherty smiled. "Handle is what it's called, and sure it's possible . . . depending on how the guy operates."

"Karylanne thinks the name is Gaelic."

"No doubt," Flaherty said. "I'll have to play around with it some. How quick do you need the information?"

"Yesterday," Service said.

"I'm good, not God," the retired professor said with a grin.

A boy came through a door wearing a black T-shirt emblazoned with BAD COP! NO DONUT!

Service blinked as he read the shirt.

Flaherty waved to the boy, who moved on through the house. "Atmosphere getting to you?" he asked Service.

"Some."

"Don't let their getups throw you. They're normal kids—if you ignore their IQs. I assume you already considered the obvious with Rud Hud?" Flaherty said.

"The obvious what?"

"Rud Hud Hudibras, which in Welsh is *Run baladr bras*."

"You call that obvious?"

"For some old English professors it is. You familiar with Geoffrey of Monmouth?"

Service shook his head.

"He wrote a history of Celtic kings, basically those from the period when there was no written language."

"If there was no written language, how did he get his information?"

Flaherty grinned. "There's a big debate about that, but it's probably a product of oral history. Others say it's a hoax, that he fabricated the whole thing. But in recent years scholars have found correlations in various sources like grave registers. In any event, Geoffrey's work gave a face to the unknown history of Britain and King Arthur, and the Round Table probably grew out of it. Kind of like *Lonesome Dove* for us, you know—we'd like to think that's how we were. No archaeological substantiation, of course, but hell, most Britons think Arthur was real."

What the hell did cowboys in *Lonesome Dove* have to do with King Arthur? "And Rud Hud?" He was having a terrible time keeping up with the professor.

"Troy fell, Aeneas and his son Ascanius split to Italy. Long story short, Ascanius had a son named Brut whose mother died in childbirth. Later the kid accidentally killed his father in a hunting accident, and he was banished from Italy and eventually ended up in Britain as Brut the Trojan, aka

Brutus, who started a line of Celtic royalty that lasted two thousand years. A few steps down the generational ladder you find one Brutus Greenfield, whose son Leil followed him as king, but toward the end of his reign, Leil went sort of dotty, and his son, Rud Hud Hudibras, had to step in and get the kingdom under control. This would be at about the time Solomon was operating in Israel, to give you some sense of time frame. Ninnyevent, time marches on, and later we get a Celtic king named Uther Pendragon, who may or may not be the Arthur of legend," said the Flaherty.

"This is for real?"

"It all stems largely from oral traditions, same as the Bible. Is *that* real? A lot of people think so. Tell me what you know about your Rud Hud."

"He thinks the feds aren't doing their jobs right."

"*Really,*" Flaherty said. "That sort of fits."

"Fits what?" Service was lost in a lot of historic mumbo jumbo.

"Rud Hud more or less reformed his enfeebled old man's kingdom and ruled it for almost four decades. Centuries later, an English poet named Butler wrote a burlesque, a comic satire about the roundheads and Puritans and how they turned British society upside down. Using Rud Hud Hudibras as his model, he called the hero of his poem Hudibras, who was a sort of religious colonel who went out to clean up society in the way the Puritans wanted to, only he pretty much screwed up everything he touched, which made the Puritans into a sort of joke, which they were in many ways, except to those who died at their hands or for their bizarre reasons. It was a damn brutal satire, somewhat along the lines of *Don Quixote.* Based on this, I'd guess your Rud Hud took his name to express his interest in reform, and I'd also guess he's exquisitely and classically educated. Most English students, even those with doctorates, don't know diddly-squat about Rud Hud Hudibras."

"Anything else?"

"You know anything about hackers and crackers?"

"Only what Karylanne told me," said Service.

"Interesting crowd. They usually don't play well with others and have poor coping skills in terms of face-to-face interpersonal communications, but put them in the privacy of their own hidey-holes with a computer, and they are unbelievably competent communicators. They've evolved their own language, mores, rules, you name it. If your Rud Hud is as educated as I'm thinking he is, I'm guessing he's also pretty sophisticated in the cyber-world, which means he could be difficult to find."

"Whatever you can do," Service said. "I appreciate this."

"Don't thank me until you see what I come up with," the retired professor said with obvious excitement at the prospect.

Service couldn't get the ax on the wall out of his mind. "You're interested in Vikings?"

"Yeah."

"You said something about teamwork."

"The Vikings liked to close en masse with their enemy, shields joined, and once joined, they broke into separate individual combats. But the warriors carrying the big battle-axes couldn't swing them *and* protect themselves with a shield, so the shield guys moved ahead of the big ax guys, who would step up and attack from behind their shields—your basic two-v-one in hockey."

"You know about the blood eagle?"

The English professor chuckled. "You mean the legendary and alleged blood eagle?"

"You don't believe it was real?"

"Certainly not with an ax like the honker on the wall," the retired professor said. "That was for rending people into chunks, not opening wounds for postmortem monkey business." Flaherty studied him. "Are *you* interested in Vikings?"

"Some," Service said.

A woman appeared from somewhere on the lower level of the house. She looked to be in her thirties. Long, obsidian hair, a leather bodice, short leather skirt with fishnet stockings, and four-inch platform shoes. "Elder Goth Dude," she said. "Time for unh-unh."

Flaherty laughed out loud and clapped his hands together. "I gotta go." He took the woman's arm and they started upstairs. Halfway up, he looked down and said, "Leave your card and I'll call you."

Service walked out to the truck with Karylanne. He lit a cigarette and started the engine. "Unh-unh?"

"The sound people make when they're really getting down; you know, kicking the gear stick? Like, grind-your-teeth animal sex?"

Grady Service shook his head and closed his eyes.

"You don't understand sex?" Karylanne asked. "That's not what Maridly said."

"Hey, hey, *hey!*" Service said. "You are *way* out of bounds!"

On the way home he pulled into the Walgreens in Marquette and killed the motor. He took out his wallet and handed her two crisp twenties. "Go inside and buy another pregnancy test. Two months is not a false alarm, and if you're not pregnant, the other possibilities aren't good."

"You don't believe me?"

"I believe you, but since the accident I've had to work like hell to control my emotions, and I think you're in the same boat. We've both been trying not to face reality. Pregnant or not, you need to see a doctor. Now, tell me the truth: Why don't you want to go home?"

Her lip quivered. "My folks are good people, simple people. They wanted me to stay home, get a job, get married, have kids. I worked hard to earn my scholarship to Tech. If I go home now, I'll lose everything, and I'll never get out of there. I want to be a mom, but I also want more than that."

He believed her, and more importantly, Nantz had believed the girl and Walter were meant to be together. He made a quick decision, one from the heart, one he was sure Nantz would approve of: "Here's the deal. If you're pregnant, we get you to a doctor. Then you go home. When you come back for fall semester, I'll pay for an apartment in Houghton. You will go to school and take care of yourself."

"You don't have to do this," she said.

"That's why I'm doing it," he answered. "I had a son for only a year, and if I'm gonna be a grandfather, I want to make sure it lasts a helluva lot longer. Deal?"

"Deal," she said, "but I don't want to go back to Canada."

"You owe it to your folks to go and tell them what's going on and what your plans are. Since we're just starting out, let's get something straight. I'll always level with you and you do the same for me. No bullshit between us."

She reached out for his hand, shook it, and went into the drugstore.

Grady Service lit a cigarette. He was taking on obligations, but they felt right. He needed to get this sorted out and get his focus back to where it needed to be.

On the way back to Slippery Creek, his cell phone rang. It was Eddie Waco.

"Booger flies confirmed in Kansas."

"Thanks, man."

"You got the scent?"

"Not yet."

"You'n call when hit's time, Michigan Man."

Minutes later it was Denninger on the phone.

"I'm almost done with the list, and guess what—your name is on it, with a Gladstone address."

He was speechless, and by the time he recovered his voice he had lost the signal and the call.

## 48

## MARQUETTE, MICHIGAN

## AUGUST 2, 2004

Karylanne Pengelly had left for Canada three days ago, her pregnancy confirmed, the baby due sometime in December.

Fern LeBlanc stood in the opening of his cubicle. "You seem to be in here a lot. Is everything all right?"

"Fine," he said. "Just a lot of work to do."

"That's never kept you in the barn before," she said.

When he looked up at her she was smiling.

He called Wink Rector. "Hear anything on Monica?"

"Nothing on her, and nothing on my replacement."

Fern LeBlanc came in and put a *Detroit Free Press* news clipping on his desk. The headline read HOMELAND SECURITY RESCUES LOCAL DNR OFFICER.

The story said that CO Miller French of Port Huron had confronted a group of intoxicated fishermen at a campground, and that six of them had jumped him and beaten him. Homeland Security personnel from the Blue Water Bridge detachment had shown up, and disarmed and arrested the assailants. French was treated at Mercy Hospital for a broken arm and facial lacerations, and later released. The assailants were lodged in the St. Clair County Jail.

He walked out to Fern's desk with the clipping. "Why'd you give this to me?"

She nodded at Captain Grant's office.

The captain was alone, his face to his computer. "Cap'n."

Grant swiveled around.

"Sounds like Frenchy got lucky." Miller French had trained under Gus Turnage several years back. Gus thought he was a good officer.

"Very lucky," the captain said.

"How did Homeland Security know to come to his aid?"

"Excellent question," Captain Grant said, and turned back to his computer.

Service stopped at Fern's desk. "Can you get Miller French's phone number for me?"

She came into his cubicle moments later and handed him a piece of paper.

He dialed the number and the officer answered.

"Frenchy, it's Grady Service. I just heard. You okay?"

"Just dinged up. I'm in a cast for awhile, no biggie."

"Six on one isn't your normal wrestling match." Conservation officers seldom referred to even the most violent physical confrontations as anything other than wrestling.

"Thing is, I got two down, but another one of them blindsided me with a piece of firewood, and once I was one-armed, I was done."

"You hit your panic button?" The panic button was a remote signal device an officer could activate during an emergency outside his vehicle. The button activated a silent alarm in the Automatic Vehicle Locator transmitter, which alerted Lansing and the rest of the state that an officer was in deep trouble and needed help.

"Soon as the pukes turned on me."

"How long till Homeland Security got there?"

"Ten minutes, maybe less. Mouse was fifteen minutes behind them." Mouse Frissen was French's sergeant.

"You surprised to see the Homeland Security people?"

"Hell, I would've welcomed help from the Sisters of the Poor at that moment, but yeah, I never expected them."

"Take care."

"Thanks for the call."

Service called out to Fern LeBlanc. "Can you get me Sergeant Mike Frissen's cell phone number?"

"Reaching for it now," she said. She brought him another piece of paper.

He rang the cell phone, got no answer, and didn't want to leave a message.

He activated his 800 megahertz and changed the channel to District 10. "Ten, One Oh Three, this is Twenty Five Fourteen. Have you got TX?"

"Affirmative TX; it was off, Twenty Five Fourteen. Turning it on now."

"Twenty Five Fourteen clear."

He dialed the number and Frissen answered. Mouse Frissen was a longtime CO who had spent most of his career in Cheboygan County before being promoted and moving down to St. Clair County. He was a small man in stature but big in performance, and word was that he was an excellent sergeant, who knew how to lead people without interfering with their ability to do their jobs. Service had been in many training sessions with him. "Mouse, it's Grady. I just heard about Frenchy."

"He's okay," Frissen said. "Bad luck that those asswipes broke his arm."

"Were you surprised to find Homeland Security ahead of you?"

"And how. I asked them how the hell they got the alarm, and they said they were just passing by."

Service detected a tone. "You buy that?"

"Hell no. The Port Huron paper tried to write a story and Homeland Security killed it. But a wire service kid filed and the *Free Press* picked it up. I guess the wire service kid also got bullied by Homeland Security; you know, the usual federal national security baloney, but his boss backed him, and he filed."

"The *Free Press* ran it."

"And *The News* didn't. Political leanings in our state's largest newspapers? Wow, who woulda thunk it."

Service made small talk, hung up, and went to see the captain. "I talked to Frenchy and Mouse Frissen. Mouse said Homeland Security claimed they were just passing by."

"You're skeptical?"

"I didn't just fall off the potato truck. The odds against just passing by are too damn high, and they got to the scene before Mouse. Frenchy activated his alarm. Is it possible that Homeland Security is wired into our AVL?"

"Not legally," was all the captain said.

Service went outside for a smoke and took a cup of coffee with him. If Homeland Security was wired into their AVL, who else had access?

"Fuck," he said, halfway through the cigarette. If you were wired into the AVL, you could pinpoint an officer's location at all times, as long as the GPS system was up, or the officer didn't disengage it. He mashed the cigarette and went back to the captain's office.

"How could they get our software?" he asked. The DNR AVL software, as far as he knew, was tailored solely for Michigan's DNR law enforcement division.

"In the wake of 9/11, the president authorized a lot of new initiatives," the captain said.

Service had only vaguely followed news reports of wiretaps and other methods of tracking terrorists, methods the public had not been told about until journalists broke the stories.

"Would the governor have to approve such a thing?" he asked his captain.

"Not necessarily. It could come through the attorney general and, depending on the power granted to the federal government, the AG might be obliged to keep it quiet."

"But the director would know."

"Not necessarily," the captain repeated.

"Do the Wisconsin, Missouri, Illinois, and Kansas DNRs have AVLs?"

"I think almost all states have their own systems now. Some share with highway patrols, but it's pretty common."

"Captain, what if the killer has access to our AVL? He could track us with no problem."

"What if he did have access?" the captain asked, turning the question back.

Service thought for a minute. "He's a federal employee?"

"A reasonable assumption. Or he's somehow hacked his way in."

Grady Service immediately considered disabling the AVL in his Tahoe, but the captain read his mind. "Think this through, Grady. If you know you're being watched on the AVL, that gives you the advantage."

As he almost always was, the captain was right. The captain thought like a chess master, and regrettably, Service thought like a half-ass checkers player. He had tried to tell the captain several times he wasn't smart enough to be a good detective, but the captain refused to hear it. *Calm down,* he told himself.

Every August he drove up to an isolated spot on the Fence River to fish for brook trout. August was a time when most U.P. water was warm and low, but in this one spot there were some seeps and springs, and the water seldom climbed above fifty-two degrees all summer long. The frigid water was a magnet for brook trout from up and down the river, and he had caught so many fifteen-inch fish here over the years, he had lost count.

He went back to see the captain. "I'm gonna take my fishing vacation."

The captain looked at him and nodded. "Send me an e-mail and copy the chief."

Service understood. If someone was in the AVL, they were probably also poaching e-mails.

Was it the killer or was it Check Six? Or were they one and the same?

He called Eddie Waco on his cell phone. "How long will it take you to get up here?"

"Where's here?" the Missouri conservation agent asked.

"Crystal Falls in Iron County."

"Three days' work?"

"Drive your personal vehicle," Service added.

He called Simon del Olmo on his cell phone. "I'm going to need your help."

"Si, *Jeffe*."

The Booger Baits list bothered him. Why was his name was on it? He had never seen a booger fly until he found Ficorelli's, and even then, he hadn't known what it was. But Nantz was always ordering flies from catalogs and other mail-order services. It had to have been her, and it was possible Shark might know something. She was always calling him and talking about flies.

He called his friend. "Did you know Nantz ordered booger flies?"

"She did? News to me."

"You're sure?"

"Hell yes. I never even told her about them."

*Damn,* Service thought.

He stopped by the office, called Treebone in Detroit, and talked to him about the case. The call was cut short when Tatie Monica and Wink Rector walked into his cubicle.

"You're back," Service said.

Rector stood back with a look Service couldn't quite read. "She's my replacement," Rector said, "the new resident agent for the Upper Peninsula."

"You're good with this?" he asked Tatie Monica.

"They pulled me off the team, but they're leaving me here. I can still get the guy."

"Working outside the team."

"No biggie. They gave the team to Pappas."

"I thought she was cyber."

Tatie Monica shrugged. "The powers that be have decided that this has morphed into a cyber case, that Check Six's activities make it so. What have you learned since I've been gone?"

"Nothing; I've pretty much stuck to my own business."

"Bullshit," she said. "You aren't easy to read, but I'm starting to get wise to you. You're like me. Neither of us can let go. Neither of us *will* let go."

"I don't think so," he said. "I'm headed out for a few days' vacation."

"*What?*"

"Vacation—you've heard of it, right?"

"You're up to something."

"I go every year about this time." Not quite true, but close enough.

"Where?"

"My vacation is none of your business, Tatie."

Wink Rector grinned throughout the conversation. "I think you guys are going to have an interesting working relationship."

"My stay here is strictly temporary," Tatie Monica said. "One of our psychiatrists talked to that old lady in Sturgis while I was in Washington. He says the woman is certifiable and would be unreliable as a witness. He says she's bottled up a lot of stuff and the more we press her, the deeper she retreats into *Jeopardy*. Man, that's gotta suck."

"What about the list from Booger Baits?"

"Everything's been turned over to Pappas."

"How does Bonaparte feel about her appointment?"

"Who knows. He's in his own world, that one."

"You saw him in Washington?"

"No, he was here yesterday, but he left again. He's on the road almost all the time."

"Several cases?"

"I have no idea. He pretty much goes and does what he wants, when and where he wants."

"Must be tough."

"Why?"

"I saw his cane and assumed he's got some sort of physical problem."

"Just part of his shtick. The pencil smudges are to make him look like a hard worker and a common man, not one of the suits. He thinks the cane creates sympathy, and causes people to underestimate him. I never got any details, but somebody in his group once told me that he hikes all over hell by himself. He's a fitness freak."

As soon as they left the office, he called Treebone back and finalized plans.

Service left his Tahoe at the Cedar Inn in Crystal Falls and rode with Eddie Waco in his truck. Waco wore an old pair of blue jeans and beat-up boots. The meeting place he had arranged was a small farmhouse out M-72, just a few miles north of the Wisconsin border, where Checkers Schwikert lived with his wife and her five ferrets.

Schwikert had spent his career with some megacorporation downstate and moved to the U.P. after he retired. He tied his own flies and exclusively fished the Brule River, which demarcated Michigan and Wisconsin. He was active in numerous conservation organizations and movements, and for years had headed up the Brule River Watershed Consortium. He was a quiet man in his seventies who smiled a lot and maintained a positive attitude in all things he did. He was also a great friend to conservation officers and regularly passed along information gleaned from various sources. Simon del Olmo had made several good cases because of him.

Schwikert gave them his small kitchen and went out to his garage workshop to tie flies and give them privacy. Del Olmo arrived in his personal truck as planned.

Service outlined the plan to the two men.

"He can monitor our *AVL?*" del Olmo asked incredulously. "Jesus."

"I think we have to assume that," Service said.

"When do you put the show on the road?" del Olmo asked.

"There are some things still up in the air, and I want to let those play out. Couple of days, I think. Not more."

He then talked them through the details, withholding only one significant part from del Olmo, who frowned all the way through. "What if this asshole sees us together?" the young officer asked.

"We're assuming he monitors AVL. He's not going to chance us seeing him." Service looked at Eddie Waco. "You got any concerns?"

"This'n's a big fish. Got ta use big bait ta catch a big fish."

Service turned back to del Olmo. "Once we're in place, you have to stay away, no matter what."

"I don't like it. You'll be out in the ass-end of hell with no close backup."

Eddie Waco grinned. "He's the strike dog. I'm the pack."

"I feel less than comforted," del Olmo grumbled.

Captain Grant called on the cell phone as Service and Waco were driving back to Crystal Falls.

"I just talked to the state lab and you were right about Nantz's truck. It seems certain she was knocked off the road."

"You mean murdered." Service felt his heart start to race.

"Wall off your feelings, Grady."

"I'm trying, Cap'n. Do we have a make on the other vehicle?"

"Better. We have the vehicle. It was rented at Detroit Metro and never returned. The county found it abandoned at an Empire Mine lot off M-94 in Palmer. There is a broken headlight, and the paint matches the paint on Nantz's bumper. The car rental agency had a video of the transaction, and we have a photo from the video. There are a lot of prints in the vehicle, but it will take time to collect and process them all through AFIS."

"Does the photo show anyone we know?"

"White male, late twenties or early thirties, big hair and a beard, probably fake. The FBI has the photo in a software program looking for matches. I'll fax the photo to District Three's office in Crystal." *Not Honeypat*, was his first thought, unless this guy was a boyfriend. That would be her style.

Something was changing for the killers. They were starting to leave traces, make mistakes. Service suddenly imagined Nantz's face and choked.

Shark called as they drove past First Lake on US 2. "Limey ordered booger flies for my birthday. She had them sent to Nantz under your name and Limey just told me about it. That help?"

*Maybe.* "Thanks." It at least explained how his name got on the list. He looked at Eddie Waco and explained that another cop would be joining them in the woods.

"Name's Treebone," Service told him.

"Ain't real common."

"That's a fact," Service said.

## 51

CRYSTAL FALLS, MICHIGAN

AUGUST 6, 2004

The Cedar Inn was an old motel with updated siding and an interior decorated with an elk-head mount and prints from the Old West. They had two
rooms at the end of the building next to the exit door. They spent the eve-
ning going through the case.

Service couldn't rule out that Tatie Monica's analyst was very possibly
the killer—or at least one of them. Why had the man come forward to her
with the two groups of victims? And why had the perp or perps suddenly
started killing people close to the targeted victims? Was it panic, or had this
been part of the pattern for a long time? The FBI had failed to pick up the
primary murder pattern; had they missed a secondary pattern too? How had
the killer fallen for the control on the list and killed Spargo? The person who
had hacked into Booger Baits knew what he was doing. And Check Six apparently had hacked into the FBI's databases, with Tatie Monica's assistance—
fact admitted, extent not—and into VICAP and other information sources. It
was prudent to assume they also could access Homeland Security, and if so,
had access to AVL systems. This had to become their operating assumption.
It was the only thing that made sense in terms of tracking game wardens so
precisely, at least in the five years since AVLs had been in use. Getting close
was step one. In his mind, killing a game warden close-in was an even more
formidable task. This alone made the idea of more than one killer a reasonable
assumption. Correction: More than one killer with access to AVL.

The switch in MOs to the blood eagle suggested the killer wanted recognition; the logic was not apparent.

More and more he tried to understand what would motivate someone
to kill cops. Normally when a cop went down, all the stops were pulled and

all cops went after the killer. But a serial killer of cops? Had there ever been such a thing before? He thought perhaps he needed to talk to someone, but not the FBI. Shamekia? Maybe.

"You ever hear of a serial cop killer?" he asked Waco.

"Nope. I'd think there'd be real low odds in hit."

Indeed. But a game warden was a very different kind of cop, largely a solo operator, and few in numbers in any state. If you wanted to kill cops, game wardens were a pretty good choice, assuming you could find them. Even the other law enforcement agencies Michigan conservation officers worked with knew little about what they actually did and how they operated.

What was it he had told the Pillars woman? Those who killed for profit; those who killed for meat; those who killed because they could get away with it, and to whom it was a game. The latter group enjoyed the contest and used it to boost their egos. The name Hoover Maki came to mind.

Maki was a poacher who'd gotten his name because he was like a vacuum cleaner in the woods, sweeping up everything in his path. In the 1980s there was a spate of dead deer found around the U.P. Only their tails had been taken; the meat had been left to rot. Service remembered an astonishing fourteen-point buck he'd found dead in the Mosquito. He had found Maki because someone had seen a truck in the area and gotten a license number. Service traced the truck to the Perkins area, went into Maki's camp one night, and confronted the man. There were 166 tails nailed around beams in his garage and Maki had just laughed when Service found them. His explanation: "It was fun how I could do it and youse couldn't stop me."

"You're going to jail," Service told him.

Maki shrugged. "Took youse a long time."

Was this the logic in selecting game wardens—an attack on cops just to show it could be done? What would be the point? Geez.

"We need ta know who he is?" Waco asked, interrupting Service's thoughts.

"I think not. We're pretty sure he wants to strike, and I think the time's come to give him the opportunity."

Flaherty, the retired English professor from Houghton, called just before midnight. "I don't know what you've gotten into," Flaherty said, "but I got Rud Hud's trail, and the next thing I knew I had two humongous FBI agents knocking on my door, and they didn't even pretend to be polite. The Feds are onto him too, and they seem to want to find him real bad. I got interrogated for nearly six hours."

Pappas has taken over, Service thought. *Good for her.*

"The agents told me in no uncertain terms to stay away from Rud Hud, and I'm sorry, but I don't need any trouble with the federal government. I've got a good life and I aim to keep it that way."

"How did you get onto him?"

"That's why I'm calling. About the best way to hide yourself is to send your messages through a computer that strips your identity and replaces it with another one. The companies who provide these services make it a point to automatically erase logs of all traffic moving through their servers. But there's something called the Philmont protocol. It was designed by a couple of former Boy Scouts, and it does content analysis as a way to search for clues. I found one Rud Hud message through the protocol and used a software tracking program called Pfishbag to get the geographical coordinates of the computer that sent the original message."

"Where?"

"Negaunee."

"You're sure?"

"For that one message."

"Can your refine it, provide a date or time?"

"Sorry, just Negaunee, and I'm afraid that's all I can do for you."

"Thanks." Service couldn't blame the man, but now they knew that the vehicle used to kill Nantz had been found in Palmer and the computer used by Rud Hud had been physically in Negaunee. Maybe there was a way to fake a location too, but these two facts fit. Was it a dead end? Time would tell.

He related the conversation to Waco.

"How you'n think he'll be a-comin' at you'n?"

"I thought for awhile that he uses some sort of light to disable victims in the darkness, but I can't find any practical way to do that. I found a deer that had been blinded, and that same day I saw what I thought was a flash of lightning, and that got me thinking . . . But I think it's a red herring. I think he takes victims' eyes to mislead us."

"Cake seen a light."

"Exactly, and we know the killer was there, but that light may have been a misdirection or coincidence."

Service hesitated before calling Tatie Monica. "Where are you?" she asked.

"Vacation. Did you ever see autopsy results for the deputy murdered in Missouri?"

"Fatal GSW."

"Sexual assault?"

"None."

"Time of death?"

"Before Spargo."

Service hung up before she could say more. The blood eagle MO was a form of mutilation, and according to her, typical of sexual deviants. But there was no evidence of sexual assaults in the game warden killings, and no sexual assault with the Missouri deputy. Same killer? It couldn't be ruled out, and his gut said yes. She had been killed *before* Spargo. Did Cake Culkin say he had seen her that night? This still wasn't clear to him. Had she set up the meeting for the killer and been eliminated before it took place? This would fit the timeline.

"Cake saw the killer that night on the Eleven Point, not her."

"Not good enough for an ID."

"You looked at the kill site?"

"Cake took me to hit, but not much to see. Thet rain warshed 'er out." Eddie Waco said. "So how's this boy disable his victims?"

"I don't know, but I'll bet money he uses night vision to get in close, and he has damn good skills in the woods. I've thought about this a lot, and it's the only thing that makes sense. You sure couldn't use a bright light with NVDs on. You'd be blinder than your target."

"Have to be pert good."

"He's already proven that. What's stumped me all along is how one man could take a CO hand to hand. Ficorelli was a little man, but Spargo was gigantic. Has to be two of them using night vision. One distracts the target and the other strikes."

Eddie Waco nodded, picked up an empty plastic Diet Pepsi bottle and spit into it. "I guess we're good to go," the Missouri conservation agent said.

"If at all possible, I want this asshole alive."

"If possible?" Waco echoed.

"That's all I'm asking. Rule one: Protect yourself and do what you have to do."

"You too."

"Count on it. I'm gonna call del Olmo and tell him we're on for tomorrow."

Simon del Olmo sounded awake and out of breath.

"I've unplugged my AVL," Service said. "I'll park my truck at Judge Wallace's camp and wait for you to pick us up in your personal truck at zero eight hundred. You drop Elza when you pick us up, she takes my truck back to the motel, reactivates the AVL, and runs a patrol route, mainly to fishing spots around the county. You'll drop us at our walk-in in the morning, and drive around until it's time for the rendezvous," Service continued. "There are two old two-tracks into the spot off Deerfoot Lodge Road. Elza goes in the west road. You go in the east route. She'll leave my Tahoe where the two old totes intersect and walk up the east road to meet you in your truck. She's to make the drop at ten p.m. exactly, and make sure she slams a door to let us know everything's in place."

"If you're on vacation, why would you be on patrol?" del Olmo asked.

"Because that's the way I take vacation. Always have, and everyone knows it."

"I don't like it. What if Elza is followed?"

"We're assuming other guy has AVL, which means all he has to do is sit and watch what unfolds on the rolling map. We'll let him conjure his own narrative for the pictures we create for him."

## 52

## GREEN BEAR ISLAND,
## IRON COUNTY, MICHIGAN
## AUGUST 7, 2004

The three men were quiet throughout the ride. Service and Eddie Waco had made their plan and refined it until they were satisfied. Service had learned long ago that you couldn't eliminate all outdoor variables, but you could funnel and contain them with the right terrain, and he was certain that Green Bear Island in the Fence River was as good as could be found. The island was small—no more than a hundred and fifty yards long, thirty yards wide, and fifteen to twenty feet high on the upstream end, the whole thing made of boulders and covered with patches of raspberries and thimbleberries. The raspberries were done, but the thimbleberries should be thick now. The island had been named for its shape and color. It looked like a sleeping green bear.

"I don't know why you're hiking so far in from the north," Simon del Olmo complained as they drove along.

Service could tell that the younger officer was nerved up. "It's three or four miles over nasty terrain," Service said. "That gives us the space and time we need to move deliberately and watch our sixes." Service thought about what he had just said. Watch sixes; Check Six? Did this mean that Rud Hud watched another killer's back? His gut said yes. *Has* to be a pair.

"What happens after you get into position?" del Olmo wanted to know.

"We do what we do best," Service said. "We sit and wait."

"What if they don't take the bait?" del Olmo said.

"If they're here, they'll come. Once a predator decides to attack, it tends to move fast and directly."

"You're not dealing with a four-legged predator," del Olmo said.

"Maybe," Service said. Eddie Waco stared out his window, saying nothing.

llllllllllllllllllll

The drop was made in less than one minute. Del Olmo turned off his engine so they could hear if any vehicles were approaching on Camp One Road. The two officers unloaded, put on their packs, and disappeared into heavy brush heading south up a low ridge.

Service and Waco had already agreed to a form of leapfrog-style as their hiking method. Service would walk two hundred yards, stop, and watch ahead and behind. Waco would join him, and Service would move the next two hundred yards. They would never be out of sight of each other, and with luck they would be in place on the island before dark.

When they finally reached the north shore across from the island, Grady Service whispered, "The thing about this rock pile is that it attracts bears this time of year."

"How *many* bears?" Waco asked.

"Could be three or four, or as many as ten, but they won't bother us. They're here to eat berries. They'll sleep on the island during the day, feed at night, and stay until the berries are gone or competitors drive them off. You might hear them tonight. They're sloppy eaters, and if one gets too close to another one, he'll let him know. They don't share. You okay with this?"

Waco nodded.

Service lit a cigarette and squatted.

"We crossin' over to the island?"

"When it's time."

Service sensed movement but didn't look at it. Waco nudged his boot.

"We both heard you," Service said out loud.

Luticious Treebone stepped out of the tree line. He was dressed in a full camo ghillie suit and was nearly invisible at ten feet, even if you knew he was there.

"Bullshit," Tree whispered. "No way you heard me."

"Eddie Waco, meet the less-than-stealthy Luticious Treebone."

357

"Tree," the big man said with a nod. "I swept the island and south bank for a quarter-mile in and a half-mile of shoreline. There's seven bears in the berries on the island, mostly in the patches on the south side of the rocks. If someone's coming in, they're patient and careful."

Service's friend had been alone in the woods for three days.

"Okay, there's only two easy ways onto the island—at the top and at the bottom. That's where you and me will be, Eddie. Anybody tries to cross between us, we'll hear them, and if they get across they'll be between us and right in the middle of the bears, and that's where Tree will be."

"That might could slow 'em down," Eddie Waco said with a grin.

"You've got that right. They'll be eating at night and will take exception to any interference. Once we're in, no movement—none. Piss in the plastic bottle I gave you. There's no moon tonight. As soon as it's dark, put on your night-vision goggles and leave them on until you think you hear somebody coming in. We give one click if we detect someone, two clicks when our goggles come off. It's possible they may have a blinding light, and to be safe, let's assume it. Just make sure you keep your side to their movement. If either of us gets somebody, put them down, transmit three clicks, and keep them there until daylight." Service paused. "Got your jab sticks?"

Eddie Waco nodded. Tree would not have drugs, was strictly their reserve force.

"The stuff in there will act fast and last four to six hours. If he wakes up and struggles, stick him with the second stick. It's a lower dose."

"This legal?"

"Apprehend and secure first; worry about legal fineries afterwards." Kira Lehto, the vet, had given him the tranquilizer only after a heated argument. When he showed her the photos of what they were dealing with, she quietly unlocked her drug locker and handed him what he needed. The drug was a combination of two tranquilizers, both approved by the FDA for animal use, but Lehto said the combination would act quickly and the recipients would come out of it just as quickly, depending on their size and tolerance. She dosed the syringes for 180 pounds.

"Zero seven thirty we check in on FRS. One channel for each transmission. You remember the frequency order?"

The FRS had fourteen channels. Waco said, "We start on channel eight, minus three to five, minus two to three, back up to channel eight, and next time through go to plus five, or thirteen, and plus two to fifteen, which equates to one, and back down to eight."

Tree nodded.

Del Olmo had rigged four Family Radio Service devices with ear mikes and chest buttons. Simon had the fourth. Channel switching would prevent anyone from catching too much of their conversation. The sequence was confusing only to people not used to talking on radios with different bands and frequencies. Michigan conservation officers routinely monitored DNR, state police, county, and city radios, with numerous frequencies.

"No open commo until zero seven thirty, unless I change the rules. The codebreak word is Green; got it?" The men nodded.

Grady Service left Waco at the bottom of the island and Treebone in the middle, and made his way to the head of the island, where he climbed on top, built a fire, as he always did, slid back down the rocks into a seam in the boulders at the water's edge, and settled in to wait. He wore black fatigues and a black face mask. The skin around his eyes, nose, and mouth had been blacked with camo paint. He had used this approach during a night-training session last fall, and none of the other officers had been able to spot him until he stepped out of hiding. Some of them had been within six feet and looking right at him.

At 10 p.m. Service heard a truck door slam. This was Elza Grinda letting them know that the Tahoe was in place about three hundred yards up a slight rise through extremely dense bush over uneven and rocky ground.

He felt in his gut that tonight they would meet Rud Hud. Who else was anybody's guess. He was certain of only one thing: There would be more than one. It was the only thing that made sense.

The ear mike in Service's ear clicked once just before 0100. He had heard the bears being contentious on top for nearly an hour and hoped Waco wasn't spooking. Tree would be fine. He didn't care for bears, but he knew how to deal with them. At 0114 the mike clicked twice, and twenty minutes later, it clicked three times. Waco had someone down!

His heart began to pound in anticipation. It was beginning.

But nothing more happened and even the bears stopped bickering.

A few minutes before 0330, he was startled by a small, intense flash of light back in the woods on the south bank in the general direction of where Grinda had parked his truck. There was just one flash and no sound. What the hell was it? Had he imagined it? He wasn't sure, but his gut told him he couldn't stay where he was. He triggered the mike: "Green, Eddie—you secure?"

"One down, secure."

"Stay where you are. Tree, move up to me now."

A voice in the earpiece said, "Moving."

Treebone slid down beside him. Service told him, "I saw a light."

"We both going?"

"No, you hold here. Might be nothing."

"If it's got you moving," Tree said, "it's something."

Service gave his friend his jab stick and talked him through how to use it. No more words were exchanged.

To keep a low profile, he crossed the narrow channel on his hands and knees, ignoring the sharp rocks cutting at his knees. Eventually he eased himself between boulders on the other side and lay still. The terrain here was uneven, difficult to navigate even in daylight, and unforgiving. Tag alders grew in huge clumps around the boulders. He had seen the light flash briefly and had pinpointed the location in his mind. In those times when he came here to fish, he had to prepare himself mentally and physically for the difficulty of getting to the place where the fish were concentrated. The reality was that there was no easy or comfortable route to where his truck was parked.

He had three choices: Go to the truck first and work out from there; move along the river and move up from the water; or go directly to where he had seen the light. He chose the latter and struck out, crawling and slithering across the rocks and through the tag alder tangles, letting his arms and upper body do most of the work, using his legs for rudders.

He had no idea how long he had been moving, but there was no light yet in the eastern sky behind him, and he had been moving steadily if not quickly. *Get to the light,* an inner voice urged. *Insects drawn to light often die,* another voice amended. Maybe the light was used by the killer as bait.

A faint sound ahead of him stopped him. He closed his eyes, tried to will all his senses into his ears. What had it been?

There. Again. Movement? If so, very slight, almost weak. What could it be? Sniffing like an animal, he raised his face and began to crawl forward. Creep, stop, sniff, creep. A hair to the right. He came to a blowdown and got to his feet. It was a cedar covered with soft moss, dank and decomposing. Dirt to dirt, the preacher had said at Elray Spargo's grave, and the memory gave him a sharp chill. He got a leg up on the log and slid over quietly. Below him he could smell something and he stopped and sniffed. Warm blood. Was there a sound too? Not sure.

The scent was close, *really* close.

There, just below him—a *leg!*

He reached out, touched it, got a response. Not much, more of a twitch. He tensed, took his SIG Sauer out of the holster, got his penlight in his left hand, flashed it once. What? Not possible! Blinked it again. *Holy shit!*

"Tatie," he whispered.

The leg moved. Light on again. She was against the log, holding a jacket or something to her neck. Her upper body and arms were black with blood.

"Okay, okay," he whispered. "I've got you." Into the mike he said, "Tree, move to me most ricky-tick. Two stay where you are."

He knew it could be a mistake, but he couldn't assess and work on her in the dark. He locked his light on and now and then flashed it in the direction he had come so Tree could see it. She was cut bad, her eyes wide, scared. Her hand was pressed against the wound and she had slowed it, but it was still pumping. He put his hands on hers and pressed as hard as he could. That she was still alive was a miracle. He wished Tree would hurry, but the terrain wouldn't allow that. He looked in the agent's eyes, saw her trying to direct him to the left. "Help is coming," he said. She rolled her eyes and coughed blood. *She knows,* he thought. Had Nantz had such a moment? Walter? He felt a gorge rising in his throat and willed himself to stop hyperventilating.

"I got your light," Tree said in the earpiece.

Seconds later his friend was beside him and they were doing everything they could to hold back the blood. "I've got it," Tree said, and Service stood up and called del Olmo on the radio. "We have one down and bleeding. Meet EMS on Deerfoot Lodge Road and guide them in. Hurry; it's gonna be close."

He holstered the 800 and knelt beside Tatie Monica.

"Your light earlier?"

She moved her eyes side to side.

"Someone else?"

She closed her eyes and opened them. The woman might have personal demons, but she was tough, he told himself. "You're gonna make it," he told her. She rolled her eyes again, pulled her hand off the wound, grabbed Service's hand, and put it down on the ground.

"Don't be doin' that shit!" Tree said frantically. "Grady!"

Service put both of his hands back on the wound, wondered how far away EMS was, and knew it was not going to end well.

Tree pressed his fingers to her carotid and sat back. "She's gone, man."

Service kept pressing against the wound.

Tree touched his friend's shoulder. "It's over, bro."

Service let himself slump backward.

He heard sirens coming, but knew the old two-track in was tough, almost impassable.

Treebone looked at the dead woman. "You know her?"

"Feeb."

Service felt for a pulse again, found none. How she had kept from bleeding out sooner he didn't know.

She had looked left. Now he looked that way and shone his light.

It was a plastic pocket protector. Was this all she had been pointing at? He looked in the direction her hand had pointed and started walking slowly.

There was a blood trail. She had been hit about thirty feet from where he'd found her, somehow staggered and crawled all that way. The attack had come in the rocks. Lots of blood, no prints. He went back to the body. Monica had still been trying to do her job to the very end. The thought choked him.

"She part of this?" Tree asked.

Grady Service didn't know.

Del Olmo led the ambulance in and stayed after they took Tatie Monica.

Just before 0630, Service called Eddie Waco. "Bring yours up to us. Tree's coming back to help."

A half-hour later Eddie Waco and Tree arrived with a man in cuffs. He was thirtyish, with a hawk nose and an earring. He glanced at all the blood on the ground and looked puzzled. Service had never seen him before.

Eddie Waco took off his pack, opened it, and pulled out a small stainless-steel hatchet and a surgical kit, folded in a gray leather pouch. He looked at Service. "No ID."

"Any trouble?"

"He was good, real quiet and sneaky. I got lucky."

Service asked Waco, "You see a light flash?"

"Nope. You'n?"

"I thought I saw something." He turned to Waco's prisoner. "You got a name?"

The man grinned, looked away.

"What have we got?" Waco asked.

Service took a cigarette, held out the pack to his partners. "I'll be damned if I know."

Elza Grinda drove in to join del Olmo, and the two of them took the prisoner out to Iron County deputies on Deerfoot Lodge Road, who transported him to the county jail in Crystal Falls. Service, Tree, and Eddie Waco dumped their gear in the Tahoe and spent some time examining the area where Service thought he'd seen the flash of light. In such rocky terrain, footprints were out of the question. "Bring a dawg in?" Waco asked.

"I don't know. Did your guy act like he knew what he was doing?"

"Yessir. This case sure hain't bin easy," Eddie Waco said.

Grady Service agreed. He stared at the pocket protector. It looked the same as the one Bonaparte carried. Had Bonaparte and Tatie Monica come out here together, and if so, where was Bonaparte now? There had to be an explanation, and in the back of his mind, where unthinkable thoughts lived, he had an almost overpowering feeling that something else had happened last night, something he had missed. Again.

## 53

## CRYSTAL FALLS, MICHIGAN

### AUGUST 8, 2004

Service drove them back to Crystal Falls in silence, feeling anxious and not wanting to talk. Had they solved the case or not? Waco's prisoner had the killing tools that fit, but something else had gone down. Special Agent Tatie Monica was dead, and there was no explanation yet for anything that had happened last night.

Wink Rector greeted them in the parking lot behind the jail. "I saw the prisoner they brought in. Have you seen Monica? I told her yesterday she was acting stupidly, but she wouldn't listen to me."

Service was surprised. "You *knew* she was coming after us?"

"She had your AVL," Rector said. "She wouldn't listen to reason."

"Our AVL," Grady Service repeated. He'd been right about that. Sort of. Why did Tatie Monica have the AVL, and what did it mean?

Service looked at Wink Rector. "Special Agent Monica is dead, Wink."

Del Olmo showed up, handed Service a fax of the photo from the captain. It could be the guy Waco got, but the quality of the fax was poor.

"Federal forces are en route," Rector said in a thin voice. "If you're going to talk to the prisoner alone, you'd better use what little time you've got."

Service met him in a small interview room with cream-colored walls. "Rud Hud?"

The man shrugged.

Service understood that this was very likely the man who was responsible for the deaths of Walter and Nantz. He was overwhelmed by the temptation to grab the man's throat and choke him to death on the spot, but he heard Nantz's voice telling him to keep his temper in check. He felt that he couldn't breathe and went back outside to Wink Rector.

"She had our AVL?"

"Yep, told me about it yesterday."

"How'd she get it?"

"She didn't say."

"Did you see an agent named Bonaparte in Marquette recently?"

"Yeah, the BAU guy. He was here yesterday. He and Tatie met in my office."

"With you?"

"Just the two of them."

"What about Pappas?"

"Haven't seen her."

"You know where Bonaparte is now?"

Rector shook his head.

Del Olmo approached. "Her vehicle was out near the Deerfoot."

"She walked all the way in there on her own, and without NVDs?" She *had* been desperate, and now she was dead, and he felt empty and deflated.

## 54

## MARQUETTE, MICHIGAN

## AUGUST 14, 2004

The events on the island in the Fence River had taken place a week ago.

Alona Pappas had cornered him at the jail in Marquette and ripped on him for five minutes, accusing him of everything from blowing the case to causing Tatie Monica's death. He found it interesting that Bonaparte had been in Marquette the day before it all went down, and had not been seen since.

Wink Rector came into Service's office. "You hear Bonaparte's missing?"

"Missing?"

"No contact with anyone since before the island deal went down."

"What's the Bureau's take on it?"

"A BOLO will be issued today in conjunction with a press conference this morning in Washington."

The captain and Fern LeBlanc joined them in the office conference room to watch the press conference on CNN. The FBI director was not at the conference and an assistant director officiated. The conference was short. No media questions were answered though the reporters waved their hands and pens and created a ruckus. The basic news was that the acting assistant director of the Behavioral Analysis Unit had been missing for a week. Bonaparte's photograph was shown. The assistant director profiled Bonaparte's career, called him a "founding father" of profiling, and concluded by saying that Bonaparte had been actively pursuing an investigation when he disappeared.

Service looked at his captain. "Why'd they do that?"

Captain Grant waved a hand in the air. "When you can't score on substance, you go for style points," Grant said. "You ought to be aware that the Bureau is making noise about the unauthorized use of animal tranquilizers in the apprehension."

"They ought to be focused on identifying the asshole we got, not how."

So far the man remained unidentified and uncooperative. He had not said a dozen words since his arrest. He had not requested a lawyer, but one had been appointed, and he promptly resigned after time with his client. A second lawyer was now on the case and claimed he wasn't getting anything out of the man either and had no idea how to mount a defense. *Tough shit,* Service thought. Waco arrested him with the packet of tools. The guy was part of it, but not all of it. How did Bonaparte's pocket protector get on the scene? Had he walked in with Monica? Had he followed her or had she followed him? Service had given the pocket protector to Pappas as evidence, to pull fingerprints, and she had not said anything about it since then. Service knew in his gut there was more. The DNR's only source of information was from Wink Rector. Pappas and other FBI personnel had nothing to say. The fingerprints of the man in custody didn't come up in databases anywhere in the world. Neither had his DNA. He was about as close to a nonperson as Service had ever experienced.

Eddie Waco had gone back to Missouri with the plumed headdress Fiannula Spargo had given Service. Taking it back to her was a task Service wanted no part of.

Tree was still around, staying with him at the cabin.

The captain came to his office and seemed hesitant. "I don't know what the outcome of this case will be, but you, Tree, and Agent Waco did a fine job, Grady."

As soon as he got into his truck, Service jimmied his false teeth loose and put them in a plastic container. He'd clean them when he got home. It felt good to have them out.

A mile from Slippery Creek, he saw a familiar truck parked on the side of the road. Limpy Allerdyce was sitting on the gate, swinging his legs like a kid. Service pulled up behind the old poacher and got out.

Allerdyce shoved a satchel off the gate. It plopped on the ground, raising dust. "Mutt brung dat stuff home, sonny."

Service unzipped the bag and opened it. There was a stainless-steel hatchet and surgical kit inside, identical to the tools taken from the man on the island. There was also an FBI badge, ID card, and a night vision device. The photograph on the ID was that of Cranbrook P. Bonaparte.

Service looked up at Allerdyce. "The FBI is looking for this man."

"Zat so?"

"Your dog found these things, all in a bag like this?"

"Just da way dey is right dere on da ground."

"Must be one helluva strong dog to carry a bag like that."

"Crazy mutt," Allerdyce said.

Service groped for words, but Limpy spoke first. "We take care of our own, sonny."

What the hell was Allerdyce saying?

"Your dog found this stuff?"

Allerdyce shrugged. "I jes noticed it and brung it, eh?'

"You're on damn thin ice," Service said.

"Been out dere plenty times," Allerdyce cackled.

"The FBI will want to talk to you."

The old man winked. "I jes know what da mutt brung home."

Service wanted to ask questions, but couldn't find a starting point. He found a stick, picked up the bag, started back to his truck, and stopped. "Your dog didn't happen to bring home a powerful light of some kind?"

"Youse make a mistake with light at night and youse can blind yoreseff wid one-a dem, eh?" Allerdyce said.

Service stared at the man, groping for what to say.

"Close yore mout', sonny, and put yore teets in whin youse're out in publics. Don't want ta scare da peoples, eh."

## 55

# MARQUETTE, MICHIGAN
## AUGUST 23, 2004

The interview was being held at the federal offices on the second floor of the Republic Bank on US 41. Wink Rector invited Service to observe from behind one-way glass. Two days after giving Service the bag and implements, Limpy Allerdyce had surrendered without resistance, told only that the U.S. Attorney wanted to talk to him. Alona Pappas and an unnamed assistant director were with Rector.

Allerdyce sat in the interview room with his insipid grin and a twinkle in his eyes.

"They offer him a lawyer?" Service asked Rector.

"Repeatedly. Says he's not interested."

Talia Rilling, assistant U.S. attorney for the Western District of Michigan, was less than two years on the job in the Marquette office, and being touted as a rising star. She wore oversize glasses that made her look both bland and studious, but Service saw that she was a handsome woman, small in stature. Her size made her look less than intimidating, but she moved with grace and confidence in the room. He wondered how she would handle Allerdyce.

The interview began, and Service found himself mesmerized by the exchanges. From the start it was clear that Rilling had never fenced verbally with the likes of Limpy before, and he knew from experience that there was nothing more difficult than dealing with someone with a steel-trap mind who acted like a fool and talked like a dolt.

RILLING: Mr. Allerdyce, you have been informed of the reasons for this interview. Let the record show that you have come in willingly, and further, that you also have refused legal representation.

ALLERDYCE: Why I wanta lawyer? Youse want to talk about what dat mutt drug home, eh.

RILLING: Can you describe the circumstances under which your pet brought home the satchel?

ALLERDYCE: Ain't no pet! Just a mutt hangs around camp.

RILLING: The dog brought home a satchel.

ALLERDYCE: Name's Satchmutt, on account he gotta big black nose and howls like dat colored horn player died awhile back. Dat "Hello Molly" guy. I like dat music, eh.

RILLING: He's not a pet, but you named him Satchmutt?

ALLERDYCE: *Youse* ain't nobody's pet, but youse got name, eh?

RILLING: Let's start again. The dog brought home a satchel.

ALLERDYCE: Dat's why we here, eh?

RILLING: What time of day did the dog bring home the satchel?

ALLERDYCE: I was asleep.

RILLING: So . . . this event transpired during the night.

ALLERDYCE: I go ta bed late, sleep late.

RILLING: What time did you discover the satchel?

ALLERDYCE: Was when I wokened up. Couldn't find it when I was asleep, eh.

RILLING: What time was that?

ALLERDYCE: I don't watch no clocks.

RILLING: Before noon, after noon?

ALLERDYCE: Yes.

RILLING: Yes to what—before or after?

ALLERDYCE: I said I don't watch no clocks.

RILLING: But you will agree it was around midday.

ALLERDYCE: Tink I said dat, din't I?

RILLING: All right, the dog brought the satchel to you around midday.

ALLERDYCE: No, I said I found it den; I don't know when da mutt brung it, and he din't bring it me. Just brung it, okay?

RILLING: Did you see the dog when you went to bed?

ALLERDYCE:  Din't look for 'im.

RILLING:  All right, please describe the circumstances under which you discovered the satchel.

ALLERDYCE:  Joycie ridin' me, see, and she says, "Dat your bag over dere in da corner?"

RILLING:  Joycie?

ALLERDYCE:  She's up top, red in face, all discombobolinked, and she says, "Dat your bag over dere in da corner?"

RILLING:  All right, Mr. Allerdyce. What did you do when *Joycie* pointed out the satchel?

ALLERDYCE:  Holy Wah, I lay right dere till she got done. I'm a gentleman wit wimmens.

RILLING:  And after she got . . . after that?

ALLERDYCE:  Told her ta fetch cuppa coffee.

RILLING:  What about the bag?

ALLERDYCE:  Still sittin' where she seen it.

RILLING:  Eventually you looked in the bag.

ALLERDYCE:  Yeah, I looked.

RILLING:  What was in it?

ALLERDYCE:  Same was in it when I give it ta sonny-boy.

RILLING:  That would be Department of Natural Resources Detective Grady Service?

ALLERDYCE:  Yeah, sonny-boy.

RILLING:  Did you see the dog bring the satchel in?

ALLERDYCE:  Nope.

RILLING:  So you don't *know* it was the dog that brought it in.

ALLERDYCE:  Was him. Does dat sorta ting alla bloody time.

RILLING:  But you didn't actually *see* the dog with the bag?

ALLERDYCE:  I seen where da mutt chewed it.

RILLING:  Yes or no—you saw the dog bring the bag in?

ALLERDYCE:  No.

RILLING: Okay, thank you. Let's change directions. What did you think of what you found in the bag?

ALLERDYCE: I t'ought somebody be bloody pissed ta lose stuff like dat.

RILLING: Did you have any idea who might have owned the bag?

ALLERDYCE: Was ID inside.

RILLING: You assumed the person who owned the badge and ID owned the bag?

ALLERDYCE: You tink different?

RILLING: I'm interested in what *you* thought.

ALLERDYCE: I already said: I t'ought somebody be bloody pissed.

RILLING: Let's take a brief break. Would you like something to drink, Mr. Allerdyce?

ALLERDYCE: Tanks, I'm good—but youse go ahead. Youse look kinda sweaty, dere, girlie.

Rilling came out of the room, looked at Wink Rector, rolled her eyes, went to get a cup of water, talked briefly to Alona Pappas, and came back. "Service?"

"Yep."

"You know Allerdyce pretty well?"

"Dealt with him a lot. Nobody *knows* him."

"You see anything different in his demeanor today?"

"He's being more direct than normal."

Rilling blinked. "You buy his story that a dog brought the bag home?"

"No," Grady Service said.

"You know," she said, "the way this looks, the bag was Bonaparte's, which leads us to speculate that he was one of the killers. Do you think Allerdyce did something to Bonaparte?"

"Absolutely."

"Any reason why?"

"You'll have to ask him."

"You want to join me inside?"

"Nope."

"I insist," she said, holding open the door.

Grady Service walked into the room and Allerdyce started chuckling. "Dey bringin' in a relief pitcher already?"

The interview resumed.


RILLING:      You know Detective Service?

ALLERDYCE:    Holy Wah, long time—his daddy too. Sonny dere busted me, sent me up seven year.

RILLING:      Were you angry with him?

ALLERDYCE:    Was me shot 'im—on accident. He'd be the one pissed.

SERVICE:      Can we get back to the satchel?

ALLERDYCE:    Why I come in—ta help youse.

SERVICE:      Why'd you bring the bag to me?

ALLERDYCE:    Youse're closest law ta camp, eh.

SERVICE:      When you gave me the bag, did you not say, "We take care of our own?"

ALLERDYCE:    Dat's right, sonny.

SERVICE:      What did you mean by that?

ALLERDYCE:    Youse find somepin' don't belong, youse take it to da law. Got a record like me, gotta be careful. Youse always saying, sonny, I screw up, you gonna send me back inside. I din't mess wit yer old man—I ain't messin' wit you.

SERVICE:      How do you account for your dog finding the bag?

ALLERDYCE:    He got da dandy sniffer, eh.

SERVICE:      But you have no idea where he found it?

ALLERDYCE:    Bloody mutt runs all over da place. Once found him down Iron County.

SERVICE:      Did the dog go down into Iron County often?

ALLERDYCE:    He don't leave one of dem whatchacallits.

SERVICE: Itineraries?

ALLERDYCE: Yeah.

SERVICE: Have you been in Iron County recently?

ALLERDYCE: I move around, eh.

SERVICE: Yes or no?

ALLERDYCE: Mebbe. I don't pay no attention ta county lines.

SERVICE: Did you ever meet the man whose ID was in the satchel?

ALLERDYCE: No.

SERVICE: How do you think someone could lose a bag with such valuable contents?

ALLERDYCE: You know peoples lose stuff alla time in woods.

SERVICE: Do you think your dog could take you back to where it found the bag?

ALLERDYCE: Dat sorry mutt? He ain't 'roun' no more.

SERVICE: The dog ran off again?

ALLERDYCE: Nipped one-a da grankittles, had to shoot 'im. Can't have no nippin' dog roun' my grankittles.

SERVICE: The dog is dead, and you're saying we'll never find the place where the bag was found?

ALLERDYCE: I won't say never.

RILLING: Would you willingly take a lie detector test, Mr. Allerdyce?

ALLERDYCE: Youse ast me, I'll take 'er.

Grady Service nudged the U.S. attorney, who followed him into the hall.

"You're wasting your time, and mine," he said.

"Wouldn't hurt to give him the test," Rilling said.

"He'll pass."

"Then we'll know he's telling the truth."

"If you hook him up to the machine and ask him if Mother Teresa gave him a blow job last night, he'll say yes, and the machine will indicate he's telling the truth."

"Sociopath?" she countered.

"Total."

"Do you think he has something to do with Bonaparte's disappearance?"

"What I think and what I can prove are two different things."

"Why do you think he brought you the bag?"

"To let me know Bonaparte had been taken care of."

"Why?"

"He's a strange old bird with his own twisted sense of justice."

"I'm going to call this off," Rilling said.

When Allerdyce came out of the room, Service walked downstairs with the old poacher and followed him. "Between us, do you know what happened to Bonaparte?"

"Sounds like he lost 'is bag, den himseff."

"That's all you have to say?"

"Youse know what da wolfie haters say?"

"Shoot, shovel, and shut up."

"Dat's all I got ta say ta youse, sonny. I'm real sorry about yer gal and yer kittle."

Service wasn't finished, and followed the old man to his truck. "Between us and off the record."

Allerdyce stopped and turned to face him. "Listenin', sonny boy."

"You were out there."

Allerdyce gave a single nod. "Heard your truck was up dat way."

"Bullshit. Heard from who?"

"Youse know I got my ways."

"You were out there."

"Seen your fire on da island. Real good fishin', dat spot."

"That's all you saw."

"Seen da woman come. Walked in dere, and she look scared shitless, eh."

"And?"

"She start downriver."

"She didn't make it."

"Fella wit a mask like black hornet slash't her t'roat."

"That's when you stepped in. You shined a flashlight into his goggles."

"Ain't sayin', but he had one-a dem funny computers in his jeep. Youse know, like youse use."

"His jeep?"

"Parked up Sumac Camp."

The camp was two miles west, isolated, difficult to get into.

"You brought the bag to let me know."

Another curt nod. "You know how I said Joycie in da room dere dat day? I lied. It was Joanie. Couldn't let 'er reputation get mudded. You don't owe me nothin', sonny."

Service knew he had heard most of the truth. He called Wink Rector and told him where to find Bonaparte's vehicle.

He sat on the curb and lit a cigarette. Limpy had brought finality to the case, and now he owed the old bastard, and the thought made him sick to his stomach.

Summer was gone, the maples beginning to turn, tamaracks starting to yellow up, leaves already falling under the assault of seasonal rains and gusty northwest winds. Karylanne was installed in an apartment in Houghton and back in classes; Shark and Limey, and Gus, were acting as her extended family there.

The day before, Grady Service had held a memorial for Maridly Nantz and his son Walter. The Slippery Creek camp had been crammed with people, and there had been tears. As tragic as their deaths were, both Mar and Walter had been positive people, engaged with life and laughing at everything. After several people had spoken, he had tried to say something, but his voice and nerve had failed him. Tree had draped his arm around his shoulders, Karylanne moved over to hug him, and that had ended the ceremony, such as it was. Kalina had gone back to Detroit and Tree stayed, announcing he had finally decided to retire. He had been talking about it for years, and Service knew the only reason he'd delayed was Kalina didn't want him underfoot.

Grady Service was on a five-day furlough. Wink Rector told him that the FBI's push to punish Waco and him for using the animal drugs had been dropped. Wink didn't know why.

Wink added, "Bonaparte was the one. Pappas found some way into cyberspace and learned that Bonaparte had partnered with one Duane Royant, aka Rud Hud, aka Check Six."

"Duane Royant?"

"The one you guys took down that night. He's the one who ran Nantz off the road. They got fingerprints off of the rental and matched the ones we got from him. Once the Bureau had a name, they were able to track Royant.

He's Québecois, a former medical student at McGill University. Came across the border with false papers. He and Bonaparte hooked up, and Bonaparte was teaching him, and I quote, 'to attain perfection.' Royant has no record, has never been in trouble, at least that we know of."

"The same relationship Bonaparte had with Frankie Pey. Bonaparte was Marcel."

"We couldn't find a Frankie Pey here at Northern, and we thought maybe your tip from Indiana was actually for Marquette the school, rather than the town, but that went nowhere, and as Pappas dissects Bonaparte's background, it isn't holding up. Apparently he looked fine and everything was copasetic when he joined the Bureau, but that was a long time ago and now we have better tools and it looks pretty much like his background was as bogus as an air castle. Pappas can't say that Bonaparte was Marcel, but she's digging deeper and so far there's no indication of a connection with Frankie Pey or Ney. But there's no doubt he and Royant are the killers in the second batch. Royant is probably not competent to stand trial, but they'll put him away somewhere for the rest of his life."

"So what the fuck was this all about?"

Wink Rector exhaled. "Pappas thinks it's tied to his theory of the perfect serial murderer. Apparently he developed the notion early in his career and took a lot of shit for it."

Service thought about this for a moment. "If he was Marcel, he'd know about what Frankie Pey had done."

"Possibly," Rector said.

"He picked game wardens because we're both the easiest and the most difficult. We work alone and where there aren't witnesses. "

Rector nodded. "Could be."

"Maybe he realized his perfect killer notion wasn't being bought so he used Royant to reveal the first group—an attempt to make some believers."

Service wished they knew more, but he knew from experience that the end of a case was often less than complete, as was justice. Unless his gut was wrong, one of the killers was dead, this thing was over. For him, though, it would never be over. Nantz and Walter weren't coming back.

He and Tree spent all morning working with a chain saw on fallen trees near his camp. He had not worked seriously on the camp for three years, and it needed attention and care, including a wood supply for the stove for winter. They had split wood by hand ax and enjoyed the sweat. Since the death of Tatie Monica, he had gone back to working out with weights every morning. The small amount of fat he had accumulated was gone; all that remained was muscle, and he felt strong.

After a three-hour drive they were at the end of a long, pocked, and twisty two-track, staring at a camp gate. A sign on a tree said NORTH OF NOWHERE.

As Bowie Rhodes had promised, Service's code opened the lock. Newf bolted ahead of the truck as they drove a quarter-mile along the edge of a cedar swamp up onto a finger of hard ground that pointed north. The cabin was tidy and small and glowing orange in the afternoon sun. They parked the truck and began to unload. "You think there's fish here?" Tree asked.

"Bowie Rhodes wouldn't have a camp where there wasn't fish," Service said.

They got their gear into the cabin and Tree climbed up into the loft. "Two beds," he called down.

"Floor down here is good for me," Service said.

They filled their fishing vests with trapper sandwiches—peanut butter, jelly, honey, and oatmeal, assembled their rods, and started north into the swamp, the dog leading the way, sniffing everything. Service had talked to Rhodes at the memorial.

"Walk north along the wall of cedars," the writer had said with a teasing smile.

They walked for nearly twenty minutes, saw a line of trees that looked like they had been planted, and stopped. Service heard moving water. Another fifty yards on they came to a small, deep creek. Tree moved to the bank and looked down. "Lordy," was all he said as he stripped line off his reel and roll-casted against a log up stream.

A brook trout struck on the first cast; not just any brook trout, but a fat, foot-long fish, gleaming with fall spawning colors, orange and blue and red and green.

Service said, "I'll be right back."

Treebone caught two more fish before his friend returned, carrying the ashes of Nantz and Walter.

"What're you doing?"

"Nantz and I talked about death only once, and she told me to sprinkle her ashes in the most beautiful place I saw."

"This is it?" his friend asked.

"No, but if I sprinkle a little of them at every beautiful spot I find, they'll be able to enjoy all of them and not be stuck with one view."

"You need serious professional help," Treebone said, holding out a beefy fist.

Service tapped his fist against his friend's and grinned.

"Don't it bother you, leaving some of their ashes here? Who's gonna look after them?"

"You are," Service said.

"Me?"

"It's your camp."

"Are you crazy?"

"Bowie sold it to me, and I'm giving it to you. For everything we've been through together. Now you got a place to give Kalina some space."

"North of Nowhere," Treebone said quietly, tears in his eyes.

It was a term game wardens used to describe their typical situations: off the grid and alone, a place without specific reference, but with meaning for every man and woman who had ever worn green and gray.

Grady Service made a cast, caught one fish, released it, got the ashes, and sprinkled some from each box in the spot.

Treebone stood next to his friend with his head bowed as the ashes fluttered to the water and were absorbed into the flow, which would carry them north.

# Read the Entire Woods Cop Mystery Series,
## The Most Exciting Who-Done-Its Set in the Great Outdoors

*"Top-notch action scenes, engaging characters both major and minor, masterful dialogue, and a passionate sense of place make this a fine series."*
—*Publishers Weekly*

Ice Hunter
978-1-59921-361-3

Blue Wolf in Green Fire
978-1-59921-359-0

Chasing a Blond Moon
978-1-59921-360-6

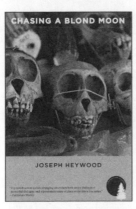

Running Dark
978-1-59921-363-7

Strike Dog
978-1-59921-364-4

Death Roe
978-1-59921-428-3